The Life She Deserves

A GRANITE SPRINGS NOVEL

Maggie Christensen

Published by Cala Publishing 2019

Sunshine Coast, Qld, Australia

This publication is written in British English. Spellings and grammatical conventions are conversant with the UK.

Cover and interior design: J D Smith Design

Editing: John Hudspith Editing Services

To my wonderful husband and soul mate without
whose support none of this would happen.

Also by Maggie Christensen

Oregon Coast Series
The Sand Dollar
The Dreamcatcher
Madeline House

Sunshine Coast books
A Brahminy Sunrise
Champagne for Breakfast

Sydney Collection
Band of Gold
Broken Threads
Isobel's Promise
A Model Wife

Scottish Collection
The Good Sister
Isobel's Promise
A Single Woman

Check out the last page of this book to see how to join my mailing list and get a free download of one of my books.

Prologue

Joanna Slater knew the bedside vigil was nearing its inevitable end.

Her best friend, Alice, had managed to survive through Christmas, but the doctors weren't hopeful she'd live to see January out. The cancer she'd been battling for the past three years was finally winning. Now, Jo sat with Alice's husband, Col, one on each side of the bed, watching, waiting, the overhead fan only managing to move the already hot air around, and doing little to cool the room.

Jo saw Alice's lips move and moved closer to hear her friend's words.

'You'll look out for Col, won't you, Jo?' Her thin hand grasped Jo's. 'Don't let him grieve too much. Make sure he…' But she was too weak to continue.

'Of course, dear Alice,' Jo whispered. 'Hush now. I'll always be here…' She squeezed her friend's hand and watched as Alice's eyes slowly closed.

Jo's eyes misted and she turned away as Col's fingers moved down Alice's cheek and he leant over to kiss her. She stood up, walking to the window to gaze unseeingly out at the garden which, starved of both water and Alice's ministrations, was now dry and unkempt. The small Australian country town of Granite Springs had turned into a ghost town. It was that time of year when the few families still in town headed for the local swimming pool or the river. Most had set off right after Christmas for the coast, preferring to see out the worst of the summer heat on the beach, where there was at least a chance of a cool breeze from the ocean.

Jo was seized with a feeling of desolation, one she'd already had to deal with. And now, without Alice, how would she cope?

She heard a gasp behind her and, turning quickly, saw Col knuckling his eyes.

'She's gone!'

'Oh, no! Col!' Jo moved to lay a hand on his shoulder, unable to stop her tears.

'I know it's a blessing, but…' Tears streamed unchecked down his cheeks. 'What am I going to do without her? These past three years…' He rose, and the two clasped each other in grief, friends sharing their anguish.

Jo remembered the good times, the years they'd been a foursome before Alice's illness and Jo's husband's defection.

Now there were only the two of them left.

One

One year later

Alice died exactly one year ago today, and Jo had missed her every single day. Tonight, they were celebrating her life with an exhibition of her paintings. A talented artist, Alice had, before her death, extracted a promise from both Col and Jo that they'd arrange this exhibition of her work and give the proceeds to cancer research.

It was a typical January morning in Granite Springs. Looking out of the kitchen window, Jo could see the heat haze glimmer on the neighbouring paddock where a herd of goats grazed, unheeding of the glare of the sun.

She was preparing breakfast when the phone rang. Seeing her elder son's face on the screen, Jo sighed. Danny would be calling to reproach her again. *When had her son started to behave as if he was the adult, and she was the child?*

'Morning, Danny. You're an early bird. No sport today?'

'It doesn't start till later, Mum. You know why I'm calling. Have you thought over what I said?'

Danny had said so many things to her over the past five years, but she knew exactly to what he was referring.

'I have, and the answer's still "No". I love this house, Danny. I've lived here all my married life and I intend to live here till they carry me out.'

'I know that's what you said. But I can't believe you really thought it through. You've been rattling around in that big place since Dad left, and one of those nice villas we've been building on the estate would suit you much better. Kylie says…'

Jo didn't want to hear what Kylie said. She could imagine. Her daughter-in-law had coveted this house since the first day she saw it; when Danny had brought her home to dinner and to show off her engagement ring. Back then, there had been no thought of her and Danny moving into the family home, but Jo had seen the way the younger woman's eyes had wandered around the place, as if calculating the cost of everything and refurbishing it more to her taste.

'I don't want to hear any more. This is a busy day for me. As you know, it's Alice's memorial exhibition this evening, and I have a lot to do. If that's all you wanted to say?'

She hung up regretfully, trying to remember when she'd last had a productive conversation with her oldest child, the little boy who'd followed her around this kitchen, demanding to be hugged, who'd told her she was the best mum in the world. That had all changed in his teenage years, of course, but he'd still been the loving son she remembered.

It had only been in the last few years, since Gordon left, that he'd started to take on this overtly overprotective role and, more recently – no doubt at Kylie's urging – insisted he knew what was best for her. He'd begun to treat her as if she was on her last legs, instead of a woman still in the prime of her life.

While those thoughts were running through her head, the toast popped up. Jo spread it with lime and ginger marmalade and prepared a cup of Earl Grey tea to accompany it, before carrying both out onto the veranda.

Sitting in one of the cane chairs overlooking her rose garden, she began to plan her day. This was her favourite time, when the sun hadn't yet reached its peak. Jo had always brought her breakfast out here, even when she and Gordon were together. It allowed her thinking time. Sometimes, especially when the children were little, it had been the only time she could be alone. Now, she still liked to start the day this way. It helped blow away the cobwebs or, in this instance, the worry Danny's call managed to create.

Today she planned to spoil herself with a visit to her hairdresser and the local beauty salon. It was something she and Alice had often laughed about – their monthly visits designed to, as Alice said, *keep old age at bay.* And the day would end with the event she'd been both looking forward to and dreading – the retrospective exhibition of Alice's paintings and sketches at The Riverfront, the restaurant Jo co-owned with her younger son, Rob.

Jo's phone buzzed again. This call was more welcome.

'Col!' Her face broke into a wide smile at her old friend's voice.

'I know we got everything set up yesterday, but there's something I need to run past you. Could you drop by the restaurant this morning?'

'Sure thing.' Jo mentally reviewed what she'd planned for the day – nothing that couldn't wait. Her beauty appointments weren't till the afternoon, and she'd planned to pop in to see Rob sometime during the day anyway. She'd wanted to take one last look before tonight's opening, before the room was filled with people, and the paintings would hopefully be sold to eager buyers.

As she drove into the carpark, Jo saw Col's car already there and hurried inside, waving to Rob as she passed through the bistro on the lower level. Entering the gallery – a large function room, with floor-to-ceiling windows looking out onto the river – she found Col standing in the middle of the room, looking somewhat lost.

'Col!'

He turned quickly. 'Jo. Good of you to come. Alice wanted…' his eyes misted, '…she wanted you to have one – to choose one you'd like for yourself.'

'I couldn't…' Jo began before realising this was just what her old friend *would* have wanted. She knew which one she'd choose and went unerringly to a small sketch of the river path below the restaurant where the pair had often walked together. She remembered when Alice had painted it – how her friend had pointed out the two indistinct figures in the background. *That's you and me,*' Alice had said. '*and no one else will know.*

'This one,' she said sadly, as Col's arm went around her shoulders, giving her a warm hug.

'She thought you'd want that one, but said it had to be *your* choice, not hers.'

Jo turned to smile at him, her eyes filling with tears, which she immediately brushed away. 'She wouldn't want to see us weeping for her either.'

'No.' There was a pause, then Col spoke again. 'It's hard. Sometimes I find it difficult to conjure up her face. It's only been a year, yet…'

'I know.'

Suddenly, it was as if Alice was there with them, telling them not to be silly, that they needed to move on, to enjoy life. Jo had promised her friend she'd help Col arrange the exhibition and make sure he looked after himself when she was gone.

She'd tried her best to keep to her promise, finding Col easy company. Their shared grief had brought them together, and they'd fallen into the habit of sharing a meal together on Mondays and Thursdays. It was on one of those evenings, she'd shared her uneasiness about Danny's urgings for her to downsize, to move into one of the modern villas on the estate on the outskirts of town – part of the new development her real estate son was marketing.

Col had been supportive and encouraged her to stand firm, understanding how much Yarran meant to her. But it was hard to accept that her son and his wife wanted to turf her out of her own home – even though they planned to buy it from her.

*

'Thanks, Col.' Jo accepted the glass of wine, took a sip, and shifted from one foot to the other. She'd been standing all evening and would die for a seat. That was probably the wrong word to use on this occasion, but Jo wasn't in the mood to be politically correct.

Alice was gone, and tonight was to be a fitting memorial – one which Alice had planned in minute detail.

Jo looked around the room, seeing all their friends happily engaged in drinking champagne and chatting. Alice would have laughed and encouraged them to enjoy themselves. If she'd been here, she'd have been the life of the party, moving from group to group, her infectious laugh rising above the chatter, her smile encouraging an answering one from everyone she met.

Everything had gone to plan. Here, in the function room on the top floor of the restaurant, and not without a few tears, she and Col had arranged Alice's paintings. The walls were filled with the seascapes, river scenes and bird drawings that had been her special talent, many of them already sporting red sold stickers.

Gazing around, Jo caught sight of her former husband. Of course, he'd be there. As Col's best friend and business partner of more years than either of them cared to remember, it would be an occasion he wouldn't miss. And there, by his side, wearing the most inappropriate outfit, was his new wife. Not so new really. It had been five years since Gordon had left her to marry Carol Landry – Carol Slater she was now – the second Mrs Slater.

It was just difficult to accept he'd moved on. He was now married to the blonde thirty-year-old bimbo who'd arrived in his law office in a whirlwind and swept him off his feet. At least, that's how he told it.

Jo saw it differently. She saw a grey-haired middle-aged man flattered by a woman half his age into leaving a perfectly good marriage for some misplaced idea of eternal youth.

Jo glanced surreptitiously at the woman who'd ousted her in her husband's affections, glad she was now able to view her without the bitterness of five years earlier. Back then, she'd have liked nothing better than to have torn out the hair of the woman who'd arrived in Gordon's office and immediately set her cap at the senior partner. But time had brought her to her senses, made her see reason. Now, she almost pitied the woman who'd taken her place.

'Jo, how are you, my dear?'

Jo turned sharply to see the well-meaning face of Gordon and Col's practice manager smiling at her. Except for the brief period Jo tried to forget, Dot had worked for the pair ever since they'd set up their practice. Gordon had often joked she ran the office single-handed and he and Col were only there for show.

'I'm good, Dot. Just missing Alice. She'd have loved this.'

'Don't be too sure she's not here. Can't you feel her presence?'

Jo felt a shiver run through her, though whether at the thought of Alice's ghostly presence or at Dot's words, she wasn't quite sure. She put a hand to her upswept hair, glad she'd chosen to wear the new hot pink outfit she'd been talked into by her daughter. Despite being mother to four-year-old twins, Eve still managed to put in a few days a week in her fashion boutique and had insisted on helping Jo choose her outfit for the evening.

'Okay, Mum?'

As if thinking of her had helped her materialise, Eve was at her elbow. 'I know it must be difficult for you tonight – for you and Uncle Col. Where is he?'

Jo pointed to the other end of the room where Col was in the middle of a noisy group. Although normally quiet and thoughtful, tonight he was making the effort to be more sociable. It was what Alice would have wanted.

In the early years of her marriage, she and Gordon, Alice and Col, had been a foursome, dining together regularly and spending part of each weekend together. Then, after her divorce, it had been the three of them – Alice, Col and Jo. Now only Col and Jo were left.

Jo looked fondly across the room to where Col appeared to be expounding the merits of one painting over another. How delighted Alice would have been to see her normally taciturn husband in this role. Jo sighed. Alice and Gordon had been the outgoing ones, with her and Col more introverted. They used to joke that was what kept them together – until Gordon left.

Finally, the crowd thinned and soon there were only Col and Jo left. Rob and his staff had disappeared downstairs.

'It went well. She'd be pleased,' Jo said, looking at the red *sold* stickers on every exhibit. 'I guess we should go home too, now.' She glanced at her companion, seeing signs of weariness in his eyes, the lines beside his mouth more noticeable than usual. 'It's still early. Why don't you come back for a hot drink?'

'Thanks.'

After mugs of hot chocolate drunk in Jo's living room, Col rose to leave. At the door he turned, almost bumping into her. 'I don't think I want to be alone tonight.'

Jo wrapped her arms around him in a warm hug. 'Then stay here.'

They walked upstairs together, past the spare room and into the main bedroom. Without speaking and still fully dressed, the pair lay down on the king-sized bed Jo had been meaning to get rid of ever since Gordon had left.

It felt strange to have another body there; over the past five years she'd become accustomed to having the large bed all to herself. But the glasses of champagne followed by the hot chocolate meant she immediately fell into a dreamless sleep.

As dawn was breaking, Jo awoke with a start to the awareness she wasn't alone. She turned to look at the familiar face on the pillow and a wave of tenderness swept over her. Col moved towards her and their lips met in what was more than their usual friendly kiss on the cheek – the one they greeted each other with when they met, had done for years. For a moment, she was startled, then a paroxysm of desire flooded her. As their bodies moved together with an urgency of their own, she had no time to wonder if this was a wise move. There was no way she could have stopped the upsurge of passion that engulfed them.

Two

Exhausted, they stared at each other wide-eyed.

'What just happened? Was I dreaming?' Col propped himself up on one elbow and gazed down into Jo's eyes, a smile slowly forming on his lips.

'If you were, I must have been there too. I never imagined…'

'Me neither.' With one finger, he traced the outline of Jo's face before pushing back her hair and kissing her cheek.

Knowing he'd never get back to sleep, Col considered what to do next. He was out of practice at this stuff. He and Alice had met at university and, since then, he'd never made love to anyone else, never wanted to – until now.

He felt bewildered. When he'd said he didn't want to be alone last night, he had no intention of doing anything other than going to sleep and enjoying the company of a warm body beside him, tired of his cold, lonely bed. Did Jo think he'd taken advantage of her?

Looking into Jo's eyes, he saw a similar confusion. Then her face erupted into a warm smile and he relaxed. This was Jo, not some stranger. But did that make it better? As if she was there in the room with them, he heard Alice's voice telling him this was what she'd wanted – to see her two favourite people get together. This was immediately followed by an image of Gordon, his friend and partner. He wouldn't be pleased.

'I don't think I can go back to sleep now,' Jo said, turning into his arms again, and pulling the doona over their nakedness.

Her skin felt soft to his touch, different in a good way. He remembered how elegant she'd looked last night in her pink outfit, her hair upswept. He knew they'd lain down fully dressed, but somewhere along the line, they'd rid themselves of their clothes. Looking across the room, he could see garments lying on the floor as if tossed there carelessly.

'You don't…?' he asked.

'Regret it? No. I feel…' She stretched her legs down to entwine with his. 'I feel as if I've found something I didn't know I was looking for.'

'What do you think Alice would say if she could see us?' Col knew he was saying what was on both their minds.

Jo seemed to consider for a few moments before replying, 'I think she'd approve. Though I'm not sure this is what she was thinking of when she told me to look out for you. Do you…? Is this…?'

Col sensed Jo's reluctance to put into words what he was thinking, too. *Was their coming together a result of the melancholy they both felt the night before – or was it something more, something to build on?*

'I'd like to think this wasn't a one-off,' he said daringly. 'Do you…?'

'Let's take things as they come. This has been a surprise. A nice one,' she added, clearly seeing a flash of disappointment cross his face. 'It wasn't premeditated. We were overwrought. Maybe we should wait and see how we feel in the cold light of day. I don't want this to spoil our friendship.'

'Nothing could do that. And it's morning already.'

The low sun was now streaming in through the blinds, the promise of another hot day. Jo moved restlessly. 'I should get up. Tea?'

Disappointed, Col agreed.

'What have you on today?' he asked, when they were settled in the large family kitchen with cups of Jo's favourite Earl Grey tea, accompanied by hot buttered toast and marmalade.

'I promised to look after the twins. Eve's bringing them round at…'

Col saw her glance at the clock.

'I should be making tracks.' He drained his cup, took a last mouthful of toast, and rose to go. 'Thanks. That really hit the spot. I guess it wouldn't do for Eve to see me here at this time in the morning?'

Jo only smiled, but Col knew how Eve idolised her father – always had. And, even though Jo might not admit it, his staying the night would have been a blow to his old friend's pride. No matter that the old friend had already moved on, had been married to another woman for nigh on five years. He saw Gordon in the office every day and knew he still took a keen interest in his ex-wife's life.

'I suppose you'll be going back to the gallery?'

Col could hear a note of longing in her voice and wondered if she wanted to be there with him just as much as he'd like her to be. But her family must come first. The three children she and Gordon had borne was something he and Alice had often envied. But they'd never admitted it and had been grateful to be honorary aunt and uncle to the trio.

Col wondered how his life would be different now, if they'd had children of their own. He dismissed the thought. It was what it was. There was no point in pondering about what might have been. 'I'll need to see the paintings get packaged up and be there for the buyers to collect them,' he said.

'Of course.' Jo joined him and they walked to the door. 'It went well,' she said repeating her words of the previous evening. 'Alice would be proud. You should be able to make a substantial donation.'

'Yes.' But her words reminded him of the reason he was here. If there had been no retrospective of his late wife's paintings, if he hadn't felt so desolate afterwards, he'd never have come back with Jo last night, never have experienced such heights of passion. And they'd have carried on as before – as friends who shared some wonderful memories. Would that have been such a bad thing?

But now they'd shared a bed, there could be no going back, and Col had a strong sense that the future would not all be smooth sailing.

Three

Jo watched Col get into his black Subaru Forester and drive off, then closed the door and stood with her back against it. What had she done? What had *they* done?

Yesterday had begun like any other day. There was no indication that by the end of it, her life would have changed forever, that she would have slept with her ex-husband's best friend, that Colin Ford would end the day in her bed.

She'd always found him attractive. She and Alice had often laughed about that, her friend suggesting that, if Gordon hadn't been so persistent in his pursuit of Jo, the two couples might have ended up with different partners. But that was history. They'd made their choices and they'd been good ones. Col and Alice had had a happy marriage, as had she and Gordon – until he'd been led astray by a combination of blonde hair and full breasts.

She continued into the kitchen to load their breakfast dishes into the dishwasher before heading to the bedroom and ensuite. Showered and dressed in a strappy sundress, Jo was already feeling the heat when she heard Eve's car draw up and the excited chatter of young Charotte and Olivia – Lottie and Livvy as they were known to the family.

'Thanks, Mum!' Eve walked straight to the kitchen and dropped a large bag on the table. 'They insisted on bringing all these toys, though I know you keep a collection here for them. You're a lifesaver. I have to be at the shop today and...'

'Good morning to you, too.' Jo hugged her daughter. 'I'm delighted to have them. I don't see nearly enough of them – or of Danny's two.' She frowned remembering her son's phone call. 'Last night went well, don't you think?'

'It was brilliant. I loved Uncle Col's tribute. I don't think I was the only one with tears in my eyes.'

'No.'

Col's speech to open the event had brought a tear to Jo's eyes too. His sometimes humorous, sometimes nostalgic, review of Alice's life brought her back as nothing else could. 'I wish she could have been there to hear it.'

They stood silent for a moment, then Eve said, 'I must be off. See you around five?'

'Fine.'

'What shall we do today, Gramma?' one of the twins asked – Lottie, Jo thought. She sometimes had trouble telling them apart, and Eve delighted in dressing them in identical outfits to compound the problem.

'You can help me make some chocolate crackles,' she said.

'Yay!' they said in unison.

Before long, Jo's kitchen was filled with the smell of melted chocolate. With the aid of two high stools, both Lottie and Livvy were "helping" their grandmother stir the melting chocolate, while Jo's old golden Labrador was lying at their feet hopeful of some titbits. Scout had really been Gordon's dog, but there hadn't been a place for him in his master's new life, and now Jo had come to depend on the dog's companionable presence.

'I think it's ready, Gramma,' one of the twins said, peering into the bowl which was sitting precariously in the saucepan of boiling water.

Jo checked and took it off the heat. 'Now for the fun part,' she said, taking the bowl to the benchtop and opening the packet of rice bubbles she'd bought especially. Once the stools had been moved over, the girls took turns in pouring the small balls of puffed rice into the bowl, getting more chocolate on their faces than on the cereal.

Scout padded over to join them, Jo taking pity on her pet to give him a dog biscuit which he carried off to enjoy in the solitude of his basket by the Aga.

When they'd filled several patty pans with the mixture, the girls were eager to try them, but Jo managed to distract them with a jigsaw while the crackles were cooling. She was in the midst of pouring out the apple juice to accompany their cooking efforts, when the phone rang.

'Rob?' she asked, seeing her younger son's number. What could he want? She wasn't due to be at the restaurant till evening when she'd agreed to do her usual Saturday night stint on front-of-house. It was something she enjoyed and kept her up to date with what was happening. She might be co-owner, but The Riverfront, Granite Springs, was really Rob's baby.

'Mum. Can you get away?'

Jo looked across the room to where her grandchildren, their faces covered in chocolate, were engaged in a competition to see who could eat the most crackles before she packed some away. 'Not really. I have Lottie and Livvy today. Eve had to work. 'What's up?'

'It's nothing I couldn't normally handle, but…' she heard Rob sigh. '… the new girl didn't turn up this morning and we're fully booked for lunch.'

'What about your usual casuals?' Jo knew Rob kept a list of potential staff, mostly students at the local university who were always glad to earn some extra cash.

'Tried them. It's holidays. They've either gone away or are busy doing other things. I'm at my wits' end.'

Jo could picture Rob standing in his kitchen, his red hair sticking up in its usual spikes, his freckles standing out on his pale skin – so like that of his grandmother – Jo's mother, now long gone. She racked her brains. 'Do you need someone with experience or just another pair of hands?'

'Anything would be good.'

'I know your Uncle Col planned to be over there this morning to finalise the sales from last night. Maybe…'

'Uncle Col?' Rob laughed. 'What does he know about running a restaurant?'

Maybe more than you think, she thought, remembering times over the past five years when she'd shared some of her worries with him, and together they'd hashed out possible solutions. The restaurant had overcome those early challenges and become a going concern and the most popular local venue for weddings and other celebrations before suffering a recent downturn due to the drought. But business was gradually picking up again.

'I thought you just needed a pair of hands? And I'll be there as usual for the evening shift. That's enough,' she said to the girls, pushing the tray of goodies out of their reach.

There was silence at the other end of the phone while Rob seemed to be digesting her suggestion, then, 'No, Mum. That won't work.'

Jo had a sudden idea. There were the twins to be looked after, there were the paintings to be organised, and there was the restaurant to be staffed. 'Leave it with me, Rob. I think I have a solution.' She hung up before he could ask any questions.

'How would you like to come to see some pictures with Uncle Col?' she asked. 'We can take your toys with us and find you a nice quiet corner. And maybe Uncle Rob can find something special for lunch?'

It was the perfect solution – if Col would agree. The girls could play quietly in a corner while Col did his thing, she could help Rob out and… the presence of the girls would surely prevent any awkwardness she and Col might feel when they met again.

As she expected, Col agreed, saying he was almost finished up there and would love to spend time with the twins. Breathing a sigh of relief, Jo wiped the two chocolatey faces and packed the girls into the car with the bag of toys and games Eve had brought along, thanking her lucky stars at her daughter's insistence she keep two child seats in the garage in the event of just such an occasion. They'd be fine with Col. They were good kids and would be starting school this year.

By the time they reached the restaurant and climbed up to the gallery level, the twins were chatting excitedly about painting their own pictures, making Jo doubly glad she'd decided to add paper and crayons to the bag Eve had left.

'Jo.'

'Col.'

They stood apart as the girls ran from one end of the room to the other, sliding on the bare wooden floor.

'Well.'

'Yes.'

It was silly to feel so awkward with each other after years of friendship, but that's what they'd been for the past thirty-odd years – friends. Now the axis had shifted. It was as if she was seeing him for the first time – in a light she hadn't seen him in before. Now she knew how his lips felt against hers, his body on hers, his… Flustered, she turned away.

'Rob's expecting me.'

She could feel Col's eyes on her back as she went through the door, imagined him still watching as she went down the stairs. When Rob greeted her at the bottom, Jo realised she was holding her breath.

Four

Col was surprised how disappointed he was. Jo had clearly felt awkward. What had he expected? He rubbed his chin. Not a hug, they were a bit old for that – or were they? He knew exactly how old Jo was. She would be sixty on the twenty-sixth of January – Australia Day – the same day as he would. When the four had first met they'd laughed, joking that the entire country stopped to celebrate with them.

Alice had often said that's why Jo and Col were so alike. And the four had celebrated together every year, three of them after Gordon left, and last year he and Jo had spent the day alone – hardly a celebration with Alice so recently gone. He wondered what would happen this year – it was only two weeks away.

'Uncle Col!' one of the little girls called, and he turned his attention to the picture she was holding up, showing two stick figures with a house behind them.

'Is this your mum and dad?' he asked.

'No!' she said reprovingly. 'It's you and Gramma, and you're here.' She pointed to the house in the picture, then to the room around them.

Her sister was still happily crayoning away, so Col took Lottie's picture – he knew it was her, from the *LO* squiggle at the bottom of the picture. 'Shall we put it up on the wall?' he asked, 'with the other pictures?' There were only a couple left, one the buyers had asked to pick up later in the week, plus the one Gordon and Carol had bought. He'd seen the pair bickering over the decision and wasn't sure why.

Maybe Carol hadn't felt it fitted with her new décor. Alice had never taken to her, nor Carol to Alice. That was understandable, given their history. The few times they'd met for dinner – at Gordon's suggestion – conversation had been stilted. He hadn't seen Carol at all in the past year – not till last night.

Since Alice's death, he and Gordon had continued to play golf together on Wednesdays and had, of course, seen each other every day in their chambers, and sometimes lunched together. But there had been no socialising which included Carol.

Col's phone buzzed, and he saw his friend's face on the screen. *Talk of the devil!*

'Hello, mate,' he said, holding the phone with one hand, while attempting to affix Lottie's drawing to the wall with the other. He was rewarded with a grin as she danced off to join her sister and do another.

'How are you this morning? I drove past your place and it looked deserted.'

'I'm at The Riverfront. You were to pick up your painting this morning – remember? The others have all gone.'

'And I'm holding you up?' Col heard Gordon chuckle.

'No. I'm actually minding the twins here. Jo…'

'The twins? What are they doing there?'

'Long story. Jo was taking the day shift for Eve, but Rob needed her here, so I've stepped in to free her up.'

'Hmph.'

'I'll be here for a bit longer if you want to collect your purchase. Otherwise I can bring it into the office on Monday.'

'That would be good. I might hang it there.' Gordon coughed. There was a pause during which Col wondered if he'd guessed correctly, if Carol hadn't wanted to give a painting of Alice's houseroom. 'It's a bit awkward,' Gordon said. 'Look, mate. I need to talk with you. Can we meet for lunch tomorrow – at the golf club? Carol has one of her ladies' meetings on, so I'd be fending for myself anyway. And about the painting, Monday'll be fine.'

'Suits me. Twelve?'

Col scratched his head as he hung up. Something was bothering

Gordon, and it was more than a disagreement about where to hang a painting.

He forced himself to forget about his friend's marital worries. He'd predicted this marriage wouldn't be all smooth sailing; that his old friend and partner had been hoodwinked by a pretty face and flirtatious manner, flattered by the attentions of the younger woman, and unable or unwilling to see the razor sharp and manipulative creature that lay hidden under the outward charm.

By the time Jo appeared to pick up the twins, the wall was festooned with their drawings and they were all engaged in a noisy game of snakes and ladders. Jo – or Rob – had sent up plates of sandwiches and juice for lunch, with a welcome beer for him, but he was beginning to feel exhausted. Looking after two young children was a tiring business.

'Hey,' he said, getting to his feet and stretching. 'Ouch!' He put his hand to his back.

'Serves you right for getting down on the floor with them,' Jo laughed. 'Had fun, twinnies?'

'Yes!' they chorused. 'Come and see our exhibition.' Stumbling over the word, the girls took her by the hand and led her to the wall, while Col followed slowly.

'You have a couple of budding artists here,' he said, noting Jo had failed to make eye contact with him. Surely she wasn't still embarrassed about last night?

'Beautiful. Shall we take them home to show Mummy?'

'I want you to choose one, and Uncle Col, too,' one of them said.

Finally, Jo's eyes met his. 'You first,' she said with a grin.

'It's too difficult,' he said. 'What if I close my eyes and point?'

That made them laugh and they chortled as he closed his eyes and waved his hand in the air, his finger finally settling on one with red dashes on a blue background.

'Mine!' Livvy yelled gleefully. 'Now you must put it up on your fridge. That's what Mummy does. See, Gramma. We have our names on them.'

Col saw Jo peer at the bottom of the drawings where the twins had scrawled either *LO* or *LI*.

'I'd better choose one of Lottie's, then,' she said, and indicated the one with the two figures.

'Good choice,' Col said, detaching them from the wall. 'You'll be off home now?' he asked Jo.

'Yes. Eve's picking them up around five, so we need to get going.'

Col picked up the bag of toys and followed them down to the car. When Jo had fastened the girls in safely, she turned to face him. 'I need to go now.'

'Do you? Can I…? Tonight?'

'I'm on duty here.'

'Oh!'

Then she seemed to take pity on him. 'I'll be finished by ten. If that's not too late for you, I could drop in for a nightcap…' Her voice tailed away as if she regretted the offer.

'No. That'll be good. I'll see you then.'

Jo got into the car and closed the door. Col heard the engine start, gave her a wave, then put his hands in his pockets and walked to his own car, a sudden gust of air blowing up a whirlwind of red dust.

They needed to talk. Tonight!

Five

'Mum!'

Eve arrived just as Jo was preparing a snack before she went to the restaurant. The twins were seated at the kitchen table with milk and some of the remaining chocolate crackles, and Scout was lying hopefully below the table. At the sound of the shrill note in their mother's voice, both the girls looked round.

'Oh, good. You're here. I need to get off to the restaurant shortly. Rob's expecting me.'

'How could you?' Eve marched into the room, her eyes flashing.

What had she done now? It was sometimes difficult for Jo to keep up with her daughter's long list of expectations and rules. She often thought Eve forgot she'd managed to bring up three children without mishap. But it seemed things were different these days – helicopter parenting, Jo had read it was called. She waited for Eve to explain.

'I spoke to Dad.'

Still Jo waited. *What had Gordon said to get Eve so riled?*

'He said you'd left the children in the gallery with Uncle Col – alone!'

Jo sighed. 'So?'

'Uncle Col doesn't have any children of his own. What does he know about taking care of them properly?'

Jo took a deep breath before replying. She seemed to be doing that a lot lately where her children were concerned. Not with Rob – he was still her lovely baby – but both Danny and Eve tended to treat her as if she was on a different planet. Maybe she was.

'He knows a lot, honey. Remember how many times he and Aunt Alice took care of you and your brothers? They treated you like their own children – the children they weren't able to have.'

'That was different. Uncle Col is a man.'

'There's no argument on that front.' *He'd proved that very ably the previous night – or was it this morning?*

'But, Mum! You know what people might say – might think. A man, on his own, with two young children…'

Jo couldn't believe her ears. This was Col Eve was talking about – a man she'd known all her life, her parents' best friend, her mother's…

'Anyone who thinks there's anything wrong with that is an ass! I'm surprised at you even contemplating such a thing.'

Eve looked embarrassed. 'I know it's Uncle Col, but…'

'What exactly did your dad say?'

'That you'd dumped the girls on Uncle Col while you did something else – something you obviously thought was more important than looking after your granddaughters.' The stubborn look on Eve's face was reminiscent of her teenage years.

Jo pressed her lips together. 'Did he also tell you that I was just downstairs helping Rob out with a staffing issue, that Col was already at the gallery finalising things from last night, and that he kindly offered to mind them for a bit while I helped your brother out?'

'No…oo.'

Jo felt her tension ease. 'He was great with them. They had a lovely time. We made some chocolate crackles first, then they drew a bundle of pictures for him and he had them all displayed on the wall when I picked them up.'

'We made an exhibition,' Livvy said, sliding down from the table and thrusting a bundle of drawings into her mother's hand.

'Oh!' Eve sounded surprised. 'Well, it's just… you can't be too careful.'

'Eve, this is your uncle we're talking about. And do you think I'd do anything to risk harming these two?'

'Sorry, Mum. I…' Eve had the grace to look embarrassed as she tucked a strand of hair behind one ear.

'And so you should be. Now, I *do* need to go.'

*

By the time ten o'clock came, Jo was dead on her feet. She was getting too old for this. Maybe she should suggest to Rob he find someone to cover her shifts. But it was the wrong time of year to look for new staff.

All she wanted to do was go home, have a long bath, and fall into bed. But she'd promised Col. She fingered her phone, wondering if he'd mind if she chickened out, then sighed. They'd have to talk about it sometime, and putting it off wasn't going to help matters. At least, she assumed he wanted to talk, not… She felt a flutter in the pit of her stomach, remembering the passion that had appeared seemingly from nowhere, a level of desire she'd thought never to experience again. But it was Col, her best friend, Gordon's best friend, and her children's godfather. Maybe it had been the result of the alcohol they'd consumed. But, deep down, Jo knew it was no such thing. It was as if the strong pull she'd felt last night had been there all along, just waiting to spring to life.

Jo refreshed her lipstick, tidied her hair, made a face at herself in the mirror, and headed out to her car.

Col's house – she'd only recently been able to say Col's instead of Alice and Col's – was an older style brick house with a corrugated iron roof, a front veranda and a large courtyard at the back. It wasn't far from The Riverside. She could have walked there but preferred to drive at this time of night. As she drew into the driveway, Jo thought of all the times she'd been here in the past, the dinner parties, the birthday events, the times when she and Alice had taken tea together. But, until Alice's death, never just her and Col.

Even now, it was an unusual occurrence. They tended to meet in cafes or restaurants, sometimes briefly at her home if he picked her up for a movie or a concert. It felt odd to be driving here alone at this late hour.

The door opened almost before she'd shut off the engine, and a beam of light shone down the steps and across the pavers. Col must have been waiting and had heard her car. He stood at the top of the steps. 'You came!'

So, he'd doubted her?

He leant forward to give her the usual peck on the cheek, triggering a slight quiver of anticipation which she tried to suppress. She followed him into the living room she knew so well but which seemed empty without Alice's lively presence.

'I was just having a port while I finished my book,' Col gestured to the glass sitting on the coffee table and the book lying open beside it. 'Have one?'

'Thanks.' She went over to pick up the book, while he reached for the decanter and filled another glass. 'Oh, you've got the new Jane Harper. I loved *The Dry*.'

'I did, too. She has a way of describing the Australian countryside that…' He spread his hands. 'Here you are.' Col handed Jo her glass and carried his own back to a well-worn chair.

She settled into the floral covered armchair opposite Col and took a sip. 'Mmm. Nice.'

'It's one Gordon gave me for Christmas.'

Jo nodded. Her ex always knew his ports.

She took another sip. *What was she doing here?*

Col took a swig from his replenished glass, leant over to close his book, then his eyes met hers. 'I thought we needed to talk… about last night.' He coughed. 'I know what you said – that we should take things as they come, but… I haven't been able to stop thinking about it – about you.'

Jo looked down into the tawny liquid, its sweet taste on her tongue. 'I haven't either,' she admitted, then looked up, a smile etched on her lips. 'This is crazy, Col. How can we…?' She fell silent, then tried again. 'There are the children to think of…' Her voice tailed away.

'Last time I checked they were all grown up.' His words were accompanied by a chuckle.

'Yes, but…' Jo thought of Eve's comments that afternoon. 'They… I don't know how… Oh, hell, this isn't easy. What if we…?'

'You have your own life to live,' he said gently. 'Pardon my saying, but you've let others rule your life for too long. First Gordon, then Danny and Eve.' He paused.

'Not Rob.' Jo smiled at the thought of her younger son.

'No, not Rob. He's had his own challenges to face.'

Jo nodded. As a gay man in a country town, Rob had faced a few of those, but he'd come through unscathed and now he and his partner,

Steve, who taught at the local university, lived in a house in the centre of town, not far from the restaurant.

'Talking of the kids, I had a run in with Eve this afternoon.'

Col raised one eyebrow.

'She queried my leaving the twins with you.' Jo didn't want to go into details. 'You're right, of course. She and Danny treat me like I have one foot in the grave.'

Col smiled in agreement. They were silent. Jo stroked the arm of the chair wondering what to say next.

The silence lengthened. This was crazy. She'd known Col for most of her life. She knew this house almost as well as she knew her own. But last night he'd surprised her. She'd surprised herself with the depth of the passion she and Col had experienced.

After over thirty years of marriage she and Gordon had fallen into a routine, sex had become a habit far removed from the passion of their early years. She'd supposed that's what happened as you grew older, more accustomed to each other, less desirous of sex, more willing to turn over and fall asleep. She'd missed the warmth of her husband's embrace, but comforted herself with the fact that, even after a fraught few years when the children were in their teens, they were still together. Until Carol came on the scene.

Jo had been surprised, but not alarmed, when Gordon began to take his weekly cycling more seriously, had started to regard it as a competition against himself, to measure his performance. Little had she known he was basking in the admiration of the new office siren.

Then Gordon had gone, and she'd been left with long nights and a lonely bed. Till last night.

She came back to the present to see Col with a speculative glint in his eye. 'Maybe we should check,' he said. 'Check we weren't mistaken, that it wasn't a fluke.'

'You mean?'

Col rose, took Jo's hand, and helped her up. Their lips met with an intensity that sent tremors through her entire body, proving the previous night had been no accidental coupling.

Six

'This could become a habit.' Col propped himself up on one elbow and gazed down into Jo's sleep-filled eyes.

She smiled and stretched her arms above her head. 'Good morning.'

'Sleep well?'

'I did.'

Jo looked so lovely lying there, her silvery blonde hair spread over the pillow, so different from the usual tidy arrangement she wore in daytime. It felt like he was seeing a secret part of her, a part she rarely revealed. As Col buried his nose in her hair and inhaled her unique scent – a heady mixture of a floral fragrance with underlying notes of musk and incense, her warm body moved against his, and they came together in a frenzy of desire.

It was some time before they emerged to gaze into each other's eyes.

'My God!' Col said. 'Who was it who said the earth moved?'

'Hemingway,' Jo chuckled. 'It *was* pretty good, wasn't it?'

Jo sat up against the bank of pillows, and Col was glad to see she didn't feel the need to cover herself. He enjoyed looking at her mature body, her womanly body. His fingers traced her curves, finally coming to rest on her breasts. He could feel her quiver under his touch. Then she moved away.

'It's late.'

Col reached to his watch on the bedside table. 'Eight-thirty. Do you have to be anywhere today?'

'No, but…'

'Damn!' He remembered. 'I'm having lunch with Gordon. He has something he wants to talk to me about.'

'Something that can't wait till Monday?'

'Seems not.'

The moment was gone. Col swung his legs out of bed. 'You rest there while I take a shower, then I can make you breakfast.'

'Sounds good.'

Col watched her slide back down the bed, then he headed for the shower – a cold one.

The coffee maker was hissing and gurgling, filling the kitchen with a strong aroma by the time Jo appeared. She stood in the doorway for a second before coming in.

'Can I do anything?'

'All organised.' Col gestured to the bacon and eggs sizzling in the pan. 'But if you'd like toast, maybe drop a couple of slices into the toaster.'

'I don't usually eat this much for breakfast,' she said. 'But it does smell good.' She sniffed. Familiar with the kitchen, she turned unerringly to the bread bin and extracted two slices of bread before putting them into the toaster.

'It feels odd,' she said, leaning against the sink.

Col knew exactly what she meant. This was Alice's kitchen. Whereas he'd changed things around in the bedroom to help him sleep, the kitchen remained exactly as it had been when Alice was alive. It still retained her stamp – the collection of pottery mugs on the wooden stand, the gaily patterned canisters on the shelf which had held her various teas and biscuits, but were now empty, the stand that had always held the recipes Alice had been planning to try out – one day.

He drew a hand through his hair. 'Sometimes I can imagine she's still here,' he said.

The toast popped up and Jo placed it on a plate and sat down at the table. 'I shouldn't be here.' Her hair fell out of the band she'd attempted to secure it with – a cloud of silver tumbling around her shoulders. He wanted to run his fingers through it. It was so different from Alice's dark locks. For a moment he imagined Alice sitting there with them, could picture her laughing. Then the image was gone.

'Thanks for a lovely breakfast. But I really should go now,' Jo said, but made no move to leave. 'Don't…'

'I won't say anything to Gordon.' Col read her mind. He could imagine what his old friend would say if he knew they'd been to bed together. Jo and Gordon might have been divorced for five years, Gordon remarried for almost that long, but Col knew he still felt proprietorial about his ex-wife.

'No. Not a good idea.' She gave a conspiratorial smile. 'What he doesn't know won't hurt him.'

'Our usual Monday dinner?'

Jo nodded her agreement, though Col knew there would be nothing usual about their dinner the following evening.

*

Col saw Gordon's BMW as soon as he drove into the golf club carpark and slid his own car alongside. He found his friend leaning on the bar, a beer in one hand.

'What's up?'

'It's Carol.'

'Is she sick? She looked well on Friday.' But Col could barely remember what she'd been wearing or how she'd looked. He only knew she'd have been dressed to the nines, probably in something tight and – in her opinion – sexy.

When Carol had joined the staff of their legal practice, her flirtatious ways had been obvious. She tried them on both Col and Gordon. But Gordon was the one who succumbed. Col had recognised her immediately for what she was – a woman on the make, looking for a sugar daddy. A demanding woman who knew what she wanted and went all out to get it. As unlike Jo as she could be. Gordon had fallen right in.

'Let's order first.'

It was only when the pair were seated in a secluded corner with a second beer and plates of steak and chips, that Gordon broached the subject again.

'Carol,' he said. 'She wants to start a family. Can you imagine? At my age? A baby?'

'Oh, I don't know. Might keep you young. I had a good time with your two granddaughters yesterday.' He chuckled at the memory, then remembered how bushed he'd felt afterwards.

'It's not funny. She's determined. What the hell do I do?'

'It's a tough one.' Col forbore saying it was what Gordon got for marrying someone half his age. He knew he'd get no thanks. 'What have you told her?'

Gordon put down his knife and fork and took a slug of beer. 'So far, I've tried to avoid the subject, but I can't do that for much longer. Help me, Col. I'm too old to be starting again with babies, nappies and the whole up-all-night thing.'

Col took a gulp of beer before replying. He had no idea what to advise Gordon. He'd never had to deal with a woman like Carol. 'Why don't you just tell her what you've told me? Surely she'll understand?'

Gordon drew a hand through his hair. 'That's just it. I don't think she will. She's been so used to getting her own way – all her life, I think. And… I may have spoiled her, given in to her when I shouldn't – but that was over little things. This…' He let out a long breath. 'This would finish me. I'd be almost eighty when the child finishes school.'

Col could see where his friend was coming from but could think of no other solution.

'Ah, you and Alice were lucky,' Gordon said, then seemed to realise how that must sound. 'I mean… No kids, a good marriage.'

'You had one too – you and Jo.'

'Yes.' Gordon sighed.

Unable to suggest anything further, Col concentrated on his meal, and the conversation revolved around the contenders for the new committee at the golf club, and a knotty problem Gordon was experiencing with a case on which he wanted Col's opinion.

But as Col drove off, Gordon's dilemma was at the forefront of his mind. If his old mate did succumb to his wife's demands and started a new family, how would that affect Jo, and what would his grown-up children make of it?

Seven

The sun beat down on Jo's head and the deafening sound of cicadas met her ears when she stepped out of her car in the parking lot at the nursing home. Tuesday was her day to deliver library books to Val Brennan. She'd been doing this every three weeks for the past six years. The older woman had seen her through a lot, and Jo knew she was one of the few people she could confide in. Nothing shocked Val who'd been married to the town doctor for over fifty years, until he'd died from an aneurism. For much of her married life, she'd also acted as practice manager and had been privy to many confidences. She knew how to keep a secret.

Last night with Col had been good. He was restful company. They'd had a nice dinner at Pavarotti's as usual then she'd pleaded the need for an early night. Two nights of strenuous lovemaking was more than she'd been used to for years, and the combination of her aging body and lack of sleep was beginning to tell. She'd sensed Col's disappointment, but he hadn't tried to dissuade her. Maybe *he* needed a good night's sleep too.

Jo made her way to Val's room, knocked gently on the door, and pushed it open. Val was sitting in her usual spot – in a maroon velvet armchair. A book was lying in her lap, and she was gazing out the window to where two galahs were fighting over a crust lying on the parched grass. The old woman looked up at Jo's entrance.

'Jo! I thought I'd see you today. I'm on the last one.' She held up the book from her lap. 'Another great selection. You're kind to an old woman. I don't know what I'd do without my regular supply of books.'

'How are you?' Jo gave Val a peck on the cheek. 'You're looking well.'

'Not so bad, today. But what about you?' The old woman looked her up and down. 'You have a… a glow about you. What have you been up to? If I didn't know better, I'd say you've found yourself a man.'

Jo felt her cheeks warming.

'You have? Well, about time. How long has it been since that no-good husband of yours did the dirty on you?'

'Five years.' Jo's voice was subdued.

'Now, sit down and tell me all about it. You're a breath of fresh air, after the dull routine in this place. They try their best, but… Anyway, enough of my troubles.'

Jo drew a chair to sit opposite Val but didn't immediately begin to speak. She looked down at her hands twisting in her lap, then up to meet the other woman's eyes. 'It's Col,' she said. 'Col Ford.'

Val's breath exhaled noisily from pursed lips. 'Gordon won't like that. Does he know?'

'He… no, we've barely begun to…'

Val chortled. 'I don't know why some of your generation is so coy about sex. We lived through the seventies – free love and all that – and now here you are acting as if it was some kind of new age thing. So, Gordon doesn't know yet? Well, well. They share an office – and now you.'

'It's not quite like that. We're both free agents,' Jo said defensively.

'And you've all known each other forever. Duke and I used to see the four of you around town and we admired your youth and resilience. Of course, it would never have happened while Alice was alive,' she mused, 'but I've often wondered if you married the wrong man.'

Jo's eyes widened. This was so close to her earlier thoughts. Was Val a witch? 'We became closer when Alice was so sick, and then, last Friday, after the retrospective of Alice's paintings… I'd never… We'd never…'

'I don't expect you had, my dear. It's often the onlooker who sees things more clearly. But I'm happy for you, if it's what you want.' She patted Jo's hand with her own age-spotted one.

'That's just it. I don't know that it is.' Jo looked down at their hands – at the frail, timeworn one and her own firmer flesh. Hers would be like Val's one day. Did she want to spend her days like Val, alone? Should she grasp what fate was offering her, make the most of what might be her last opportunity at happiness?

'You need to think about yourself. I may be an old woman, but I've seen a lot, and it seems to me that you've always done what others expected of you – your husband, your children…'

Jo opened her mouth to speak, but Val held up a hand.

'Hear me out. There are no medals given out for being compliant. At your stage of life, you need to start thinking about what *you* want, about what's good for *you*. You have a lot of years left, God willing, and you deserve to have a good life. If Col can give you that, I say you should go for it.' She sat back, studying Jo.

Jo was lost for words. She didn't know what she'd expected Val to say, but not this. How did she know?

'How did…' she began.

'I'm pretty good at reading people. Had to be in Duke's medical practice. And I'd be willing to bet those children of yours still expect you to be running around after them. Am I right?'

'Well…' Jo thought about the three of them, so different in many ways, but essentially Val was right. It was almost exactly what *Col* had said.

'I suppose… Eve treats me like the clothesline, expecting me to be always available when she needs me to babysit. Oh, I love my two granddaughters, don't get me wrong, but sometimes, if I've made other plans…' Jo thought back to Saturday, and Eve's annoyance. '…and Danny…' she drew a deep breath, '…he always thinks he knows better. He's been on at me to sell the house to him and Kylie, and move into one of those villas he's been developing outside town – the other side to here.'

Val tutted. 'What about your youngest – Rob?'

'Oh, Rob's no bother.' Then Saturday came to mind again. 'Though he does expect me to fill in at the restaurant at the drop of a hat.'

'Maybe you should take a holiday. Go away for a bit. See how they manage without you. And with Danny… Is it such a bad idea?'

'Yes! Sorry, I didn't mean to yell, but we… I've lived at Yarran since Danny was born. The children all grew up there. It's my home.'

'Well, give it some thought – all of it. You're the only one who can decide what's best for you. All I can say is, don't allow yourself to be swayed by what others want, by what *they* think is best for you, whether they be your ex-husband or your children, or even Col. And – something I learned long ago – don't worry what people think. In most instances they're so busy worrying about themselves, they don't think at all.'

'Yes, you're right.' Jo lifted her eyes to meet Val's. 'Thanks for that. You've certainly given me food for thought.'

'Why don't I see if they'll bring us some tea?' Val asked. She rose, getting stiffly to her feet before Jo could answer, and moved to the door. Jo heard her ask if the carer could bring her a pot of tea for two.

'We're lucky,' Val said, when she returned to her chair with a grateful sigh, 'It's the lovely Della on duty. Some of the others wouldn't give you the time of day, never mind a cup of tea. Now tell me about those lovely twins of yours.'

The tea arrived, and for the next half hour or so, Jo entertained Val with the latest exploits of Lottie and Livvy, making her laugh at the way Col had managed to keep them occupied.

'But Eve didn't like my leaving them with him,' Jo said ruefully. 'She's becoming a bit too protective and concerned about "what people might think".'

Val shook her head. 'Those modern parents,' she said. 'Col wouldn't harm a hair on their heads. I hope you told her so.'

'I did. Now I must go. It's been lovely to see you and thanks for the tea.'

'Not Earl Grey I'm afraid, but a passable drop.'

Jo rose to leave. 'Thanks for your advice too, Val. It's much appreciated. I'll see you in another three weeks,' she added, before leaving and closing the door behind her.

Once in her car, Jo sat for a few moments digesting Val's advice. She had no doubt it was sound, but it would be difficult to change the habits of a lifetime.

Eight

Jo had barely arrived home and was about to fill the electric jug when the phone rang. She checked the caller ID – Danny! What did he want now?

'Mum,' he said, before she had time to greet him. 'Great news. Phase one of the development is almost complete, and the display home is going on the market. I've booked an advance viewing for you tomorrow at ten. I can meet you there. Four Myrtle Avenue.'

Jo counted to ten before replying.

He was just like… his father, Jo realised. And what had been attractive in the younger Gordon had become annoying as they'd grown older, as she'd become more independent and developed her own opinions about things. But stating her opinion didn't work with Danny who brushed off all her objections as if she didn't know what she was doing – as if she was an idiot.

Remembering Val's advice, Jo was tempted to tell Danny exactly what she thought of his high-handed arrangement, but knew he'd ignore her yet again. It wouldn't kill her to look at the damned place. She took a deep breath. 'Ten o'clock tomorrow. I think I can make that.'

'Good. See you there.' He hung up. No "thank you". No "love you, Mum". He'd got his way and was satisfied. Though he wouldn't be when he discovered she still had no intention of buying into the development, no intention of selling, no intention of turning this house over to him and Kylie.

Jo walked through Yarran, the house they'd built on those twenty acres when Danny was still a baby. They didn't build them like this these days – double brick walls, high ceilings, a wide veranda surrounding the entire house to provide shade in summer and looking out over the paddocks, now a mass of purple – the dreaded weed, Patterson's curse. Since Gordon left, she'd leased the paddock to a neighbour, keeping only the land around the house and her well-tended garden – though it was difficult to keep up the watering in the present drought conditions.

Her neighbours, John and Bernadette, reared goats, and the animals provided Jo with hours of pleasure as she watched their antics from her kitchen window or from the cool of the veranda while she sipped her morning cup of tea or her sunset glass of chardonnay.

Jo made herself a sandwich, poured a glass of chilled water from the fridge and settled down with her book club book. But today, the book selected by the group – Anne Gorman's *The Country Wife* – failed to hold her attention. Her body was remembering how she felt in Col's embrace.

Although still a youthful and energetic woman in her late fifties, Jo had assumed that part of her life was finished, never again expecting to experience the passion of her youth. But with Col, she'd felt a sense of renewal, a realisation it wasn't over, that it was still possible to feel intense rushes of emotion – emotion that took her breath away.

*

Jo peered out the car window at the small villa with a single window and single garage door. It looked no different to the others she'd passed on the way into the estate, either already occupied or still being built. She was reminded of a song she'd heard many years ago – something about little boxes. That's exactly what they were. And Danny wanted her to give up her comfortable, spacious home for this?

'Mum!' Danny stepped out of his dark blue BMW and came towards her, opening her car door, bending in to give her a kiss on the cheek, and holding out his hand to help her out. *As if she was elderly*, she thought as she took the outstretched hand.

'What do you think?' He gestured towards the boring white house with a smile.

'It's… very modern.' Jo couldn't think of anything else to say about it.

'Isn't it?' he enthused. 'Wait till you see inside. You'll fall in love with it. I know you say you want to hang on to the old place,' he continued to talk as they walked up the front path, 'but imagine having so much less to look after, of being able to get rid of some of those old pieces of furniture that are well past their best. You could furnish this in a new modern style. Kylie thought…'

Jo closed her ears to what Kylie thought. If her present home was in such a sad state, why was her daughter-in-law so keen to get her hands on it?

'I agreed to look at this place, Danny,' she said. 'But I haven't changed my mind. I'm happy where I am. Yarran isn't too big for me. It's my home.' She recalled having said that before.

By this time, they were inside the villa, and Jo could see that, although it might be well designed, the rooms were small and poky. She'd feel claustrophobic living here after the airy rooms she was used to.

'You're being selfish, Mum.'

Jo gasped. Selfish to want to stay in her home? Selfish to refuse to turn it over to her son and daughter-in-law in some misguided act of generosity? She bit her tongue and allowed Danny to lead her through all the rooms, opening cupboards and extolling the advantages of downsizing. Downsizing! She'd rather die! She might as well end up in a nursing home like poor Val as move into this little box.

She realised Danny was still talking. Now, he was praising the virtues of having near neighbours '…in case anything happens to you, Mum.'

Jo had had enough. She drew herself up to her full height – still a full head and shoulders shorter than her son – and said firmly, 'I'm not in my dotage, Danny. I'm quite capable of managing by myself and I *have* neighbours. Bernadette and John are just over the fence – a phone call away. Now, are we done here? I have things to do, and you must have to get back to the office. It's been good of you to take time to show me around but, as I said, it's not for me.'

Danny only smiled, giving Jo the impression the discussion about the villa wasn't over.

Jo drove home in a daze. How could Danny ever imagine she'd contemplate living in a place like that? How little he really knew her. She wondered idly if he'd spoken to his dad about it. They'd been close once, but Jo had the feeling that these days Gordon was closer to Eve. She thought even Gordon was unimpressed with Kylie's delusions of grandeur, though she knew he enjoyed spending time with Danny and Kylie's two boys. Tim and Liam were ten and eight now and turning into little replicas of their dad.

The house closed around Jo when she walked in, welcoming her, almost as if it was a living thing. She sighed with relief and, making a cup of tea, carried it out to the veranda with her book, determined, this time, to make a dent in it. She was enjoying the true story of the country wife who'd led such a difficult life but managed to overcome her challenges to bring up five children and establish her own business. She was at the part where the author joined the Country Women's Association when her phone buzzed with a text. Smiling to see Col's name. Jo pressed *open* and read the message.

Tomorrow as usual? Cx

Jo found herself smiling as she texted her agreement. She felt like a young girl. She couldn't wait to see Col again.

Nine

'Busy?'

Col looked up at his partner standing in the doorway, embarrassed at being caught texting Jo. Though why he should feel that way he had no idea. He quickly shut off his phone. 'An appointment in fifteen minutes. What's up?'

Gordon took the chair normally reserved for clients and leant his elbows on his knees. 'I tried what you suggested,' he said. 'It was no good. She came up with all sorts of reasons to start a family, shot down all my objections, even suggested I might think I was past it – was firing blanks. A man can't let that go.'

'So?'

'We seem to be at an impasse.' Gordon frowned. 'How can I…?'

'I'm the last man to advise you on that one.' Col rubbed his chin. 'I suppose the only way to disprove her on that is to go ahead with what she wants. Didn't you discuss all this before you married?'

'It all happened in such a rush. I thought… Hell, I don't know what I thought.'

You thought you were a lucky bastard and couldn't wait to dash down the aisle – or into the registry office as it happened – leaving a perfectly good wife.

'Hmm.'

Col had always liked Jo. In fact, if things had been different, it might have been them who had married all those years ago. But Gordon had been the more outgoing of the two and had made his intention clear.

Col had been happy to hook up with Alice, and they'd had a good marriage, the only blot being their inability to have children. Maybe that had been the glue that had held them together. Gordon and Jo's three hadn't done much for their marriage, though Gordon had at least waited till the kids were grown before kicking over the traces – or had he? Col had sometimes wondered about his friend and partner, but never said anything.

He looked pointedly at his watch. Frank and Marie Beattie would be arriving shortly. The well-known local couple, owners of a popular café, had parted ways and wanted Col to expedite their divorce. It seemed it would be a straightforward affair. The only possible stumbling block might be the family business which had been in Frank's family for three generations, but which Marie had managed to pull out of a slump a few years earlier by offering baking classes and children's birthday parties in the back room.

'I'm sorry, Gordon.'

'Sure. I'll let you get on. Lunch?'

'Can do. I'll let you know when I'm free.'

Almost as soon as the door closed behind Gordon, Col's phone buzzed.

'The Beatties are here.' They'd brought Dot back from her early retirement to replace Carol. Col wasn't going to make the same mistake again. He had no idea what had possessed them to employ Carol Landry in the first place. Maybe they'd thought having a bright young thing around would be good for business. It certainly hadn't been good for Gordon.

'Send them in.' Col rose to greet the couple who entered. He'd been a loyal customer in their café over the years and was sorry to see them in this situation.

'Marie, Frank,' he said, shaking their hands. 'Take a seat.'

Once they had settled and the pleasantries had been exchanged, Col got down to business.

He peered down at the folder on his desk. 'I see you want to divorce.' He looked up. 'You're both agreed?'

'Yes,' Frank said, glancing sideways at his wife.

She nodded.

'And you've lived apart for twelve months?'

'Marie's still in the house,' Frank said, 'but I've set myself up above the café. We have a nice little flat there that we were just using for storage and…'

'Right. Shouldn't be any problems then. A no fault divorce. Irreconcilable differences?'

Both nodded.

'I just need your paperwork, and we can discuss the division of assets.'

The pair looked puzzled.

'Paperwork?' Frank asked.

Col sighed. Dot should have prepared them for this interview.

'I can provide the necessary forms, but I'll need your marriage certificate.'

They looked at each other. Frank cleared his throat. 'We don't have one.'

Col leant forward, his hands clasped. This wasn't unusual. Sometimes people weren't as careful as they might be with important documents. 'That's not a problem. You can easily get a copy from the Registry of…'

'No!' Marie didn't let him finish. 'What Frank means is that we don't have a marriage certificate. We never have. It was back in the seventies and…'

'…we never got around to it,' Frank said.

Col was stunned. This was a first. 'Well,' he said, laughing inwardly, 'If you've never married you don't need a divorce. All we need to do is decide on the division of assets.'

The discussion didn't take much longer as the couple had already worked out how they wanted to do this. Col showed them to the door with a smile and shook hands again, wishing all his clients were so easy to deal with.

He tidied up the papers on his desk and popped his head around Gordon's door. 'Lunch?'

His partner looked up and removed his glasses. 'Be right with you.' He pushed back his chair.

'We'll be back in an hour or so,' Col told Dot as they left the office, the large wooden door swinging closed behind them. 'Club or the Italian?' he asked Gordon as they reached the street.

'Italian. Less likelihood of being hi-jacked by anyone.'

Col grinned. In days gone by, Gordon loved to be caught up in conversations during lunch, drinks or dinner. This business with Carol was bothering him more than he made out.

When they were seated in the restaurant, having both ordered beer and the house pizza, Col looked across the table at his friend. 'It's getting you down? This thing with Carol.'

Gordon took a swig of the beer which had just been served and nodded. 'I'm at my wits' end. But what did you get up to today? Did you manage to arrange the Beatties' divorce for them?'

'Funny thing.' Col decided to tell Gordon the story, hoping to take his mind off his own worries.

'Wish it was that easy,' Gordon complained.

Shocked, Col glanced at his companion, surprised to see the haunted expression in his eyes. 'Surely it's not that bad, mate?'

'No. I guess not. I just wish I could get her to see sense.'

Their meals arrived and nothing more was said about Carol and her desire to have a child, the conversation revolving instead around a couple of tricky cases Gordon was handling. It was as they were drinking coffee prior to leaving that Gordon asked, 'You still see Jo, don't you?'

'From time to time. Since Alice passed, we've got into the habit of having dinner together a couple of times a week.' He mentally crossed his fingers.

'Right. Glad it's you, mate. If it was anyone else, I'd be worried.' He chuckled in a way that left no room for doubt that Gordon still wanted to keep tabs on his ex-wife. 'She's still hanging on to the house? The lad says he and Kylie want to buy her out. Has she said anything?'

'I think she mentioned something about it. But you know Jo – it'd take more than Kylie to move her out of that place.'

'Mmm. It'd be good for the boys.'

Col agreed but felt, like Jo, that if Danny and Kylie wanted an acreage, they could find their own.

There was obviously something else on Gordon's mind, but Col knew there was no point in pursuing it. His friend would tell him if and when he was ready. He was pretty sure Jo had won the house fair and square in the divorce settlement, so Gordon had no claim on it. Why the interest?

On the walk back, Col thought to ask, 'Have you hung that painting yet?'

Gordon seemed to cheer up immediately. 'I have. Didn't you notice it? Come in and see for yourself.'

Back at their chambers, they went into Gordon's office where the painting hung on the wall beside the window, clearly visible to anyone entering; Col hadn't looked in that direction earlier.

'Looks good,' Col said, going towards the depiction of a beach scene. 'Tathra. That was one of the times we all went there when your kids were little.'

'Good times,' Gordon said with a sigh.

Col gave him a swift glance.

His friend was gazing at the painting with a nostalgic expression. Then he seemed to collect himself. 'Long gone. They're all grown now with children of their own – except for Rob.'

'I won't keep you.' Col left to return to his own office and the mass of paperwork that awaited him. Some legal things still had to be in hard copy.

But as the afternoon passed, he wondered exactly what had been in Gordon's mind when he asked about Jo.

Ten

Jo was enjoying her early morning cuppa on the veranda when her phone ringing attracted her attention. She dragged her eyes away from the two kookaburras sitting on the fence-line and smiled to see her friend's cheerful face on the screen. Kay had been gone over Christmas, visiting her daughter in Brisbane, and she'd missed being able to confide in her.

'Hi Kay. Are you back?'

'Late last night. It's good to be home.'

Jo could hear the relief in Kay's voice. 'It didn't go well?'

'It was all right. Lovely to see Noah, but sometimes I wonder if Zoe's the same little girl I brought up. She tires me out. She's so difficult and… You don't want to hear all my moans. How are you?'

'I'm good.' Jo couldn't keep the smile out of her voice.

'You sound very upbeat. What's been happening while I've been gone? Has Danny finally come to his senses?'

Jo gave a wry laugh. 'No chance! But, since Alice's retrospective…'

'Oh, how did that go?' Kay interrupted. 'I was so sorry to miss it. You must tell me all about it. Coffee? What are you doing this morning?'

Jo smiled to herself. Kay would never change. Friends since their schooldays, Kay had always been the outgoing one, while Jo followed in her wake. Both had married local boys and set up home in the town they'd grown up in. They'd seen each other through marriage, motherhood, teenagers, Jo's divorce and, two years earlier, the death of Kay's beloved husband, David. Over the years, they'd fallen into the habit of meeting for coffee at least once each week. Jo had missed her over the past few weeks.

Coffee with her old friend was exactly what Jo needed.

'Sounds good. I could make it at ten. I need to exchange my books.'

'See you then.'

There was no need to specify a meeting place. For years, the pair had met in the café just around the corner from the library. Although changing hands several times, Mouthfuls had retained its original ambiance and the quality of the coffee left nothing to be desired. The present owners were new to the town, having moved there from Sydney several years earlier. Melody and her husband Jason had fitted into the community right away, Melody becoming a popular member of Friends of the Gallery, while Jason had added his strengths to the cricket club.

Jo finished her tea, threw the remnants of her toast onto the grass where a flock of galahs immediately arrived to fight over them, and headed inside, Scout padding loyally behind her. She bent to ruffle his ears. She'd have been lost without this faithful companion during the past five years, and had often shared her worries with him, his soulful eyes suggesting that he understood even if he couldn't answer back.

By nine-forty, she was dressed in a loose blue and white caftan and, slipping her feet into a pair of flat white sandals, was ready to go.

'Won't be long, Scout,' she said, as she shut the gate behind her, leaving her pet lying in a spot of shade on the veranda. The once lively dog was now content to lie around, lazily moving from one spot to another as the sun moved around the house.

Parking her Volkswagen Golf in a side street, Jo made her way to the café where Kay was already seated in the back courtyard under a shade umbrella. The two women hugged, then Kay said, 'I already ordered. Skinny cap for you?'

'Thanks.' Jo took a chair, but her bottom had barely touched the seat when Kay began to speak.

'How was it – Alice's exhibition?'

Jo laughed. Kay would never change. But that was one of the things she liked about her. She refused to let anything dampen her enthusiasm for life. Jo knew she'd spent months grieving when David passed away, and still hadn't fully recovered, but she'd managed to put a brave face on it. Jo suspected she was the only one who really knew what Kay had suffered.

'Give me time to sit down,' she said, laughing, but recognising Kay's eyes still held a shadow.

'Here you are, ladies.' Melody placed two cups of coffee on the table along with a chocolate brownie neatly cut in two.

'Thanks,' Kay said, then turned to Jo. 'I thought we deserved a treat since we didn't see each other at Christmas.'

'Thanks.' Jo looked at the brownie with a jaundiced eye. She'd sworn off such treats after noticing she'd gained two kilos over the holiday, but picked up her half and took a bite, the cloying sweetness reminding her of what she'd foresworn.

'The retrospective?' Kay prompted.

'It went really well – exactly as Alice planned. I think half the town turned up and all the paintings were sold.'

'I hope you got in first.'

'Col had me choose one before it opened. Said it had been Alice's wish.' Jo felt her eyes moisten at the thought of her friend.

'And Gordon?' Kay raised an eyebrow. 'I suppose he was there with his floozie.'

'She's his wife,' Jo corrected her with the glimmer of a smile, 'and, yes, they were both there. She was dressed up to the nines as usual.' She shook her head. How had Gordon managed to be taken in by a woman who was so flashy?

'Now, what happened in Brisbane?' she asked.

'You don't want to know,' Kay said, but clearly didn't mean it as she continued, 'I don't know why I bother. Oh, I do, really. Noah is a delight. But Zoe!' She wrinkled her nose and leant back, her coffee cradled in both hands. 'It's like she's on autopilot all the time. She never stops. Poor Noah's life is organised from the minute he wakes till he goes to bed. It's as if she can't turn off. I know she has a responsible job managing the Human Resources department at that hospital, but really! She wants to manage everyone in her life, too.'

'What about her husband?'

'Eric? He's lovely. But she tries to manage him as well. I don't know how he puts up with it.' She fell silent for a moment, then took a gulp of her coffee. 'Anyway, we had a nice Christmas Day with his parents, then it was a whirlwind of gallery visits, walking on South Bank and Mount Cootha, coffee and lunch in a few trendy cafes. I'm glad to get home to relax.'

Jo chuckled. She had trouble imagining anyone trying to manage Kay. 'The apple doesn't fall too far from the tree.'

'Hmm. But enough about me. What's been happening with you and your three?'

Jo sighed. 'Danny took me to look at one of his villas.'

'You mean you actually went along with him? You're too eager to please that one.'

'It was easier to go along, but I told him it wasn't for me.'

'And did he accept that?'

Jo sighed again. She had no way of knowing, but doubted she'd heard the last of it. 'Probably not. Kylie's pretty determined. And I had a lovely morning with the twins, then Col took care of them while I helped Rob out.' She frowned remembering Eve's annoyance.

'And you and Col are still having those dinners? If you ask me…'

Jo felt a blush in her cheek, and picked up her cup, taking a long sip of coffee. *Had Kay guessed?*

But it seemed not as her next words were, 'He's a good man, but I guess it'll be a while before he's ready to move on.' Then she peered at Jo, who felt her face must be giving her away. 'What have I said. He's not… You haven't…'

Jo placed her cup carefully on the table and raised her eyes to meet Kay's amazed gaze. 'We…' she stuttered. 'After the retrospective… Col came back for a drink and…' she nervously pleated the material in her lap, '…he stayed.'

She wasn't sure what sort of response she'd expected, but it wasn't the one she got.

'He what?' Kay almost yelled, then glanced around to see if anyone had heard, but the only other occupants of the courtyard – a couple of old dears – were totally engrossed in their own conversation. 'But it's far too soon – Alice is barely cold in her grave! Maybe it's different for men,' she sniffed.

Shocked by Kay's obvious disapproval. Jo couldn't think of anything to say. She'd been so looking forward to sharing her newfound romance with her old friend, to confiding how she was unsure if it was the right thing to do, how Gordon might react, how she'd decided to take things slowly.

It had never occurred to her that Kay would find it distasteful for her and Col to get together.

Eleven

Still smarting from Kay's response, Jo decided to spend the afternoon in the garden trying to repair the ravages of the summer heat and forget the stunned look on her friend's face and her subsequent tight-lipped farewell.

When she finally stood up and put her hand to her aching back, she was glad she had a massage booked for late afternoon. She'd discovered Magda Duncan soon after Rob had been born and had fallen into the habit of having a monthly massage. Lying on Magda's massage table was a way of ironing out her problems as well as the knots in her body, and the pair had become good friends over the years.

Magda was the daughter of a Hungarian couple who'd emigrated to Australia after the Second World War. She'd married a local man who'd died young and had set up a massage business in her home to enable her to be there when her children were little. Like Jo's they were all grown now and had flown the nest.

She was older than Jo, but Jo had never been able to discover her age. Magda kept some things to herself – her age, her memories of Hungary, her marriage – and she was mindful of other people's need for confidentiality.

Jo drove up the back laneway stopping at the little stone cottage surrounded by an aromatic herb garden. As she walked up the pathway, the scent of lavender, mint and thyme assailed her nostrils, promoting a sense of wellbeing and relaxation. Kay's harsh words began to fade, as she inhaled deeply, knowing an hour of Magda's therapy was exactly what she needed.

'Welcome!' Magda's beaming face greeted her at the door and Jo immediately felt as if her cares were dropping from her shoulders.

'I need your tender care today,' she said. 'I spent the afternoon in the garden and… I'm not as young and supple as I used to be.' She laughed as the image of her and Col, bodies entwined, flashed before her eyes.

'Well, you've come to the right place.' Magda led her into the purpose-designed room. The massage bed stood in the middle of the room which was lit only by a dim table lamp and candles which emitted the relaxing aroma of lavender, geranium and bergamot. Some soft music was playing.

Jo felt better already.

'I'll leave you to get settled,' Magda said, as she withdrew, closing the door behind her.

Jo quickly stripped down to her underwear and climbed onto the massage table face down, pulling a towel over her. She could easily fall asleep here – and had done on several occasions in the past.

She barely heard Magda re-enter, only aware of the towel being moved, another being placed on her legs and Magda's firm but gentle hands massaging all the knots out of her tired body.

An hour later, Jo sat up slowly, her eyes gradually becoming accustomed to the dim light.

'Take your time,' Magda said, handing her a glass of water. 'Come through when you're ready.'

Jo gratefully sipped the drink, before sliding off the bed and dressing. Then she picked up her bag and made her way through the house to Magda's large family kitchen. This room, like Jo's, overlooked the surrounding acreage, the difference being that three horses were lazily grazing on what was left of the grass in this paddock.

Two cups of sweetly smelling camomile tea were sitting on the table and Magda was cutting slices of a delicious-looking sponge cake.

'Feeling better?' she asked.

'Much.' Jo turned her head from side to side and stretched out her arms, delighted in the ease of movement she now experienced. 'I feel wonderful. You've worked your magic again.'

Magda only smiled.

'Now tell me,' Magda said, when Jo had taken a seat and was

enjoying the soothing tea, 'How's Danny behaving himself? Is he still intent on moving you into one of those villas of his?'

'Don't get me started. Kylie has always had her eye on the old place and she has him wound round her little finger. Who'd have thought it?' She helped herself to a piece of cake. 'This looks delicious, Magda.' She bit into the soft, sweet confection.

'He always did have a soft spot,' Magda reminded her. 'When they were little, he was the one to follow my Kenny's lead. Remember the time they decided to swim in the old dam at Miller's place?'

'And almost drowned,' Jo grimaced, remembering how worried they'd been. 'How is Kenny?'

'He seems to be doing well – he and Laura and the three kids. I don't see much of them, of course. Not since they moved to Adelaide. And he's not the great communicator. You're lucky having your three so close.'

'Hmm.' Jo wondered if she was. But it was nice to be able to enjoy her grandchildren growing up. If only… 'Sorry, you were saying something?'

'I was asking about your other two. Eve's twins will be going to school this year, won't they? I bet they're looking forward to it.'

'Can't wait. I won't know what to do with myself without Eve dropping them around on a regular basis.'

'Oh, you'll soon fill your days. But I wouldn't get too carried away. My guess is you'll be on school pick-up when Eve gets too busy in her shop.'

'You're probably right.' Jo had been planning to get her life back, maybe join a pilates class, spend more time in her garden, catch up on her reading. At Magda's words, she could see the free time she'd been looking forward to disappearing.

'You need to take a stand,' Magda advised. 'You make yourself too available. You and I didn't have parents to help us bring up our kids and we did okay.'

Magda was the second person in as many days to offer this advice. But what could she do? 'You're right,' she said. 'And I'm thinking of cutting back on my hours in the restaurant. It's time Rob employed a proper front-of-house person for weekends. I just can't figure out how to tell him.'

'Do I detect a hint of rebellion? Is the worm finally going to turn?'

Well…' Jo spread her hands. 'You're right – it's lovely to have them living so close, but… sometimes I yearn for a bit of space. Since Gordon left, all three of them seem to have made it their mission to fill my life. Kylie is a different matter – she just wants my house.'

'What about your son-in-law?'

Jo chuckled. 'Brad is something else altogether. He's a nice lad and a good father, but tends to be obsessive about things – his current passion is cycling. It seems to rule his life.' She exhaled. 'But I don't see much of him. If he's not working all the hours God gave him, he's off scouring the countryside with his cycling mates. I don't think Eve sees too much of him, either.' She bit her lip. That was another of her worries, and one over which she had no control.

Sensing her disquiet, Magda asked, 'Everything all right there?'

'I think so. But Eve would never say if it wasn't.' Jo remembered how her daughter had married the handsome young computer technician at twenty-one despite her parents advising her to wait a few years. Now Brad owned his own firm and had become a successful businessman.

'I should go,' Jo said at last, when the tea was finished, and the plate of sponge slices was almost empty. 'It's been good, and I feel marvellous. I need to have a shower and change.'

'You and Col are still doing that dinner thing?'

Jo felt a tremor in her stomach at the thought of the evening ahead. Kay's words were still fresh in her mind. Would they make love again or not? She knew it was up to her. Col was too much of a gentleman to insist. But whereas her body told her there was nothing she'd like more than a repeat performance, her mind told her it was madness to even contemplate it.

'Yes,' she said. 'He and Alice have always been good friends to me, and he's been very kind since Gordon left.' She mentally crossed her fingers. Kind wasn't exactly how she'd describe his behaviour last weekend.

'He's a good man,' Magda said, nodding. 'They aren't too many like him. You wouldn't…?' There was a speculative expression in her eyes. 'No, of course not. He's Gordon's partner, isn't he?'

'Always has been,' Jo said bending down to pick up her bag to hide any giveaway expression in her own eyes. Magda could be very perceptive. There was no way she was going to confide in her. Maybe Kay was right. Maybe it was a bad idea. Maybe it was too soon – for both of them. It was true Alice had only been dead a year, but she'd been sick for much longer, hadn't been able to be a wife to Col for years. Did that make it better?

Jo couldn't think straight. What had been a delightful surprise, a late reawakening, had been tarnished. But had it been tarnished beyond repair?

Twelve

Col whistled to himself as he prepared for dinner with Jo. Although they'd been meeting for dinner twice a week for just over a year, this time it felt different.

He knew Alice had only been gone a year, and some might think it too soon for him to even imagine bedding another woman. But he knew Alice would be pleased. She and Jo had been best friends and she'd left him in her care. Had she guessed what might happen?

Jo and he had become closer over the years as they shared caring for Alice, and even closer in the past year through their regular dinners. It had seemed only natural to take her in his arms, as if, by fulfilling Alice's last wish to hold the retrospective of her paintings, they were also fulfilling her desire to see her two best buddies get together. But had they been wrong?

Relegating these thoughts to the back of his mind, Col selected a favourite pale blue chambray shirt and his best jeans, noting as he glanced in the mirror that his hair was now almost completely white. Where had the years gone?

Driving down the main street of Granite Springs, he reflected how the town had changed. It was no longer the peaceful country town he and Alice – and Jo and Gordon – had grown up in. The establishment of a university, closely followed by a fruit processing plant had revitalised the town, turning it into a bustling regional centre. Now a fast food joint had replaced the old grocery store on the corner of Main and Grafton, groups of teenagers hanging around the entrance. The old Station Hotel was still there but it had received a much-needed facelift and was now decked out in bright yellow and black and attracted a younger crowd, leaving the older members of the community to frequent the older and dingier Royal Hotel close to the edge of town. It had also led to the establishment of several trendy cafes and eateries, one of which was The Riverside and another the Italian to which he was now headed.

By the time he reached the car park of Pavarotti's where he and Jo always met, he was feeling nostalgic for the old days. As he locked the car, he noticed Jo's yellow Golf was already there and smiled, remembering how she'd wanted to buy a low sports model when Gordon left – eager to show her independence. But good sense had prevailed, and her car was now able to fit the two child seats she needed to ferry around the twins on a regular basis.

Jo was sitting at their regular corner table, her eyes on the menu. Col took a moment to study his dinner companion before joining her and bending down to plant a kiss on her cheek.

This was nothing new – they'd greeted each other this way for years – but the face that glanced up at him tonight held an unfamiliar expression. It was fleeting and quickly followed by her usual smile, but he registered it before taking his own seat opposite.

'Something wrong?'

'Wrong? No.' Jo returned her gaze to the menu.

Col reached over to take it out of her hands. 'You can't fool me, Jo. We've known each other too long for that. Something's wrong and the sooner you tell me the better. Then we can enjoy our meal.'

'Not really.' Jo folded her hands on the table, then said, 'Kay's back.'

Col stared across at her. He knew Kay, though not well. She'd always been a friend of Jo's, grown up with him and Alice too, but a few years younger, not part of their inner group. What did her return have to do with them?

'Did she have a good Christmas? I missed seeing her at Alice's do. I guess she must still have been away.'

'Yes. She was disappointed to miss it,' Jo said vaguely. 'I'm sorry, Col. This must seem odd to you, but she said something…'

Col dragged a hand through his hair, uncomfortable with the way this was going, but not sure why.

He saw Jo take a deep breath and waved away the hovering waiter. He needed to hear what Jo had to say.

'I've always confided in Kay,' she said, 'Her and Alice – and now there's just Kay. She asked about the retrospective, and what had been happening, and…' he saw her glance sideways at him, '… I told her about us – that we…'

Col gave a sigh of relief. Was that all? He'd been imagining… he didn't know what he'd been imagining.

'That's okay. We couldn't keep it a secret forever.' Granite Springs was still a typical small country town full of small-minded people. It was impossible to keep things secret and soon everyone knew everyone else's business. Though he did hope to keep it from his partner for a bit longer, unsure how Gordon would react.

'But it's what she said. She said it was too soon for you – for us. She… she spoiled it – what we have, had, and I don't know…' Her voice tailed off and Col could see a tear form in the corner of one eye.

He reached across to cover Jo's hands with his. 'It's none of her business. I know she's your friend, but… Hell, Jo, what does she know about how we feel, about how Alice would feel about us?'

'D'you think?'

'I do. She practically threw us together. I did most of my grieving before she left us.' He rubbed his chin, remembering the long years of watching his beloved wife become gradually weaker and fade away – a lingering death was not one he'd wish on anyone.

'She said…' Jo continued, with a wry smile, '…that maybe it's different for men.'

Col gave that serious thought then, still holding Jo's hands, spoke gently, 'It was different for her. It was sudden – a shock. David took his own life. I can imagine that would take a long time to accept and adjust to. It's two years now, isn't it?' He squeezed her hands

'Yes. It was January. I guess she feels it most as the anniversary looms.' He felt an answering pressure, then Jo withdrew her hands. 'You're probably right, but…' She bit her lip.

'Why don't we order before Tony gives up on us?'

Jo gave a small smile and retrieved her menu, her frown clearing. Col watched her as she bent her head over the menu, a strand of her blonde hair falling over her face, the few silver streaks only adding to her appeal.

'Have you decided?'

Col looked up again as the waiter returned, his tablet at the ready.

'Tonight's specials are on the board.' He pointed towards the far wall. 'And the fish is bream.' He hesitated, as if wondering whether to stay or go.

'I think we've decided.' Col raised an eyebrow in Jo's direction.

'I'll have the Spaghetti Carbonara,' Jo said, choosing her favourite.

'The Gnocchi Pavarotti for me,' Col said, 'And we'll have a serving of garlic bread.'

'And for wine?'

'Red, I think.' Col looked across at Jo who nodded. 'The McLaren Vale Shiraz.'

By the time their meals arrived, Col was glad to see Jo appeared more relaxed. She'd even managed to find some humour in Kay's stunned response. But he was aware she still harboured a few doubts about the wisdom of their new relationship.

'You feeling better?' he asked when their meals were finished.

'I am. But…' She picked up her glass then put it down again, '…I think maybe we should…' She folded her arms on the table. 'Col, you know how I feel about you. I'd love to continue what we started, but…'

'You want us to take our time?'

'Exactly.' She seemed relieved and, although Col couldn't understand her reasoning, he was happy to go along with it – for the time being at least.

Thirteen

Early Saturday morning, Jo pulled up in the driveway of her daughter's house to be greeted by a whirlwind of blue and white. It took her a moment to realise Lottie and Livvy were dressed in their new school uniforms.

'Look, Gramma!' they shouted in unison. 'We have school dresses!' They twirled proudly to show off the new outfits.

'You both look lovely,' Jo said, gathering them into a hug, before they slipped off again to run around the garden.

'Now, into your play clothes,' Eve said, chasing the girls back into the house.

The two women followed them and settled in the kitchen from where they could hear the twins arguing upstairs.

'They insisted on getting dressed up for you,' Eve said, filling the electric jug. 'Tea, Mum?'

'Thanks, dear. It was lovely to see them in their uniforms. I remember how excited you were at their age.' She thought back, picturing the young Eve and her enthusiasm at the prospect of joining her brother in *the big school.* 'You were just the same.'

She saw Eve give her a disbelieving look, as if she'd never been that young.

'I just don't want them getting their dresses dirty before school starts. I have enough to do without an extra load of washing.'

Jo bit her tongue. Sometimes she wondered what had happened to the eager little girl, the excitable teenager. There were times when this edgy, self-controlled woman seemed to be a stranger.

'How are things at the shop?' Jo asked, to change the subject.

'I'm glad you asked. I needed to speak with you about that. Lemon and ginger all right?' When Jo nodded, she dropped teabags into a couple of mugs and joined her mother at the kitchen table.

Jo picked up her mug and looked enquiringly at her daughter.

'Good – really good. But Rache is going off on maternity leave, so I'll need to be there on a more permanent basis.'

Jo knew Rachel Armstrong was Eve's senior member of staff who had been with her since the beginning. Her capable manner had enabled Eve to cut back to working part-time when the twins had been born.

'Well, with the twins at school, you'll have more time, I expect.'

'That's just it.' Eve drew out an A4 sheet of paper. 'I've drawn up a roster.'

Curious as to what this might have to do with her, Jo took the proffered sheet to see it held a chart of times and events.

She raised her eyes to meet Eve's. She couldn't be expecting… She was!

'You'll see all the twinnies' schedule there. I can drop them off in the mornings on my way to the shop, but they'll need to be picked up and ferried to swim lessons, ballet and…'

Jo felt a twist in her gut. She could see her leisurely afternoons disappear, her book club, the planned pilates class. She'd have to re-organise her life to fit more things into her mornings. She loved her granddaughters and the time she spent with them, but this chart made it look like a full-time job. She took a deep breath before speaking, wondering what she could say that wouldn't alienate Eve.

'This looks very thorough,' she said at last. 'But, Evie, I'm not sure…'

'I knew you'd be like this!' Eve's voice rose a notch. 'You jump every time Rob needs you at the restaurant, but when it comes to your own granddaughters… You're going to say you're too busy, aren't you?'

'No,' Jo was quick to respond. 'Of course, I'd love to do this for you. But it's a lot. What you're asking is…' she scanned the list, '…a commitment every day of around three hours. I'd be able to do some of those, but maybe you need to have someone in reserve – for when I can't manage it.'

'There's no one else.'

'I'm sure we can find someone.' She thought for a few moments. 'What about a student? Doesn't Steve teach education students? Maybe he could recommend someone, and she and I could share the load.'

'Maybe.' Eve sounded doubtful. 'But the girls are expecting you to be there for them. They're excited about it. We had it all planned.'

Jo was sure she had. Eve was good at planning things, especially for other people – and could be very self-centred. She was like her dad in so many respects. Jo sighed. 'Well, let's start with your schedule and see how we go, but okay if I sound Steve out when his classes begin?'

'If you must.'

Any further discussion was stymied by the boisterous arrival of the twins who claimed hugs, and stated they were hungry. While Eve filled plastic mugs with milk and doled out one biscuit per child, Jo folded the chart and slipped it into her bag, determined to do more about it later. The room was filled with joyful chatter while Lottie and Livvy ate and drank, wrangling over the size of their respective biscuits. Then they slid down from the table and were off again, the sounds of their voices fading as they went outside to play.

'Have you heard?' Eve said in a hushed voice in the ensuing silence. 'About Dad?'

Jo sighed again. *What now?*

'I haven't seen him since your Aunt Alice's retrospective. What's he been up to?'

'You mean you haven't heard? I heard it from Sue at yoga – she knows Carol's sister and…'

Jo held up a hand. 'If it's gossip about your dad and Carol, I'd prefer not to hear it, Eve.' She had enough to worry about without the doings of her ex and his new wife.

'But Sue says Carol is trying to get pregnant. She wants a child. It's gross! Can you imagine?'

Jo could imagine – very well. It wasn't a surprise – not really. Carol was young, it was only natural she'd want to start a family. But Gordon? At his age? How would he cope? How would that work out?

*

It was a busy evening at The Riverside. Jo had been on her feet since before five and could barely raise a smile when Col walked in close to closing time. She showed him to a corner table and handed him a menu.

'I didn't expect to see you tonight.'

'I have to eat. And Rob puts on a good meal. Besides,' he said, grabbing hold of her hand as she was leaving, 'It was an excuse to see you.'

Try as she might, Jo couldn't suppress a surge of excitement.

'You look tired,' he said. 'Is all this getting too much for you?' He gestured at the busy restaurant.

Just what a woman wants to hear. But it was exactly what she'd been thinking.

'Maybe.'

'Join me later?'

Jo glanced around at the few tables still occupied. Apart from one couple who'd arrived a few minutes earlier, they'd all be gone soon. She nodded and hurried away.

'On you go. I can take care of the rest.' Rob handed Jo a plate of lasagne and a glass. Gratefully, she accepted. She'd be glad to get off her feet. She really was getting too old for this. She'd tell Rob, she decided. It was time.

She slid into the seat opposite Col, and he filled her glass from the bottle of Cabernet Sauvignon he'd ordered.

'You'd better help me out with this,' he said. 'Busy tonight?'

'Packed. Things seem to be looking up.' Jo bit her lip. She hadn't intended to let that slip.

'They haven't been so good?'

'The drought has affected all the town's businesses,' Jo said by way of explanation. That had been one of the reasons she'd always been ready to fill in for Rob, but maybe now things were improving she could ease off. 'Thanks,' she said, picking up the glass of red wine and taking a sip. She looked at the lasagne, then pushed it away. She'd been surrounded by people eating all night and it had taken the edge off her appetite. She'd fix something simple when she got home.

'How was your day?' Col asked, pushing aside his own, now empty, plate and leaning his elbows on the table.

'Good. I called in at Eve's this morning and the twins treated me to a display of their new school uniforms. They looked so cute.'

'School already? So, they'll be out of Eve's hair soon.'

'Yes, and…' Jo bit her lip, remembering the full schedule Eve had prepared for her.

'Don't tell me – Eve wants you to ferry them around?'

'How did you guess?'

'I've known her all her life and I'm aware her manager is pregnant. It makes sense.'

'Yes, it does, but… I'll need to rearrange my own schedule to fit it.' She sighed. 'Well, we'll see.'

'Talking of children and pregnant women, I wondered if you'd heard the latest of the Gordon and Carol saga?'

'Eve mentioned it. Carol wants to start a family. Gordon told you?'

'He's worried sick.'

'Surely he's going to talk her out of it? I can't imagine him with a baby or a young child at his time of life. He was never good with the kids when they were small and he was much younger then. And…' The full implication of Carol's choice hit home. Any child of Carol's would be an aunt or uncle to Eve and Danny's kids. 'We have grandchildren and, much as I love them, it's always a relief to hand them back. I don't even think Gordon has taken much notice of them beyond being proud of the boys' exploits on the footie field and, of course, the continuation of the Slater name,' she said bitterly.

'He's not happy about it,' Col replied, 'and he's not finding it easy. Seems he's always given in to Carol till now, so she can't accept he won't do so on this issue.'

Suddenly Jo burst out laughing. 'It serves him bloody right. Sorry, that came out wrong. But really! What did he expect? Carol's a young woman. It's no surprise she'd want a family of her own. Eve's furious. She's always been her dad's little girl, his favourite. What if he has another daughter?'

'Well, it may never come to that.'

'Hmm.'

'Now finish up your wine and let me take you home.'

'I have my car,' she said, but the thought of being taken care of was tempting. She hesitated.

'Leave it here. I'll drive you. I won't come in if you don't want me to, although…' There was a twinkle in his eye.

'Thanks,' Jo said with a sigh. It had been a hectic day. It would be nice to be cossetted and maybe she would invite Col in – for a nightcap, nothing more.

But, after a cup of hot chocolate and a glass of brandy, it was comforting to feel Col's arms around her, his lips on her neck.

All of her good intentions began to falter.

Fourteen

Wakening to the sound of the resident pair of kookaburras, Jo could smell coffee. She was about to snuggle down again when she remembered and sat bolt upright. She and Col – it had happened again! Despite all her good intentions, she'd succumbed to her baser urges. Well, maybe not so base. She smiled, remembering the way Col had made her feel. It had been a long time since Gordon made her feel that way.

'Coffee?' A fully dressed Col appeared at the bedroom door carrying a tray with two cups of steaming coffee and... Were those chocolate croissants?

'You're spoiling me,' Jo said, propping herself up against the pillows, while Col joined her, deftly manoeuvring the tray so that it lay between them on the bed. 'You must have gone out to get them.'

'I wakened early, and you looked so peaceful, I didn't want to disturb you.'

'Thanks.' She took a sip of coffee and a bite from a croissant, then remembered. 'Hell. The kids are coming to lunch. I can't...' She looked wildly around.

'No worries. I'll be gone long before then. I guess it wouldn't do for them to find me here?' Col chuckled.

'No. Sorry.' Jo was embarrassed at wanting him to leave, but she could imagine Eve and Danny's faces – not to mention Kylie's – if they found Col here on a Sunday morning. Brad probably wouldn't notice. He'd be too engrossed in checking his early morning ride on Strava and sharing it with anyone who'd listen. She sighed, knowing that, if this thing with Col turned out to be serious, they'd have to know – Gordon too. But she didn't want to think about that right now.

'Do you want a ride into town?'

Jo gave him a puzzled look.

'Your car.'

'Oh!' Her very identifiable yellow golf was still sitting outside the restaurant. By now… As if her thoughts made it happen, her phone buzzed, and Rob's face appeared on the screen.

'Darling!'

'Good morning to you, too, Mum. You left your car here.'

Jo thought quickly. 'Yes, I was exhausted and…'

'I saw you leave with Uncle Col.'

Jo glanced at Col whose eyes widened. She moistened her lips and was trying to work out what to say when Rob continued, 'It's okay, Mum. You deserve some happiness. So does Uncle Col. I think Aunt Alice would be pleased.'

Jo exhaled in relief. 'Thanks, Rob. But don't let your brother and sister know just yet. I need to decide how to break it to them.'

'Yeah.' Jo could hear the amusement in her son's voice. 'Better keep it from Dad for a bit, too. I can bring your car back sometime this afternoon – after the lunch crowd. Steve and I can drop over. Will the others be there?'

'Yes, they're coming to lunch – which reminds me, I should be getting it ready.'

'Okay. See you later. Love to Uncle Col.' He hung up, leaving Jo staring at the phone.

'Rob sends you his love,' she said to Col who had paused, his cup half-way to his mouth.

'Trust Rob. I wondered how long it would be before he guessed. And he's okay with it? With us?'

'Seems to be. He's a lovely lad – my baby boy. Always wants what's best for me, not like…' She sighed, thinking of her recent altercations with both Danny and Eve, who always seemed to put themselves first.

'Well, guess I should be making a move.' Col rolled off the bed, leaving behind a trail of crumbs and broken pieces of pastry.

Rob's call had effectively put an end to their cosy breakfast together, so Jo rose too and, picking up the tray, followed Col into the kitchen. At the door, he gave her a warm hug and kiss. 'I'll be in touch,' he said.

After packing the dirty dishes into the dishwasher and dithering around, Jo showered and dressed in a loose sundress. She could tell it was going to be another scorching day. She fed Scout and let the dog out into the yard but, true to form, he chose to lie on the veranda, his body across the doorway, barring it to all comers.

Given the heat of the day, Jo decided to put together a couple of quiches, use up the remains of a leg of ham she had in the fridge, and prepare a salad from some fresh vegetables from the garden. Despite the drought and the water restrictions they'd been suffering for the past months, she'd managed to keep the vegetable garden watered using what was called grey water – collected from the shower and washing machine – and her lettuce, potatoes, tomatoes, corn and capsicum continued to flourish.

It didn't take long, and she even had time to make herself a cup of tea and sit down with the papers Col had brought back from town earlier. All too soon, the sound of a car crossing the cattle grid at the entrance to the property met her ears. She folded the paper and got to her feet.

'Gramma!' Lottie and Livvy leapt out of the car, closely followed by Eve, with Brad trailing behind, peering at his phone. Some things never changed.

'Aren't you a sight for sore eyes,' Jo said, picking the girls up one by one and whirling them around. 'Good to see you again, darling,' she hugged and kissed Eve, 'and you too, Brad.' She gave Brad a peck on the cheek. 'Come in and have a cold drink.'

They'd barely reached the kitchen before there was the sound of another car, and Danny walked in followed by Kylie and their two boys. Liam and Tim were so like Danny at that age, Jo could almost believe she'd gone back in time and was seeing double.

'Dad, can we...?' Tim looked beseechingly at his dad, while Liam pulled on his mother's arm.

'Mum,' Danny said, 'the boys want to know if they can have a swim before lunch. Is that okay?'

Jo hesitated. She hadn't planned on this, but it made sense. It was hot already, heading towards the forty degrees centigrade forecast. A dip would cool everyone down. 'Sure. We can take drinks out to the pool and those who don't want to get in can join me in the shade.'

The boys grabbed their swimmers from a bag and whooped off to change, while Eve fussed with the twins who started to yell, 'Swim!'

Finally, everyone was settled. Most opted for the pool, only Kylie and Eve choosing to join Jo under the large shade-cloth and Scout settling at Jo's feet.

'They love it here,' Kylie said, sighing and sipping her white wine spritzer. 'I wish...' she threw a pointed look in Jo's direction.

Eve looked puzzled. 'You have a pool too, Kylie.'

'Yes, but we don't have all this space. The boys need to let off steam; they need exercise. This place would be wonderful for them.' She sighed again, theatrically. 'I don't know why you're being so stubborn. It's not as if you need this big place.'

She tapped her manicured nails on the glass-topped table and Jo wondered, not for the first time, how she'd cope with living so far from town if she and Danny did live here. She supposed Kylie would organise a host of helpers and sit around playing Lady Muck. But Jo dreaded to think what would happen to her carefully tended vegetable garden. It didn't bear thinking about.

'You're not suggesting Mum moves out?' Eve sounded outraged.

It was Jo's turn to sigh. Until now, she'd managed to keep Danny and Kylie's demands from her daughter.

'Why not?'

'It's our home.'

'How old are you, Eve? You haven't lived here for years.' Kylie snorted.

'But it's still my home. It's where I grew up, where all my memories are, where Mum and Dad...' Her voice trailed off. 'You're not thinking of moving, are you, Mum?' Her shocked voice rose causing Lottie to jump out of the pool and rush to her side.

'Mummy?' she wailed, pushing her face into Eve's lap.

'It's all right, sweetheart,' Eve murmured, then threw a look at Kylie. 'Now look what you've done. I think swim time may be over. Livvy! Brad!' she called, rising and carrying her glass and the dripping Lottie inside.

Leaving Kylie alone, Jo followed, calling, 'Lunch in ten minutes,' to the rest of the family still frolicking in the pool.

While Eve was towelling the twins dry, she called out to Jo, 'How long has Kylie had her eye on this house?'

'Oh, since she first saw it, I guess,' Jo replied, taking the green salad out of the fridge and adding a dressing, then carrying it through to the dining room. When she returned for the ham and quiches, the little girls were dressed again and Eve was standing, back against the sink, her arms folded. 'But it's only since your dad left that she's become more insistent.'

'And Danny's going along with it?'

'You know Danny.' Jo pushed a stray lock of hair out of her eyes. 'Kylie has him wrapped around her little finger. He took me out to see one of those villas in the development he's marketing.'

'He what? But you're not…? You wouldn't…?'

'No chance. But it was easier to go along with him and have a look. They're tiny – like little boxes.' Jo shuddered, remembering the claustrophobia she'd experienced. 'No, don't worry, darling. I have no intention of leaving here.' She stroked the well-worn and often-scrubbed kitchen table – the one all three children had eaten at, done their homework on, at which they'd spent many hours of their childhood. She and Gordon had discovered it at a farm clearance sale soon after they'd built the house and she'd fallen in love with it. It and the oak dresser were still two of her most prized possessions. They would never fit into one of those villas.

At that moment, the rest of the tribe arrived in the kitchen dripping, with Kylie following up in the rear carrying her drink. 'Anything I can do to help, Mother Slater?' she asked, Jo cringing as usual at this title. It made her feel like Methuselah, or, at best, completely out of touch with the modern generation.

'There's a potato salad in the fridge,' she said. 'You could put that out, and,' she looked around wildly, 'Eve, could you slice that loaf on the table? I'll just…' She left them and made her way to the cloakroom where she held onto the edge of the basin and stared at herself in the mirror. A well-preserved woman with fading blonde hair looked back at her. Her face was flushed with annoyance at Kylie's having brought up the whole house thing in front of Eve – there had been no need for her to know – but her features were good, her clear skin bearing testament to a lifetime of skincare and sun protection.

It took some time for everyone to gather around the dining table. First, Liam couldn't find his tee shirt, then he didn't want to sit next to his brother. Danny finally sorted them out, then Eve had to extricate the twins from the dress-up basket, which they'd decided to upend, sending clothes everywhere.

Eventually all were seated, and Jo looked around at their faces with pleasure. Despite their differences, they were family – her family.

But Kylie had to spoil it.

'We've been telling the boys we might move here,' she said, when Eve was helping Jo clear away the plates. 'They're looking forward to it.'

Jo's lips tightened. This was too much. She looked at Danny who was surreptitiously checking his phone under the table, then at Brad, who appeared stunned. It was he who spoke first.

'I didn't know you were moving, Mum.'

'I'm not.' Jo spoke so forcefully that both Tim and Liam's eyes widened and they looked from their mother to Jo and back again.

'You promised,' Liam said.

Danny looked up. 'I thought I told you not to mention it to Mum,' he said to his wife. 'I'm handling it.'

'Not very well, it seems,' Eve said, stopping midway to the door. 'This has been your home, too. I can't imagine what you're thinking of – trying to push an old woman out of her home.'

Jo stared at her, a heavy feeling in her stomach. Is that how her children thought of her – as an old woman? It would be funny if it wasn't so sad.

The table cleared, Danny and Brad gave in to Tim and Liam's demands to go yabbying in the dam which still held a little water. All four set off across the paddock carrying the requisite lengths of string along with a container of raw meat and a bucket. The boys were optimistic they'd catch a bucketful, but Jo thought they'd be lucky to find any at all. Kylie had looked pointedly at her heels before retiring to the living room with a magazine and another glass of wine, while Eve joined her mother in the kitchen with a cup of tea and the girls returned to their dress-ups.

'Not a word,' Jo warned Eve, before she could say any more about Kylie's demands. 'Tell me about Rachel. When's she due?'

But Eve had barely started to talk when there was the sound of two cars crossing the cattle grid.

'That'll be Rob and Steve,' Jo said, rising.

'Two cars?'

'I left mine at the restaurant last night. I was exhausted and got a ride home.'

She crossed her fingers, hoping Eve wouldn't ask where she got her ride, but instead Eve said, 'You do too much. It's time you slowed down. Tell Rob to get someone else.'

'Maybe.' Even though Jo had already decided to do just that, she resented Eve taking it upon herself to assume she was too old. Her earlier remark still rankled.

'Hi there!' Rob's six-foot bulk filled the kitchen doorway, his equally tall partner following. Jo hugged both men before whispering, 'Thanks, honey,' then asking in a louder voice, 'Drinks, you two?'

'Wouldn't say no to a beer,' Rob replied. 'Where is everyone?'

'Uncle Rob!' Livvy emerged from the spare room, dressed in a cast-off purple blouse of Jo's and with a red scarf wrapped around her neck.

'Wow! Look at you,' he said, hoisting her up in his arms.

'Me too,' Lottie yelled appearing behind them. She had wrapped an old curtain around herself and was tripping on the edges.

Steve picked her up and whirled her around, sending her into a fit of the giggles.

'That's enough, girls,' Eve said. 'Let your uncles have a drink in peace.' But their arrival seemed to relax her. She fetched a couple of beers from the fridge, leaving Jo to get caught up on news about the lunch crowd.

'Things have picked up?' Eve asked, overhearing their update on their busy morning. 'I thought you were having difficulties.'

'Where did you hear that?' Rob was quick to ask.

'Oh, around.' She waved her hand in the air.

'Local gossip. Not true,' Rob said, swigging his beer, settling himself astride a chair and leaning his elbows on its back.

'So, what's new at William Farrer?' Jo asked Steve. 'When does semester start?'

'Not till March,' Rob replied for him. 'Some folk have it easy.'

Steve nudged his elbow. 'You know that's not true. The students don't start till then, but we have orientation week in February and I'm back already, planning lectures and writing a conference paper. It's not all beer and skittles, I can tell you.' But he grinned at his partner. This was clearly a well-worn debate.

'So, March…' Jo said, giving Eve a sideways glance. 'Maybe one of your students would be interested in doing some part-time childcare?' She ignored Eve's angry expression.

'Sure,' Steve said easily. 'They're always looking for ways to earn more money. The twins?' he asked Eve.

Eve's lips tightened. 'Mum seems to think so.'

Both men looked from one woman to the other, then back again.

'Eve has asked me to take over afternoon duty for the twins once they start school,' she explained, 'but I thought it would be useful to have some backup. That's all.'

'Makes sense,' Rob said. 'You looked pretty tired last night, too. Are you wanting to slow down?'

Jo felt her anger rise. First Eve referring to her as an old woman, then this! But Rob was right, and hadn't she been thinking the same thing? It was just that, coming from her children, it rankled. She took a deep breath before replying, 'Maybe. But how would you manage?'

'I can step in,' Steve said, much to her surprise. 'Keep an eye on what my other half gets up to when I'm not around,' he chuckled, his warm smile in Rob's direction belying his words.

'Really?' If Steve was serious, it would take a weight off her shoulders; save Rob having to employ someone else. Things might be looking up for the restaurant, but Jo kept the books and knew the salary of even one more employee would strain the budget.

'Really. I think I'd enjoy it.' He covered Rob's hand with his. 'What do you say?'

'Keep me on my toes,' Rob grinned. 'I'm up for it if you are. Looks like you're off the hook, Mum.'

Kylie walked in, just as Jo was hugging the pair. Her eyebrows rose, but she didn't say anything, merely carried her empty glass to the sink and rinsed it.

'Now, Mum. The birthday is coming up,' Rob said. 'It's a big one. We need to celebrate.'

'Oh, I don't know,' Jo hedged. 'Last year…'

'Last year, Aunt Alice had just died,' Rob said, 'and no one felt like celebrating. But this is the big six-oh. You and Uncle Col have to do something to mark the occasion.'

Was Jo the only one who saw his sly wink?

'Steve and I have been talking,' he continued, 'and we know you may not want a big bash, but how about we set aside the gallery level at the restaurant and we just do family and a few friends? What do you think, Eve?' he asked, turning to his sister.

'Maybe,' she replied. 'It *is* an important birthday, Mum.'

'You can't let it pass without a party,' Kylie put in. The others, who had forgotten she was there, turned to look at her. 'I'm only saying,' she said.

'Well, if you're prepared to do all the work.' Jo felt herself weaken and the idea of a small gathering at The Riverside did have some appeal. 'We'll have to check with Uncle Col.' She shivered slightly at the thought of her and Col being the star turn at their joint birthday celebrations. They'd done it for years, but this year it would be so very different.

When the boys arrived back from the dam, both Tim and Liam were muddy and wet through, causing Kylie to demand what Danny had been doing to allow them to get into that state. All three looked woebegone, and Jo heard Liam mutter, 'It'll be like this all the time when we move here.'

She decided to say nothing, while wondering exactly how much the boys had been told about Kylie's plans and how she proposed to make the transformation from a town dweller to a country wife. No doubt, she had visions of herself lording it over the members of the Country Women's Association, a group which Jo herself had strenuously avoided joining.

By four o'clock, they'd all left, and Jo was able to relax. *When had having the family over become such a chore?*

But when Col rang later that evening, she was able to laugh about it with him. When she finished the call, she gazed unseeingly into space. He understood. He knew her children almost as well as she did, had been there for all their growing up, their successes and disappointments. They'd been the children he and Alice never had.

Then she remembered – their joint birthday. She'd forgotten to mention it to him. Would he agree – or would it be too much of a reminder of birthdays past?

Fifteen

Col closed his mobile with a wry smile. He and Alice had often envied Jo and Gordon their trio. But now he wasn't so sure. He rubbed his chin, then went to the fridge to fetch a beer, taking it out onto the veranda where a cool breeze had blown up, breaking the heat of the day.

He settled himself in one of the Adirondack chairs he and Alice had purchased many years ago. They were now worn with age, the once-white paint, yellowed, cracked and peeling. The call with Jo had unsettled him. He wished she was there with him, sitting in the other chair – Alice's chair. He sighed. That was part of the problem. In his mind – and no doubt in Jo's, too – this was still Alice's house. No matter how much he told himself it had been their house – belonged to both of them – it was her touches that had made it a home.

He liked to see Jo here, busying herself around the kitchen, sitting on the sofa. She'd spent a lot of time in this house over the years. While Alice was so sick, she'd taken it on herself to spend most of her days here, helping out with Alice, cooking and even cleaning – though he'd brought in a cleaner to do that.

He sighed. He had no idea where this thing with Jo was headed. But whatever happened in the future, he couldn't see them being together in this house. In his mind it still belonged to Alice and, although he was sure she'd approve of his relationship with Jo, it still felt wrong.

He was on his second beer, when his phone rang again.

'Col,' he said without looking at the screen.

'Hi, Uncle Col. It's Rob.'

He felt something twist in his gut. Jo had told him her youngest had discovered their secret and was cool with it. *What if she was wrong? What if Rob was calling to tell him to fuck off?*

But he needn't have worried.

'You and Mum? Huh? Not before time. I always thought you'd make a good couple. Even when…' Col heard someone speak in the background and assumed Steve was counselling Rob to be tactful.

'Anyway. Did she tell you about the birthday bash? She said she'd check with you, but I need confirmation to get things rolling. It's only a couple of weeks away.'

'Birthday bash?' *What was he talking about?*

'You and Mum. We've always had a celebration, and this is the big one. I know we let last year go, but we thought… Steve and me… a smallish family do in the gallery. Aunt Alice wouldn't want the two of you to miss out on this one.'

Col considered what Alice would think. Rob was right. She'd always enjoyed a party and made much of the fact that Col and Jo shared a birthday.

'You may be right, son,' he said. 'A small gathering, you say?'

'And neither of you need to do anything. I've got it under control. I suppose…' he said hesitantly, '… you'll want Dad to be there?'

It was Col's turn to hesitate. Gordon was Col's partner and best friend. But he was also Jo's ex, and she and Carol had never seen eye-to-eye. But they did cross paths frequently. The town – and their social circle – was too small for it to be otherwise.

'I guess.'

'Do you want me to…?'

'No,' Col exhaled, 'I'll do it. I'll mention it to him tomorrow. Just family, you said?'

'Mostly. But Mum may want to invite that friend of hers, Kay, and maybe a couple of others. Let me know if there's anyone you want to come, too, so I can work out the catering.'

'Right.' Col finished the call and took a long draught of beer. He'd all but forgotten about their annual celebration, perhaps hoping the others would forget about it too. If he'd considered it at all, he'd imagined he and Jo celebrating together, in private like last year. He'd prefer that. Now it would be a public affair, he'd have to hide his feelings for Jo, pretend to be the old family friend.

Could he do that? Could they pull the wool over the eyes of the rest of Jo's family and Gordon? Wouldn't their newfound happiness be obvious to everyone? Didn't Jo say she'd told Kay – and had suffered her disapproval? What if the woman let the cat out of the bag? And that wife of Danny's had sharp eyes. It would be difficult to fool her. Maybe they should just come out into the open and be done with it.

It was all too much, and beer didn't hack it. Rising, he took his now empty glass into the kitchen and stared at the whisky bottle. But that wasn't the solution.

'Alice, what am I to do?' he wailed, his voice echoing back at him, the emptiness of the house no more noticeable than now, when he needed someone to talk to. Wandering back through the house, he picked up a photo from the bookcase. It was one taken on a holiday to Airlie beach ten years earlier. Alice was standing in front of a low stone wall, behind her was the marina filled with yachts.

He could remember that day as if it was yesterday – the warmth of the sun on their shoulders, the aching feet they'd had from their long walk, the refreshing cold beer at the end of the day, the way Alice had teased him about being out of condition.

'Why did you have to leave me?' he asked, uselessly. 'It was way too soon. And now, look what a mess I've got myself into.'

Sixteen

'You wanted a word?' Col looked up to see Gordon in his office doorway. He'd been busy with clients all morning and had almost forgotten leaving a note on his partner's desk.

He checked his watch – close to lunchtime.

'I did. Why don't we grab a bite at the club and talk there?'

Gordon raised his eyebrows, clearly wondering what on earth Col had to say that couldn't be said here. It could have, of course. He could have just told him about the birthday do and left it at that. But Col was unsure of his old friend's reaction. He was conscious Gordon had become touchy recently on the subject of his ex-wife, and wanted to choose a more neutral setting for their conversation.

'We should do this more often,' Gordon said, as he cut into a large T-bone steak and took a gulp of the latest craft beer on offer. 'Not a bad drop, this.' He held his glass up to the light, admiring its clarity. 'Now, you had something to say?'

Col gazed out the window of the clubhouse to where a group of older men were teeing off and wondered what it would be like to have time to play golf on any day of the week, not to have to go to the office, to deal with difficult clients. He pictured a day when he'd be in their position, coming home to be greeted by a smiling Jo, eager to hear how his game had gone.

'Col?'

'Sorry.' He pulled himself back to the present. "I had a call from Rob last night.'

'Rob? What did the young fellow want with you? Haven't seen hide nor hair of him since the night of Alice's retrospective. He put on a good spread. The place seems to be doing well.' He sounded doubtful.

Col remembered how disappointed Gordon had been when none of his children chose to follow him into the legal profession. Rob had been his last hope, and when the youngster had chosen to become a chef, then had come out as gay and elected to take Steve as his life partner, he'd had trouble coping. It was as if he felt he'd been a failure as a father.

'We – Jo and I – have a birthday coming up.'

'So you have.' Gordon took another sip of beer. 'Australia Day as ever. Don't know why they changed to celebrating the holiday on the actual day. It was better when it was held on the nearest weekend.'

Col sighed. That was beside the point, but when Gordon got on his high horse, it was difficult to shift him. He cleared his throat.

'Rob wants to arrange a small do in the gallery.'

'Where Alice's thing was? For Australia Day or your birthday?' Gordon chuckled. 'It's a holiday. I'd have thought they'd have a full house – no time for family gatherings.'

'That's as may be. But he wants to do it. Seems he's already spoken to Jo…' Col let his voice trail off.

'That'd be right. He was always closer to his mother. So, what did she have to say?'

'Seems she agreed – as long as it was kept small. But I… he… assumed you'd want to be there.'

'What about Jo? Does she want me there?'

'I guess so. I haven't spoken to her about it.' Col was glad he could honestly say this, glad Jo hadn't mentioned it last night, though he wondered why not. She hadn't mentioned their birthday at all. Did that mean she wasn't happy about it? Was she regretting their impetuous coming together? Or had it just slipped her mind?

How would she feel seeing Col and Gordon together in such an intimate setting? How would *he* feel, now that he and Jo were lovers? Would people be able to tell? Would it be written on their foreheads – like the adulterers of old? But they weren't adulterers. She and Gordon were divorced. He'd been remarried for years. And Col was a widower.

'Well, have to check with Carol, I suppose. But it'll be good to see the family all together again. Don't know when…' He furrowed his brow as if trying to recall. 'I see Danny and the boys, of course, and Evie and her two, but Rob… not so much, unless Carol and I go to that restaurant of his. I don't see Jo often either, unless we happen to run into each other by accident.' He sighed as if filled with regret, then took a deep breath. 'I guess that's life.'

Col cut into his own steak, chewing it slowly before speaking again. 'You'll let Rob know?'

'What we decide? Yes. I expect we'll be there. Carol likes a party.'

And likes to lord it over Jo, Col thought, but it was none of his business.

'Right,' he said.

*

The phone rang just as Col was finishing dinner. Living on his own, he often chose to eat out, finding the noise of other diners in the club or the local hotel helped stave off his loneliness. But tonight, after the hearty lunch he'd enjoyed with Gordon, he'd decided to make do with popping a ham and cheese sandwich into the microwave and accompanying it with a glass of wine.

Seeing Jo's face on the screen, he pressed to accept the call.

'Jo!' he said, 'I was just thinking about you. He'd actually been rehashing his conversation with Gordon in his mind, but didn't want to say that.

'Really?' He heard the smile in her voice. 'There was something I meant to mention last night.'

'Rob's idea for our birthdays?'

'You knew?' She accused him.

'Not when we spoke. But your dear son chose to call me to enlighten me.'

'Oh!' There was a pause, then, 'What do you think? Is it a good idea?'

So, Jo was having the same reservations as he was? He scratched his head. 'From what Rob told me, it's a done deal. He wanted me to ask Gordon if he'd come.'

'Gordon?' Her voice rose. 'But, he said… a small family affair.'

'Gordon's his dad. No doubt he considers him still part of the family.'

'Yes, but… Oh, what a mess. It was easier when Alice was here, and she arranged it. Rob… he means well, but… And I suppose Gordon said "yes". And that means Carol, too.'

'He said he'd let Rob know but did say how Carol likes a party.'

'Does she ever.' Jo paused again. 'But I'm not going to let her spoil my birthday. I'm just afraid that… seeing us together… everyone might guess…'

He should have known Jo would be worried about that side of it. She wasn't ready to bring their relationship into the light of day. Thinking about it gave him a slight inkling into how Rob must have felt when he and Steve got together.

'Rob's cool with it,' he said.

'Rob's cool with everything. In his eyes, I can do no wrong and he likes you a lot. He and his father, on the other hand…' Col heard her sigh. 'Still, if he wants Gordon there… And I suppose Eve and Danny will expect to see him, too. Can you handle it?'

'I see him every day, Jo. He's my best friend.'

'Of course.' He could almost hear her brain working. 'Sorry. I tend to forget. He's…'

'He still cares for you too, Jo. He'll want to be there.'

He heard her sigh.

'Sometimes I think he cares too much.'

'Maybe.' Col thought back to his conversation with Gordon a few days earlier. Jo was right. Gordon still felt a proprietary interest in his ex-wife. It wasn't natural, was it?

'You're not regretting…?' he asked.

'No, I could never regret what we have together.'

But Col heard a slight hesitation in Jo's voice and wondered if she was being completely honest with him.

Seventeen

Jo hadn't seen much of Col in the days leading up to their birthdays, so it was with some trepidation that she dressed in the new turquoise strappy dress she'd bought especially for the occasion. As she turned around to check herself in the mirror, she wondered if it had been a mistake. It looked okay in the shop – she'd chosen to go to the large department store in the neighbouring town rather than take Eve's advice this time – but now her upper arms appeared flabby. Could she really carry off those straps? She sucked in her stomach, but no amount of sucking in could get rid of the roll of fat that seemed to have appeared as if by magic.

Jo stroked the soft material and admired the way it floated around her hips. This is what she'd seen in the tiny fitting room mirror, not the rest. She sighed. It was too late to change now.

Making sure Scout had plenty of food and water and leaving the outside light on for when she got back, Jo got into her car and set off. As she bumped over the cattle grid on the way out, she reminded herself to check her tyres before too long. On the way down the lane, she passed Magda, walking her pair of rescue greyhounds. She stopped and wound the window down.

'Hey. How're things?'

'Pretty good. Off to celebrate with the birthday boy?'

Jo almost choked. One thing Col certainly wasn't was a boy. He was all man. But Magda must be close to ten years older, so she supposed she had a different perspective. 'A family celebration,' Jo corrected her.

'Oh, that's right. My mistake. That's what you're all gussied up for?' she chortled. 'You're looking good.'

Jo put a tentative hand up to her hair, checking her upswept style was still in place. 'Is it too much?'

'Just about right, I'd say. If he's not in love with you already, that should do it.'

Jo felt herself redden. How did Magda know? The woman was a witch. 'I'm not…'

'Go away with you. Of course you are. I'd do the same if I were your age again and had a man like Col interested in me. What do the family think?'

'They don't know – apart from Rob.'

'And Gordon's going to be there tonight?'

'Yes – and Carol.'

'Hmm. Well, mind you behave yourself. That one would try the patience of a saint.'

Not the words Jo wanted to hear on her way to her birthday dinner. But Magda was right about Carol. She hadn't realised they knew each other.

As if in answer to her unspoken question, Magda added, 'She booked a massage with me one time, then has looked down her nose at me ever since on the odd occasion we've passed each other in town. Don't think I was classy enough for her. Though what she has to put on airs about, I don't know.'

'She's married to Gordon.' Jo laughed.

'There is that.'

*

Jo was still smiling when she drove into the restaurant car park. As predicted, it was already almost full, ensuring a busy night for Rob's staff. She slid her car into a space next to Col's, checked her face in the mirror, took a deep breath, and headed inside.

'Mum!' Rob was first to greet her, giving her a hug and kiss and handing her a glass of champagne. 'We were beginning to wonder if you'd chickened out. You look stunning,' he whispered, 'Carol will be green with envy.'

Fat chance, Jo thought, seeing her ex's wife's eyes glitter from across the room, her arm tightly entwined with Gordon's.

As if I was interested in him any longer, Jo thought with a shudder.

Her mood changed as her granddaughters rushed to greet her.

'Happy birthday, Gramma,' they called in unison, with Lottie adding, 'We have a present for you, but Mummy said we had to wait till after.'

'That's lovely, girls,' she said, hugging them, then looking up to see Eve bearing down on her.

'Happy birthday, Mum.' Eve kissed her. 'We thought we'd do the present thing after dinner – they're over by the window.'

Jo followed the direction of Eve's pointing finger to see a table covered with multi-coloured packages.

'Open ours first, Gramma,' Livvy said, hopping excitedly from one foot to the other.

'I will.'

Jo raised her eyes to search the room and immediately caught sight of Col. Her stomach lurched as she took in his broad shoulders straining at the blue chambray shirt, his tanned arms and neck, and the thick thatch of almost entirely white hair. She'd known him for so long, but he'd never had this effect on her before now. The image of him as she'd last seen him – naked and tousled, his eyes blurred with sleep and desire – rose unbidden into her mind.

She took a deep breath, hoping her emotions didn't show on her face. 'Happy birthday, Col,' she said as he joined her, wished her happy birthday, and kissed her on both cheeks. Something moved deep in her gut and she stifled the urge to throw her arms around him and kiss him properly.

'Mother Slater!'

'Stiff upper lip,' Col whispered as Kylie took his place and air-kissed her, followed by Danny who hugged her warmly.

'Happy birthday, Mum,' he said. 'Boys?'

Tim and Liam came forward, self-conscious with their hair unnaturally tidy and wearing what looked like new white shirts. 'Happy Birthday, Grandma,' they said very correctly, accepting her hugs awkwardly and making her wonder where the exuberant boys of the previous Sunday had disappeared to.

Finally, after much jostling, everyone was seated, Gordon and Carol politely wishing her happy birthday as they took their places. She was just pulling in her chair when Kay appeared at her elbow and kissed her on the cheek. 'Happy birthday, old friend,' she said with a grin.

'Thanks, but less of the old. It'll be you, too, in a few years' time,' Jo replied.

Despite Col's attempts to sit beside her, he was placed at the far end of the table. 'Guests of honour at each end,' Eve said gaily, ushering them into their places. He sent her a rueful glance.

'Thanks, darling,' she said when Steve refilled her glass. She looked around the table. Her family. Already, it felt as if Col was part of it. She watched him joking with Danny at the other end of the table and wished she could tell them. But she knew very well that would put a dampener on the evening.

Beside Danny, Kylie was fussing over the boys who looked as if they'd rather be anywhere but here. Opposite, Brad's face held much the same expression as the boys. Jo threw a glance at Eve, sitting beside him, but she showed no sign of her husband's discomfort. Jo wondered again if all was well there. It had to be, with two small girls to bring up.

Then her eyes fell on Gordon and Carol, sitting together halfway down the table. He was looking good, but that tan didn't come from the sun. Carol must have persuaded him to visit the tanning studio she frequented. Jo hid a smile. He was trying too hard. And Carol did look somewhat stressed, her normally self-satisfied expression missing, replaced by a faint frown. Maybe her desire for a child was eating at her.

Jo was glad she'd invited Kay after all. She was a good friend and they'd shared a lot together. She caught her friend glancing speculatively at her and Col a few times during the evening and wondered what she was thinking. No doubt she'd find out next time they met.

She couldn't wait till it was over and she and Col could talk. Was that unkind of her? This was her birthday – hers and Col's. Her children had gathered to celebrate with her. She should be grateful – happy, even. So why did she feel as if there was something simmering just under the surface, waiting to erupt?

Eighteen

Rob and Steve were clearing the table, leaving Jo and Col alone for a few moments. The others had all left, Gordon claiming another engagement, and Eve and Kylie citing the need to get the children to bed.

Col helped Jo gather up her gifts asking, 'Do you want all the wrappings, too?'

'I don't think so, though…' her eyes fell on the special wrapping paper on which the twins had written Happy Birthday in large, untidy, coloured lettering, '…maybe I'll keep this one.' She picked it up and folded it carefully. The mechanical purple kitchen witch it had contained bore all the signs of being chosen by Lottie and Livvy themselves. She knew it would make her laugh every time she saw it. And she knew just the spot for it – on the old-fashioned oak dresser in her kitchen.

'You're looking lovely tonight. I wasn't able to tell you earlier. Put Carol to shame.' Col took Jo in his arms, her hands holding the wrapping paper crushed between them. He kissed her forehead, sending a swift surge of desire through her body. *How could she resist this man?* Regardless how often she told him – and herself – they should take things slowly, she knew in her heart he was what she wanted. They were too old to play games. What they had was real. They should enjoy it while they could.

'One last one, Mum? Uncle Col?' Rob and Steve appeared with a bottle of champagne and four glasses.

'Oh, don't you think we've had enough?' Jo laughed.

'It's not every day you turn sixty,' he said, popping the cork and pouring out the sparkling liquid. 'To you – both of you,' he said, raising his glass.

'Oh!' Jo said, picking up her own glass. For the first time tonight, she felt able to look at Col without dissembling. 'Thanks, honey.'

'When are you going to tell Eve and Danny?' Rob asked without preamble.

'You don't beat around the bush,' Col said, taking a sip of his drink. 'It's up to your mother.' He raised an eyebrow in Jo's direction.

'Not yet,' she said decisively. 'There's nothing to tell, and…'

Both Rob and Steve began to laugh. 'Been there, done that,' Rob said. 'There's never a good time and Dad will have to know some time – before he finds out.'

Jo knew he was right, but she was loath to spoil things by having Gordon turn their relationship into some sort of one-upmanship thing. He and Col were best friends and had been partners forever. But beneath the bonhomie, she'd always detected an underlying sense of competition. Maybe that's even part of the reason he was so quick to fall under Carol's spell – to prevent Col from being tempted and getting there first? No – she wouldn't go there.

'There's time enough for that,' she said, picking up her glass and taking a gulp as if doing so would dismiss her speculations.

'Time to go?' Col drained his glass and stood up.

'Thanks, you two,' Jo said rising unsteadily to her feet, only to find Col's reassuring arm around her shoulders. 'It was good of you to arrange this for us.'

'Any time, Mum,' Rob said, giving her a hug before linking arms with Steve. 'We're always here for you.'

His words sent a warm glow through Jo. Rob was one child she could count on – maybe the only one. What was it that happened to those little children who'd hung on her every word? They'd grown up. They had their own issues to deal with. And their parents – because she wasn't immune to the realisation they treated Gordon in exactly the same way – came way down their list of priorities.

But that didn't mean they wouldn't be incensed to discover about her and Col, she reasoned, her champagne-fuelled brain going into overdrive.

'Let's get you home.' Col steered her to the car – hers, this time, she noticed – and belted her in.

Jo leant her head against the head-rest and closed her eyes, opening them again when she heard the engine start. 'I think I may have overdone the champagne,' she muttered indistinctly, and heard Col chuckle. She closed her eyes again, only opening them when a waft of cool air indicated they'd reached her home and Col had opened the passenger door.

*

Jo opened her eyes and gazed blearily around the room, then at the sleeping figure beside her. She carefully lifted the single sheet to check – she was naked and had no recollection of undressing or coming to bed. She made an attempt to focus, noticing the dress she had been wearing was hanging on the back of the door and, on the chair, there was a neat pile of what she took to be her underclothes. A shirt and pair of khaki pants hung over the chair's back.

At that moment Col's eyes opened and he smiled at her obvious confusion.

'Did I? Did we?' she asked.

Col chuckled, took her in his arms and dropped a kiss on her hair. 'Of course not. It would have been like making love to a corpse. You conked out as soon as we got through the door.'

'And you…' She nodded towards the door and the chair, embarrassed to think he'd had to undress her.

'I couldn't let you spend the night in your good outfit.'

'But…'

'It's okay. I've seen you naked before – remember? And I got plenty of practice in handling women's clothes when Alice was ill.'

While both of these statements were true, Jo still shuddered to think he'd managed to remove all of her clothes without her knowledge. And it reminded her of Alice's final weeks and days.

'I should get up. I'll probably feel better after a shower.' And the way her mouth felt, she didn't want him kissing her until she'd brushed her teeth. 'And I'd imagine you'll need to get to the office. What's the time?' She tried to see around him to the bedside clock.

'I think I'll play hooky today.' Col leant back and clasped his hands behind his head. 'Maybe we could go for a drive?'

Jo stretched. 'Sounds good. But what will Gordon say?'

'He's my partner, not my boss.' He gave her a nudge and, suddenly feeling more awake, Jo slipped out of bed and headed for the shower.

The strident ringing of her phone brought her out of the shower just as she was turning on the water.

Col was holding up her mobile and looking embarrassed. 'I didn't think I should answer it,' he said.

Seeing Eve's face on the screen, Jo sighed. *What did her daughter want now?*

'Good morning, Eve.'

'Mu…um.' Eve's tone immediately sent shivers up Jo's spine.

'What's wrong? The girls?'

'It's Brad. He… he's…' Eve's words were incomprehensible, muffled by tears.

Jo threw an anguished look at Col and mouthed, 'Brad.'

'Calm down, darling. I can't understand you. Take a deep breath. What's happened to Brad?'

Her words seemed to do the trick. Jo heard her daughter inhale. When she spoke again, her words were clearer. 'He's had an accident. He was out on his morning ride when… I need to go to the hospital… The girls…'

Pinching the skin at her throat, Jo looked apologetically across to where Col was rising and getting dressed. 'I'll be right there. I can see to them and stay as long as you need me. Is he badly hurt?'

'I don't know,' Eve wailed. 'The hospital called and…'

'Stay put. I'll be with you as soon as I can.'

'Accident on his bike?' Col asked, when Jo hung up the phone.

'How did you guess? I'm surprised it hasn't happened before now. But I need to get over to Eve's. I'm sorry.'

'No worries. You can drop me off on the way. I'll shower at home.'

'Thanks.' Jo rose to her toes and kissed Col on the lips. 'I can have breakfast when I get there.' In her mind she was already at Eve's place, working out how to deal with the two little girls who would be wondering why their mother had to dash off. All thought of a day with Col was forgotten.

*

'Why don't I pop over once I've showered and dressed,' Col suggested as he stepped out of Jo's car. 'I'm sure you could do with an extra pair of hands.'

'Would you? Wouldn't you rather go into the office?' But the thought of having some assistance with what would no doubt be two upset and inquisitive little girls did have some appeal.

'I'd already decided to take the day off, if you recall,' Col said with a grin. 'Call me when you know what's what and let me know if you need me to bring anything.'

'Thanks.'

Driving off, Jo was suffused with a warm feeling – one she hadn't experienced for years. Even before Gordon had left, she realised, their lives had been moving in different directions. It was nice – better than nice – to have someone who cared, who wanted to help, to be there for her, even when all she had to do was spend the day with her grandchildren.

'Mum. Thank God!' Eve greeted her at the door.

'Are you sure you're okay to drive?' Jo asked, shocked by the state of the normally immaculate Eve. This morning, her hair looked uncombed, she wore no makeup and appeared to have thrown on the first garments that came to hand – a pair of baggy khaki shorts and an oversized tee-shirt which looked as if it belonged to Brad.

'I'll be fine. I just need…' With a quick hug of her mother, she was off.

'Let me know…' Jo called after her, but it was too late.

She watched the car drive away, a worried expression on her face. This was so unlike Eve who usually left Jo with a long list of things to take care of; of activities the twins should do and not do and instructions on what they were and weren't allowed to eat.

'Gramma!' Jo looked up to see Livvy trailing out of the kitchen, still wearing her pyjamas. 'Mummy went to see Daddy.'

'Yes, she did.' Jo gathered her up in her arms, only to find Lottie had followed her through to join in the hug.

Jo set about organising breakfast, instructed by the twins as to where their favourite cereal was stored. When they were settled, she made coffee and toast for herself, glad Eve and Brad had invested in a state-of-the-art coffee maker. Sometimes even her favourite Earl Grey didn't do it. She was in desperate need of a caffeine hit.

She had only just finished and chased the girls into their bedroom to dress, when Col rang.

'No more news,' she said in response to his inquiry. 'I'll try to call Eve later if I don't hear anything. But I don't want to disturb her yet.'

'Are you feeling better? Have you eaten?'

'Yes to both. You don't need to come over. I'll be fine. The girls…'

But the twins chose that moment to begin arguing and their screams could easily be heard on the other end of the phone.

'Sounds like you *could* do with some help,' he said. 'I won't be long.'

Despite her protestation, Jo was relieved. She hung up and in the bedroom she found two red-faced children quarrelling over the ownership of a yellow pair of shorts. Jo sighed. This wasn't going to be an easy day. Eve's sudden departure had upset their routine and, although they'd been kept in the dark about their dad's accident, they sensed something was wrong.

'I know,' she said, carefully extricating the crumpled shorts from one pair of hands, 'Why don't we go for a swim.'

'Yay!' they said together. 'In your pool? Oh, please, Gramma!'

Jo thought for a moment. She was sure Eve expected her to remain there until she got back. But that could be hours from now. And Jo would certainly feel more comfortable in her own home. She made an instant decision. 'Okay. But no more arguing.'

Her words worked like magic. No sooner had she texted Col to let him know of the change in plans, than two angelic-looking little girls appeared in the doorway.

'We're ready,' Livvy said with a grin. 'Can we go now?'

Five minutes later, they were strapped into the car, and in another thirty they drew up at Jo's home. Col's car was already parked under the large pepper tree – a remnant of the earlier occupants of the acreage which had once been two adjoining soldier settlements. After the First World War, the Australian government had deeded ten acre parcels of land to returning soldiers, and Jo and Gordon had bought this block, long abandoned by its original owners who'd have had to work miracles to make a living from it.

They'd been delighted with its peaceful aspect and Jo had been thrilled when she discovered remnants of an old garden. For a time, Gordon had been amused to turn up rusting horseshoes and nails, but that had soon palled. However, Jo had persevered to develop what was now a flourishing flower and vegetable garden, albeit much diminished by the drought.

'Uncle Col!'

Col rose from the wooden bench on which he'd been sitting. He was already in his swim togs and Jo did a double take. He was in good shape for someone who'd turned sixty only a day ago, putting her own flabby body to shame.

'We're going swimming,' Lottie informed him. 'Will you come in with us?'

'That's the plan.' He rose to give Jo a hug and kiss. 'You joining us?' he asked with a grin.

'Oh, I don't know.' It was one thing for him to see her naked in bed or in the bedroom, but for her to don a swimsuit in front of him in broad daylight was something else altogether. 'I might just sit and watch.'

'You look beautiful whatever you wear,' he whispered, so quietly the girls weren't able to hear, clearly reading her innermost thoughts.

'Well…'

'Swim with us, Gramma,' Lottie urged, pulling her hand to drag her inside.

Reluctantly Jo allowed herself to be led into the bedroom where she changed into the black swimsuit she'd purchased before Christmas, intending only to wear it when she was alone. She examined herself in the mirror, much as she had done the previous evening. But this time, she was aware of her bulging thighs and the hint of a stomach that even the firm control panel of the suit failed to hide.

She heard the girls run outside, and loud splashing and squeals as they joined Col in the pool. Scout had joined them, too, but was lazily lying on the steps, with only his hind legs in the water. Taking a deep breath, Jo wrapped a towel around her waist and joined them.

It was cool in the pool, the shade cloth providing protection from the strong sun. The morning passed quickly.

Jo was drying off the twins when her mobile buzzed. Picking it up, she was relieved to see Eve's face. 'How is he?' she asked, shooing the girls off with a wave of her hand.

'Not good.' But at least Eve wasn't crying. 'It's his spleen. The doctor thinks he's ruptured it.'

Jo thought quickly, trying to remember what she knew about the spleen. She thought you could live without one but… 'Are they going to operate?'

She heard Eve take an indrawn breath. 'Not at the moment. They've been doing tests and think it may heal by itself. Brad's pretty out of it at the moment, so I want to stay here for a bit. Are you all right to stay with the twins?'

'Of course. They wanted a swim, so I brought them home with me. We've just got out of the pool.'

'Right.' Jo could tell she was distracted.

'They're fine here. Just let me know when you'll be home, or you could come here.'

'Thanks, Mum. I might do that.' She hung up.

*

Col had left, and Jo and the girls were having dinner – a quick spaghetti bolognese she'd whipped up – when they heard the sound of a car and Scout lumbered towards the doorway.

'Mummy!' Lottie screamed and, followed by her sister, ran to the door almost tripping over the dog, heedless of Jo's warning to slow down and let their mum get into the house first.

She was standing by the stove when Eve, a child hanging on each arm, walked in. Right away, she could see how exhausted Eve was.

'Some dinner?' she asked gently. 'Have you eaten?'

'I just wanted to pick the girls up. I don't think I could swallow anything.' She sank into a chair, her head drooping.

'Why don't you all stay here tonight? You look too tired to drive back into town, and I can bath the girls and put them to bed.'

'I…' But Eve was too tired to argue. 'Thanks, Mum.'

Jo ladled out a serving of spaghetti and poured a measure of brandy. You get yourself round that. We don't want you getting sick too. I'll see to the girls.'

Eve looked at the bowl of food, seeming about to refuse, then she slowly picked up a fork while Jo cleared away the dishes and sent the girls to undress, promising them ice cream after they had their bath.

'Uncle Col was here. He came swimming with us,' Lottie burbled as soon as they returned to the kitchen.

'How could you, Mum? After that time at the gallery. What's he doing sniffing around you, anyway? You want to be careful.'

Jo bit her tongue, knowing Eve was hurting, worried about her husband. But to think her daughter felt she needed to warn her about Col – her old friend. She couldn't believe it.

Nineteen

Jo tossed and turned, her mind returning to Eve's words – to warn her about Col! How could she even imagine…? But it was another example of how patronising her two older children had become. She'd been right to keep her budding relationship secret from them. But how could she tell them now? Maybe she and Col had been wrong to imagine they could defy convention and become a couple in this town.

She sighed and turned over again, trying to find a comfortable position, only falling into a light sleep as dawn was breaking.

At breakfast, both she and Eve were bleary eyed, while the twins were full of life.

'You'll be wanting to get to the hospital,' Jo said, when she and Eve were on their second cup of tea and the girls had been sent off to get dressed.

'Yes.' Eve looked up from where she'd been studying her empty plate. 'They should have the results of their tests today. I need to be there.'

Eve's obvious distress at Brad's accident had completely disabused Jo of any idea there might be something wrong in her daughter's marriage. Eve's behaviour was consistent with that of a wife who loved her husband – regardless of how distant or censorial he might be at times. And Eve could give lessons in being censorial too, Jo acknowledged, remembering her restless night.

'The girls are good here.'

'Yes, but…' Jo saw Eve's face take on the stubborn expression she knew so well, '…it would be easier all round if they were in their own home.'

Easier for whom? Jo thought, but Eve's distraught face prevented her voicing her feelings.

'They start school on Tuesday,' Eve continued, 'and I don't know how...' She gazed pleadingly at her mother.

Jo sighed. She should have expected this. Part of her wanted to tell Eve to grow up, to take responsibility for her own family, to work something out. But another part, the part that allowed her to be coerced into falling in with whatever plans Eve had devised for her, knew now wasn't the time to make a stand. She decided to pre-empt Eve's request. 'Why don't I move in while Brad's in hospital?' she asked. 'Then you'll be free to come and go as needed. We can reconsider the arrangement when he gets home.'

'Oh, Mum, would you?' Eve's face immediately brightened. 'It would set my mind at rest.'

'Scout would have to come, too,' Jo warned, knowing how houseproud her daughter was, and wondering how she would react to having the old dog in her spotless, modern, two-storey townhouse in the centre of town.

'Oh!' For a moment it seemed Eve was going to refuse, then Lottie, who'd returned to hear the last part of the conversation, pleaded. 'Oh, can he, Mummy? Please!'

'Well…' Eve hesitated for a moment, then gave the glimmer of a smile. 'If he... I know you'll take care, Mum. It's just that…'

'We'll be good,' Jo promised. 'Now, my dear, why don't you get ready and be off? We'll head into town when I've cleared up here and packed enough for a few days. You can call me when you have any news.'

'Can we come to see Daddy, too?' Livvy asked, appearing in the kitchen wearing her shorts, her feet bare. She ran over to cling to Eve's knees.

'No, honey. Not today. Daddy…' she teared up, '…he needs to rest. Another day. You stay with Gramma today, and I'll see you later. Be good for Gramma, won't you?'

'Yes,' Livvy said, doubtfully.

'Scout's coming home with us,' Lottie said, proud to be the bearer of good tidings, and sliding a sideways glance at her mother as if fearful she'd change her mind.

'Yay!' Livvy ran to hug the dog who licked her face enthusiastically.

Seeing Eve's doubtful expression, Jo immediately pulled Scout away from Livvy. 'We'll be fine,' she repeated. 'Don't you need to go?'

'Yes.' Eve stood up.

Finally, Eve left, and Jo turned her attention to the twins. It took her almost an hour, but eventually they were all ready and packed into the car, Scout fastened into the back seat between two delighted little girls.

They had just reached the outskirts of town when it began to rain. The rain the town had been looking forward to for the past four months had decided to fall when Jo had two active four-year-olds for the entire day. She parked in the garage and hurried everyone into the house, Scout taking his time to sniff around all the corners before deciding to settle beside the French doors leading out into the garden, head on his paws.

To Jo's surprise, the girls soon disappeared into their room, content to continue with what they now referred to as their 'art work', and she was able to make herself a cup of tea and call Col.

'I'm at Eve's,' she said without preamble. 'She thought it less unsettling for the girls to come home. She's at the hospital.' She tugged at the edge of the loose shirt she'd thrown on that morning and wound a strand of hair around one finger. 'I think… it might be best…' How was she to say this?

But Col knew her so well. 'You want me to stay away?'

Put like that it sounded so blunt.

'Eve,' she began.

'Doesn't she trust me with the twins?'

'She doesn't trust you with *me*.' There, she'd said it. She heard Col chuckle.

'I don't know whether to be insulted or flattered,' he said.

'Oh, flattered, I think,' Jo said, relieved he could see the funny side. 'She warned me to watch out for you – to be cautious about your possible nefarious intentions.'

'She didn't actually say that?'

'No, not exactly. I think she actually said something about warning me to be careful of your sniffing around.' Col snorted, and Jo began to laugh too, finally seeing the funny side of her daughter's concern.

'She's worried about Brad. He has a ruptured spleen. It's not clear if they'll have to operate. We have to make allowances. I said I'd stay here while he was in hospital. It shouldn't be for long. But the twins start school on Tuesday and…'

'You've been co-opted to fill in as usual.' *Was there a note of bitterness in his voice?*

'They *are* my grandchildren.' As soon as she'd said it, Jo felt guilty. This was Col. She had no reason to be angry with him. If she was going to be angry with anyone, it should be Brad for not taking more care, for riding down the hill so fast he was unable to stop. But there was really no one to blame. It just irked her that her life was on hold for one of her children yet again. One thing was for sure, she was going to remind Steve about his promise to check out his students. And Eve would have to accept that her mother wasn't always going to be there when her life went into freefall. Should she feel guilty about thinking this way? Jo knew there were many grandparents who welcomed the opportunity to spend time with their grandchildren – and she did too. But not quite so much time.

'Are you still there?'

'Yes. Sorry. I was thinking. You're right, of course. Maybe…'

But it seemed Col had heard enough. 'Call me when you have time,' he said.

Jo heard the phone go dead and stared at the blank screen. Now what had she done? She'd managed to upset the normally placid Col. Damn Eve! Damn Brad!

'Gramma! What can we do now?' She was brought out of her musings by two woebegone faces, and had to quickly force herself into a more cheerful frame of mind.

By lunchtime, Jo was exhausted. She'd helped the twins make paper lanterns, played innumerable games of Uno, and finally resorted to turning on the children's programme on television, despite knowing Eve would disapprove.

Eve's call was a welcome diversion, and Jo was glad she could tell her daughter the girls were having a nap – she would love one too but was making do with a cup of tea and putting her feet up.

The news was good. The doctors had decided against surgery for the time being, preferring to monitor Brad for a few days to ensure there was no more bleeding, and believing the spleen might heal itself with rest.

'He could have died,' Eve said, with a break in her voice.

'But he didn't.'

'Oh, Mum. I know he sometimes makes me so angry, but I don't know what I'd do without him. How do you cope?' she asked, as if suddenly realising Jo had lost her husband.

'Well, I didn't have two young children to contend with. But it's not easy when you've been part of a couple for years. Be grateful.'

'Oh, I am.' There was a pause, then Eve said, 'He'll be here for another few days before we know... Can you…?'

'I can stay as long as you need me.' *And there go all my plans to turn over a new leaf with my children.*

'Thanks.'

But Jo could tell Eve's mind was already elsewhere.

'I'll need to make some arrangements for the shop. And I did want to be with the twins when they started school, but…'

'You need to be with Brad. I understand.'

Jo hung up. Almost immediately her mobile rang again. Danny.

'Mum. What's this I hear about Brad?'

Jo told him what she knew, only to have him berate her for being too ready to drop everything for Eve. 'I bet you'd let her have the house if she and Brad wanted it,' he said, bitterly.

Where had that come from? Jo could hear her daughter-in-law's words coming from Danny's mouth. She took a deep breath before replying.

*

The rest of the day passed quickly, and Jo managed to have the girls bathed and fed before Eve came home. She was a ghost of her usual self, and Jo hugged her tightly, before making her sit down and eat the mushroom risotto she'd prepared. Despite Eve's protests, Jo also poured her a glass of red wine and drew her a bath, knowing it would help her sleep.

By the time she fell into bed herself, Jo was completely exhausted.

How was she going to manage however many more days it took for Brad to be declared well enough to come home? She didn't dare consider the alternative. Just before her head hit the pillow, her phone buzzed with a text.

I'm sorry. Hang in there. Love you. Colx

Jo closed her eyes with a smile.

Twenty

Col wakened on Tuesday morning with a sense of loss. It took him a few moments to work out why. Then he remembered. He'd argued with Jo. Well, not argued exactly. But his reaction to her dropping everything yet again for Eve had stung him, as had the younger woman's comments. Warning her mother to be cautious!

Maybe he'd over-reacted by hanging up on her so suddenly but, although he'd managed to see the funny side of Eve's warning, he'd been angry at the thought of her blatant manipulation of her mother – and Jo's willingness to be used in that way. He'd regretted it afterwards and sent a text to apologise. But Jo hadn't replied. Sunday and Monday – the day they usually had dinner together – had passed, and he had no idea what was happening. He tried to tell himself she was busy, staying at her daughter's, and that her son-in-law was in hospital, but he still felt something had gone wrong between them – something he needed to fix.

His morning coffee tasted bitter. He had no appetite for breakfast but managed to choke down a piece of toast with vegemite. He could almost hear Alice reprimanding him, telling him to take more care of himself but, for once, he paid no heed. What if he'd completely screwed things up with Jo? How could he live with himself?

In his office, he gazed unseeingly at the computer screen trying to raise some enthusiasm for the task, only looking up when his partner walked in.

After discussing a knotty problem he was having with a property dispute, Gordon rubbed his hands together. 'The twins start school today,' he said. 'It doesn't seem so long ago that Eve was running through the school gates for the first time. Where have the years gone? These young ones are so full of energy. I don't know…'

Col didn't reply. He didn't want to get into another discussion about Carol's longing to start a family. That was Gordon's problem – and one of his own making. Col allowed his gaze to return to the screen and Gordon took the hint.

'I'll let you get on,' he said before leaving.

Once he'd gone, it occurred to Col that, with the girls at school, Jo would be freed up. Maybe he could persuade her to meet for lunch? Maybe he was worrying needlessly? She'd been busy with Eve and her grandchildren. He sent off a text inviting her to lunch and waited.

'There's a woman here to see you,' Dot's voice on the intercom was an annoying interruption. He felt like a foolish teenager waiting for Jo to reply. Why hadn't he just rung her like any sane person?

'Does she have an appointment?'

'No. She says her name is…' there was a pause while Dot no doubt checked, 'Sally Anderson. Do you want to see her?'

Col checked his diary, then the document he'd been attempting unsuccessfully to make sense of for the past ten minutes. 'Give me five minutes, then send her in,' he said.

Five minutes later a tall dark-haired woman who looked to be in her early thirties walked in. There was something vaguely familiar about her.

'How can I help you, Miss Anderson?' he asked when she had taken a seat, perching nervously on the edge of the chair.

'I… You're Colin… Colin Ford?'

'I am.' He laid down the pen he'd been fiddling with and leant back in his chair. 'Do we know each other?'

'No… yes… my mother…'

Col waited patiently. He was used to clients taking some time to come to the point.

Two red spots appeared in her cheeks before she uttered her next words, 'You're my father.'

Col was too shocked to reply. Her father? What was she talking about?

'That's not possible,' he said without thinking, only to see her break down in sobs. Hell, he was no good with weeping women. He reached for the box of tissues Dot made sure was always by his desk and, walking round to her side, handed it to her.

'I'm sorry,' she sobbed, dabbing at her eyes and blowing her nose. 'I don't usually fall apart like this.'

Safely back behind the desk, Col tried to gather his thoughts. The woman clearly believed what she had said, but she was mistaken. She must have been born when he and Alice were married, and he'd been faithful to his wife throughout the marriage.

He waited till she appeared to have recovered, then said gently, 'Why don't you tell me all about it?'

She scrubbed her eyes with a tissue and hiccupped.

Col went to the water cooler in the corner, filled a paper cup, handed it to her, then resumed his seat and waited again. This could take all morning. He watched her gulp gratefully, then crush the empty cup before beginning to speak.

'My mother was Glenda Darling,' she said, looking at him questioningly. 'She attended a ball here in the eighties. I was born in 1998. She died last year. She wrote it all down. Your name. Everything.'

Col racked his brains. The name meant nothing to him. He and Alice had been in the habit of attending the winter balls held after the picnic races every year. But he knew he'd never met this Glenda Darling. Yet there was something about the woman that seemed familiar, that tugged at his memory.

'It wasn't me,' he said with a sigh. 'I'm afraid you've come here on a wild goose chase.' He felt sorry for the woman, but this was all a pack of lies. What was she hoping to gain by her wild accusation? Money? He didn't have enough of that to make it worth anyone's while to make such a claim.

'Why would my mother lie?' Her voice hardened as she glared across the desk at him.

'I don't know.' Col pulled on his ear. 'But I assure you, I've never heard of her.'

'Colin Ford. Solicitor. Granite Springs. That's what she wrote. Is there more than one of you?' Her voice rose, making Col worry Dot would hear her and come in to check all was well. It wouldn't be the first time a client became angry and threatened him or Gordon when things didn't go according to plan.

'No, just me. But your mother must have been mistaken.' He exhaled loudly. This was going nowhere. His phone beeped. Was it a text from Jo? He cursed silently, knowing he couldn't check till the woman had left.

'But you *were* there,' she accused.

Col drew a hand through his hair. He and Alice would have been at the ball, but what did that prove?

'My wife…' he emphasised the word *wife*, '…and I regularly attended the balls back then. But we didn't meet your mother. I'd have remembered.' But would he? There had been so many social occasions back then. Alice loved the atmosphere, whereas he'd just tagged along, content to bask in the glow of her popularity. She'd often been the centre of a noisy group while he looked on, knowing that, while she needed the surge of adrenaline it gave her, she was content to return home with him.

'I believe my mother. I thought… I hoped… you'd be pleased to meet me,' she said, rising to leave. 'You haven't heard the end of this,' she threw at him as she walked out, head held high.

The door closed behind her with a thud. Col shook his head. What had that been all about? While the woman was clearly mistaken, she obviously believed what her mother had told her.

Had this Glenda woman been here in Granite Springs in what must have been 1987?

Where had she got his name?

And why did Sally Anderson look vaguely familiar?

Twenty-one

The weekend passed uneventfully for Jo, with Eve spending her time at the hospital and Jo taking care of the twins who seemed to be becoming accustomed to this arrangement, beyond the odd question of why their dad wasn't coming home.

Tuesday dawned a bright, sunny day. The rain of the weekend had disappeared, leaving behind the special freshness in the air that comes after a heavy deluge. Breakfast was a nightmare with two excited little girls running around the kitchen, and Eve anxious to get to the hospital.

Finally, Eve left, and Jo managed to calm the girls sufficiently to pack them into the car and drive to school. Once there, they became part of a group of other four and five-year-olds, some eager, some reluctant, to start their education.

'I'm Miss Lang,' said a young woman with brown curls tied back from her face and an infectious smile. Jo thought she looked about sixteen. 'All you mums can come with your littlies for the first ten minutes, then it's best if you leave quietly.'

Jo joined the group standing at the side of the room while the young woman settled the twenty or so children on a mat at the front of the classroom, introduced herself, and began a singing game. It was soon clear that the adults standing around had been forgotten. Jo quietly crept out.

For the first time since Saturday, Jo felt free. It should have been a heady feeling, but there was a niggle at the back of her mind. Col hadn't been in touch – not since his brief text on Saturday evening. She'd expected him to call, to arrange to meet on Monday for dinner as usual. She'd have refused. She couldn't have left Eve – not with the state she was in – but it would have been good to hear his voice.

She checked her mobile and gave a sigh of relief to see a message from Col. The text suggested they meet at Mouthfuls at twelve. Texting back with a smiley emoji, Jo grinned. She'd missed their Monday dinner, spending the evening reassuring Eve everything would be all right, even though no one knew if it would be.

Lunch with Col would cheer her up.

But first, she had arranged to have coffee with Kay. Jo knew her friend would quiz her about Col and wondered how to combat her disapproval. She didn't like being at odds with her, but Kay didn't understand. Or maybe she did – maybe she understood all too well.

The two women greeted each other amicably and ordered coffee with the day's special banana and walnut muffin. Jo had too many other things to worry about to be concerned about adding extra kilos. She waited for Kay's interrogation about Col.

But, instead, her friend was excited about news of her own.

'You'll never guess?' she said with a grin.

Jo didn't even make an attempt, waiting for Kay to explain.

'I've got a job!'

'You're going back to work?' Jo was surprised. 'Where?'

Until her husband's death, Kay had managed his dental practice, handling reception and accounts. But she'd left soon after David died, preferring to lead a quiet life out of the limelight.

'At the university. I heard they were having trouble filling an admin position in the School of Education. I met the Dean's PA at a choir practice,' she explained, 'so I applied. I start next week.'

'You're sure?' Jo asked, knowing how Kay had shunned company, fearful of being reminded how David had taken his own life and the recriminations of members of their close-knit community.

'I think so. I can't hide forever. And it'll be good for me to get out of the house more.'

'Well, congratulations.'

'It would do you good, too.'

'A job? Me?' Jo laughed. 'I've just managed to get out of helping

Rob at the restaurant and now I'm caught up minding the twins. When would I have time for a job?'

'It would take your mind off... You *are* still seeing him, are you?'

Jo should have known it was too good to last. 'I don't have much chance to see anyone but Eve and the girls at the moment,' she said, ignoring the fact she was about to meet Col for lunch. *That didn't count as "seeing" in Kay's terms, did it?*

'Well, mark my words, no good can come of you and Col Ford. For one thing...'

But Jo didn't want to hear. She blanked out the rest of Kay's words, focussing instead on cutting her muffin into bite-sized pieces.

She managed to change the subject to the upcoming church fete, relieved when Kay looked at her watch.

'I need to go. I have a hair appointment in ten minutes. Thought I should smarten myself up for the new job. I realise I've been letting myself go since...' Her eyes moistened.

The pair rose and hugged.

Jo watched her friend leave, pleased Kay had decided to move on with her life, then walked around the corner, deciding to use the time until her lunch with Col to go to the library. She really hoped she'd be able to return home soon. Eve's house was nice, very modern, but it wasn't her home. Then there was Col. She felt as if her insides were vibrating just thinking of him. It was crazy to be behaving like a teenager. But that's exactly how she felt – the same way she'd felt when Stu Lawrence asked her out on her first date in Year Nine at Granite Springs High School. She hummed to herself as she walked along, enjoying the warmth of the sun on her back.

Jo browsed the shelves, chatted to the librarian she'd known for most of her life, and finally went to the checkout with a couple of the latest books by two of her favourite authors, Joanna Trollope and Marcia Willett. She looked forward to starting them but wasn't sure when she'd get an opportunity.

Her phone buzzed as she was leaving. Surprised to see her daughter-in-law's number, she sat down on a nearby bench to answer.

'Mother Slater,' Kylie began.

Jo cringed. She wished Kylie wouldn't call her that.

'Kylie. This is a surprise.' It was most unusual for Kylie to ring her, most of their communication being through Danny.

Jo heard an indrawn breath, then, 'I hear you've moved in with Eve.'

She almost laughed out loud. Word got around fast, but Kylie had got it wrong.

'Not exactly. Brad's in hospital and I'm staying at Eve's to help out for a bit. The girls started school today and…'

But Kylie didn't let her finish. 'Since you're in town, why don't you come to lunch?'

Jo was glad she was sitting down. An invitation like this was unheard of. Kylie wanted something. Was this about the house again?

'That's very kind of you, but I do have a luncheon engagement today. Maybe another time?' she said, tongue in cheek.

'Oh!' Kylie sounded deflated, but quickly recovered. She agreed to wait until Brad was well again, leaving Jo wondering what Kylie really wanted.

*

'How are you, my dear?' Col greeted Jo with a kiss, making her look around to check no one was watching. She hated the secrecy, but it was of her own making. Col would have been happy for the world to know they were an item.

As if reading her mind, he said, 'They'll find out soon enough. You can't keep a secret for long in this town.'

Jo knew he was right. 'Just till I move back home,' she said.

'What you need is a break from all this.' Col waved his arm to encompass the restaurant, the town, her family.

'That sounds great, but…' She hesitated, remembering Val had made the same suggestion.

'Tell you what,' Col continued. 'I haven't taken any time off since Alice…' he faltered, then went on in a stronger voice. 'The weather will be cooler on the coast. Why don't we go there together for a few days – a weekend or maybe a week? Tathra's nice at this time of year.'

Jo felt her breath catch, and a smile twitched at her lips at the thought of spending a few days away from the demands of her family, the gossip of the community; to be with Col where no one knew them. It sounded wonderful, but…

'I couldn't. Not with Brad so ill.'

Col reached across the table to cover her hands with his. 'I don't mean tomorrow, or even this month. When you're ready. When Eve has things back on an even keel. What do you say?'

'Yes.' Jo knew it was exactly what she needed; time to be alone with Col; time to work out whether this was something real, something lasting, or merely a flash in the pan – a sudden flare up of lust that would die if they spent any length of time together.

They ordered lunch, Jo choosing a chicken wrap with salad, while Col opted for a burger with fries. As they waited for their meals to be served, Jo began to fill Col in on Brad's condition, but noticed Col was distracted, gazing into space.

'Is something the matter?' she asked.

Col shook his head. 'Not really. There was a client this morning. Not exactly a client… A woman came to see me. She seemed to think… Oh, it's probably nothing,'

Jo longed to stroke away the frown which had appeared between his eyes. 'Tell me.'

'She thought I was her father.' Col's eyes met Jo's in bewilderment. His honesty shone through. Jo knew it was a ridiculous claim. Col would never have been unfaithful to Alice.

'How old is she – this woman?'

'Around thirty. She said her mother visited Granite Springs in the eighties. Oh, it's nothing. She's obviously mistaken. Just odd.' He gazed off into the distance again. 'I told her it couldn't be me.'

'Did she believe you?'

'I'm not sure.'

Jo felt uncomfortable. She believed Col. Of course she did. But it was an odd thing to happen. She wanted to know more. 'Who is she? What did she look like?'

'Tall. Slim. Dark hair. Her name is Sally Anderson. She said her mother was Glenda Darling. The name means nothing to me. I'm sure I'd remember if I'd ever met her. It's an unusual name. But we were probably all at the ball she was referring to. Alice spoke to so many people. She loved to be the centre of attention. I suppose *they* could have met, but why…?' He pushed a hand through his hair.

Jo reached her hand to cover his on the table. 'Don't let it worry you. The poor woman is trying to find her father. By now she'll have worked out she's come to the wrong place. We can have no idea what her mother was thinking of. Maybe she saw your name somewhere and decided to use it. Maybe she was never at the ball, never even in Granite Springs. She's dead now, you say?'

Col nodded.

'So, we'll never know.'

'You're right,' Col sighed. 'Now, you were telling me about Brad.'

Jo started to recount Brad's injuries, and they didn't touch on the woman's appearance again.

But, later that evening, Jo began to wonder if Col was being completely honest with her.

Was this Glenda woman really the stranger he made her out to be?

If they'd never met, where would she have heard his name?

And why would she have told her daughter he was her father?

Twenty-two

The stifling summer heat had returned, making it difficult to sleep. It was as if the rain had never happened. Town and country alike sat glued to the television forecasts each evening and the danger of fires was on everyone's mind. Jo worried about her house, set as it was in the middle of dry paddocks on which the few days of rain had barely made a dent. She'd spoken to Magda who reported that the only result was a few puddles on the lane where the red dust had turned to mud.

It shouldn't be long now. After a full week in hospital, with Eve spending most of her days there, Brad had been given the all clear to come home. Jo had been hesitant to broach the subject with Eve the night before, her daughter's exhausted face giving her cause for concern. She didn't want to have two invalids on her hands. But she was keen to get home, back to her routine, albeit with Eve's dreaded schedule to fulfil – at least until Steve could come up with a replacement.

As she waved goodbye to the twins at the school gate, she reflected how quickly they'd settled into the school routine. That was one thing to be grateful for. But they'd missed their dad. After one disastrous visit to the hospital during which Lottie had broken down in tears, and Livvy had wanted to get into bed with Brad, Eve had been forced to admit it had been a bad idea.

Now they were excited he was coming home and had spent the previous evening painting a welcome home banner which was now hanging somewhat lopsidedly in the kitchen. Eve had left for the hospital early as usual, but this morning Jo noticed she'd taken time with her appearance, wearing a pink striped sundress and high-heeled white sandals, her hair carefully styled, and a perfectly made-up face.

Unsure when Brad would be discharged, Eve instructed Jo to stay home and have lunch ready. A request would have been nice, but Jo was still making allowances for her daughter. At least she'd been relieved of her evening duties at the restaurant, with only the accounts to look after. She could do those at home.

Deciding to make a salmon and rice dish for lunch – one that could be eaten hot or cold or even do for dinner if Brad and Eve were delayed, Jo turned on the radio. She was stirring the cheese sauce when the music programme was interrupted by an announcement warning of more rain and possible flooding. Jo didn't pay much heed. She was more worried about fire than floods. Although the town was built along the river, she could barely remember the last time it had burst its banks. She'd been only seven or eight at the time and had been kept home from school.

Back then, they'd lived in the centre of town, and she and her friends had been caught up in the excitement of watching from afar while a legion of men worked steadily to stack sandbags along the riverbank. It had been to no avail. Their temporary levee had been breached, causing untold damage to nearby homes. The year after, the town council had built a more substantial levee, one which had prevented a repeat occurrence.

Jo had just closed the oven door on the salmon dish, and was about to throw together a salad, when her phone rang.

'Mum!'

'Rob?' Jo wondered why he sounded so distraught.

'Have you heard the weather warning?'

'You're not worried, are you?' Jo pictured the restaurant hugging the edge of the river, just beyond the levee. 'It'll hold. The town hasn't flooded since…'

'You haven't seen the way the water is gushing downstream. The BOM says we're due for another deluge. If that happens, then the water coming from further upstream may be too much for even the levees. They haven't been renewed in years.'

Jo knew her children set great store by the predictions of the Bureau of Meteorology. She preferred to rely on checking the sky. She supposed she was old-fashioned in that regard. 'I'm sure it'll be fine,' she said, gazing out of the window at the clear blue sky. Although she was aware how quickly things could change, she thought Rob was worrying needlessly.

It was almost lunchtime when Eve called to say there was a delay and it looked like a late afternoon discharge. Jo put the cooling salmon dish in the fridge, made herself a sandwich for lunch and decided to take Scout for a walk. She could drive to town, take a walk along by the river, check out what Rob was talking about, and maybe call into the restaurant to try to dispel his fears.

It was hot and humid with the threat of rain, and they hadn't walked far before she was regretting her decision. But she persevered and soon reached the narrow beach that was featured on Alice's painting. She unleashed Scout to let him wander into the water and found a shady spot to sit. It wasn't long before the dog found a stick for Jo to throw, but he soon tired of the game and lay down beside her, panting.

'You're getting on, too, old fellow,' she said, stroking his wet coat. She gazed across the river, remembering happy times here with Alice when they'd been in their teens. Their crowd had spent most of the summer holidays by the river, swimming and swinging on a rope which had hung out over the river. That had long gone, removed in the interests of safety. But Jo couldn't recall any accidents back then. Had kids been more careful – or had they just been lucky?

The river was fuller than she'd expected, heavy rain upstream contributing to the flow, and Jo could see that the normally placid flowing water was gushing down from upstream. Rob had been right. Re-attaching Scout's leash, Jo made her way to the restaurant. She was surprised to find it a hive of activity, when normally this would be the lull between lunch and dinner service.

'Jo!'

It was Steve who greeted her, his arms full of tablecloths.

'What are you doing here?' Jo asked, surprised. 'Shouldn't you be at work? Didn't you say your holidays were over? Has something happened to Rob?'

'Not when I last looked.' Steve gave his lopsided grin. 'He rang about the weather warning, so it's all hands on deck. If the river overflows, we're right in its path here. The conference paper can wait. This can't.'

As he was speaking, Rob appeared behind him, carrying a load of chairs. 'Mum. What are you doing here? And Scout, too? Didn't you listen to me?'

'I thought you were exaggerating, so I came to see for myself. Do you really think…?' Jo realised it was a stupid question. Rob wouldn't be carrying chairs around, have enlisted his partner's aid, if he didn't believe they were in danger of being inundated with floodwater. And to think she'd been worried about fire. That was Australia for you.

'Unless you want to help, Mum, you should go. We need to get as much as we can to the upper level before it's too late. We'll be closed tonight in any case. I don't expect anyone will be interested in eating out. Shouldn't you be picking up the twins?'

Jo checked her watch. Rob was right again. By the time she took Scout back and drove to the school, Lottie and Livvy would be waiting at the gate. It seemed no time since she'd dropped them off. Where had the day gone? Was this what happened when you were older – time seemed to disappear?

*

The girls wriggled excitedly in the car all the way home, eager to see their dad again, even though Jo had warned them he might not be back till later. She breathed a sigh of relief when Eve's car was already parked in the driveway.

'It looks like your daddy's here,' Jo said, as she parked. The girls couldn't wait for her to unbuckle them, managing to do it themselves and diving out of the car to run to the door.

By the time Jo entered, they were regaling a tired-looking Brad with the details of their day and wanting to drag him into the kitchen to see the banner they'd made.

'Leave your dad be,' Jo said. 'He'll see it over dinner. I'm sure he needs to rest for a bit. He's only just out of hospital, remember.' But her words fell on deaf ears. The girls were too excited to care. It took Eve's appearance and her firm voice sending them to their room to change to have any effect.

'How are you feeling, Brad?' Jo asked, when the room was quiet again. 'I expect you'll need to take things easy for a while.'

He gave a long sigh. 'The doc says no form of exertion for at least six weeks. I can go back to work before that, but no cycling.' He made a face. 'I was training for the Sydney2Canberra in April and was all set for the King of the Mountain this year. Six weeks will put me back. Shit, I may miss it altogether.'

Jo pressed her lips together. Brad and his blasted bikes. That's what got him into this mess, and all he can think of is the next race. 'It's hard, I know. But your health must come first,' she said.

'I guess.' He sighed again.

Eve came bustling through in time to hear his last words. 'Is that him complaining about the race? I'd like to take the damned bike to the tip.' She glared at him, seemingly forgetting her worry of the past week.

Caught in the middle, Jo felt awkward. What was she doing here?

Her salmon dish proved popular, with Brad asking for a second helping and saying how sick he'd been of hospital food. When the girls had excused themselves and escaped to their room, Jo decided to broach what had been on her mind. 'Now Brad's home, you'll be wanting some time together. I should go back home too.'

Eve's face dropped. 'Mu…um,' she began.

Jo was sure she was about to object, to say she still needed her to be here, but before she could open her mouth, Brad spoke. 'Good idea,' he said. 'I heard them talking in the hospital. They're predicting more heavy rain, saying the levee mightn't hold, that the road might be cut at the bridge. You should get back while you still can.'

The bridge? It hadn't occurred to Jo. But, of course, if the river overflowed, the road out to her place would be flooded.

Twenty-three

'They need some help out at the levee.'

Col looked up to see Dot's worried face appear round the door. He'd been engrossed in drafting a property settlement for most of the afternoon and hadn't noticed the sky darkening.

'You and Gordon,' she said, a frown etched on her forehead. 'The river's gushing down and more rain's expected. They need all the hands they can get to fill sandbags and bolster the embankment. Some have been at it since lunchtime, since the weather warning. You didn't…? No, of course you didn't.'

'You up for it, mate?' Gordon joined her at the door. 'Hope young Rob's okay. That restaurant'll be right in its path. Told them they were fools to buy there, but why would they listen to me? I remember the floods when we were kids. We thought it was good entertainment then, but it's not funny for people to lose their homes and livelihoods. The council should have done more, but no sense berating them now.'

'Right.' Col turned off his computer and joined them. 'We're hardly dressed for it,' he said, looking down at the knife-fold in the beige pants he'd donned fresh this morning, and at Gordon who was similarly attired and sporting a pristine white shirt. But he loosened his tie and, with a burst of energy, feeling like the young man he wished he still was, said, 'Let's go.'

Across town, the pair joined a group of other businessmen who were busy filling sandbags which were then being hoisted into place by a team of volunteers who appeared to come from all walks of life.

There was a camaraderie about the group that reminded Col of his days as a Boy Scout. He supposed this was what it felt like to be part of the military – a group of men working together for a common goal.

It was completely dark when they finally came to a halt.

'That's it, guys,' the Mayor said. He'd rolled his sleeves up and dug in with the rest of them, adding sandbags to the levee as if he did it every day of the week. He wiped his brow. 'It'll have to do. Let's hope it holds. Now off you go home and make sure your families are safe. Good luck.'

Gordon turned towards Col. 'I'm going to check on the restaurant. Want to come with me?'

'Sure.' Col grinned to himself in the darkness. Gordon might disparage Rob and Jo's venture, but when the chips were down, Rob *was* his son and he *did* care about him.

The pair headed towards the restaurant which showed a few lights on the upper level. The door was locked and the CLOSED sign visible in the glimmer coming from above. Gordon knocked, and they heard a voice yell, 'We're closed.' He knocked again and shouted, 'It's me. It's your dad, Rob.'

Eventually, they heard a bolt being drawn and Rob's pale face looked out. His red hair was standing on end and his freckles seemed to be even more prominent than usual. 'What do you want, Dad?' he asked, opening the door further. 'Look at the state of you. And Uncle Col, too. What the hell have you been doing?'

Col looked at Gordon, then down at himself in the stream of light coming from the open door. They were a sorry pair, covered in wet sand. Gordon's face was streaked with sand and grime and he was sure his must be, too. 'We were helping sandbag the river. Your dad wanted to make sure you were all right before we left.'

Rob essayed a smile. 'We're fine. We moved as much as we could upstairs, and Steve and I decided to stay and wait it out. Best we know the worst and we'll be on hand to do what's needed, in the event it does flood. Want a drink? You both look as if you could do with one.'

'Thanks, son.' Gordon nodded and sent a questioning glance towards Col, before the two men followed Rob into the now empty restaurant and upstairs. What had once been the elegant gallery level was now crowded with tables, racks of chairs and boxes spilling kitchen equipment and stores.

'Hi there,' Steve said, rising to greet them from one of two chairs set just inside the balcony. 'You look as if you've done a hard day's work.'

'Sandbags,' Rob said. 'They've been trying to save our bacon. Scotch?' he asked.

Col and Gordon nodded and collapsed into the chairs Steve unloaded from one of the racks. They gratefully accepted the drinks, knocking them back in one gulp.

'Thanks,' Col said, the liquid burning down his throat to the pit of his stomach. 'That hit the spot. You guys are prepared then?'

'As much as we can be,' Rob said. 'Now we just have to wait.'

'Mmm.'

It seemed that, now they were here, Gordon didn't know what to say.

'You've been busy,' Col said to fill the silence. 'Let's hope it doesn't come to…'

'Mum was here,' Rob said, after a pause. 'I think she planned to go home. Brad was being discharged today.'

His words didn't appear to make any impact on Gordon, but Col felt a chill in his gut at the thought of Jo alone in that big place outside town. For a moment he wondered if he should drive out there, be with her, before dismissing it as a mad idea. She'd be fine. She was a long way from the river, and if water flowed over the bridge, the road out of town would be cut.

'Do you want something to eat?' Rob asked. 'We've got plenty of food.'

'No, son. I should be getting back. Carol will be wondering what's happened to me. But thanks for the offer.'

He rose, and Col joined him. Rob saw them downstairs, waving them off, before closing the door behind them. Col heard the thud of the bolt and stood looking up at the tall building. It seemed only yesterday they'd all been there celebrating Alice's retrospective – and such a lot had happened since then. He turned away reluctantly.

'Why don't you come back with me for a bite to eat?' Gordon asked. 'We're not as young as we used to be, and you won't be wanting to have to start cooking a meal. Carol will have one ready, and I'm sure there'll be enough.'

Col heard the implicit message that his company might save

Gordon from the tongue-lashing he'd get for being so late. He didn't want to be caught in the middle of a domestic dispute.

'Thanks, but I'll get something…'

'Everything'll be closed.'

Col looked around and, sure enough, there were no lights in the street which housed the town's cafes and small restaurants. Like The Riverside, they were all closed and shuttered against the predicted storm.

'You've convinced me.' He held his hands up in mock surrender.

As Col got out of his car outside Gordon's opulent blond-brick home in the most expensive part of town, Col wondered if he'd made a mistake. He could have been home by now. Although close to the river, his house was on a rise so out of any danger. What had possessed him to accept Gordon's invitation?

Not the offer of a hot meal. He'd have been perfectly happy with a sandwich thrown together from some odds and ends he had in the fridge. Was it some sort of morbid curiosity? He'd only been in Gordon and Carol's home on one previous occasion, and that had been for a birthday party – Gordon's – after Alice died. She'd vowed never to set foot in it, and Col wasn't Carol's favourite person. He supposed she reminded him of Gordon's first marriage – and maybe there was the memory of how he'd spurned her early advances, before she set her sights on Gordon.

'You're back! I was so…' Carol's words dried up as she caught sight of Col standing behind her husband. 'Col! What are you doing here?' She wrinkled her nose. 'You've been drinking,' she accused. 'I can smell it, and you're both filthy.'

Col didn't know if her distaste was due to the smell of alcohol or their dishevelled appearance. He wished he hadn't come.

'Come on, Caro,' Gordon said in a wheedling tone Col had never heard him use before. 'Can't you see we're exhausted? We helped with shoring up the levee bank in town, then called in to make sure Rob was okay.'

Carol's lips tightened, forming a hard line. Col could see what a lucky escape he'd had. Though not lucky – he'd never been tempted. He'd been happy with Alice. It had been Gordon who'd been willing to kick over the traces. And now look where he was.

'I suppose you'd better come in,' she said grudgingly and stood aside to let them pass.

'I invited Col back for a bite to eat,' Gordon said. 'Everything's closed up in preparation for the big storm that's supposed to be coming our way. I guess we should clean up a bit first?'

Carol nodded, evading Gordon's attempt to kiss her on the cheek. Col followed his partner's directions to a cloakroom off the hall while Gordon made his way upstairs.

In the small room, Col grimaced when he caught sight of himself in the mirror. His white hair was caked with dirt and his shirt creased and covered in particles of grey sand. He'd seen how Gordon looked at the restaurant, now he could see he looked even worse. Washing off the worst of the damage, he patted down his hair and made his way back to the hallway.

Hearing voices coming from the direction he knew to be the kitchen, he headed towards them, faltering when he realised the loudest voice was Carol's, and she still didn't sound happy. There was a sudden silence as he reached the doorway.

Carol was standing by the stove filling two plates with chicken and salad. 'Take a seat, Col,' she said in a tight voice. Gordon rolled his eyes behind her back. 'I've already eaten,' she continued, 'but I'll have a glass of wine. I suppose the pair of you would like a beer?'

'I'll get it, honey,' Gordon said, in an obvious attempt to mollify her.

They ate in silence.

'This is good, Carol,' Col said, trying to smooth over whatever was still clearly eating Carol. 'I don't often get a homemade meal these days.'

'Thanks, Col.' She flashed him a false smile, then threw a glare at her husband. 'It's good to be appreciated.'

Col forked up a piece of chicken, wondering how quickly he could finish and leave. He'd been caught up in exactly what he wanted to avoid. This wasn't *his* quarrel.

'You'd know what it's like,' she said suddenly. 'You and Alice.'

Col was puzzled. What did he and Alice have to do with it? Her beef was with Gordon.

'You must know what it's like to want to have children,' she said. 'Can you persuade this idiot? It's only fair that we have a family.'

Col didn't know where to look. It was as if Gordon shrank in front of his eyes. He just wanted to get out as soon as he could. But Carol was waiting for him to reply. He took a last mouthful of food, and a final swallow of beer. 'It was different for us,' he said at last, with an apologetic glance at Gordon. 'We both wanted children, but we weren't blessed. I think this is something between the two of you. I don't want to get involved. I should go.' He stood up awkwardly, pushing his chair back. 'Thanks for the dinner. I appreciate it. I'd better get back before…' As he spoke, the lights flickered, dimmed, then came back on. 'Looks like I won't be a moment too soon.'

'I'll see you out.' Gordon got to his feet and led the way to the door. 'Sorry, mate,' he said as they stood in the open doorway. 'I don't know where that came from. I had no idea she'd bring it up. Not your problem.'

As he drove back through the deserted town, Col caught a glimpse of the torrent raging down the river and prayed they'd done enough. He thought of Jo, alone on her acreage and wished he could be with her. He even drove towards the bridge, but it was too late. The water was already lapping over the road. He just hoped she was safe.

Twenty-four

The sky was darkening as Jo turned onto her property. Scout gave a yelp of pleasure at the familiar sight which greeted them, and Jo had a sense of relief.

The television reception failed several minutes before the power went off. Jo fossicked under the kitchen sink to find the candles she kept there for just such an emergency. It wasn't an uncommon occurrence. In a stiff wind it sometimes happened that a branch would fall on the power lines – one of the hazards of living outside town. She turned on the radio which worked on a battery, but all she could hear was static. It was time to go to bed.

She was wakened by a loud crack of thunder and the sound of Scout whining and scratching at the bedroom door. Rising and opening the door, a bolt of lightning flashed across the sky, its bright glow illuminating the bedroom, before another peal of thunder followed.

Although it wasn't cold, Jo shivered, while Scout whimpered and scrabbled to find a corner in which to hide. She picked the poor animal up and hugged him tightly. She'd forgotten how heavy he'd become. 'It's all right,' she whispered into his ear, stroking his trembling body. 'It's only the storm. It'll be over soon.' Scout wriggled out of her grasp and crawled under the bed, where he lay panting. Kneeling down, Jo tried to persuade him to come out, but he obstinately refused.

She went through to the kitchen and opened the French doors. A rush of air met her, but no rain. Lightning flashed again, the rumble of thunder following faster this time. There was a red light in the neighbouring paddock where a bolt of lightning had set the grass on fire. In the glare, Jo could see the goats huddling under a tree. The stupid animals. Not the best place to shelter in a thunderstorm. There wasn't much she could do about the fire, apart from worry it might spread. She picked up her mobile to call the rural fire brigade, but the phone rang out. They'd be busy tonight. She could only hope someone had already called in this fire.

Deciding she wasn't going to get any more sleep that night, Jo poured herself a glass of scotch, slid her feet into the pair of gumboots sitting on the veranda and sat down to watch, telling herself it would be over soon. She coughed as the acrid smell of smoke from across the paddock assaulted her nostrils and caught her throat.

For the first time since Gordon left, she felt alone. Suddenly what had been her secure home – her refuge – had become fraught with danger. What if the fire in the paddock came this way? What if the power didn't come back on again? She chided herself for being a foolish old woman and, for the first time, she felt that – old. She shivered again and knocked back the scotch.

Then, suddenly, it came. Pounding down in torrents, bouncing on the dry earth before forming rivulets which made their way along unseen depressions in the ground, drenching the earth with life-giving rain – enough to extinguish several fires. Maybe the goats had known something after all. The roar of the thunder disappeared into the distance and the rain kept pouring down.

Rob had been right. The storm had arrived with some force. Jo went back inside. In the bedroom Scout's nose peeped out from his hiding place. At the sound of Jo's movements, he slowly crept out and she picked him up again. Lifting the dog into bed with her, Jo curled up and tried to get back to sleep.

*

After a fitful night's sleep, Jo awoke to the sound of her phone buzzing somewhere in the house. She followed the sound to discover her mobile lying on the kitchen bench and to see Col's face on the screen. She picked it up.

'Col.'

'Jo, are you all right? That was a terrible storm, but it seems the levee held. I went out earlier. There's a lot of damage, trees uprooted, branches over power lines, but no homes flooded that I could see. How did you fare out there? I wanted to come out, to be with you but…'

'I expect the bridge was under water. I just made it in time. The power went out, so I went to bed, then was wakened by the thunder and lightning. It was fearsome. But all seems calm now.' Jo peered out the window to see the sun shining. It was almost as if the storm had never happened. The only evidence of damage was a large branch hanging on top of the boundary fence and a thick layer of leaves washed up on the back veranda. Looking further afield, she saw her rose garden had been denuded of blooms and the nearby apricot and nectarine trees had lost their fruit which now lay ready to rot on the ground. She made a mental note to collect the fruit for bottling and jam.

'I...'

Jo heard an intake of breath.

'I had dinner with Gordon and Carol last night.'

'You did?' Jo moved to the family room and curled up in one of the cane chairs, Scout appearing to settle at her feet. 'I didn't think you were on those terms with him and Carol.'

'I'm not,' he laughed, 'but we'd been working on the levee and Gordon took pity on me and invited me back to eat with them. I should have refused.'

'Why?'

'You could have cut the tension with a knife. Maybe I arrived at a bad time. But your ex's life certainly isn't a bed of roses.'

Jo didn't reply immediately. Gordon's life was none of her business, but she couldn't help the hint of satisfaction she experienced to learn he wasn't having it easy with his young wife. She immediately suppressed it, saying, 'Well, what did he expect? There's such an age gap. They're bound to have differences. I'm sure they'll manage. I suppose it's about her wanting to start a family.'

'That and… I'm not sure, but there seemed to be some longstanding differences.'

There was a pause, then Col said, 'I'd like to drop over if I can get there. I took a wander earlier and the water over the bridge seems to be diminishing. There's a lot of debris around, some large branches down, and the council workers are out trying to clear the mess and the mud that's accumulated along with it.'

'Only if it's safe.' Jo held her breath, remembering how alone she'd felt last night. She'd have given anything to have his company then. Now, with the sun shining, all she wanted to do was to get out there and start cleaning up. 'Don't you need to go into the office?'

'I doubt many businesses will be open today. I'll be there as soon as I can.'

*

Dressed in a pair of baggy shorts and gum boots, Jo was struggling with the fence when she heard Col's car. She wiped the perspiration from her brow and wished she'd tidied herself up. Col had seen her like this many times over the years– when she'd been gardening or when they all went camping together – but it seemed different now they were… lovers. She rolled the word round in her mouth. That's what they were. There was no denying it. And the very thought made her want to leap for joy.

She laid down the wire strainer she'd been using and called to Scout who was chasing some new scents the rain had stirred up in the far paddock. At the sound of her voice, the dog came running. She patted his head. 'Good boy,' she said as they made their way towards the house, Jo pushing back the stray strands of hair that had become loose while she was working. She wished Col had given her more warning. She knew he said he'd be there as soon as he could, but she hadn't expected him before noon.

As she neared the house, Jo checked her watch, surprised to see if was half-twelve. She'd been out here much longer than she thought. That damned fence! She shouldn't have attempted it on her own. She was too independent for her own good – as Danny was always telling her. Just as well he couldn't see her today. He'd use it as one more reason for her to move into town and let him have this place.

'You survived the storm without too much damage?' Col wrapped his arms around her and gazed around.

'Thank goodness. I've just been trying to fix the fence.'

'Looks like you need a man around here.'

Jo grimaced and leant into his arms. 'Don't let Danny know,' she said. 'I thought I knew how to do it. I helped Gordon when we built the fences.' Jo thought back to those early days of her marriage. They were happy times – times when she and Gordon had worked together to build a home for their family. When had it all started to unravel? Danny had been a good baby, content to lie in his carry cot while his parents worked together on the property – they'd utilised the full twenty acres back then, making plans to become self-sufficient.

It was when Eve came along that things changed, she realised. She'd been a sickly baby, demanding more of Jo's time, and Gordon had lost interest in their plans to develop lavender, nuts, pigs, bees, whatever the latest fad was. He'd become busier and busier in his legal practice and she'd been left home to bring up the children pretty much on her own.

'That was years ago.' Col released her gently. 'It wouldn't be a sign of weakness to get some help.

'You're probably right.' Jo sighed and pushed her hair back again. 'Come on inside. I can offer you lunch but let me get cleaned up first. There should be some beer in the fridge. Help yourself.'

Jo led the way inside, leaving Scout with Col while she went into the bedroom, the mirror only confirming what she already knew. She scowled at her image and headed for the shower.

After a cool shower and dressed in a pair of white capri pants with a blue tank top, Jo felt more prepared to meet Col.

'That's more like the Jo I know,' he said, rising to give her a lingering kiss on the lips. Her heart lurched as she inhaled the unique blend of aftershave and soap he always carried with him. It was a heady mix and one she'd come to love. 'You said something about lunch?'

'I did. We lost power last night, but I think I can still rustle up a salad. Will that do?' She extricated herself from his grasp as she spoke and opened the fridge door to hide what she was sure were her flaming cheeks. 'Another beer?' she asked.

'Not yet. I may have one with lunch.' Col resumed his seat by the window and picked up the beer bottle again. One hand dropped to stroke Scout's head, and the dog wriggled in appreciation. 'You have a good place here,' he said. 'I can see why your daughter-in-law has her eye on it. I can also see why you don't want to let it go.'

'You don't think I'm being selfish?'

'Selfish?'

'Wanting to stay here. It *is* a big place for one person. And, I can tell you, I did have a touch of the wobbles last night during the storm.'

'Anyone would. But, to answer your question. Selfish? No. You haven't a selfish bone in your body. Is that what Kylie's saying?'

'She hasn't actually used the word to my face – though Danny has.' Jo recalled her son's anger when they were in that horrible little villa. 'And she wants to have lunch with me.'

'Is that so unusual?'

'Unheard of. She's bound to have some agenda, most likely how she can change my mind about this place.' Jo looked around the room. 'But it's my home.'

'And she and Danny could well afford to buy property elsewhere if she's so set on an acreage to bring up the boys on.'

'You're right, of course. It's what I've been telling myself, but…' Jo bit her lip and began to slice tomatoes, cucumber and lettuce as if her life depended on it. She wasn't going to allow Danny and Kylie to drive her out of her home due to some misguided sense of family loyalty.

It wasn't until they'd finished eating and were sitting on the veranda with coffee, Jo having filled Col in on Brad's progress, that he brought up the idea of their going away together again.

'I can't,' Jo said regretfully. 'Until Steve comes up with some sort of a replacement, and I've no idea when that will be. But not until classes start again at the earliest. I promised Eve I'd follow this schedule of hers. Once the schools re-open again, I'll be tied up every afternoon.'

'Well, how about a weekend? Surely you don't have to be on grandparent duty 24/7?'

'No…oo,' Jo said slowly. Could she really take a weekend off, get away from all this, from the petty quarrels and demands of her grown children, spend time with Col, find out if these feelings she had were real or if she was deluding herself?

Twenty-five

Col was buoyant as he drove back into town. He'd have preferred to spend the rest of the day with Jo, but Dot had called him to say the office was open again and his presence was required.

He couldn't stop thinking about the proposed weekend with Jo, thrilled she'd agreed. He knew her life was pretty chaotic at the moment and hoped she'd be able to relax once they were away from Granite Springs and her children. He was beginning to realise how much strife he and Alice had been spared, but regardless of the potential for conflict, he still wished they'd had children of their own.

If he and Jo decided to make a future together, he'd fall heir to her kids and all the attendant challenges. A low whistle escaped from his lips. A future together. This was the first time he'd actually envisioned it. But it was what he wanted. It might be too soon – it probably was – but he knew he wanted to spend his remaining years with Jo.

'Thank goodness you're here!' Dot greeted him. 'I came in at lunchtime to find Gordon had been sleeping in his office. He doesn't look well. I couldn't get any sense out of him. I didn't know what to do, so I called you.'

'Thanks, Dot. You did the right thing.' Col rubbed his chin and went into his own office where he dropped his briefcase before heading next door to Gordon's.

He knocked, then pushed open the door to find his partner sitting at his desk with his head in his hands. Gordon glanced up as Col entered. There was a glazed expression on his face. He looked as if he hadn't slept.

'You look as if you could do with a strong coffee,' Col said. 'There won't be any clients today. On my way here, I noticed the Bean Sprout is open for business. A cup of Frank's strong brew is what you need. And maybe something to eat. Did you have any lunch?'

Gordon shook his head.

'Breakfast?'

He shook his head again.

'Then let's get you fed.' Col led the other man out of the office and, with a nod in Dot's direction, out the door. They walked down the street to Frank and Marie's café and found a seat in a secluded corner.

When they'd ordered two coffees and a toasted ham and cheese sandwich for Gordon, Col folded his arms on the table. 'Now, what's up? Dot says you spent the night in the office. What happened after I left?'

'Oh, mate, you don't want to know.' Gordon avoided Col's eyes.

Col wasn't sure he did want to know. Gordon and Carol's private life was just that – private. But he couldn't bear to see his old friend so distressed. 'Probably not. But try me, anyway.' He took a gulp of coffee, the caffeine soothing his throat and having its usual stimulating effect. He hoped it would do the same for his friend.

Gordon sighed and took a sip of his drink before replying. 'It was the usual stuff, but this time,' he shook his head. 'I think my bringing you home exacerbated it. After you left, she… she threw everything at me – all the grievances that have been boiling up in her. My long hours, her desire for a child, Alice's painting, Jo's birthday, even my continued friendship with you. Things got heated and… she told me to leave.'

Col was shocked. He'd heard Gordon whinge about Carol's demands before, but nothing like this.

'Have you tried to call her?' he asked. 'Maybe she spoke in the heat of the moment.' He remembered she'd consumed the best part of a bottle of wine at dinner. 'Could it have been the wine talking?'

Gordon rubbed the back of his neck. 'Maybe. She's been drinking a lot lately. But it's more than that, Col. Am I too old for her? Was I a fool to think I could hold onto a woman like Carol?' He sighed and pulled on an earlobe. 'I tried calling her, but she's not answering. It could be she's out with some of her women friends, or she sees my number and…' He took a small bite of the sandwich before pushing it away.

Col didn't know what to say. If he agreed with Gordon that he *was* too old and should never have been taken in by Carol's machinations, then how would his old friend react when the couple made up. He decided to say nothing.

The pair sat in silence, Col drinking his coffee while Gordon stared into space.

Then Gordon seemed to recollect himself. 'You and Alice,' he said. 'You had a good marriage. You never felt the need to…'

'Look elsewhere,' Col finished for him. 'No, never.'

Gordon shrugged. 'Jo and I… we were good together, too. I don't know why I… Maybe I should have stayed with her. She's a good woman. We never quarrelled, not like this. She'd never have… And she's out there all on her own in that big house – our house.'

'Not anymore,' Col reminded him gently. 'She got it fair and square in your divorce settlement.' He didn't like the way this conversation was going. Gordon was about to start reminiscing about the good old days of his marriage with Jo. Although Col had nothing to reproach himself with, a curl of something akin to guilt made his chest tighten. What would Gordon say if he knew about him and Jo?

Col managed to get through the next few minutes without incident. His attempts to get Gordon to eat something were unsuccessful, but he did manage to persuade him to keep trying to contact Carol to apologise for whatever sins – real or imaginary – he'd committed and try to effect a reconciliation. He stopped short at telling Gordon he'd made his bed and now had to lie on it, but that was the gist of his advice.

By the time they returned to the office, Col thought he'd convinced his friend all would be well if *he* pleaded the effects of alcohol and took all the blame.

He scratched his jaw as he pulled out his desk chair and fired up the computer, glad he wasn't in Gordon's shoes. He was pretty sure Carol would take him back – and probably make him suffer for his imagined misdemeanours. He wondered if the end result would be the child she seemed to want so desperately.

But he had more on his mind than Gordon's marriage woes. Jo had agreed to spend a weekend with him at Tathra. The small seaside town was one the four of them had often visited when Jo and Gordon's children were small. He had happy memories of them all swimming and building sandcastles on the beach when the children were little then, as they grew older, spending hours surfing, bushwalking, or hiring mountain bikes.

As they grew up, the small town failed to hold their attention. When it was clear they preferred to spend time with their friends, the two older couples had ventured farther afield, exploring other parts of the country and even taking trips to holiday venues in nearby south-east Asia. It was years since either Col or Jo had visited the South Coast.

Col opened up a holiday booking site. He needed to find accommodation. In years gone by they'd camped or stayed in neighbouring caravans with the three children running between them. They had been good times. Now, he wanted to find something more romantic.

After almost half an hour of searching Col found what he was looking for. It wasn't in Tathra, but further down the coast at Eden, originally the site of a whaling station and located on one of the deepest harbours in Australia. It probably wouldn't do any harm to avoid stirring up those old memories anyway. Col grew excited as he read details of the accommodation, clicking to book a deluxe suite with a spa bath.

Twenty-six

'Steve!' Jo had a smile in her voice when she heard Steve on the phone. Rob had chosen well with his partner, which was more than she could say for her other two children, though maybe she was being unfair where Brad was concerned. 'How can I help you?'

'It's *I* who can help *you*,' Steve's deep rumbling voice said. 'You asked about a babysitter for the twins. I think I've found you the very person.'

Jo dropped into a nearby chair with a sigh of relief. She loved spending time with her grandchildren – she did. But it was too much. She wasn't as young as she used to be, and to have the girls every day was tiring. 'Tell me!' she said.

'It's one of my final year students. Allegra's a lovely girl. The twins will love her. She's a bundle of energy and is really keen to meet them. Should I contact Eve or…'

'No. Better I do it. Thanks, Steve. I really appreciate it. You're a gem.'

Steve's infectious laugh echoed down the phone. 'I've been called many things in my life but that's a first,' he chuckled. 'Okay, will you get back to me or will I give you Allegra's contact details?'

'I'll get back to you,' Jo began, then thought better of it. 'No, on reflection, better give me her details. I'm happy to take your recommendation, but I should probably meet the girl before I talk with Eve.' She bit the inside of her lip, wondering how to approach her daughter without giving offense. It was crazy to have to feel she had to tiptoe around her daughter, the little girl she'd brought up. But that was Eve these days – touchy was putting it mildly. She'd have to choose her moment. 'Thanks, Steve. I really appreciate your doing this for me.'

'Any time,' Steve said easily. Jo wished all her children's partners were as easy to deal with.

As soon as she hung up on Steve, Jo dialled Allegra's number, reassured to hear the girl's bubbly voice on the other end of the line. After a short chat Jo was convinced she'd work well, but arranged to meet the girl for coffee that afternoon. She could drive out to the college before picking the girls up from school and, with a bit of luck, broach the subject with Eve later.

Jo breathed a sigh of relief as she finished the call. She'd still do the school run herself one or two days a week, but it would be a relief to have a few days to herself. And it would be good for the girls to have someone younger to run around with them.

She pottered around all morning, singing to herself as she watered her plants and swept the cork tiles on the kitchen and family room floor, disturbing Scout who, this morning, had chosen to remain inside. Last night, Col had shown her the website of the accommodation he'd booked for their weekend and she'd been blown away. She knew he was more romantic than Gordon had ever been, but to see his idea of a romantic weekend boded well for the future of their relationship. She was really beginning to believe they had a future together and, all going well this weekend, she planned to break the news to Eve and Danny.

After taking Scout for a walk along the lane, she fixed herself a quick lunch of bread and cheese and set off to meet Allegra. As she drove through town, Jo reflected how the university had changed the town demographics. Now, instead of the streets being filled with locals and countrywomen in town for the day from their outlying properties, there was the buzz of young people. The university students brought life to the old place with their trendy clothes, variegated hair colours and the tattoos which, she had to admit, she disapproved of. Maybe another sign she was getting old and out of touch with the younger generation. But she did hope that, when her grandchildren were older, either the trend had changed or they had more sense than to spoil their natural good looks with those horrible tatts and piercings.

Jo turned into the university grounds and headed for the visitor's carpark close to the Banjo Patterson Café where she'd agreed to meet Allegra. Driving along the avenue of wattle and gum trees which had grown tall in the past few years, she regretted she didn't visit the campus more often. Maybe she should take Rob's advice. He had often suggested she enrol – or audit – one of the Australian History classes. It seemed she'd be able to attend the class and enjoy the content without the added stress of having to complete assignments. There would be no qualification at the end, of course. But she didn't need any more qualifications. She'd leave them to the younger generation.

A stiff wind was blowing up as Jo locked the car. The university was built on a hill on the north side of town which had always been renowned for its ability to catch every breeze. Before the campus had been built there, the locals called the high ground with its outcrops of exposed granite Windy Hill. Glad she'd thrown a pashmina over her long-sleeved cotton top, Jo pushed open the door of the café. There was the sound of jazz music being played low in the background and the delicious aroma of coffee beans wafted towards her.

At this time of day, the café was almost deserted, except for a group of male students in one corner and a girl with long dark hair sitting alone by the window texting on an iPhone. She must be Allegra. Jo walked towards her smiling.

'Allegra?'

The girl closed her phone and looked up, her wide brown eyes twinkling. 'That's me. You must be Mrs Slater.'

'Call me Jo.' Jo was about to reach out her hand before realising this generation probably didn't do handshakes. 'Lovely to meet you,' she said instead, taking a seat. 'Can I get you a coffee?' she asked, seeing the other's cup was empty.

'That would be good, thanks. An almond milk chai latte for me.'

Jo rose again to place her order, musing how the ordinary coffee had changed beyond recognition these days, but happy to stick to her own favourite skinny cappuccino.

'You're not what I expected,' Allegra said, when she returned to the table.

Jo raised one eyebrow. What *had* the girl expected?

'When Steve said you were his partner's mother – and the grandmother of the two little girls – I was expecting…' she grinned,

'…someone like my own grandmother. But you're much more…' She waved her hands in the air as if trying to describe the indescribable.

Jo laughed.

The coffees arrived almost immediately and, as Jo spooned up the chocolate from the top of her drink, Allegra proceeded to give her a potted history. Born in Melbourne from Italian immigrants, Allegra was studying teaching and had ambitions to teach overseas to satisfy her desire to travel. She appeared to be an intelligent girl with a pleasant personality and full of fun, confirming Jo's earlier impression that the twins would love her.

'So, will I do?' Allegra asked at last, holding her cup in both hands and smiling tentatively across at Jo. 'I love the idea of taking care of twins. I always wanted little brothers or sisters, but I'm the baby in our family with four older brothers. That's one of the reasons I didn't want to study in Melbourne. At home I'll always be the youngest Moretti. Here I can be myself.'

'I think you'll do very well,' Jo said, meaning it and trying to avert her eyes from the edge of a tattoo peeking out from the neckline of Allegra's shirt – no doubt one sign of her *being herself*. Jo wondered what her no doubt very conservative parents thought of it. If they even knew.

'So what happens now? When do I meet the girls? I love their names.'

'I need to talk with my daughter first,' Jo said, a knot in her stomach reminding her Eve might not be quite as eager to welcome Allegra into the family, 'then I'll call you again and arrange for you to meet Lottie and Livvy.'

'Cool.' Allegra checked her phone and rose. 'Thanks for the chai latte. I have a class now. I'll look forward to hearing from you.' And she was off like a whirlwind, leaving Jo gazing after her in admiration at the exhilaration of the young.

Checking her watch, Jo realised she must go too, if she was to be at the school gate in time for the girls.

'Gramma!' the pair greeted her with a combined hug. 'We painted and had a story and… and…' Livvy began excitedly.

'And Tommy Banks was sent to the naughty corner again!' Lottie added with a smirk.

'Naughty Tommy,' Livvy chortled. 'And *we* got stamps.' She held out her hand to show the smiley stamp on the back of it and Lottie did the same.

'What did you get those for?' Jo asked.

'For being good,' Lottie stated in a self-important tone.

Jo chuckled. She loved them so much. They were so like Eve had been at that age. Thinking of Eve reminded her she'd need to broach the idea of Allegra with her, and she should do it today.

'Home now, girls,' Jo said, taking their hands and leading them to the car. As she was strapping them in, she noticed them share a glance then, 'Gramma, can we stop for ice cream? We did get stars,' Lottie said with a beam.

'Ice cream? Mmm. We'll see.' Jo smiled to herself. The girls loved their ice cream and almost always managed to find a reason for them to stop at the recently opened Ben and Jerry's on the way home. And Jo almost always succumbed.

Today was no exception but, when the girls had finished their cones – chocolate fudge brownie for Lottie and cookie dough for Livvy – Jo knew she couldn't put their trip home off any longer. There were no extra-curricular activities this afternoon, so she might be able to rest a little while the girls played quietly.

The twins were still engrossed in a game of Minecraft on their dad's computer when Eve's car drove up. The door slammed and Eve appeared in the kitchen where Jo had just turned on the electric jug.

'What a day!' she said, dropping her bag on the floor and glancing around the room. 'Where are the twinnies?'

'On the computer. I was about to make a cuppa. Want one?'

'I think I need something stronger. You wouldn't believe what happened in the store today. Wine for you, too?' Eve opened the fridge and held up a bottle of sauvignon blanc.

Jo nodded and joined her daughter at the kitchen table. She chewed on the inside of her cheek, wondering how best to approach Eve about Allegra. This might not be the most propitious time, but if not now, when? The time might never be right.

Once Eve had regaled her about the trials of her day – the difficult customers, the sickly assistant, the awkward supplier – she took a deep breath. 'Eve, darling, there's something I want to talk with you about.'

'Yes?' Eve sounded disinterested. She finished her wine and poured herself another glass while Jo was still only halfway through her first.

'This schedule of yours,' Jo began, but got no further because Eve's eyes flashed.

'You're not going to renege on me now, are you? I can't handle any more.' Her eyes began to glisten.

'No, but… Just hear me out,' Jo said, as Eve opened her mouth to speak again.

'It's a good schedule, and I appreciate the time and effort you put into it. And you know I love spending time with the girls, but I do have a life and I need some time to myself.' She held up a hand to stymie Eve's inevitable objection. 'I spoke to Steve.'

'Steve? What's *he* got to do with it?'

'Just listen.' Jo sighed. Eve was behaving exactly as she'd expected. 'I spoke to him,' she repeated, 'and asked if he knew of any of his students who'd be willing to take on some child-care duties – look after the twins occasionally to free me up and...'

'But…'

'It pains me to say it, but I'm not as young as I used to be and they're an energetic pair.'

'Well, if it's too much for you…' Eve sounded annoyed.

'Not at all,' Jo lied – a small white lie. 'But I thought they'd benefit from the company of someone younger – not every day, of course. I'd hate to give it up altogether.'

'So how much is this going to cost? I'm assuming whoever you and Steve get isn't going to look after them out of the goodness of her heart.'

Trust Eve to go straight to the bottom line. It would never have occurred to her that this was exactly what Jo was doing. But Jo was family, making it different, she supposed.

'I'll be happy to pay Allegra,' she said.

'Allegra? So you've already chosen someone? Without telling me? What if…?' Eve's voice rose.

'I've spoken to the girl Steve recommended – yes. We met for coffee this afternoon, actually. But I told her you had to okay it first – her, and the arrangement.'

'Hmm.' Eve took a gulp of wine.

Jo ploughed on. 'She's a lovely girl. Final year. Comes from Melbourne. Youngest of a large Italian family. I think the twins will love her. What I thought was…' Jo gave her daughter a quick glance, '…I could arrange for you to meet her, then, all being well, she could meet the twins and we could go from there.

'Well…'

Jo could see Eve was weakening.

'Maybe…' She seemed to be considering. 'But, if I don't like her, or the twinnies don't take to her…'

'We'll forget the whole thing.' Jo crossed her fingers under the table. She was sure Allegra would win Eve round.

'Okay,' Eve said reluctantly.

'Thanks, sweetie.' Jo patted Eve's hand, seeing her daughter give a cautious smile.

No more was said at that time, but before she left, Jo made sure they'd made arrangements for Eve and Allegra to get together. Eve had agreed she could slip out of the store for a brief coffee, and a text to Allegra had confirmed the young girl was free late morning the following day.

*

'I'm still not completely sure about this,' Eve said. She and Jo were sipping coffee in the café next door to Eve's shop, waiting for Allegra to appear. 'She's late,' she said checking her watch for what must have been the tenth time. 'I don't have all day.'

'It's only ten minutes past the time we arranged, and she has to come all the way from campus.'

'Hmm.'

Just then, Allegra rushed in. 'Sorry, sorry,' she said, breathlessly, throwing a smile in Jo's direction. 'My class went over time and…' her voice faltered seeing Eve's expression, then she gave her winning smile. 'You must be Eve,' she said, 'or would you prefer I called you Mrs Tait?'

Jo could see Eve thawing.

'Eve's fine,' she said. 'Mum's told me a bit about you already. You're in your final year, so you're used to young children?'

'I love the littlies best,' she said disarmingly, 'and I brought this for you.' She drew several foolscap sheets held together with a bright yellow bulldog clip from her bag. 'It's a sort of CV and I've included by prac teaching reports. I thought you might find it helpful.' She handed it to Eve and sat back.

Jo smiled. She could see Eve was surprised – maybe even impressed. Allegra was proving to be even more prepared than she'd anticipated.

'Thanks,' Eve said, looking bemused.

'I'll get you something to drink,' Jo said to Allegra. 'It was almond milk chai latte?'

'You remembered!' Allegra beamed.

While Jo drank her cappuccino and Allegra her chai latte, Eve perused the documents carefully, only looking up when she reached the foot of the last one.

'Well, that's very impressive,' she said. 'Did you know Allegra did a stint with Miss Lang at Granite Springs Primary last year?' she asked Jo. 'The twins are in Miss Lang's class,' she explained to a bemused Allegra.

'She's a wonderful teacher,' Allegra enthused. 'I learnt so much from her. So?' she asked, leaning forward. 'What's your decision? I'd really like to meet your twins. They sound delightful. Twins – wow! I'd love to have been a twin. They must have such fun together.'

Eve definitely softened at this. 'They do,' she said, 'and they can be real terrors at times.' Her eyes moved from Jo to Allegra and back again. 'I'm happy for you to meet them, then we can take it from there. Why don't you come to tea – maybe on Sunday? You can meet Brad then too – my husband. I'm sure he'd like to talk with you before we go any further. But, if the twins take to you, I can't see why we can't give it a try, at least.'

Jo let out a breath. It had worked. Allegra had worked. She – Jo – was going to get some of her life back again and what's more, the twins would have this lovely young woman in their life.

Twenty-seven

Jo lay in the spa, leant her head back, a glass of prosecco in one hand, Cols' arm around her shoulders, and gazed out at the distant ocean. She wished she could stay here forever. But they only had the weekend, and one day had already gone. She had to be back to pick up the twins from school on Monday afternoon. Although Allegra had begun her childcare duties, she had classes on Monday afternoons, so Jo did the pick-up. But she wouldn't think of that now. Today there was just her, Col, and this glorious view.

'Penny for them.' Col's voice broke into her thoughts.

'I was just thinking I could stay here forever,' she said, wriggling closer, enjoying the way their bodies fitted together and the smooth feel of his skin against hers.

'Me, too.' Col kissed the top of her head and pulled her tightly towards him. 'But we should make a move if we want to catch the restaurant before they stop serving. The sun will be going down soon. We can watch the sunset while we have dinner.'

They watched the sun sink in the west as they toasted each other with more prosecco, before deciding to take a stroll along the beach in the moonlight. Jo slipped off her sandals and dangled them from one hand while the fingers of the other were interlaced with Col's. She loved to feel the soft moist sand on her bare toes. It was a glorious balmy evening, the only sounds the gentle lapping of the waves and voices far off in the distance.

Jo sighed with delight.

They had returned to their luxury apartment and were getting ready for bed, when a thought struck her. 'Did you ever hear any more from that woman who claimed to be your daughter?'

'No. I didn't expect to. She no doubt had second thoughts, decided her mother was mistaken, or found someone else to hassle.'

'It was odd, though.' Jo wondered again if Col was being entirely honest with her. She wanted to believe him, but something didn't ring true. She put down her hairbrush and swung round to face him. 'What year was it again?' she asked, a dreadful notion occurring to her.

'1987. You'd have been there too, at the ball – you and Gordon.'

'1987? No, I wasn't there that year. It must be the only year I missed. Danny was five and Eve only three. I remember it, because it was the year Eve had such a high temperature. We were afraid it was meningococcal. She was in hospital and they kept Danny in for observation, too. I never left their sides. Luckily, it was a false alarm. But I'll never forget those two days of worry. Gordon went to the races and the ball, though. *He* might remember.'

For an awful moment Col and Jo stared at one another, each thinking the same thing.

Gordon.

'He wouldn't…'

'He couldn't have…'

Both spoke at once, unable to grasp what they were thinking.

'I always had a suspicion Carol wasn't the first,' Jo said, 'but I was never sure, and Gordon was so good at dissembling. Did you know?' she asked Col with a probing gaze. 'You two were always close.'

'Not that close. He'd never have confided in me about other women. But I did suspect… Oh, my dear!' Col drew Jo to him, his lips on her forehead.

She sank against him, unable or unwilling to believe what until now had only been vague suspicions. After a few moments she drew away again. 'Do you really think it could have been him – with this Glenda woman? Do you think that while I was in hospital with our two sick children, he could have…? And pretended to be you? How… how… despicable!'

'I can think of a few other words,' Col said grimly.

Secure in Col's arms, Jo couldn't bear to imagine Gordon had been so heartless, so coldblooded as to give his best friend's name to the woman with whom he was committing adultery. 'Will you speak to him?'

'I most certainly will. But I can't really believe it. Surely not even Gordon would stoop so low? There must be some other explanation. Anyway,' he drew her closer, and Jo could feel the warmth of his body, his need for her, 'let's forget about the bastard. Don't allow him to spoil our weekend together.'

*

The remainder of their weekend passed without incident and without any mention of Gordon or the possibility of his having pretended to be Col. Though it did cross Jo's mind to wonder whether – if it *was* true – it had been the first or only time he'd used such a subterfuge to avoid discovery.

They drove back slowly, sorry the weekend was over so soon and relishing their final hours together. They stopped en route for a sandwich which served as lunch, Col dropping Jo off with an hour to spare before she had to pick up the twins.

'I'll see you tonight,' he whispered as he hugged her before getting back into his car and driving off. Jo stood waving till the car had driven over the grid and into the lane, then called to Scout and went inside. They'd picked up the dog from Magda on their way back. Although he usually got on well with Magda's two greyhounds, Scout was an old dog and set in his ways. Magda's house could be noisy, and he much preferred the peace and quiet of his own home.

'You're like me,' Jo said to her pet as she filled up his food and water bowls. 'There's no place like home – and we're not going to move out for anyone.'

Delighted to see Jo at the school gates, the twins immediately began to regale her with news of their day. It was good to see they'd cast off their worry about Brad, now they had him home again.

'Thanks, Mum,' Brad said when the girls tumbled out of the car and ran to the door, followed more slowly by Jo. 'I don't think Eve appreciates how much you do for her. I'll be right with them now.'

'Are you sure?' The twins didn't have any further activities today and had disappeared to their room, but Jo was mindful Brad was still recuperating and needed to take things easy – and that Allegra would have stayed to play games with them. 'Aren't you supposed to be resting?' She knew how tiring her two grandchildren could be, but Brad was their father and she had to respect his independence. It was tricky to know how much she could insist.

'I know they can be a handful sometimes,' he grinned, 'but they're well aware how weak I am at the moment and they mind me when I tell them to behave. Eve and I had a long talk with them. They're good girls, really.'

'Of course they are. Well, if you're sure, I'll just go and say goodbye.'

Ten minutes later, Jo was on her way back home. Although she'd only parted from Col just over an hour ago, she couldn't wait to see him again. Her fears about the weekend had proven unfounded. The more time she spent with Col, the more certain she was that it was the right thing to do. Right for her, right for Col, and, she believed, exactly what Alice had in mind when she asked her to take care of him. She and Col had talked about this on the weekend, and he'd assured her there was no need to feel any disloyalty to her friend. It was almost as if they had Alice's blessing.

The chief flies in the ointment were Eve and Danny. She had no idea how they'd react to her new relationship. Then, there was Gordon. Col had been very noncommittal when she'd wondered about his reaction. She shook her head at her foolishness. What on earth did it matter what Gordon thought? He was Col's business partner and friend. But Col had even suggested it might be time for him to retire – turning sixty had been a watershed moment for him and he intended to make the most of the rest of his life, hinting he wanted to spend it with Jo. She felt a flutter in the pit of her stomach at the prospect.

It was time to tell everyone. They'd kept it secret for too long.

*

Next morning, Jo had barely waved Col off when she heard a car driving up. Thinking he'd forgotten something, she slid open the

French doors, stepping over Scout's recumbent body on the way, only to see, not Col's Subaru, but Gordon's sleek black BMW.

'Gordon! What are you doing here?' she said, inwardly quaking and hoping he hadn't passed Col's car in the lane.

'That's a fine welcome,' he said, gazing around in a proprietorial manner. 'You've kept the place up well.'

She stiffened, standing stock still. Gordon hadn't been here since they split five years ago. What did he want now? Had Danny sent him? Was he an emissary to try to force her to move?

'Now, now,' he said, moving towards her and smiling. 'That's no way to greet an old friend. Aren't you going to invite me in?'

Jo thought quickly. Was there any evidence of Col's presence in the house? She didn't think so. They'd cleared up the kitchen after breakfast. The bed was made. But there was no way she was going to let her ex get anywhere near the bedroom. She breathed a sigh of relief before saying, 'I guess you'd better, now you're here.'

She led the way into the kitchen, remaining standing while Scout, recognising his old master, lumbered up to Gordon to settle at his feet. 'I was about to make some tea,' she said, hoping her voice didn't shake.

'Lovely. Missed me, have you, old fellow?' he asked Scout, scratching the dog's head.

Inwardly fuming at the animal's betrayal, Jo turned on the tap more violently than she intended, with the result that she managed to splash water over herself. 'Damn,' she muttered *sotto voce*, asking aloud. 'Earl Grey?'

'You haven't changed – and this place hasn't either.' He gazed around with a look of satisfaction and leaned back in his chair for all the world as if he'd never been away.

Jo tried to ignore him as she made the tea and took two mugs from the cupboard, automatically putting two spoonsful of sugar into one before handing it to him.

'Well,' she said, joining him at the table, 'you didn't come here for the good of your health or to check the maintenance of the property. If you have something to say to me you could have called or emailed, though any business we had together was settled long ago. Is Danny behind this?'

'Danny?' Gordon's eyes widened.

Not Danny, then.

Gordon took a sip of tea, then replaced the mug carefully on the table. He leant forward, hands clasped. 'It's hard for me to say this, Jo. I made a mistake, a terrible mistake.'

Twenty-eight

Jo clasped her knees tightly together and swallowed hard. There was a lump in her throat and her stomach was doing summersaults. What the hell did he mean?

'We were good together once, Jo. We could be again.' Gordon's wheedling voice made her cringe. This was the man she'd been married to for years, the father of her children, the man she now felt nothing for – not even pity.

'No, Gordon. We're finished. We were finished years ago – when you left me, left *us*. You need to go back to your wife – to Carol.' She almost spat out her name.

'Jo! I made a mistake. If I could have my time over again, I'd never…'

It was too much. Jo could barely believe this cowering creature was the same person she'd fallen in love with, borne three children to. 'And what about Glenda Darling?' she asked.

'Who?' He recoiled as if he'd been struck. 'Where did you hear that name?'

'So you do know her? Col and I wondered.' She was too angry to try to hide the fact she and Col had been discussing him. 'Was she the first of your whores?'

'That's putting it a bit strong. Glenda was… an indiscretion.'

'An indiscretion? Did you know there was a child?'

'A child? But that was more than twenty-five years ago.' He began to tremble and shrink.

'Thirty-one to be exact. It was 1987. A woman turned up in Col's office – your partner's office – claiming to be his daughter. Your *indiscretion*, as you call her, gave Col's name to her daughter on her deathbed. How could you involve an innocent man in your…' Jo was lost for words. She looked across the table at Gordon's now bowed head and cradled the mug in her hands. She held it tightly lest she give in to the temptation to throw its contents at him. How could she have failed to see his inherent weakness? Col was ten times the man he was.

'Why did you give her Col's name? That was inexcusable.'

'I… It was a spur of the moment thing – started out as a bit of a joke, then… I didn't mean anything by it.'

'How could you?'

Gordon shrugged.

'I think you should leave,' she said. 'Don't you have to be at the office?'

Gordon checked his watch and rose. 'You're right. But we're not done. Think about it, Jo. We have three children together, four grandchildren. We can't write that off as if it didn't happen.' He looked around. 'This place needs a man. It's too much for a woman on her own. Danny's right about that.'

Scout followed him to the door, gazing after him with longing, then as if realising he was really leaving, the dog slumped down on the doorstep, head on his paws.

'You're a fine one,' Jo berated her pet. 'Who's the one who's looked after you since he left, who feeds you, walks you? He gave no thought to you when he walked out on both of us, but you still think you're his dog. I saw you making up to him.'

Hell, she thought. *Here I am taking my anger out on a helpless animal. Of course Scout went to him. He was always Gordon's dog. The poor animal's been missing him, wondering where he's gone. I've probably only been a poor substitute.*

Gordon had caught her unprepared. She hadn't taken time to shower, her body was still warm from Col's morning caresses, her hair mussed from her night's sleep. Had he even noticed? He'd been too intent on his own agenda – until she'd put an end to that with her question about his whoring. She smiled to herself. Let him try to get out of that one. She couldn't wait to tell Col.

Jo set about her household chores. They had piled up when she was at Eve's and she hadn't had a chance to catch up till now. But as she filled the washing machine and vacuumed the living area, she was distracted by Gordon's visit and his unexpected declaration.

Had she been too hard on him? This couldn't have come at a worse time – just as she was preparing to come out into the open about her relationship with Col. What would the children think? What would Col say? Would he laugh? Be angry? She'd find out tonight. Despite the fact they saw each other most days, spent most nights together, they still kept to their routine of dining at Pavarotti on Mondays and Thursdays. These dinners were their tribute to Alice's memory. It was strange, Jo mused. To stop doing that would seem a betrayal of her memory, while sleeping together didn't.

Jo's phone beeped causing her to jump. Checking, she saw it was Kylie reminding her of their lunch together. Damn! With everything else going on, she'd forgotten the promise to her daughter-in-law. She knew she'd been hoping if she put if off long enough, Kylie would have forgotten. She should have known better. When Kylie put her mind to something, she didn't give up. As soon as she'd heard Jo was home again, she'd been back in touch, and today was the day they'd settled on.

Jo sighed. She really could do without having to face her daughter-in-law after Gordon's revelation. But she'd promised. What could Kylie have to say that Danny hadn't already said? She put the vacuum away, hung out the clothes, and made herself a cup of tea, before changing into an outfit more suitable for meeting her daughter-in-law.

Showered, with her hair caught up on top, her face fully made-up, and dressed in a pair of white pants and a pink and white patterned shirt, Jo felt ready to face Kylie. She left Scout lying by the door, the old dog merely opening one eye as she walked past, before closing it again and emitting a loud snore.

*

Jo glanced up at the two-storey townhouse where Danny and Kylie lived in the top end of town. It wasn't dissimilar from Eve and Brad's, the main difference being the two bikes lying at the side of the wide driveway and the basketball hoop above the garage door. She sighed and locked her car, before heading up to the front door.

'Mother Slater – come in,' Kylie greeted her with a peck on the cheek. The younger woman was impeccably dressed as usual. Why was it that Kylie always managed to make Jo feel dowdy? Unlike Eve who owned a boutique and dressed fashionably, Kylie always seemed to have that extra edge.

'Do call me Jo, Kylie,' Jo said for what must have been the hundredth time. 'Mother Slater makes me feel old.'

'But you *are* Mother Slater to me,' Kylie objected. Jo waited for her to add 'And you *are* old', but she didn't – at least not aloud.

Taking a deep breath – she could do this – Jo followed Kylie into her immaculate kitchen, the white laminated cupboards and granite surface looking as if nothing was ever cooked there. Jo knew that wasn't so. Kylie was a good cook, had gained a Cordon Bleu cooking qualification before her marriage to Danny, and regularly held chic lunches and dinner parties for their friends.

But Jo wondered how she'd fare in her country kitchen if Danny did succeed in prising it from her. She supposed they'd do a complete renovation, get rid of the beautiful old wooden table and dresser, her faithful Aga, maybe even the cork tiled floor which Jo loved. It wasn't going to happen.

'I thought we could eat in the courtyard.' Kylie slid open the floor-to-ceiling glass doors to reveal a small round table set for two. In the centre of the table was an antipasti platter along with a basket of bread, a bowl of salad, and a quiche – clearly of the home-cooked variety. All were covered with the sort of net cloth Jo remembered from her grandmother's kitchen. She'd heard they were back in fashion. This was proof, if any was needed. Trust Kylie to keep up with all the trends.

'This looks lovely, Kylie,' Jo said, taking a seat, and accepting the glass of white wine Kylie offered.

'Thanks.' Kylie joined her, sitting down carefully to avoid creasing the white linen pants she was wearing. Jo looked down at her own already wrinkled pair. She'd never win with her daughter-in-law in the fashion stakes if it came to a competition. But there was no reason why it should. Older and wiser, she reminded herself.

The conversation during the meal was desultory, Jo filling Kylie in about Brad's health and Kylie recounting the boys' achievements at school and on the sports field and talking excitedly about her plans for a lunch she was organising for the picnic races.

The reference to the races brought the whole Gordon catastrophe to mind again and she found herself pursing her lips.

'Something wrong?' Kylie asked.

'No. Someone walked over my grave.' *What a stupid saying*, Jo thought, but it stopped Kylie from asking anything else.

Jo was waiting for Kylie to reveal the reason for this lunch, but it wasn't till they were drinking coffee which Kylie served with delicious bite-sized chocolate covered slices of orange, that she began.

'Mother Slater – Jo,' she said. 'I know Danny has spoken to you and taken you to see one of his luxury villas. And I know how much you love the boys. I hope I can persuade you to be reasonable about this. It would mean so much to them to know they were growing up in the same house their dad did – to continue the Slater tradition.'

Jo almost choked. Yarran, the house she and Gordon had built, was nice. She loved it. But it was no grand stately mansion with enormous grounds and a history going back for generations. It was a typical Australian country home surrounded by a veranda and twenty acres of pretty useless paddock. She waited to see what Kylie would say next.

Perhaps emboldened by Jo's silence, Kylie ploughed on, 'Just look at the size of this backyard.'

Jo's eyes followed Kylie's pointing finger, the silver painted nail shimmering in the sunlight. What she saw was a standard-sized back yard. Surrounded by a narrow edging of shrubs the main feature was a large pool. A trampoline was located to one side of it, while on the other it appeared someone had attempted to set up a cricket pitch with a set of rather wobbly looking stumps at one end.

'The boys are becoming more boisterous as they get older. They need more space. Surely even you can see that?'

Jo bit her tongue, the word 'even' really getting to her. But Kylie was her daughter-in-law, the mother of her two grandsons, and she didn't want to upset her. 'It's a pretty normal type of backyard, Kylie,' she said, trying to sound calm while feeling heat flash through her body, 'and, as I've told Danny, I have no intention of moving.' She smiled, hoping to soften her words.

But Kylie was in no mood to be placated. 'Why are you being so selfish?' she asked, her eyes narrowing, her lips pressed into a tight slash. 'I should have known you'd be like this. If you were *my* mother…'

Jo let that statement hang, knowing Kylie's parents would most likely take the same view. But they didn't live in Granite Springs, so it was a moot point.

'I think I should go, Kylie. Thanks for a lovely lunch. I'm sorry if I've disappointed you, if the only reason you invited me was to try to get me to change my mind. If you and Danny want an acreage for the boys, I'm sure with his real estate contacts, Danny can find something suitable.'

'But that…' Kylie seemed to think better of what she was going to say and fell silent.

It wasn't till Jo was in her car and driving off, that she let out the breath she'd been holding.

Twenty-nine

It was Thursday and time for dinner with Col again. Jo hadn't seen him since he left on Tuesday morning. That night she'd been so distraught after Gordon's unexpected appearance – and his even more unexpected declarations – and lunch with Kylie, that she'd pleaded a headache and told Col she wanted a night to herself.

She'd immediately regretted it and her hand almost went to the phone to tell him she'd changed her mind, but some innate sense of self-preservation stopped her. She'd be no company to anyone the way she was feeling and needed to spend time thinking about her day – especially the conversation with Gordon. On Wednesday, Col had some legal dinner. So it wasn't till tonight she'd have the opportunity to share her worries with him.

Jo couldn't wait to see him. She wanted him, ached for him – his lips on hers, his fingers on her skin, his… She felt the heat course through her body just thinking about him.

Glad to have arrived at the restaurant first, Jo settled at their usual table and ordered a glass of white wine. She wasn't sure why she felt the need for some Dutch courage before Col appeared, but the thought of telling him about Gordon's visit struck the fear of God into her.

'I've missed you,' Col whispered into her ear, his hair tickling her cheek as he bent to kiss her.

'Me too,' she said, wondering how to tell him.

Col was full of the challenges of the day and his meeting the previous evening, regaling Jo with amusing anecdotes she normally would have enjoyed. But not tonight, when her mind was filled with thoughts of her ex-husband.

It wasn't till they were well into their main course, that Col said, 'You're very quiet tonight.'

Jo laid down her fork, her eyes filling with tears.

'What's wrong, sweetheart? Is it something I've said? Have you told the children about us? Is that what's the matter?'

'No, nothing about you. And I haven't told anyone about us yet. It's…' She looked across the table to meet Col's concerned face. 'After you left on Tuesday, I had a visitor.'

Col raised an eyebrow.

'Gordon.'

She heard Col's indrawn breath. Had he guessed? What did he know?

'What did he want?' Col's voice was calm, but with an undertone of bitterness.

'I think he wanted to come back.' Jo drained her glass so quickly she almost choked. Now she'd said it out loud, it made it real.

'And what did you say?' Col sounded brittle. His eyes had dulled. His brow had creased.

'I told him to leave, of course.'

'But?'

'Why must there be a *but*?'

'It's not like you to get upset over Gordon making a fool of himself.'

'Well, he certainly did that. He all but admitted to using your name with that woman back in the eighties. He's Sally Anderson's father all right. How could he? And I'm not sure she was the first – *or* the last. Though I guess Carol was the last.' She tried to laugh but it came out as a croak.

'You don't think? No, Carol would never stand for it.'

'If she knew. But I think you're right. Carol keeps him on his toes.'

And I didn't, Jo thought. *All those years and it never occurred to me. What does that say about me? Am I blind? Stupid?*

Col seemed to read her mind. 'There was no way you could have known,' he said.

'Is that supposed to make me feel better?'

'Getting back to this visit. Did he mention Carol?'

'No. I did wonder. Has he said anything to you?'

'Not this week, but there have been his usual complaints about her demands, how difficult she is…' He pulled on his ear. 'He *has* harked back to the past a bit, but I didn't anticipate this. Anyway…' he covered Jo's hand with his, '…don't let it get in the way of our dinner. He's history as far as you're concerned, isn't he?'

'Ye…es. Yes, you're right.' Jo determined to relegate Gordon and his visit to the past where it belonged. She was with Col now, and she knew he'd never let her down. But there was still that little niggle at the back of her mind telling her she hadn't heard the end of this.

'What else has been happening with you?'

Jo pulled herself together and related the story of her lunch with Kylie. '*Am* I being selfish?' she asked, when she'd finished.

'You asked me that once before, and my answer now is the same as it was then. Kylie's the one who's being selfish – she and Danny. I can't believe they're hassling you so much about the house. Would you like me to talk with Danny?'

'No!' Jo knew she should be able to handle her own children. It just seemed to get more difficult as they got older, exactly when you would think it would be easier. She tried to remember her relationship with her own parents. She thought she'd been supportive, helpful even, but was that how they'd viewed it? 'This getting older sucks,' she said.

'You're not wrong there. But there are some advantages.' Col wiggled his eyebrows, his eyes twinkling.

'Oh, you!' But his actions took the tension out of the conversation and allowed them to finish their meal without further discord.

Their coffee had just been served when Jo saw a familiar face across the room. It was unusual for Kay to dine out, preferring as she did to maintain a low profile and avoid the Granite Springs social scene.

She must have winced, because Col asked, 'Something the matter?'

'No.' Jo twisted in her seat and waved in Kay's direction. 'It's Kay. Maybe I should…' Col laid his hand on hers. 'Best not. She's sending baleful looks over here. She doesn't approve of me, does she?'

'It's not you. It's… She thinks it's too soon for us, as I said. I'd hoped she'd change her mind, once she'd had time to consider, but it seems not – not yet anyway.'

Jo managed to put Kay's presence out of her mind while they

enjoyed their coffee, but as they passed her table on their way out, her tight-lipped, 'Kay. Col.' Left Jo feeling uncomfortable.

Why couldn't her friend be happy for her? Was this reaction what she might expect from her children too?

*

Gordon and Kay were both far from their minds when they awoke next morning, and Col was able to help Jo with staking up a couple of trees that had become unstable in the recent storm. But, after he'd left and she was alone again, Jo couldn't dismiss her worry that Gordon might put in another appearance.

Relieved to have books to deliver to Val, she made sure Scout had food and water before setting off for town.

When Jo arrived at the care home, she knocked on Val's door, and was about to push it open, when she heard a voice from inside asking her to wait. It wasn't Val's voice and immediately Jo's heart sank. Had something happened to her friend? She perched on the edge of a chair outside the door and started to scroll through her phone while trying to hear what was happening inside the room with one ear.

Jo was opening a text from Eve, when the sound of the door behind her opening alerted her. She immediately closed the phone and stood up.

'You can see Val now. We were just helping her shower. She slept a bit later than usual this morning. I'll be bringing in her breakfast shortly. Would you like a cup of tea?'

'Thanks. That would be good.' Relieved nothing was amiss, Jo went into the room where she found Val sitting in her usual chair. 'You gave me a scare,' she said, bending to give her a peck on the cheek.

Val chuckled. 'You can't get rid of me that easily. Now let me see what you have for me today and then you can tell me what you and that lovely man of yours have been up to.'

Jo drew in a breath. Although Val was stuck in this room, she saw more of life than many who walked around with their eyes open and their minds closed. She handed over the books she'd chosen and waited patiently while Val turned them over in her hands and checked them out.

'Looks like you've made a good choice again. I really appreciate your doing this for me, Jo. I'd be lost without my books to keep me company.' She stared at Jo speculatively. 'Now, you. You're not looking the best. What's worrying you? Has the lovely Col not been treating you well?'

'No, Col's good. But…' Jo felt the tears come to her eyes. She brushed them off with the back of her hand. Val handed her a tissue and waited. 'Oh, Val, it's everything,' she blurted out, then began to recount all about Gordon, the potential daughter, Brad's accident, lunch with Kylie, Kay's disapproval. When she'd finished, she felt as if a heavy load had dropped from her shoulders. What was it about Val that invited confidences?

'Well, now. That's quite an assortment of events. No wonder you're looking wan. So, what do you intend to do about them all?'

'I don't know.' Jo twisted her fingers in her lap and looked down at them as if they held the answer.

'Here you are, ladies.' A cheerful young woman wearing the care home uniform of blue pants and top, wheeled in a trolley. She handed Jo a cup of weak tea and gave Val a tray containing a similar cup and a bowl of watery-looking porridge. 'Here you are, dear,' she said to the older woman, and left with a smile in Jo's direction.

'Is that your breakfast?' Jo asked, indicating the greyish substance in Val's bowl.

'It's fine. I'm not so hungry these days. And I don't have to make it.' She chuckled. 'Don't worry about me.'

Jo couldn't still a trace of concern. Val seemed too thin. She was skin and bone. Was she eating properly – being properly cared for? But she did seem happy enough.

As if answering Jo's unspoken question, Val added, 'They do look after us very well here. It's not easy for the girls. Not all the residents are as amenable as I am. In fact… but you don't need to hear about this place. You were going to tell me what you're going to do.'

'I don't know,' Jo repeated. 'I want to be with Col. I know that, but maybe… Oh, I don't know. Sorry, I'm beginning to sound like a broken record.'

'I think you should follow your heart. Your children aren't going to disown you, no matter what you decide. And Gordon certainly doesn't deserve anything from you – not after the way he's behaved. You had no idea?'

'None.' But had she? Had there been a few instances over the years when she'd wondered, but decided she was imagining things, decided to paper over the cracks for the sake of her marriage, for the sake of the children? She'd never mentioned her suspicions – if they even deserved to be called that – not even to Alice. A dreadful thought struck her. Had Alice known, suspected? Well, she'd never know now. But Jo did recall how understanding her friend had been when Carol appeared on the scene – how she'd commiserated with Jo, told her Gordon wasn't worth it, didn't deserve her loyalty. She really missed having Alice to confide in now, even though she knew how ridiculous that was, given her present circumstances.

'But it's different now,' she said, by way of explanation.

'Different? How?'

'We're older for a start,' Jo laughed. 'And this… this woman who claims to be Col's daughter. If she *is* Gordon's daughter, she's only a few years younger than my Evie. How's she going to react to the news? My family's going to need me. I can't swan off into a new life.'

'I don't think I heard any suggestion you were going to swan off anywhere. Col lives right here in Granite Springs. You do, too. The pair of you weren't talking of moving, were you?'

'We weren't talking of the future at all,' Jo said in a quiet voice. Maybe she'd been building all this up into something it wasn't. 'You're right,' she sighed. 'I may be making difficulties where none exist. It always does me good to talk with you, Val. Helps me get things into perspective. Thanks.'

'Well, you don't live as long as I have without seeing a few things.' She tapped the side of her nose with her forefinger. 'But do keep me up-to-date. You're a breath of fresh air. Life can get boring in here despite my books and this lovely view.' She nodded to the window where a couple of king parrots were fighting over some morsel on the grass. 'Your goings-on certainly brighten up my day. It's better than the television.'

Jo didn't know whether to be insulted or flattered. She decided on the latter. 'I'm glad you find my life so diverting,' she said, rising to leave, 'I'll bring you the next episode in a few weeks' time.'

'I look forward to it.' Val chuckled. 'But,' she added on a more serious note, 'don't let the bastards grind you down. Make sure you take care of yourself – mentally, emotionally and physically. If you don't, no one else will.'

Val's words stayed with Jo as she walked through the lush gardens back to her car. It wasn't till she was sitting and had belted herself in that she remembered the text from Eve. Steeling herself for bad news, Jo opened it. It was brief.

Don't forget twins' birthday and Easter. Ideas?

Jo smiled. As if she could forget her granddaughters' birthday. She already had their presents squirrelled away. She discovered the packs containing tiny tents and sleeping bags in an online store and knew the girls would be thrilled to have their very own little houses to sleep in. They were designed like ladybugs and identical, so Jo had sewn their names on each to avoid the inevitable arguments. She planned to augment the gifts with a couple of books closer to the actual date.

Jo wondered what Eve had in mind. In previous years they had celebrated with family only, but now they were at school, the twins would no doubt be begging to have a proper party with their friends. She hadn't realised the date coincided with Easter weekend. That was usually a family time too with Jo and Gordon – now just Jo – providing brunch followed by an egg hunt on Easter Sunday.

After a brief pause, she replied,

Let me think about it. Talk tonight. x

Although Val's advice had gone some way to restoring Jo's confidence in herself, it didn't provide her with any solution. Jo knew she had to work that out for herself.

Thirty

Col had been trying to avoid his partner since Jo told him of Gordon's visit. He didn't know what to say to him. Of course, Gordon wasn't aware he knew, probably didn't imagine Jo would have told Col. They'd been so secretive about their developing relationship, there was no way he'd guess how close they'd become.

But Col felt uneasy. Although he understood – and respected – Jo's reluctance to come out into the open – he didn't like subterfuge. He wasn't made that way. And, since it seemed he'd become Gordon's sounding board about his failing marriage, he didn't want to risk hearing more than he could stomach about Gordon's private life.

It would soon be Easter, and Jo had promised she'd use the family get-together to finally say something to Eve and Danny. She'd warned him there might be ructions, but knew it had to be done.

'We can run off together afterwards,' he'd joked, to which she'd looked so sad he immediately regretted his levity. Her children's reaction to their budding romance wasn't something to joke about. It was at times like these, he was glad he and Alice hadn't had children. Imagine if there were two lots of grown children to placate? Though, maybe his would be more understanding.

This morning, he was minding his own business, having told Dot he didn't want to be disturbed, when Gordon burst into his office red-faced, wild-eyed, his hair dishevelled, and his tie half-undone.

'She's given me an ultimatum,' he croaked, before collapsing onto a chair and burying his head in his hands.

'Carol?'

'Who else? Jo wouldn't…'

'Jo? You've been talking to Jo?' Col decided to plead ignorance.

'I… I dropped by to see her,' he admitted. 'Talk over old times. You know how it is,' he said flippantly.

The trouble was, Col knew exactly how it was – and what he'd said to Jo. Hardly talking over old times.

He sighed. 'Mate! Was that a good idea?'

'Probably not. But we had a good thing going. I didn't realise what I'd thrown away till recently… till Carol… Oh, hell, Col. What have I done?'

Col refrained from telling him that he was the wrong person to ask. But Gordon appeared to come to that conclusion on his own.

'Why couldn't I be more like you? You and Alice. Your marriage lasted. Why couldn't I have…?' He shook his head in dismay.

'Your choice, mate. The question seems to be, what do you do now? You divorced Jo,' his voice almost broke on her name, 'and you're married to Carol. Doesn't that say something about where your loyalties should lie?'

'But I can't…' Gordon began, then seemed to consider Col's words. 'You mean I should give in to her ridiculous demands?'

'Seems to me that's what you've been doing for the past five years. Maybe it's what you've led her to expect?' Col raised an eyebrow.

'I've been a foolish old man – thinking I could keep a young woman like her satisfied.'

Col contemplated the shell of the man he'd known and who'd been his best friend for most of his life. All he felt was pity.

'Come on, mate. You need a stiff drink. Let's get out of here.'

Gordon seemed to pull himself together. He raised his eyes, blurred with unshed tears, to meet Col's.

'We'll be out the rest of the afternoon,' Col told Dot as he ushered his partner past her desk to the door.

'The RSL, I think,' he said when they reached the street. They were less likely to meet any of their friends there. At this time of day, the club would be frequented by the returned soldiers from which it got its name.

They walked along in silence.

Pushing open the glass door at the entrance to the club, they entered the dark bar, immediately engulfed in the unfamiliar atmosphere. While Gordon settled at a table in the far corner – away from other patrons who were either watching a sports program on the large wall-mounted television screen or engaging in a game of Keno, Col went up to the bar.

Several glasses of scotch later, they were no further forward.

'You don't think Jo and me?' Gordon asked, after a long diatribe about Carol's failings as a wife and his own needs.

Col hadn't realised quite how self-centred his friend was.

'No, I don't,' Col replied with a certainty he was far from feeling. Regardless of what Jo had said about her ex-husband, she'd loved him for all those years, he was the father of her children. Surely that counted for something? But he couldn't bear to think of his own budding relationship going up in smoke.

They were interrupted by a voice instructing them to be upstanding followed by the sound of a bugle playing. Col checked his watch. Six o'clock already. They'd been here for almost two hours. Along with all the other patrons, the two men rose to their feet as, with the bugle playing *The Last Post* in the background, a sonorous recorded voice announced the daily litany of the club: '*They shall grow not old as we that are left grow old. Age shall not weary them, nor the years condemn. At the going down of the sun and in the morning, we will remember them. Lest we forget.*' Then they joined in the muttered chorus of '*Lest we forget*', before returning to their seats.

Gordon rubbed his hands over his face. 'Sorry, mate. I've taken up too much of your time. Thanks for listening. You're right. I have to sort this out for myself. Not your problem.' Gordon rose unsteadily to his feet, the alcohol seeming to have affected him more than it had Col, making Col wonder if Gordon had been drinking earlier in the day, too.

'You okay to get home?' Col asked as the fresh air hit them. 'I don't think you should be driving.'

'I can walk from here. Give Carol something else to complain about.' But Gordon straightened up as he set off along the main street and out of sight.

Col took out his mobile intending to call Jo, and saw several missed calls from her. It was Thursday night. While he'd been trying to talk sense into her ex-husband, she'd been waiting for him in their usual restaurant, wondering what was keeping him.

He sighed and pressed to return her calls.

Thirty-one

The sun was shining through the curtains when Jo opened her eyes, and the resident kookaburras were offering their usual morning chorus to all within earshot. She stretched her arms above her head then reached over to Col's warm body. Last night had been wonderful – a reaffirmation that whatever she felt for him was right. But she still hadn't found the courage to share her newfound love with her two oldest children.

Col reached for her, but she moved away. It was Easter Saturday and Lottie and Livvy's birthday. She had things to do before she went over to Eve's for the children's birthday party her daughter had planned.

'Must you?' he murmured, his voice husky with sleep and desire.

Jo hesitated. It was tempting to stay – to curl up in Col's warm embrace, to give in to the flood of desire that swept through her at his touch. Instead, she kissed his shoulder gently, the touch of his skin sending shivers down her spine. 'I must.'

By the time Col emerged from the bedroom, showered and dressed for the day, Jo already had a plateful of pancakes on the table, and was slipping the twins' birthday cake into the oven.

'Wow, you've been busy,' he said, wrapping his arms around her. 'What's the theme this year?'

'Frozen. It's their favourite movie.' Jo had lost count of the number of times she'd watched it with her granddaughters. 'I've made the basic cake. I'll decorate it later this morning. It's become something of a tradition – makes it more of a surprise for the girls if they don't see it till almost party time.'

This was something she really enjoyed. She'd been sad when her own children grew too old to want her homemade cakes for their birthdays, and Kylie always preferred shop-bought to homemade. Jo's lips tightened at the thought of her daughter-in-law. They hadn't spoken since that disastrous lunch. But she'd be there at the party along with Danny and the boys. Maybe Jo could avoid her, spend time in the kitchen pleading the necessity to help out.

But Jo knew that wasn't an option. Kylie was family. She couldn't avoid her forever. A phrase of her mother's came to her mind 'You can choose your friends, but not your family'. And Jo mentally added, 'And marriage and children choose your in-laws for you, for better or worse'.

'Eve is tired of hearing that song from the movie,' Jo added. 'But the girls love it. So I decided to find images of the two princesses – Elsa and Anna – and put them on the top along with the girls' names and a large 5.'

'You're so clever.'

'Not so clever. I searched the internet to find exactly what I wanted. It's amazing the things you can find there,' Jo laughed. 'I hope the twinnies will be impressed.'

'They're sure to be. And how many little princes and princesses will be there?'

'Princesses. Girls only – apart from their cousins, that is. And I assume *they'll* only be there for the food.'

'And Gordon and Carol?'

Jo hesitated. It would be difficult to face them both after Gordon's plea to resume their marriage, for that's what it had been, hadn't it?

'I expect so,' she said, 'Coffee?' She busied herself with the coffee machine, reflecting how Col enjoyed his coffee first thing, whereas she'd always preferred tea. These days she had coffee with him, then her tea later, after he'd gone. She wondered how that would change if they were ever to set up home together.

'Thanks, honey. Wow, these pancakes look delicious.'

So, Col wasn't going to speculate on Gordon either. He saw him every day. Did he know more about what was going on in her ex's life than she did? He'd never say. Men could be like that – keep everything close to their chest until it really mattered.

After breakfast, Col helped Jo clear up and stack the dishwasher, the latter a task she preferred to do by herself. It was something Gordon had never tried to help with and, over the years, Jo had developed her own method of stacking the dishes and cutlery. One more difference between the two men, and one she supposed she could get used to.

Once Col left and the cake had cooled, Jo iced it and set the decorations on top, turning it around and around to admire it, before adding the requisite five candles around the edge. It would do.

She checked her watch. Just time to drive into town and back and eat a bite of lunch before she had to leave for the party. Next day – Easter Sunday – there was to be the usual Slater family ritual. Ever since her own children had been small, the family had celebrated this day with brunch and an Easter egg hunt. While the egg hunt disappeared during the teenage years, Jo had revived it when their grandsons had been born and were able to join in the fun. She loved to watch them fossicking for eggs among the long grass of the large garden. Before he'd left home, Gordon had always taken an active part in the hunt, pretending to attempt to outdo the youngsters and to be upset when he only ended up with a couple of eggs in his basket.

Jo sighed. They'd been good years when the children were little, and the bad times which followed couldn't erase those memories.

But she still had the chocolate eggs to buy, along with hot cross buns. She'd make the quiches fresh in the morning and already had eggs, bacon, smoked salmon, hash browns and other ingredients in the fridge.

She was rushing around the supermarket, adding extra milk and fruit juice to her basket, when she heard a familiar voice.

'Jo! Happy Easter!'

Jo turned to find herself being embraced.

'Steve!'

Rob's handsome partner pointed to her basket. 'Preparing for tomorrow? I hope us big kids get a look in at the egg hunt. Rob and I are looking forward to it.'

'Get away with you. No one over fifteen. Though sometimes I wonder about the pair of you,' she said with a chuckle.

'Bye. See you tomorrow.'

He was off, leaving Jo smiling.

*

Jo was greeted by two excited little girls and a bunch of pink and purple balloons festooning the front gate.

'Happy birthday, twinnies.' Jo gathered them up in a joint hug as best she could, given the packages she was carrying. 'Let me just get these inside to your mum and we'll sort out which are for you. She moved through the front door, accompanied by two skipping girls, and headed to the kitchen where Eve was surrounded by plates of sausage rolls, mini quiches and ribbon sandwiches.

'Thank goodness you're here, Mum,' Eve said, wiping her brow and pushing back a stray strand of hair. You've brought the cake?'

'As if…' Jo held up the Tupperware cake container she'd had since Eve was a child.

'Yay!' Livvy said, trying to peer through the opaque plastic surface. 'What is it, Gramma?'

Lottie was hopping up and down in excitement. She reached up to the handle.

'Careful,' Eve admonished. 'I don't expect we'll have any peace till they see what's inside.'

Jo dropped the two packages containing the birthday gifts and lifted the cake from its container. It was greeted with awed silence, then, 'Wow, thank you, Gramma,' the twins said together and wrapped their arms around her.

Then their eyes darted to the floor as they noticed the two large packages. 'For us?' Lottie asked, turning one around to see the label. 'It has my name on it. The other must be yours, Livvy.'

They sat down on the floor and began to unwrap them.

Eve rolled her eyes. 'Mum! You might have waited or taken them into the other room. I'm in the middle of everything here.'

'Well, it's not every day they turn five. Is it, twinnies?' she asked with a grin, while the girls tore off the wrapping paper, sending it everywhere.

Jo picked up the torn pieces and began to fold them. At least that might do something to calm her daughter who looked as if she'd like to strangle them all – Jo first, then the twins.

'Look, Mummy,' Lottie shouted excitedly, the first to discover what the package contained. 'We can go camping!' She checked to make sure her twin had the same gift, then asked, 'Can we put the tents up now?'

'Maybe outside,' suggested Jo, seeing Eve's face turn red. She knew her daughter and recognised she was about to say something she'd later regret. 'Let's take them out of Mummy's way. She has a lot to do before your friends get here.'

Jo helped the girls set up their little tents facing each other in a corner of the yard. They then unrolled the sleeping bags and hid inside, peeking out to wave at each other and at Jo. Their enjoyment in this activity was curtailed, however, by Eve's arrival and her edict that they should get dressed before their friends arrived.

The twins scampered off, leaving Eve and her mother gazing after them.

'Thanks, Mum. They'll get a lot of enjoyment out of those, though if they want to sleep out here…' She shook her head.

'You can probably put them up inside too,' Jo said, in an attempt to calm her overwrought daughter. She glanced round. 'Is Brad not helping?' She couldn't see her son-in-law anywhere. He hadn't been in the kitchen either, though that was no surprise. Eve had always deemed it to be her territory.

'He's gone for a ride,' Eve said, her lips curling up in what was almost a sneer.

'Already? I thought he was supposed to be still resting.'

'He couldn't wait. He said he'd take it easy and be back in plenty of time to hang up the piñata.'

'Can I help?'

As she spoke, Brad appeared in the doorway. 'Told you I'd be back in time,' he said, clearly seeing Eve's expression. 'I'll just have a quick shower first.'

'How're you feeling, Brad?' Jo asked.

'Much better. Thanks for asking, Jo.' He threw a bitter look at Eve. 'I've been out of training for so long. I need to get back in shape.'

'Just don't try to do too much. We don't want a relapse.'

'Not you, too,' he muttered, leaving.

'See what I have to put up with?' Eve said. 'And now there's…'

Jo saw her bite her lip.

'There's?' she prompted.

'I didn't want to say just yet, but I'm pregnant again.'

'Oh, darling. How lovely. A little brother or sister for the girls.'

'Don't say anything to the girls yet. Only Brad and I know. I… I think that's why the thought of Dad and Carol having a baby really got to me. This one,' she pointed to her still flat stomach, 'could be born at the same time.'

'Carol's not already…?' Jo was stunned. She'd thought the baby thing was still up for debate. And Gordon's appearance in her home had done nothing to dispel that belief.

'Who knows where she's concerned?' Eve threw her hands up in the air.

'Are she and your dad coming today?'

'I hope so. The twins will be disappointed if their grandad doesn't make an appearance with a big gift. Not so sure about Carol. She's never had much time for the girls, and they've never taken to her. I can't imagine what sort of mother she'd make.'

'Mmm.' Jo decided not to comment. Although she had her own opinion about her ex's wife, she tried to remain neutral where the children were concerned.

They were interrupted by a whirlwind of blue satin and net as two excited blonde princesses ran towards them, grinning.

'Wow, look at you!' Jo exclaimed. 'When does the party start?' she asked Eve who was now beaming at her daughters.

'As soon as I get this thing hung.' Brad appeared carrying the multi-coloured *papier-mâché* object which he proceeded to hang from a hook on the veranda then stand back to admire it, just as the front-door bell rang.

Jo saw Eve breathe a sigh of relief. Everything was back on plan.

Soon the house was teeming with four and five-year-old girls. It was like a circus. Jo had forgotten how noisy a group of youngsters could be. But Eve was in her element and even Brad seemed to be enjoying the excitement.

Kylie had called to plead their apologies – the boys had not surprisingly baulked at being surrounded by little girls all afternoon, so Danny had taken them to a movie instead. There was no sign of Gordon and Carol.

The girls were all seated with Livvy and Lottie standing on chairs to blow out the candles together when Eve's phone pinged with a text. She glanced at it, frowned, then slid it back into her pocket while the group sang *Happy Birthday* and the twins blew out their five candles.

When Jo carried the cake into the kitchen to cut it, Eve joined her.

'Dad's not coming,' she said. 'No explanation – just *something's come up*. Damn him! He knew the girls were looking forward to seeing him.'

Jo knew that, in the excitement of their party, the twins probably hadn't even noticed their grandad wasn't there. It was Eve who was disappointed.

'Has he done this before?' Jo asked.

'A few times. More, recently. I bet Carol's behind it. I always felt she resented the twins.' Eve's mouth formed a tight line.

'Well don't worry about it now. Let's take in the cake. There's still a party to get through, then we can have a glass of wine and you can tell me all about it.'

'Thanks, Mum.' Eve seemed to cheer up.

Once everyone had left and Brad had volunteered to bath the girls and get them ready for bed, Jo joined Eve in the promised glass of wine.

'Thank goodness that's over for another year,' Eve sighed. 'I hadn't imagined it would be so exhausting.'

'And I'd forgotten,' Jo said.

'You did it for each of us – every year – until we were teenagers,' Eve said in amazement. 'How did you cope?'

'We just did. Your dad was a big help in the early years, until...' Jo thought back. When did Gordon start making excuses to avoid the children's parties? It had happened so gradually, had she even noticed? But, suddenly, it seemed, he always had a golf tournament or a big case, or some other earth-shattering event that precluded his being there, leaving all the hard work – and the subsequent rewards – to her. 'By next year you'll have forgotten the hassles and only remember the good parts,' she advised with a grin.

Jo had planned to drop by Col's on her way home. They'd agreed that, although this was to be a family weekend for her, they'd still try to catch up in the evenings. She'd been tempted to invite him to Easter brunch, but good sense had prevailed. She intended to break the news of their relationship and it was better he not be there in case of adverse comments from Eve and Danny. She hoped they'd see it the way Rob had – be glad for her. She *had* been on her own for five years and they *had* known Col all their lives. But, given Eve's recent comments about Col, and Danny's overbearing and overprotective attitude, she couldn't be sure of their reactions.

It was a shock, therefore when her phone buzzed, and she saw a text from Col.

Unexpected visitor. Best you go straight home. Good luck tomorrow. See you Mon. Cx

Thirty-two

Col poured himself a beer and wondered how the birthday party was going. He knew Jo had her family obligations this weekend and tried not to feel left out. He was looking forward to a time in the not-too-distant future when he'd be a recognised part of the family instead of an add-on – a favourite uncle who appeared at some, but not all, family gatherings.

He picked up the book he'd collected from the library only a couple of days ago, but even Tony Cavanaugh's riveting tale of police corruption failed to hold his interest. He was thinking of Jo, of how he had feelings for her he'd never imagined possible, when he heard a car draw up and there was a knock at the door.

'Gordon,' he said, surprised to see his partner there on a weekend.

His friend's face was pale, his eyes dull.

'Come in and take a seat. You look terrible.'

'Thanks.' Gordon fell into an armchair and sat slouched over. 'She threw me out, Col – threw me out of my own house.'

'Carol?'

'Who else?' He sighed. 'I thought… I thought we could have a civilised discussion. I could explain why I felt I was too old to have a child and she'd understand. I thought… I thought she loved me. But…' He dropped his head into his hands.

Col waited patiently.

'Then…' Gordon raised red-rimmed eyes to meet Col's. The man who'd been shoehorned into a younger mould by his young wife, who'd dressed in tight shirts and narrow pants, who'd been talked into using face creams and tinting his hair, now looked older than his sixty years. 'I said Jo would never have acted like that. I think that was the final straw. So, here I am.' He stretched his arms wide. 'I wondered if I could stay here for a couple of days – just until I get myself sorted out.'

Col's heart sank. What was he to do? Gordon was his friend – his best friend. But he was also Jo's ex-husband.

Before he could reply, Gordon spoke again. 'I've been thinking about Jo a lot lately, Col. I realise I made a mistake leaving her for Carol. If I could go back… do you think Jo'd have me? We were good together… And there's the three kids…'

No! Col screamed silently. *Not now – not when Jo and I are finding happiness together.* But all he said aloud was, 'I think you need a drink. I'll make coffee and maybe a glass of something stronger?'

Gordon didn't reply. He stared down at his hands.

Col went to the kitchen, busying himself with making coffee, his mind going around in circles. He needed to talk with Jo, but she'd still be at the twins' birthday party. She'd told him Gordon had called round – that she'd sent him on his way, had no intention of ever getting together with him again. But what if she weakened? He'd seen this happen time and time again in his practice. The woman who'd been betrayed, who'd turned around and taken the erring husband back for the sake of the children. But Jo's children were grown now. So surely…?

The coffee made, Col poured two mugs and returned to the living room. Gordon was still sitting where he'd left him, head buried in his hands.

'Here, mate.' He handed one mug to Gordon, putting the other by his own chair, then headed to the drinks cabinet where he poured a measure of scotch for Gordon then hesitated before pouring another for himself. He needed something stronger than coffee if he was to get through this conversation.

'Thanks.' With a shaky hand, Gordon accepted the scotch and downed it in one. 'I needed that,' he said, picking up the coffee which he'd placed on a side table. 'I can stay, can't I?' he asked with a worried look.

'Of course you can.' What else could Col say? He could give no good reason to refuse, despite the fact he dreaded to think what his old friend would say when he found out about him and Jo. Jo! She planned to reveal their relationship next day at her Easter family brunch. Gordon wouldn't be there, of course, but he'd be sure to find out. He was close to Eve and Danny, and one – if not both – would be sure to spread the news.

Where would that leave Col?

'Did you bring anything with you?' Col didn't want to sound practical, but Gordon had arrived at the door empty-handed.

'I have a bag in the car.' Gordon sounded vague, then seemed to pull himself together. 'I'll go back for more of my things on Monday when Carol's at her yoga.' He rubbed his forehead. 'I'll find somewhere else to stay then, too. I won't be a burden to you for long. Then I need to make plans.'

Plans? What did he mean by that? Was Jo to be part of his *plans*? Col felt a wrench in his gut and a thickening in his throat. But he couldn't think about himself just yet. Gordon needed his help.

By the time he'd settled his old friend into the spare room, Col realised he was feeling hungry and, when he checked the time, saw it was almost six. He hadn't had a minute to call Jo and was aching to speak with her but knew he couldn't do that while he was still in Gordon's company.

'Why don't we go out for a bite to eat?' he suggested. Maybe he could slip off and give Jo a call.

'Could we get a takeaway? I don't think I could face people right now.'

Col's heart sank. There was no getting away from the man. 'Sure thing. Indian? Chinese?'

'You choose,' Gordon said in a tired voice, so unlike the decisive man Col knew.

'Right, Chinese it is.' Col went to the drawer where he kept his collection of takeaway menus – something he'd come to rely on more and more since Alice had died and he hadn't had the motivation or the skill to cook much for himself. Picking up the phone, he ordered a dish of sweet and sour pork, one of stir fry chicken, and one of beef and black bean along with two servings of boiled rice. Then he sent Jo a short text. She'd said she might pop over and, with Gordon there, that was the last thing he wanted.

While they waited for the meals to arrive, Col poured then both a beer and turned on the sport on the television.

As the evening wore on, one beer became several and by the time the two went to bed, they were both decidedly unsteady on their feet.

Next morning, Col woke to a sore head and a mouth that felt like the bottom of a parrot's cage. He rose sluggishly, regretting the indulgence of the previous evening. A cool shower took the worst of his hangover and he headed to the kitchen knowing what he needed was a strong coffee.

He was surprised to see Gordon already sitting there, eating toast, the aroma from his coffee titillating Col's nostrils.

'I helped myself. Hope you didn't mind,' he said, sounding far livelier than he should, given the amount he'd imbibed the previous evening.

'No, that's okay. You're sounding brighter,' Col said, pouring himself a coffee and joining his friend at the table. He couldn't face anything to eat just yet.

'I've been thinking,' Gordon said. 'I have a plan.' He tapped his nose but didn't elaborate., leaving Col wondering yet again, if Jo featured in this *plan*.

Once Gordon had left, Col picked up his phone to call Jo only to realise it was out of charge. He cursed the fact he'd elected to cancel the landline after Alice passed away, reasoning he didn't need it as his mobile took care of all his needs. He set it to charge, then went out into the garden. He'd let it go recently and, although the rain had freshened the grass, the vegetable patch Alice had been so proud of had suffered from the drought followed by a drenching.

It was some time before he returned to the house and picked up the now charged phone. He was looking forward to talking to Jo, to hearing about the birthday party, and to filling her in on the latest news of Gordon.

'Jo!' he said, when she answered, the very sound of her voice sending a wave of yearning through him. What was it about this woman that made him feel like a schoolboy again?

'Col! I was just thinking about you,' she said.

'Good thoughts, I hope.'

'Always. I missed you yesterday and when you didn't call last night…'

'Something came up, I need to tell you. But first, how was the party?'

'A lovely party. Eve does these things so well. And, guess what? She's pregnant again. How she'll manage another little one, I don't know, but I guess that partly explains why she was so upset at the thought of her dad and Carol producing a child. They didn't appear, by the way. Eve thought it a bit odd as…'

Col took a deep breath. Now was the time to let her know Gordon and Carol had split. 'About that…' he began.

'Oh. Col, I have to go. I can hear the first lot arriving. Talk to you later.'

Thirty-three

Jo hung up the phone with a smile on her face. Her whole family was coming to Easter brunch and she'd just spoken to her lover. They'd get together later in the day and have time to catch up then. Right now, she had other things to take care of.

Danny and Kylie were getting out of their car when Jo opened the door, the boys running ahead to greet her with a hug.

'Are we having an egg hunt again this year?' Tim demanded. 'Last time I got most.'

'Did not,' his brother argued, bumping him on the shoulder.

'Boys!' Kylie called, but it had no effect as the pair continued to push and shove each other in typical fashion. 'You see what it's like,' she said to Jo as they greeted each other. 'They need more space to run around in – get rid of all that excess energy.'

Jo wasn't sure how a childish argument over who had collected the most eggs a year ago led to the need for an acreage – *this* acreage – but she let it go. She didn't intend to get into an argument this early in the day.

'Swim, boys?' she asked instead.

'Yes, please, Grandma.' It was Liam who answered, running inside to change. 'Beat you in, Tim!' he yelled as he disappeared.

'Everything's a competition,' Kylie complained.

'They're just boys,' Jo said. 'I remember when Rob and Danny were that age and…'

'We were never like that,' Danny said.

'No?'

'Well, maybe a little,' he allowed.

'Now, tea or coffee for you two?'

'Coffee'd be lovely.' Kylie leant against the kitchen bench and watched Jo make it, while Danny gazed around the kitchen.

'This place needs a complete reno,' he said, his eyes moving from the old Aga stove across to the scrubbed table and dresser. 'All that heavy furniture needs to go, and we could put in a modern stove and…'

'It suits me just fine, Danny,' Jo said, her temper beginning to rise.

'Yes, but…'

Jo saw Kylie shoot him a warning look and he said no more, but it left her wondering if the pair of them had already discussed plans to update the old home, assuming they'd be moving in. Over her dead body! She was saved from saying anything by the arrival of Rob and Steve closely followed by Eve and her family, the exuberant hugs of the twins removing any shreds of bitterness from Danny and Kylie's pointless plans.

'Swim, swim!' Livvy yelled, seeing her cousins already jumping into the pool.

'Brad?' Eve asked, putting down the large bag she'd been carrying. 'I brought some champagne, Mum. Thought the adults could probably do with a pick-me-up. I won't have any,' she said quickly, clearly seeing Jo's warning glance.

'Let's get changed, twinnies,' Brad said, herding the two girls into the house.

We really should stop calling them twinnies, Jo thought. *Now they're at school, we need to make sure they develop their separate personalities. It's been all too easy to link them together as if they were one unit.*

'Oh, good, coffee,' Eve collapsed onto a chair in the kitchen and gave Danny and Kylie a worried glance. 'What's going on here?' she asked, obviously sensing the atmosphere.

'Oh, just your brother trying to renovate me,' Jo said, trying to laugh it off. 'But let's not talk about that today. I want this to be a happy family day.'

'I should think so.' Rob gave his mother a hug. 'No quarrelling. It's Easter. Let's celebrate. And I, for one, am looking forward to the egg hunt after brunch.'

'You're too old for an egg hunt,' Lottie declared arriving just in time to hear his final words.

'Never too old,' Steve put in. 'But maybe we'll leave the eggs for you littlies.'

'We're not little anymore. We go to school.' It was Livvy who spoke, puffing out her chest as if to show how grown-up she was.

'So you do,' Steve replied. 'It won't be long before I see you in one of my classes at university.'

'Don't be silly!' Livvy said. 'We have all of school to do before that.'

'Silly Uncle Steve,' Rob said with a laugh, throwing an arm round his partner. 'But maybe you'd like to be flower girls at a wedding.'

'Whose wedding?' Lottie asked, eyes wide.

'You're not? Oh, I'm delighted.' Jo threw her arms around the pair. 'When did this happen?'

'After closing last night,' Rob said with an embarrassed grin. 'I popped the question and this lovely man said "yes".' He glanced fondly at Steve and they shared a private smile.

'Congratulations,' Danny said.

'From me too,' Eve said. 'The girls will love to get dressed up.'

Jo could see that, in her mind, Eve was already planning their outfits, and was pleased. A wedding would give her something positive to think about, instead of worrying about her dad and Carol.

*

They were all seated around the dining room table when there was the sound of another car driving up.

Who on earth could be arriving on Easter Sunday morning? Jo rose to check. To her dismay, she saw Gordon's car approaching the house. 'It's your dad,' she said, hearing the tremor in her voice. What was he thinking, arriving unannounced like this? It was bad enough he'd come that last time, but to arrive on what he must know was her annual Easter event was beyond the pale. She just hoped Carol wasn't with him and that she could get rid of him quickly.

At her words, Eve and Danny rose from their seats. Rob was engrossed in a conversation with the twins about the possible duties of flower girls and assuring them they could dress like flowers and carry a posy. The boys, however, seeing their grandad, slid out of their seats.

'Grandad, did you bring us eggs, too?' Liam asked.

'Liam!' Kylie remonstrated.

'Did you? Did you?' Tim repeated.

Gordon looked embarrassed.

Why had he come? Jo stood up, eyebrows raised.

'Thought I'd spend Easter with my family,' he said awkwardly, and smiled as if expecting a warm welcome.

'I'm sure there's plenty of room for one more,' Danny said, moving to slide another chair in between him and Kylie. 'Mum?'

Eve was smiling a welcome too.

Biting back the caustic comment that threatened to burst from her lips, Jo gave a tight smile. 'Plenty,' she said.

The conversation flowed smoothly during brunch, the children's comments lightening what could have been an awkward meal. When the last hot-cross bun had been eaten, Liam looked at Jo. 'Is it time for the egg hunt now, Grandma?'

Jo laughed. They'd been patient all through the meal and hadn't seemed to notice when Rob and Steve snuck out to hide the chocolate eggs all over the home paddock. Hopefully there would be an equal distribution of them but, if not, she'd kept a few back for any of the grandchildren who missed out on the search, knowing how competitive the boys could be.

'Baskets and buckets are on the kitchen bench,' she said. As part of her shopping trip she'd managed to find two baskets – one pink, one purple – and two buckets – green and blue – almost the same size. That should avoid arguments and ensure the twins had an equal chance to fill their baskets too.

'Can Scout help us search for eggs?' Lottie asked.

Scout gave Jo a pleading look.

'No, dear. Not for the egg hunt. It's best he stays inside. Dogs can't eat chocolate like you can. It would make Scout very sick. He can join us later, but make sure you keep the eggs well out of his reach.'

Lottie held her basket to her chest and nodded.

When the four children were happily engaged searching for chocolate eggs, Eve opened the champagne and filled seven glasses, topping up the sparkling liquid with orange juice and filling one with orange juice only.

'No sparkling for you?' Kylie raised an eyebrow.

'No,' Brad answered for his wife and took her hand. 'We're…' He cleared his throat and gazed fondly at Eve. 'The girls will have a little brother or sister in six months' time.'

Eve beamed. 'We haven't told the girls yet but wanted you guys to know.'

There were congratulations all round, then Jo raised her glass again. 'And to Rob and Steve.'

Gordon looked puzzled.

'I've decided to make an honest man of him, Dad,' Rob said with a chuckle. 'We're getting married. To us!' He raised his glass towards Steve who reciprocated.

Jo glanced towards Gordon, knowing that, while accepting his younger son's sexual orientation, he'd never been completely happy to see him in a same sex relationship. She saw him swallow hard and take a gulp from his glass.

'Congratulations, son.' he said, just a beat too late, then looked around. 'You all knew already?'

'Rob told us earlier,' Jo said, wondering how her own news would go down. When she'd made the decision to reveal her relationship with Col today, she hadn't bargained on Gordon being there. Her eyes roved around the table. Her family. Despite Gordon not being invited, it somehow felt right to have them all together for the announcement of Eve's pregnancy and Rob and Steve's proposed marriage. She speculated how they'd react to *her* news, and experienced a twist in her gut as she opened her mouth to speak.

But Gordon beat her to it.

'I have some news, too,' he said. 'I've left Carol,' he took a deep breath, 'and I've asked your mum if I can come home.'

There was a stunned silence, then, it seemed, they all began to talk at once.

Jo didn't know what to do, where to look. She wished the floor would open up so she could disappear. She wished herself anywhere but here. Why had Gordon said that? What did he hope to achieve? She'd shown him the door, told him she wasn't interested, now this?

Eve was first to respond. 'Oh, Dad! That's the best news ever,' she bubbled. 'We can be a real family again.'

Jo was aghast. Is that what Eve thought – that they hadn't been a real family since Gordon left? Damn the man! He'd always loved being the centre of attention. She looked round the table seeing a variety of expressions. Eve's delight lit up her face, Brad's reflected his wife's pleasure, Rob and Steve appeared puzzled. But it was Danny and Kylie's expressions that surprised her – though they shouldn't have.

'Home? You mean here?' Danny asked at last, his face ashen.

'Where else? Isn't this our family home – the house you grew up in?'

'But you have a house in town now. Surely…?' His voice trailed off. Jo saw Kylie place a shaking hand on his arm.

'But, Father Slater,' she said. 'We'd planned to…'

Danny shot her a warning glance and she subsided, but Jo could see her flush with embarrassment.

'Mum?' It was Eve who turned to Jo for comment.

Jo couldn't speak. To have this thrown at her as she was about to tell them about her and Col!

'Your mum and I still have a few things to iron out,' Gordon said.

Iron out? That was rich.

'Where are you living at the moment?' Rob asked.

'I landed on your Uncle Col last night, but I can't stay there forever. I'll find a room somewhere until things are sorted out.'

'Would you…' Eve began, but Jo saw Brad shake his head slightly. 'How's Carol taking it?' she asked instead.

'We've been having a few problems for a while,' Gordon said, with his habitual charming smile. 'She'll be fine.'

There was an awkward moment when it seemed no one knew what to say or do, then there was a flurry at the door and the four children broke through. Lottie was crying, Livvy's face was red, and the boys were arguing.

'It's not fair!' Livvy screamed, 'Tim took all the eggs and…' she hiccupped, …and…'

'I didn't. The girls did get some. Just because we're bigger,' Tim tried to explain, 'they think…'

'You did collect most of the eggs,' Liam said. 'You always do. Before, it was just me, but now there are four of us.'

'Boys!' Danny started to rise, but Jo took the opportunity to defuse one situation and get out of another.

'I'll deal with it,' she said, getting up and pushing back her chair. 'Bring all your eggs through to the kitchen and we'll see who has most.' She led the way from the table, glad to leave the now tense atmosphere in the dining room.

Once in the kitchen, she sat all the children down at the table and had them count the eggs in their baskets and buckets respectively. It appeared the boys had indeed collected more than the girls, and that Tim had a few more than his brother. Jo soon settled the disagreements by persuading Tim to give Liam two of his eggs and produced more from her supply of extra eggs for the girls.

'Happy now?' she asked.

They all nodded.

'Can we eat them now?' Lottie wanted to know, though from the chocolate rim around her and Livvy's mouths it appeared they'd already eaten some.

'Two each,' Jo said. 'Then it's up to your parents.'

'What's up to us?' Eve asked, appearing in the doorway with a pile of dirty dishes, followed by Kylie with another. 'We'll stack the dishwasher for you, Mum. You've done enough.'

But Jo didn't want to return to the dining room to face Gordon. She began to wipe down the already immaculate kitchen surfaces.

'Dad's gone,' Eve said, as if realising her mother's dilemma. 'He said he needed to book in somewhere and would get back to you later. You *are* going to agree, Mum, aren't you? It would be so good for the twins and this little one,' she rubbed her still flat stomach, 'if their grandparents were back together – a real family.'

Jo cringed at the repetition.

'I don't want to discuss it with you, Eve,' she said, realising the news of her relationship with Col had been delayed even longer. Then it occurred to her. Hadn't Gordon said he was staying with Col? Why hadn't Col told her?

'We'll head off now, Mother Slater,' Kylie said, as Eve turned on the dishwasher. 'Thanks for a delicious lunch and for arranging the egg hunt. The boys were really looking forward to it.' She paused, as if unsure what to say next, then continued, 'What Father Slater said… about coming home. Did he mean it?'

'You'd have to ask him,' Jo replied. 'But this is *my* home, not his.' *And not yours either.*

'But, Mum,' Eve began again.

'Not now, Eve.'

Not ever.

Danny and Eve drove off with their families at the same time, leaving Jo with Rob and Steve. Scout, who'd been outside farewelling the children, came back inside with them and padded around sniffing each of them in turn, before settling in front of the stove.

'Well, not quite the Easter brunch we expected,' Rob said, an arm around his mother's shoulders. 'What a turn-up for the books, eh? How about another glass of bubbly?'

'I think it's all gone,' Jo said, loving the concern in her youngest's voice.

'We brought a bottle, too,' Steve said, brandishing it. 'We thought we were going to have marriage plans to celebrate, but Eve and Gordon snatched the limelight.'

'Sorry, you two. Okay, just a small one. And I'm really happy for you both. When's the big day?'

'We haven't thought about that yet,' Rob said, opening the bottle and filling three glasses. 'It was a big enough step to make the decision. There's no rush. But what about you and Uncle Col? I take it Dad doesn't know.'

'No.' Jo ran a finger around the rim of her glass. 'I'd planned on telling everyone this morning, then…'

'There was us and Eve…' Rob laughed.

'And then your dad arrived with his announcement.' Jo shook her head. 'I don't know when I'm going to tell Danny and Eve now.'

'Eve won't be happy about it,' Rob said. 'She's always been Daddy's little girl, and getting married and having her own girls hasn't changed that. She'd love it if you and Dad got back together.'

'I suppose there's no chance of that happening?' Steve asked.

'Not a snowflake's chance in Hell.'

'Well let's drink to you and Uncle Col.' Rob raised his glass.

But Jo only took one small sip before setting her glass down again. It wasn't as simple as Rob seemed to think.

'Are you all right, Mum?'

'I will be. As soon as your dad gets rid of this mad notion he can just waltz back in here as if nothing happened – as if Carol didn't happen.'

'You know Dad. Once he gets an idea in his head, it's difficult to shift it. And he needs a woman to look after him. He'd be hopeless on his own.'

'He should have thought of that before he walked out on Carol.'

'Do you think he did?' It was Steve who'd been sitting quietly sipping his drink, who asked this.

Jo was thoughtful for a moment. Gordon had approached her about returning home several weeks ago. But Steve had a point. Her ex-husband had always had someone to look after him – first his mother, then Jo, then Carol. He wasn't like Col who, she knew, had always helped out with the housework when Alice was alive. Would Gordon really have walked out on a woman who did everything for him on the chance Jo would capitulate and let him back?

'Oh-oh,' Rob said. 'You mean the bitch threw him out?'

'Rob! You shouldn't talk about your stepmother like that.' Jo remonstrated.

'Hey, you call her that, too.'

'That's different.'

But had she thrown him out?

Col would know.

She couldn't wait to talk to him.

Thirty-four

Unable to wait till evening, Jo had texted Col when Rob and Steve left. They'd arranged he'd drop round for dinner, but she couldn't rid herself of the thought that he hadn't warned her about Gordon. It nagged at her all afternoon and prevented her from settling to anything. She wished she'd called instead of texting. Then she could have asked him outright. But she'd been afraid Gordon was with him.

Instead she'd spent the afternoon in the garden, unconsciously mirroring Col's actions of earlier in the day. Then she'd taken Scout for a walk, but the old dog much preferred to stay home, lying in his favourite spot. He'd enjoyed the day. Jo had noticed her grandchildren spending time with him and the twins smothering him in cuddles. But, to her surprise, Gordon had made no mention of the dog who'd been his pet. And he'd practically ignored Scout when he tried to attract his attention.

'He left both of us,' she said to the now recumbent animal, 'and now, when it suits him, he wants us to take him back – the bastard!' She spat out the word. 'But we're not going to let him back, are we, old fellow?' Did she imagine it, or did the old dog nod his head? He stretched out his forepaws and yawned.

*

Jo tried to suppress the niggle of worry as she showered and dressed, before preparing a tuna casserole for dinner and popping a bottle of white wine in the fridge. She'd throw together a salad later.

After her gardening and the walk with Scout, she'd found the morning drinks catching up with her and lay down for a short nap. Now, dressed in a pair of white wide-legged pants topped with a pale green tunic, she felt ready for anything. The anticipation of seeing Col brought the now familiar flutter to her stomach. She supposed she'd felt that for Gordon back in the early days, but it was so long ago, she could barely remember. His betrayal with Carol had wiped her memory.

Scout heard the car before Jo did and his ears pricked up. Although tempted to run to the door, push it open and throw herself into Col's arms, Jo took her time. She reached the door at the same time as Col did, and wrapped her arms around his neck, pushing her head into his shoulder. She felt her eyes moisten, not sure why.

'Hey. What's the matter?' Col held her at arm's length, his eyes moving across her face. 'Did something happen? Did Eve say something to upset you? Or was it Danny?'

Jo brushed away the incipient tears and remembered Col would be thinking she'd already told her children about them.

'I didn't… Gordon… You knew!' she accused him.

'Gordon was here?' Col drew a hand through his hair. 'Bloody hell!'

'He said he was staying with you.'

'Last night he did. That's why I didn't call. Then my phone was dead when he left. Then you couldn't talk, so I didn't get the chance to tell you. But I never thought he'd turn up here. So, I guess we're still a secret?' Col sighed.

'Yes. What with Eve's pregnancy, Rob and Steve's engagement…'

Col whistled. 'Wow, quite a celebration!'

'…then Gordon's announcement that he wanted to return *home*, there was no time for our piece of news.'

'He actually said that?' Col appeared dumfounded.

'He did and, of course, Eve was delighted. Though…' Jo reflected, '… Danny and Kylie were less so. I think Kylie saw her chances of moving in here going up in smoke. Not that there ever was any likelihood, but she couldn't see that.'

'Well, it's an ill wind…'

'Don't say that! What did he tell you? He announced to us he'd left Carol. Is that the way it happened?'

'Not exactly. Seems she threw him out. She wants a child. He's not prepared to go along with it. And…' he chuckled, '…I believe the final straw was when he compared her – unfavourably, I might add – to you.'

That made Jo smile.

'I'm almost sorry for him,' she said. 'But he's made his bed…'

'That's more or less what I told him last time.'

'Last time? This has happened before?'

Col rubbed his chin. 'Mmm. I didn't tell you, but after the river flooded, I found him sleeping in the office. Not sure if that was the first time, either.'

'Oh!' Jo wasn't sure how she felt about this. She knew Gordon deserved all he got, but a tiny part of her wanted him to be happy. He *was* the father of her children, after all. But, if the deterioration of his relationship with Carol was leading him to think he could go back to playing happy families with her, he needed to think again.

'Enough about Gordon. Apart from his unexpected appearance, how was brunch? Did I hear right – an engagement *and* a pregnancy?'

'You did. It was all going really well until Gordon's announcement. But now I'll have to figure out how to tell them *our* news. It's not so easy to get everyone together. Of course, Rob already knows…'

'And we have his blessing?'

'Yes. Now, let me get you something to drink,' Jo said, stroking Col's cheek and kissing him gently on the lips.

'I brought this.' Col flourished the bottle of champagne he'd been holding, unnoticed by Jo. 'I thought we'd have something to celebrate.'

'Let's have it, anyway. Seeing you after that bastard's smug face is reason enough to celebrate.' Jo took two champagne flutes out of the cupboard while Col opened the bottle, sending a sudden gush of foam over everything.

'Sorry. I must be out of practice,' he said with a grin. 'To us.'

'To us,' Jo repeated lifting her glass to her lips. 'And no more negative talk.'

*

It wasn't till they were lying in bed together, replete from making love, that Jo wondered how she could have known Col for all those years without realising how in tune they were, how their bodies fitted together so well. Then, suddenly, the image of Gordon as he had been at brunch came back into the forefront of her mind.

Damn the man! How dare he force himself into this part of her life. He was gone. He should stay gone. But, as Col slept peacefully beside her, Jo knew it wasn't going to be so simple. She knew her ex-husband so well. She should. They'd been married for over twenty-five years. And she knew that once Gordon got an idea into his head, it was difficult to shift it. He was like a bull at a gate when it came to getting his own way.

Jo knew that, if Carol didn't take him back, he'd become obsessed with the idea of returning to Jo, and she'd have to deal with it – somehow. She hadn't been surprised at Eve's reaction. She'd always been her daddy's little girl and would now, no doubt, be delighted that any risk of Gordon having another child had disappeared. She'd keep her favoured spot as the only and favourite daughter.

Her eyes were closing as a final awful thought occurred to her. That woman who'd claimed to be Col's daughter. What if their suspicions were correct? Gordon hadn't denied what he called *an indiscretion*. What if she really was Gordon's daughter? That would really put the cat among the pigeons. How would Eve feel then?

Thirty-five

Col was humming to himself when he walked into the office. Thankfully, there had been no sign of Gordon yesterday or when he returned home from Jo's again this morning, so no need to explain where he'd spent the night. Though he was a bit long in the tooth to have to do any explaining on that front. He popped his head round Gordon's office door to see his partner already hard at work.

'You found somewhere to stay – or are you back with Carol?'

Gordon grimaced. 'Fat chance. She won't even answer my calls. I've booked myself into the Grand,' he said, naming the upmarket motor inn in the centre of town. 'It'll do me till I can make other arrangements.'

Col didn't ask what these *other arrangements* might be, still afraid Gordon might be under the mistaken assumption Jo really would take him back.

Once in his own office, he found it difficult to settle to anything. If he took himself out of the mix, would it really be such a bad thing for Gordon and Jo to get together again? They'd rubbed along nicely for all those years, had three children, four – soon to be five – grandchildren together.

How would Jo have reacted to Gordon's proposal if she and Col weren't an item? If Alice was still alive, what would *she* have counselled Jo to do? He pulled on his ear. Maybe the kindest thing to do would be to slip out of the picture, leave them to it. When he'd mentioned retiring to Jo, his plan had been for them to spend quality time together

– travelling, enjoying life. But what if there was no Jo in his life? He felt a pang of something akin to grief at the thought of losing what he had so recently gained. But he shouldn't put himself first. He had to think of Jo – and Gordon.

'Oh, Alice, what should I do?' he asked his dead wife. But this time there was no reply.

He finally managed to settle to some work and, when his internal phone buzzed sometime later, he was surprised to see it was close to lunchtime.

'Yes, Dot?' he asked absentmindedly, his mind still on the case he was dealing with.

Dot's voice came in a whisper. 'It's that woman. The one you saw several weeks ago. She wants to see you again.'

Col laid down the pen he'd been using to doodle with while he worked on a tricky issue. 'What woman, Dot?' He saw lots of women every day.

'The one who calls herself Sally Anderson.'

Col started to say, 'If that's what she calls herself, then that's her name,' when the penny dropped. Sally Anderson was the woman who'd claimed to be his daughter, the one who…

'You'd better show her in,' he said with a sigh.

'Hello.' She stood just inside the door clasping her handbag in both hands, looking more confident than on her previous visit.

'Take a seat, Miss Anderson. What can I do for you this time? As I've already told you…'

'I found a photo,' she said, perching on the edge of a chair. 'It proves you knew my mother.'

Oh, shit. Here we go again. How can I persuade this woman I've never met her mother? He pushed aside the thought that perhaps his partner had.

He watched while she drew a photo from her bag. He recognised the style of the local photographers who enjoyed taking shots at local events, particularly the picnic races and the ensuing ball.

'It's not terribly clear,' she said, 'but that's my mother and that's you.' She pointed a shaky finger at the well-worn print.

Col squinted at the photo which showed a woman who was a complete stranger to him. She was dressed in a long strappy gown –

the sort that had been fashionable back then – and was standing next to the blurred figure of a tall man wearing a dinner suit. It could have been anyone, except for one thing. The man was holding a pipe.

It had to be Gordon. Their suspicions were correct. Col recalled it was the year Gordon, in his attempt to cut down his nicotine consumption, had taken to chewing on an unlit pipe – thought it made him look suave or something. Col remembered the teasing he'd got, forcing him to abandon the whole idea.

'It's not me,' he said again. 'Look, Miss Anderson – Sally – I know you want to find your father but…'

At that point the door flew open, and Gordon bumbled in.

'Sorry, I didn't know you had someone with you. I just wanted to ask…' His eyes fell on the photo which lay on Col's desk. He picked it up. 'Where did you get this? God, that was the time I tried a pipe. Didn't last, more's the pity. I still think I look pretty good with it.'

There was a stunned silence, then Sally Anderson gasped, 'You!'

Gordon gazed at her, then at Col. 'What did I say?' he asked.

'The man in the photo – is it you?' Sally asked, her voice quivering with emotion.

'Sure is. Don't know who the woman is, though,' he chuckled. 'Not a bad looker. I always could pick them.'

'That's my mother. Glenda Darling.'

Did Col imagine it, or did Gordon blanch at the name?

'Your… mother?' Gordon glanced around as if expecting her to suddenly appear.

'She died.' Sally's eyes teared up, then she drew her shoulders back. 'And before she did, she told me she met my father here in Granite Springs at a ball in 1987. I was born in 1988,' she added.

This time Gordon did turn pale. 'There were a lot of people in town for the races,' he blustered.

'But only one with Mum in the photo. Could it be you? Could you be my father? I've waited all my life to find out. I don't want money or anything. I just want…' She broke down into sobs. 'Sorry.' She scrubbed her eyes with a tissue, leaving black mascara tracks under them.

It was when she looked up that Col could see the resemblance. It was in the eyes. The two of them, side-by-side, made it unmistakable.

Sally Anderson resembled Gordon more than any of his three children – any of his *other* three children, he guessed he should say.

'I think you two need to go somewhere to talk this over,' he suggested.

Sally nodded and scrubbed at her eyes again.

'Maybe you'll want to wash your face first,' he said gently to the girl, rising and leading her to the door. 'Dot,' he called, 'can you show Miss Anderson to the ladies' room?'

Once she'd gone, Col turned to his friend who was visibly shaken and running a hand through his hair.

'I…' Gordon began, 'I… don't know… Who *is* she?'

'She's a woman looking for her father. She came here a few weeks ago to see me – thought I was him. She had my name. How could you, Gordon? Bad enough to cheat on Jo, but to pretend to be me? I knew I wasn't the one and… wasn't '87 the year Eve was sick, and you were on your own? Pretending to be single, were you? Not very fair on Jo – or the other woman.' Col couldn't keep the note of disapproval out of his voice. 'Do you even remember her?'

'Vaguely.' Gordon's eyes looked towards the ceiling. 'From what I recall she was…'

Please God don't say she was asking for it, Col thought.

'A pretty little thing,' Gordon said. 'She was passing through. Never expected to see or hear from her again. Now this! It's what Jo hinted at.' He dragged a hand through his hair again. 'What am I going to do, Col? I'm in enough of a mess as it is. What will Jo think?'

Col hesitated for a moment, stunned that it was Jo, not Carol, who immediately came into Gordon's mind. But not surprising, really. Jo was the betrayed wife, the one to whom Gordon was aiming to return. Had he already dismissed Carol from his future?

He couldn't think of an appropriate response, so said nothing.

'What am I going to say to the girl?' Gordon asked. 'Come with me, Col. You're good with people. You can help her see I can't… Oh, hell. Why did this have to happen now?'

Col hesitated. This was Gordon's problem. He didn't want to get involved. But he felt sympathy for the woman who only wanted to discover her family. And he had Jo to think of, too. They'd discussed this but had no idea of how Gordon would react. Then there were the children. It would be difficult to keep this quiet. He thought of Eve; how upset Jo had said she was at the thought of Gordon having another child with Carol. How would she take this when she found out, as she was bound to?

'Okay,' he said. 'I'll come along. But it's your show. Where shall we go?'

'Not the club.' Gordon shuddered.

'The Italian, then?'

'Okay.' Gordon took a deep breath. 'I could do without this,' he muttered.

Col felt pity for Sally Anderson. The poor woman only wanted some certainty in her life. Surely she deserved that? But Gordon… He really was a bastard. Jo was right. Jo! She needed to know about this. He'd tell her tonight.

'Hello.' A refreshed Sally peeped through the door. 'Can we…' she said hesitatingly.

'I think we're ready. Okay if I join you?' Col asked.

'Would you?' Sally appeared relieved she wouldn't be alone with her putative father.

'If we're going to do this, let's go,' Gordon said, moving towards the door. 'I'll let Dot know we're out for… an hour or so?' He glanced at Col as if for confirmation.

Col nodded, and the three left the office.

*

Once seated in the restaurant, it seemed Sally didn't know where to begin. The two men ordered lunch, but she refused food, saying she wasn't hungry, only asking for coffee. Col could see Gordon wanted a beer but managed to restrain himself, settling for mineral water instead. There was no sense in him getting tipsy. He needed all his wits about him to decide how to handle this.

In one sense, it was a pity Col wasn't the father. He'd have been able to cope with it so much better – his wife was dead and there were no children to complicate the situation.

'Well,' Gordon said, 'here we are.' He stared across the table as if seeing Sally Anderson for the first time. 'You have the look of my mother,' he said at last.

'I do?' Sally's voice was eager. 'Tell me about her.' She leant forward, elbows on the table.

'She was a farmer's wife,' Gordon said, 'on a property on the far side of town. I was her only child and I guess she spoiled me rotten.'

Col rolled his eyes. That was the story of Gordon's life. He expected everyone to treat him the way his mother had. He continued to eat his lunch while Gordon recounted selective childhood memories.

Then Sally asked, 'Are you married? Children?'

'Hmm,' Gordon appeared about to bluster again.

Col nudged him under the table.

'It's a bit awkward at the moment,' Gordon said after a long pause.

Awkward? Col grimaced inwardly. *That was one way of putting it.*

'I have three children from…' Gordon hesitated, '…my first marriage. Two boys and a girl.'

'A girl,' Sally exhaled loudly, 'a sister,' she said in astonishment. 'I've always wanted a sister.'

'No!' Gordon said, but he couldn't take back his earlier words. 'She's not… I mean…' He looked helplessly at Col who knew exactly what he was thinking.

Eve would go spare when she learned of Sally's existence.

Thirty-six

'Thanks, Eve.' Jo cradled the mug of tea in her hands. She was sitting in the back room of Eve's boutique surrounded by boxes of clothes.

'So, how's Allegra working out?' Jo imagined this was why Eve had asked her to drop by during a workday. It was a few weeks now since Allegra had taken on her duties with the twins, and Jo hoped Eve wasn't going to raise any problems. Now Jo only cared for the girls a couple of days each week, she was enjoying their company even more, and they were full of stories of the activities they enjoyed with Allegra.

They had taken to calling her Legra, and Jo had laughed only the day before when Lottie said, 'Legra's just like a teacher, but more fun.'

'Oh, she's good,' Eve replied. 'The twins love her, and I can't say I've found any issues.'

Jo smiled – Eve and her *issues*. She tended to treat everyone as if they were her employees, which, she supposed Allegra was, despite the fact Jo was paying *her* meagre salary.

'No, I wanted to talk with you about Dad.'

A sour taste formed in Jo's mouth. She'd known this moment would come. She tensed. 'What about your dad?'

'What he said at Easter – about wanting to come back home. It would be wonderful to see the two of you together again – for me, for the twins, and for this little one,' she pointed to her stomach. 'You *are* going to agree, aren't you?'

Jo felt a tingling in her chest. 'It's not that easy, honey. Your dad and I...' She took a deep breath, her fingers tightening on the mug she was holding. She looked down at them and consciously loosened her grip, fearful the mug might break. 'We've been apart for over five years now. Our marriage is finished. He chose to leave. He has a new wife. Carol…'

'I know all that.' Eve spoke impatiently. 'But he wants to come back – to you. He's our dad, Mum. He always will be. Why must you always be so stubborn?'

Stubborn? Is that what she was?

'Yes.'

Had she said it aloud?

'Stubborn and selfish. No wonder Dad left you.' Eve's voice was beginning to break. 'I don't know why I bother. All I want is to see my parents together again – happy. Is that too much to ask?'

Laying down her mug, Jo took Eve's from her and clasped her daughter's now shaking hands. 'Sweetheart, I know what you want – and I love you for it. But…' she bit her lip, '…what your dad and I had together was gone long ago. When we met and married, when you three were born, we *were* happy together, but… over the years… things changed. It was a gradual process. One I wasn't fully aware of at the time.'

Jo remembered the late nights working, the excuses that became less and less believable, the bumptiousness, the arrogance that gradually became more apparent. Then she thought of Col's solid presence, his honesty, his integrity. There was no comparison.

'But…'

'You're our child – our beloved daughter. Of course we papered over the cracks for the three of you. What kind of parents would we have been otherwise? You were all grown with lives of your own when Carol appeared on the scene. And…' she sighed, '…it seemed your dad didn't feel any more need to pretend. Or Carol wouldn't let him,' she added, *sotto voce.*

'You mean…' Eve's eyes widened, '…there were others?'

'I never knew for sure, and didn't want to admit it, even to myself. But I did have my suspicions over the years. Anyway, that's all water under the bridge now. But you do see why the idea of taking him back – letting him come *home* as he put it – is abhorrent to me? He's married to Carol now. That's where his home is. Yarran is *my* home now – and always will be.'

'But it was so nice to have us all there together on Easter Sunday – just like it used to be,' Eve wailed. 'I… I thought…'

Jo could see her holding back the tears, and wished she could make it right, just as she used to when Eve was little. But that time was long gone. Eve was an adult and needed to realise she couldn't always have her own way. She was like her dad in that respect, Jo reflected. She stiffened her resolve.

'No, Eve. It can never be the way it was with your dad and me. Too much has happened; there have been too many issues. And he's married to Carol now. That's where his loyalty should lie. You have to accept that's how it is, my darling.'

'Oh, well, if you say so, I suppose.' Eve gave a heartfelt sigh, released her hands from Jo's and started to rise. 'Now, I should be getting back through to the shop and I'm sure you have other things to do.'

Jo got up and hugged her daughter. 'It'll all work out, you'll see,' she said as she left, not at all sure it would. She had a strong suspicion she hadn't heard the end of Gordon's demands and hoped that, for once, Danny and Kylie would be on her side.

*

Jo stared at her phone. The text from Col was intriguing but told her nothing. It seemed the woman claiming to be Col's daughter had reappeared. Well, she supposed she'd have to wait till she saw him tonight. She had a lot to tell him, too. Eve's outburst had been a surprise, though, now she thought about it, it shouldn't have been. Eve had always been Daddy's girl and Jo should have known Gordon's comments would have hit a nerve. But it was going to make it even more difficult to tell her about Col.

Cooking always took her mind off things. She decided to bake a batch of cupcakes to take round to Eve's next day and a slab of chocolate brownies for her own cookie jar, before starting on the beef wellington for dinner.

The afternoon passed quickly and there was just time for a walk along the lane with Scout before changing for Col's arrival. She'd got into the habit of dressing up a little each evening – it made their dinners into something special and made her feel good about herself. As she wandered along the lane, Scout loping along at her side, Jo's thoughts took her back to the conversation with Eve. How could her daughter even imagine she'd take Gordon back?

Jo's forehead creased. She wanted her children to be happy. But it seemed that, whatever she did, she was destined to alienate at least one of them. Eve wanted her to take Gordon back, Danny wanted her to move out of her home. Rob was happy if *she* was – at the moment. But it might only be a matter of time before she managed to put him offside too. But thinking of her youngest child made Jo smile. She was so happy for him and Steve. Happy they'd found each other and happy the new laws meant they could marry – just like everyone else.

She'd concentrate on that, she decided. Focus on the positive – Rob and Steve's wedding – and the new grandchild. Maybe life wasn't so bad after all. With a new spring in her step, she called to Scout and opened the gate.

She had just closed the door behind her and filled Scout's bowls, when her phone rang. Seeing Danny's face on the screen, Jo pulled out a chair and sat down. She had a rough idea what this call would be about. She was right.

Danny didn't beat about the bush. 'What's got into Dad?' he asked, without any preamble. 'He surely can't think he can waltz back in and take over after five years away? Kylie thinks…'

Jo held the phone away from her ear. She didn't want to know what Kylie thought. She already knew. Her daughter-in-law made no bones about the fact she wanted Jo's house. When she held the mobile back up to her ear, Danny was still talking. 'So, if he's really left Carol,' he said, 'why don't you both move into town. That's a nice place he has there, and I don't suppose Carol will want it. I'm sure, with his legal knowledge, Dad can come to some arrangement and…'

Jo was aghast. She felt a chill on the back of her neck. This was her son, trying to plan out her future for her. She took a deep breath before asking, 'Is this your idea or Kylie's?'

'Well, when we got home on Sunday, we discussed possibilities.'

Kylie's, then.

'Danny,' she said patiently, 'I have no intention of letting your dad back into my life – of living with him again, either here or in that monstrosity he and Carol call home. And I doubt she'll let go of it as easily as you imagine. She always had her eye on the main chance. As I've already told both you and Kylie, I have no intention of leaving here – with or without your dad. It's my home. How often do I have to say it?'

'But…'

'Goodbye, Danny.' Jo hung up and sat looking at her phone. That was a first, and she was surprised she didn't feel guilty. But she was sick and tired of her children trying to run her life.

*

'Hi, Jo!' Col joined her in the kitchen, handed over a bottle of shiraz, and gave her a peck on the cheek.

Did Jo imagine it or was there a coolness in his manner that hadn't been there before? She shook her head. No, it was her overactive imagination at work again. 'We're good?' she asked with a frown.

'Why wouldn't we be?'

But there was something, something Jo couldn't quite pinpoint. 'Can you pour a couple of glasses?' she asked instead. 'I need to finish this.' She gestured to the salad she'd been preparing when he arrived.

'Sure.' Col took back the bottle, did as she requested, then sat down at the kitchen table and fondled Scout's head. The dog loved Col and always made a beeline for him when he arrived.

He was really a man's dog, Jo reflected, cutting a tomato more fiercely than necessary. What was the matter with her? 'You said that woman came back,' she said, sliding the chopped tomato into the salad bowl and brushing her hands.

'Yes. Let's eat first. It's quite a story. How was your day?'

'I saw Eve. She rang and asked me to drop by.'

'How is the darling girl? Is Allegra working out with the twins?'

'Yes. It wasn't about that.' Jo stopped what she was doing and leant both hands on the benchtop. 'She wanted to talk about Gordon – about what he said.'

'About coming back here?'

Jo saw Col frown and felt her stomach do a flip. She nodded. 'She thinks it's a good idea, that I should agree. Can you imagine?' she asked. But, instead of Col agreeing with her as she expected, he nodded.

'I thought she might. I get the sense she's always hoped for some sort of reconciliation.'

'No! She and Carol have never seen eye to eye, and she hated the idea of Carol and Gordon having a child together, but… Anyway, it's out of the question. Danny rang too,' she said, picking up her glass and draining it quickly, feeling the wine immediately go to her head. 'He and Kylie are of the opinion I should move into Gordon's house in town.'

'Wow. They have it all worked out, then.' Col sounded distant.

No more was said on the matter. Col wandered over to the window to admire the way Jo had managed to restore the garden and, while the beef finished cooking, Jo joined him to explain the new watering system she planned to install. Almost automatically, Col's hand reached out to squeeze her shoulder. Jo trembled with pleasure. Maybe she'd been imagining the slight coolness in his manner.

'That was delicious.' Col pushed his plate away, with a sigh of satisfaction. 'Alice always said you could beat her hands down when it came to cooking.'

'Rubbish.' Jo knew he was flattering her. Alice had been a good cook, too, though perhaps a more conventional one than Jo, who enjoyed trying out new recipes.

'You haven't told me what you meant in your text,' she said, setting a platter of cheese and biscuits on the table along with some sliced pears. She felt she'd been patient long enough. 'What happened today with Sally – isn't that her name?'

'Right.' Col took a gulp of wine before replying. 'This time she had a photo with her.'

'A photo?' A curl of something like fear twisted in Jo's gut. She licked her lips, which had suddenly become dry. 'Of whom?'

'Her mother and Gordon.'

'It was definitely him?' Jo felt her legs go weak with relief. So, she'd been right to believe Col. Then she flinched. It was one thing to suspect her ex-husband of having affairs throughout their marriage, even to have fathered a child, it was quite another to have proof. And to have gone with another woman when his wife was caring for his two young children in hospital, when anyone could have seen them… and to have used his best friend's name. It didn't bear thinking about.

'There's no doubt. He was easily recognisable. Gordon recognised himself.'

'He saw it? He met her?'

''Fraid so. Are you all right, Jo?'

Jo felt the colour drain from her face. Col placed a warm reassuring hand on hers across the table.

'It's a shock, I know. We talked about it, but to have it confirmed…' Col lifted the bottle to fill Jo's empty glass, but she shook her head.

To her surprise, her feeling for Gordon wasn't entirely disgust – though there was that. But her disgust was tinged with pity. What must it be like for him to suddenly discover a long-lost daughter at his age?

'So, what's next?' she asked. 'Does she want some sort of relationship?'

'She does, and not only with Gordon. She wants to meet her brothers and sister. She was very definite about that.'

All Jo could think about was her daughter. Eve had hated the idea of her dad fathering a child with Carol, fearful it would be another daughter who'd take her place in his affections. How would she react to discovering one already existed – one who was only a few years younger than she was?

Thirty-seven

'Mum, is it true?'

'Is what true, honey?' Jo was pouring food into Scout's bowl with one hand, her phone held in the other as she answered Eve's call.

'This woman who claims to be Dad's daughter. Rachel heard it in the café and came rushing in to tell me. I told her it was rubbish, but she seemed to be so sure. Tell me it's not true.'

Jo swallowed hard. She placed the packet of dog food carefully on the benchtop. She could picture her daughter, rocking in her chair, crossing and re-crossing her legs, the way she did when she was a child, fearful of some unnamed horror. Back then, it had been a falling out with a friend, or failing to be chosen for a sports team. This was a whole other ball game. How she wished she could allay her fear, be there with Eve to hug her and tell her it would be all right, that the bad woman would go away.

'It… I did hear… Look, Eve. It's best I come into town. Can we have coffee somewhere?'

'Coffee? You want to have coffee while you tell me… while everyone is laughing at me?'

'Of course not. No one is laughing at you. Where would you prefer to meet?'

There was a silence punctuated by the sound of the shop door opening and closing. 'I can't do this now. Allegra is picking the girls up today and they have ballet. Brad will be home late. I'll see if I can close up early and I'll come out to Yarran. And you'd better have a good explanation as to why you've kept this a secret,' she added, before ending the call.

Jo laid down her phone and found she was clenching her teeth. How dare Eve blame her! Gordon was the one who'd fathered another child. It had nothing to do with Jo. But, true to form, Eve had managed to ignore her father's infidelity and had focussed instead on what her mother might have hidden from her.

Eve would no doubt arrive in high dudgeon, angry at life, angry with her mother, when it was Gordon who should bear the brunt of her rage. Surely, when she calmed down, she'd be able to see that?

Jo spent the afternoon in the garden, Scout lying at her feet and occasionally getting in the way of her spade as she planted the hibiscus and camellias to replace those which had perished in the drought. Then she moved to the pathway leading to the house and to the selection of bulbs she'd bought earlier in the week. She was looking forward to the profusion of colour when the anemones, bluebells, freesias and jonquils came into bloom.

Rising with a groan, her hand automatically went to her back, reminding her to make another appointment with Magda and her magic hands. But right now, she needed to prepare herself for Eve's arrival. A warm shower and change of clothes might help provide the confidence she'd need to handle her daughter in the sort of mood she'd be in.

An hour later, and dressed in a smart pair of navy chinos topped with a pale blue cotton sweater, Jo felt ready for anything. Scout had been fed and watered and was lying in one of his usual spots by the French doors, enjoying the last rays of sun. Jo looked longingly at the fridge where the bottle of white wine she'd placed there ready for Col's arrival later that evening beckoned. But alcohol wasn't the answer. She needed all her wits about her to face Eve.

She heard Eve before she saw her, the loud roar of the car engine racing towards the house and the thump as Eve stamped on the brakes. She'd never been the most careful of drivers and, when in a mood like now, she was lucky to have made it without an accident.

'Now, Mum,' she began sliding the door open and pointing a finger at Jo, 'what do you have to say for yourself?'

'Why don't I make us a cup of tea, and you get off your high horse first,' Jo said in what she hoped was a calm voice. She'd seen Eve angry before, but not like this – not as an adult, anyway. Her daughter's face was red, there were dark circles under her eyes, and her makeup was streaked – a sure indication she'd been crying. Jo was reminded of the little girl who'd come crying to her, wanting her to fix something that had gone wrong, or to intervene with Gordon when he'd refused approval for an activity she'd dearly wanted to do.

This wouldn't be so easy to fix.

Eve dropped into a chair, barely acknowledging her mother. Jo nodded to herself and filled the electric jug, then set some Tim Tams on a plate. She doubted Eve would touch them, given her vow to avoid sugar, along with her current state of mind, but Jo would welcome a sugar hit to get her through this conversation.

'Well?' Eve said, when they were both seated with cups of Earl Grey tea. 'How long have you known?'

'Not long. In fact, I only found out for sure a couple of days ago.'

'How could he?'

This is more like it, Jo thought. *Put the blame where it's deserved.*

'Very easily, it seems,' Jo said bitterly. 'I must have been a fool not to have realised…'

'But this woman… When?'

'You won't remember, but when you were only three, you were hospitalised with suspected meningococcal. Danny was five at the time and I was pregnant with Rob. I spent several days in hospital with the two of you. It coincided with the picnic races. True to form,' Jo's lips tightened at the memory, 'your dad carried on as usual – the races, the ball… And it seems he met this woman – this Glenda Darling – at the ball.'

'But how can she be sure – this… what's her name?'

'She's called Sally, Sally Anderson. It seems there's no doubt. She has a photo of her mother with your dad at the ball and…' Jo bit her lip, '…they look alike – your dad and her.' Jo threw a wary glance at her daughter. She knew it was an ongoing disappointment to Eve that she didn't resemble her beloved dad in any way, taking after Jo's side of the family.

'Noooo!' Eve wailed. 'There must be some mistake. It can't be true. Not Dad!'

'I'm sorry, darling. But sometimes our loved ones do disappoint us. It doesn't make them love us any less. You're still your dad's favourite daughter.'

'But not his *only* daughter.' Eve gazed down into her still undrunk tea.

'Drink your tea, honey. It'll make you feel better.'

'Nothing will make me feel better.' Eve pushed the cup away. 'My whole life has been turned upside down, and you want me to sit here and drink tea?' She broke into heartrending sobs.

'Eve!' Jo put an arm round her trembling daughter's shoulders. 'Nothing has really changed. Your dad still loves you. I still love you. You have a loving husband, two delightful children and another on the way. Nothing about this woman can change that.'

'Have you and Dad spoken about this?'

'No.' Jo squeezed Eve's shoulders, then picked up her cup, taking a sip of the refreshing liquid. 'We don't have anything to say to each other. All this happened a long time ago. It's nothing to do with me now.'

Jo wondered how she'd have felt if she'd discovered Gordon's infidelity at the time. Would she have been angry? Undoubtedly. Would she have left him? Probably not. With two young children and another on the way, in a country town where everyone knew everyone else's business. No, she'd have put a brave face on it and carried on as if nothing had happened; been seen as *the poor Mrs Slater – the woman whose husband couldn't keep it in his pants.* Or perhaps as *the woman who couldn't retain the interest of a man like Gordon Slater, pillar of the community*? It didn't bear thinking about.

'I don't know what I'd do if Brad…' Eve seemed to finally realise this affected Jo too.

'But he wouldn't.'

'No, he's wedded to that damned bike of his.' Eve grimaced but seemed to be recovering her equilibrium. 'What's she like?' she asked.

'I've no idea. I don't know anything about her.'

'Aren't you curious?'

Jo thought for a moment. *Curious? No, that didn't describe her feelings.*

'Not really. Or… only on your behalf. I know how horrid it must be for you to discover something like this, but…'

'Horrid! You have no idea. I feel my whole life has been… I need to talk to Dad.'

'That may not be such a good idea right now. I think he's still coming to terms with it himself. Maybe give him time.'

'Time for what? Time's not going to change anything, is it?'

While Jo was considering a reply, Scout levered himself up and made his way to the door, tongue hanging out, and gave a short welcoming bark.

The two women looked up, and Jo felt her heart drop. Standing at the door, a bottle of wine in one hand, a smile on his face, was Col.

Jo saw Eve's eyes widen.

'Uncle Col! What are you doing here?'

'I…'

Jo saw Col react quickly.

'Your mum invited me to dinner,' he said.

Eve's eyes moved quickly from him to Jo and back again.

'Did you know, too?' she accused.

'Know what?'

'Don't try to hide it. About Dad and this woman – this new daughter of his. Did you cover up for him all those years? I can just see it – best friend, business partner, good mates,' she said bitterly.

'I only found out for sure this week. A woman appeared in my office several weeks ago claiming to be *my* daughter. I knew it couldn't be true, then…'

'No, the virtuous Col Ford wouldn't stoop to commit adultery. Aunt Alice was luckier than Mum.'

Col cleared his throat.

Eve's eyes moved between them again, clearly putting two and two together.

'Dinner?' she said. 'Is this a regular thing?' She turned to her mother. 'Is this something else you've been keeping from me?'

Jo quaked and looked to Col for help, but there was none to be had. He appeared as dumbfounded as she was. She took a deep breath. 'Your Uncle Col and I… since Aunt Alice died… we've been spending time together.'

'I know – your Monday and Thursday dinners at Pavarotti's.' She looked at them intently, her eyes seeming to see right through them. 'But this is more than that, isn't it?'

Jo was lost for words, but Col seemed to have regained his ability to speak.

He took Jo's hand. 'Your mum and I shared our grief at your Aunt Alice's death. It brought us closer.' He smiled at Jo. 'We've become…'

But Eve didn't want to listen. 'You're both as bad as he is!' she yelled, gathering up her bag and storming out.

'That didn't go too well,' Col said ruefully as they heard the car engine rev and drive off. 'I'm sorry, sweetheart.'

'No. It's not your fault. She had to find out sometime. I should have told her. I don't know why I didn't. Maybe…'

'Maybe you anticipated this sort of reaction?'

'Maybe. But, coming on top of the news about Gordon, I suppose it was too much.'

'How did she take it?'

'She's devastated. I wouldn't be surprised if she's off to confront Gordon now. What's she like – this Sally Anderson?'

'Seems a nice enough girl – woman I suppose. She's almost Eve's age. I guess that's part of the problem. She's been married, divorced and, now she's all alone in the world, she's desperate to find her family.'

'*Her* family!'

'They *are* her family. Father, half brothers and sister.'

'What does Gordon intend to do about it?'

'He's in a bit of a spin at the moment. But, I think, when he has time to consider it properly, he'll agree to her demand to meet her brothers and sister.'

'If they agree to meet her. Oh…' Jo half-rose then fell back into her chair again. 'Danny and Rob. Should I tell them?'

'I suspect Eve will do that, don't you?'

'You're right. It'll be like when she was small, she'll want to line up the troops, get them on her side. Though there are really no sides in this. And Gordon's the big bad wolf who's responsible.'

'Well, there's nothing we can do about it. Was there some mention of dinner?'

Jo blanched. 'Sorry, Col. I intended to put something in the oven, but with Eve…' Jo couldn't believe she'd completely forgotten to prepare dinner.

'Never mind. We can go into town. Maybe try out that new Thai restaurant on Main Street?'

'You're a gem. I don't know what I'd do without you.'

But as they drove into town, Jo wondered for the first time, if her new relationship would exact a price too dear to pay.

What if Danny took the same view as Eve?

Could she continue to see Col if it estranged her from her children?

Thirty-eight

Jo knew she couldn't let it go with Eve. She had to see her daughter, try to pacify her, though how she was going to do that, she had no idea.

Knowing Eve closed the shop at lunchtime on Saturdays – like most of the retail outlets in town – Jo headed into town to arrive after closing time, but before Eve had left to go home. She didn't want to antagonise her in front of Brad and the girls and was afraid of her daughter's reaction.

As usual, the main street was deserted after midday, everyone having completed any shopping in the morning. Jo parked outside Eve's boutique. She thought, not for the first time, what a success her daughter had made of this venture, despite the many naysayers who'd predicted a town the size of Granite Springs had no need for such an upmarket store. She opened it when she was pregnant with the twins, and it had gone from strength to strength proving everyone wrong, though Jo wondered how she'd manage when the new baby came along.

She knocked on the locked door and peered through the glass.

'Mum! What are you doing here?' Eve opened the door a crack.

Not the welcome she'd hoped for. 'Can I come in? I'd like to talk with you.'

'I suppose.' Eve opened the door sufficiently to allow Jo inside, then turned her back and walked through the shop.

Jo followed. This wasn't going to be easy. But she hadn't expected it would be.

'Well?' Eve asked, when they reached the back room. She stood in front of Jo, her arms folded.

'Can we sit down and discuss this like two grown-ups?' Jo asked. 'It was never my intention to upset you, or to keep secrets from you.'

'Well, you made a good job of it. Uncle Col!'

'A cup of tea would be nice.'

'I don't have time.' But Eve did take a seat.

Jo sat opposite and twisted her fingers, trying to find the right words.

'Okay. Uncle Col – I should have told you before now, but… It all happened so suddenly, and I didn't want to…' Jo tried to remember why she had kept it to herself. Was it because it was so new, so wonderful that she'd felt it would soil it to share it? That couldn't be right, because Rob knew – and approved. Had she been afraid of just this sort of reaction from her daughter?

'You mean you're…' Eve's mouth turned down in something like disgust. 'You and Uncle Col? You're both so…'

'Old? Is that what you were going to say?' Jo asked, only to see Eve redden.

'Well…'

'We're only sixty. Wait till you're our age. Life doesn't stop at forty, you know – or fifty, or even sixty. I can appreciate it came as a shock to you. It came as a shock to us, too. We've been friends most of our lives, honey. Your Aunt Alice was my best friend, too. And sometimes good friends are the ones you turn to when you need a bit of comfort.'

'Comfort!' Eve snorted, but Jo could see she was listening. That was a start.

'Yes, comfort. And that can – and did – lead to something more intimate. After your dad left, I never thought to find anyone I could care about again – in that way. It's been a revelation – to both of us.'

'Does Dad know?'

'No.' Jo pleated the edge of her linen top with shaking fingers. What would Gordon think when he found out? Now Eve knew, no doubt Danny would be next, then Gordon.

'When did you and Uncle Col intend to tell him? You're letting him think he can come back home when all the time you're…'

'No, Eve. I've never let your father think he can come back to the house which is now *my* home. I've made it perfectly clear to him that our marriage ended five years ago when he left. If he's now chosen to forget that, to ignore my protestations, then that's his problem.'

'But...'

'Can't you see, darling? Your dad has made another life for himself with Carol. I've been on my own for five years. Isn't that long enough for me to want to move on?'

'I suppose.'

'And now your dad has other things on his mind.'

'His illegitimate daughter.'

'Put bluntly, yes.'

'How else would you put it?'

'Have you spoken to him?'

'He's coming to dinner tonight. He called yesterday and invited himself. I don't know how I'm going to face him. First, this woman, now you and Uncle Col. I just want to hide away and come out again to find it's all over. I've invited Danny and Kylie over, too. Best they know the latest.'

'Mmm.' Jo didn't know whether to be glad or sorry. But it would all be out in the open, now – Gordon's faithlessness, her and Col. Why did she feel there should be a third item on the agenda? She shook her head. These two were enough. She'd love to be a fly on the wall at that dinner, but no doubt she'd hear about it soon enough.

'So, am I forgiven?' Jo didn't know exactly what she was asking forgiveness for, but it seemed like a good idea and would allow Eve to think she was in control – something she'd always loved.

Eve gave a tight smile, and Jo knew she'd have to be content with that slight indication all might not be well yet between them, but soon could be. She rose and hugged her daughter, feeling the tension in Eve's body and wondering if it was all due to her and Gordon or if, as she'd earlier suspected, Eve had other things on her mind – if all was well with her and Brad.

Jo sighed as she got back into her car. Raising children wasn't easy. You did the best you could, sent them out into the world and hoped they'd make it through. But there were the inevitable pitfalls to encounter, and she and Gordon hadn't helped in this instance. In their separate ways, they'd managed to alienate their daughter, and who knew how Danny would react. He'd no doubt take his cue from Kylie who'd quickly work out how to manipulate events to suit her own ends.

She was glad she was seeing Col tonight as usual but, somehow, Eve's reaction had tarnished what had been a beautiful relationship. And she couldn't dismiss the niggle of something unidentifiable in his manner last week. Had it been after he told her about Sally Anderson, when she recounted Gordon's unannounced arrival on Easter Sunday or when Eve saw them together?

She couldn't remember.

*

Something was wrong.

Jo couldn't feel the same joy in the anticipation of their evening together. It was as if all that was happening with Gordon had soured everything. She dressed carefully in a favourite pair of shocking pink pants teamed with a soft cream cashmere sweater and peered at her face in the mirror as she applied light makeup. Had all these lines been there two weeks ago? When had those dark shadows appeared under her eyes? She was beginning to look and feel old. How could Col want her?

At the sound of a car arriving, Jo patted her hair and hurried through to the kitchen just in time to greet Col at the door.

'Evening, sweetheart. You're looking wonderful, as usual,' he said, drawing her into his arms. But his words did nothing to allay the worry clouding her mind. Jo searched his face for signs of the distance she'd noticed previously as she pulled away but, to her anxious eyes, Col looked much the same as usual. His thick white hair was carefully combed back from his high forehead, his grey eyes twinkling as if with some secret. But there it was! The slight crease between his eyes that hadn't been there before. Something was bothering him.

'You look as if you need a drink. What happened today?' he asked, stroking her cheek with the back of his hand.

'Eve happened. I dropped round to see if I could resolve our differences.'

'Let me guess – you didn't manage it?'

'Not really.' Jo dropped into a chair and let Col find the wine in the fridge and pour two glasses before joining her. 'She's still incensed about Gordon and about us. He's invited himself to dinner at her place tonight – and she's invited Danny and Kylie.'

Col blew out a breath of air. 'Wow! Bet the shit really will hit the fan.'

'And she'll tell them about us, too.'

'Mmm.'

'Col?' Jo expected a stronger reaction from him.

'There's a lot going on in your family at the moment. This may not be the right time…'

Jo felt her gut twist. It was what she'd been dreading. 'What do you mean?' she asked, trembling.

She picked up her glass and took a gulp, almost choking.

'Just that. It seems to me that you – and Eve, Danny and Gordon – have enough on your plates at the moment without my involvement complicating the picture. Maybe I should bow out a bit till things settle.'

Jo's heart sank. She'd been right.

'Why did you come at all? Do you want to leave now?' she asked, her voice tight with emotion.

'Come here, you.' Col drew her to him, his lips soft on her neck. 'It's not what *I* want. It's what's best for *you*.'

'And Gordon,' she said bitterly.

'And Eve, and Danny. Maybe even young Rob, though he's been with us all the way.'

'I think you'd better leave,' Jo said stiffly, watching Col's expression change before he turned away.

'If that's what you want.'

He rose and left, his wine still untouched.

Jo sat stock still listening to the sound of the car engine disappear into the distance. Scout padded up to her and put one paw on her lap.

'Oh, Scout,' she said in despair. 'What have I done?'

Thirty-nine

'Hey!' Col was surprised to see Gordon at his door so early on a Sunday morning.

'Where is she?' Gordon blundered past him and stopped in the hallway as if unsure which way to go.

'Good morning to you, too,' Col said, his heart thumping. If all had been well, Jo could have been lying upstairs in bed waiting for him to bring up their morning coffee, before climbing back into bed with her. But, more likely, he wouldn't have been here at all. They'd have been cosied up out at Jo's house – the one Gordon still referred to as home.

The gurgle and hiss of the coffee maker reminded him what he'd been doing when the doorbell rang. 'Coffee? I presume by 'she' you're referring to Jo. She's not here. Come through.' He led the way into the sun-filled kitchen.

Gordon gazed around, clearly seeing all the reminders of Alice.

'Sorry, mate. I thought… Eve said…' Gordon raked a hand through his hair. 'Oh, hell. I don't know where I am or what I'm doing.'

'Eve said something that made you think you'd find your ex-wife here?'

'Yeah. Coffee smells good. Thanks.' He took the proffered mug bearing the golf club logo and leant against the sink, his bulk almost dwarfing Col.

'Sit down.'

He did, taking a sip of the steaming liquid. 'Thanks,' he said again. 'They don't know how to make decent stuff at the Crown and it's only instant in my room.'

'You're still there, then?'

'Where else, until… So, you and Jo – it's all a furphy? Eve seemed to think…' he blustered.

'As you can see, there's only me here.' Col held his hands wide, thankful Jo had shown him the door. Or was he? Gordon had to know sometime. He couldn't continue to live in a fool's paradise where the ex-wife welcomed the erring husband home with open arms.

Col decided to change the subject. 'So, dinner at Eve's. How was it?'

'Not good, mate. I set it up so I could tell her about Sally, maybe arrange to introduce the girls – they're about the same age.'

'But…?'

'She'd invited Danny too. So, there I was with the four of them – Eve and Brad, Danny and Kylie. And that Kylie, she has a sharp tongue.' He shook his head and took a gulp of coffee. 'I don't know what I was thinking, but Eve!'

'She didn't take kindly to the idea?'

'That's putting it mildly. You'd have thought I was an axe murderer. She accused me of… Oh, you don't want to know.'

'And Danny?'

'He didn't say much. His wife made up for him. Talk about strident! You'd have thought it was her who was the wronged wife.'

'Hmm.' Poor Gordon. It seemed everyone was against him. He didn't deserve this. He might have acted unwisely, okay, like a fool, but they were his kids, and Jo had been his wife.

'Do you think…' Gordon swirled the remaining coffee in his mug. 'Do you think I have a chance with Jo? Will she take me back? I know I don't deserve it – don't deserve her, but it would go a long way to resolving the issues with Eve at least. Not too sure about Danny. That wife of his has a bee in her bonnet about…'

Col stopped listening. He was the last person to advise Gordon on this subject.

Jo! The woman who was balm to his soul, who'd made him come alive again after losing Alice, who'd brought him out of the darkness, who'd… who'd told him to leave, he remembered. And *he* was the one who'd precipitated it with his stupid idea of making her life less complicated.

'Col?'

His friend was looking at him askance.

'Did you hear what I said?'

'Sorry, I was miles away. Better tell me again. Promise I'll be all ears this time.'

'I was talking about Jo. I was a fool to leave her, a fool to do all the stuff I did over the years. She deserved better. I've learnt my lesson.'

He sounded sincere. Col wondered how it would be if Jo and Gordon did get back together. It would break his own heart, but perhaps would be for the best. They'd been friends and partners for a long time; their children were the ones he and Alice had never had.

'Your call, mate. There's something I wanted to say to you, too.'

'Yes?' Gordon appeared surprised.

'I've been thinking about it for a while, but turning sixty convinced me it's time to take things easier. I'm planning to retire.'

'Retire? But we're the same age.'

'We are. But seeing Alice…' Col swallowed. 'It taught me we need to make the most of the time we have.' This much was true, and Col *had* planned to retire – but those plans had included Jo. He sent her a mental apology. 'We never know how many years we have left. I know you have enough going on in your life without this added complication, but it's time.'

Gordon blinked rapidly, shaking his head as if in denial. 'I can see how Alice's death might have made you think of the future but… Your health is fine, isn't it?'

'And I intend to make sure it remains so.'

'But…' Gordon blustered, his own challenges seemingly forgotten, '…what about you just take time off? A few weeks, even months? See how things pan out?'

Col could see Gordon's mind working overtime. Would he have to buy Col out of the practice? Would Col remain in Granite Springs? He knew the latter would be impossible if Gordon and Jo reconciled. He wouldn't be able to bear seeing them together, knowing… feeling…

'No,' he said decisively. 'I need to make a complete break.'

He felt guilty he'd kept his relationship with Jo hidden from his best friend, but was mindful of her wishes and fearful of Gordon's reaction should he discover it was true she'd moved on – and with Col. It was better to do it this way – better for all of them.

Forty

The early morning chorus from the kookaburras came as a relief. Jo hadn't slept all night, hearing the clock in the living room chime every hour. Her eyes were bleary when she stumbled through to the kitchen to let Scout out at the crack of dawn. She felt like death warmed up, as her mother would say. She stood in the open doorway in the half-light, inhaling the scent of the lemon gum trees and watching the dog make his morning pilgrimage round the fence line, stopping occasionally to make his mark, before returning eagerly for the breakfast he knew was his due.

With her dog fed and watered, Jo made herself tea and toasted a slice of bread she doubted she could stomach. As she sat, curled up in an old armchair, her cup cradled in both hands, she wondered how dinner at Eve's had been last night. Had Gordon managed to mollify his son and daughter regarding the unexpected – and unintended – addition to the family? How had Danny reacted?

And how was Col this morning? She almost picked up the phone before remembering… Jo shivered, although the house was warm. She should have been waking up in Col's arms this morning, planning a lovely day together, discussing the chaos of her family. Instead, she'd sent him off, pretended it was for the best. She sighed and decided to shower and dress, then call over to see Rob and Steve. They wouldn't have left for the restaurant yet. She knew they'd welcome her, listen to her woes and offer sympathy.

*

Leaving a sad-eyed Scout to mind the house, Jo drove off. The house had seemed too large again this morning – something she hadn't felt since she and Col… no, she mustn't think of him. She focussed on her family. Eve – how was she this morning? Would she welcome a call from her mother, or would it seem too invasive? What had matters come to that she worried about whether or not her daughter would welcome hearing from her?

Jo was pulling up outside Rob and Steve's renovated cottage a few streets back from the river when her phone buzzed. Danny's face flickered on the screen. So early? She sighed and pressed to accept his call.

'Hello, darling. I know you were at Eve's last night,' she said to forestall what he might have to say.

'You knew?'

So, he was focussing on Gordon's act of infidelity? Maybe Eve hadn't shared anything about Jo and Col. His next words disabused her of that notion.

'And you and Uncle Col? Who'd have thought? What a dark horse.'

Jo wondered whether he was referring to her or Col. How was she to handle this, now that she and Col were – what? Over? They couldn't be. She needed to talk to Col, too. But best to give him time to simmer down – and time for her to work out how to apologise for her appalling lapse of judgement.

'Your dad,' she said.

'Eve's furious. She's always been Dad's favourite – the only girl. Now she's not – the only girl, I mean. Dad says…'

Jo pricked up her ears. She was keen to hear what Gordon had said, how he'd explained it away. He'd always been good at that, papering over things he didn't want to discuss.

'He says he wants us to meet her.'

Jo drew in her breath. Even for Gordon, surely this was expecting too much?

'And how do you feel about that?'

'I don't have any feelings. Kylie thinks it's a good idea. She's curious. Maybe this woman is just out for what she can get. Dad's pretty well-heeled and…'

'From what I've heard, she's not looking for money.'

'She would say that. Kylie thinks we should suss her out. There's the boys' inheritance to consider.'

Trust Kylie – always looking at the bottom line.

'I think you should be there, too.'

'Me? Oh, darling I don't think so.' Jo couldn't think of anything worse. She was about to finish the call, seeing Rob's face at the open door, when Danny said, 'and about Uncle Col… good on you.'

Jo almost choked. To be given the okay for another relationship by her ultra-conservative son was a shock. But, as she hung up and waved to Rob to indicate she'd be right with him, it occurred to her it would probably suit Danny and Kylie just fine if she and Col got together and moved into Col's house in town.

'Mum, good to see you. What brings you here?' Rob pulled her into a warm hug and drew her inside. 'Just in time for coffee, and Steve's taking a batch of his famous chocolate brownies out of the oven.'

'Hi, Mum,' Steve greeted her, with another hug. Jo loved the way he'd taken to calling her Mum. His own mother had passed away a few years earlier and he'd asked if Jo would be his honorary mum. She'd been delighted to agree, telling him he could be her third son.

Jo felt so welcome in this house, with no need for subterfuge or worrying about giving offence by saying the wrong thing.

'It's so good to see you two. I needed a dash of your positive vibes this morning.'

Jo saw the pair exchange a warning glance. 'What? Is there something I don't know?'

'Not sure.' Rob filled three mugs with coffee, then placed three chocolate brownies, still warm from the oven, on a plate and pushed it towards Jo. 'We had a guest at the restaurant last night who says she's my sister.'

'Oh!' A part of Jo had wondered how long it would be before this Sally took matters into her own hands. 'And?'

'That's it. But she looked a lot like the old photos of Grandma Slater, and her eyes… Has Dad been playing away?'

'Rob!' Steve cautioned.

'Well, that's what it amounts to, isn't it? Question is, did you know, Mum?'

'Not at the time.' Jo was tired of answering this question. It had been so long ago. Rob hadn't even been born.

'I'm sorry, Mum.' Rob enfolded her in a warm embrace designed to assure her of his undivided love. 'He's an asshole.'

'You shouldn't talk about your father that way,' Jo objected, but knew her tone didn't convey any certainty. It would serve Gordon right if he alienated all three of their children. But, now he'd left – or been thrown out – by Carol, who would he have, other than this newfound daughter?

'Where's Uncle Col? He's not with you this morning?'

Jo swallowed. She should have known Rob would pick up on this. 'No. We're having, what do you call it – a break?'

'Uh oh. Doesn't sound good. Does Dad have anything to do with it? All this talk of his about *returning home*.'

'Maybe,' she said carefully. Gordon's comments may have been the catalyst, but was there more to it? Had it all happened too quickly?

'I know,' Steve said, coming round to Jo's side of the table, a brownie in one hand, his mug in the other. 'What you need is time out. Why don't you put your feet up here today, then pop over to the restaurant for dinner? We're never too busy on a Sunday. Meantime, I'll call over to Yarran to make sure Scout has a walk and is fed.'

'I don't think…' Jo began and tried to rise, but Rob pushed her gently back down. The thought of doing nothing all day, then eating a lovely meal she didn't have to prepare was an attractive proposition. 'If you're sure,' she said weakly.

'We're sure,' Rob replied.

*

Jo stretched and opened her eyes to absolute silence. It took her a moment to remember where she was, then she recognised the sofa she was lying on, a fine wool throw carefully placed over her legs. She was at Rob and Steve's. She'd been asleep and the light was beginning to fade. What time was it?

As she struggled to rise, the door opened a crack to reveal Steve's cheerful face.

'You're awake.'

'I fell asleep. What time is it?' she peered around, then at her wrist, trying to see her watch.

'You were exhausted, so we decided to let you sleep. Rob's gone to the restaurant, and I was about to leave. There's no rush,' he said as she tried to rise again before falling back against the cushions. 'You can lock up here and come when you're ready.'

'I…' Jo put a hand to her forehead, recalling their earlier conversation. She was to dine at The Riverside.

'How about I make you a nice cup of tea before I go? The jug's boiling. Earl Grey?'

'Lovely.' Jo sat up. How could she have slept away most of the day? She guessed her lack of sleep last night had caught up with her. She pushed a hand through her hair. She'd need to smarten herself up before dinner. The tea would help.

Once Steve had left, Jo sat quietly sipping the refreshing tea, and nibbling on one of the thin chocolate digestive biscuits he'd provided. She was hungry. She'd completely missed lunch but knew dinner at The Riverside would more than make up for it.

She finally roused herself sufficiently to make her way to the cloakroom where she refreshed her makeup and tidied her hair. She glanced down at the outfit she'd hastily dressed in this morning – the straight-legged washed denim pants and matching jacket covering a white skivvy was hardly the outfit she'd have chosen for dining out. But it would have to do.

Feeling refreshed by her long nap, Jo decided to walk to the restaurant and pick her car up later. The fresh air completed the effect of her long snooze, and she was feeling invigorated as she pushed open the large glass door and breathed in the familiar aroma. Although Steve had taken over her front-of-house duties here, she was still co-owner and felt part of the place. She nodded acknowledgement to familiar members of staff as she made her way to the table in the back corner which was always reserved for family.

As she studied the blackboard menu, Jo's eyes roamed around the room. Despite Rob's assurance that Sundays weren't busy, she noted most of the tables were occupied, a sign the drought was finally over, and people were feeling confident enough to spend money again.

Relieved this signalled a successful future for Rob – and herself – Jo concentrated on deciding what to order.

'Mum! You're looking better – more rested.' Rob appeared at her side and kissed her on the cheek. 'We have a special lamb dish which I know you'll love. Maybe you'd also like the Moreton Bay Bug and Prawn entrée?

'No entrée for me.' Jo had never been a fan of Moreton Bay bugs though she knew many found them to be a delicacy. 'But,' she checked the menu reading, *Roasted lamb backstrap, slow cooked belly, charred zucchini, buckwheat, black garlic labna,* 'the lamb sounds delicious.'

'Steve'll be out in a sec with a glass of wine for you.' Rob disappeared again, to be replaced almost immediately by Steve with the promised wine.

'You're spoiling me, boys,' Jo smiled, taking a sip of the wine she immediately recognised as one of her favourite shiraz blends.

'You deserve it.' Steve disappeared again.

This would be perfect if only Col was sitting opposite, Jo thought, before dismissing it as wishful thinking. *She* was the one who'd told him to leave and *she* was the one who had to apologise.

Jo was still regretting her words when she noticed a familiar figure entering the restaurant followed by a tall dark woman who was a stranger. She watched Steve show them to a table and the man take a seat with his back to her. What was Gordon doing here and who was his companion? Could it be his newfound daughter?

'Your meal, Mrs Slater.' The young waitress placed the dish carefully on the table, the garlic aroma wafting up to tease her taste buds.

'Thanks. Could you ask Rob to come to speak with me for a moment?'

'What is it, Mum? Something wrong with your meal?' Rob's forehead creased.

'Your dad's just walked in with a young woman. Is she…?' Jo gestured towards the couple who were now studying their menus.

Rob's eyes moved in the direction Jo indicated and nodded. 'That's her. A bit blatant of him to bring her here tonight.'

'I suppose they have to eat, and this is the best restaurant in town.' But Jo agreed with her son. What was Gordon thinking? The answer was, he wasn't thinking – he never did.

Although conscious of the pair's presence, Jo didn't allow it to spoil her meal, even deciding to complete it with the restaurant's signature dessert dish of passionfruit soufflé with vanilla crème fraiche, white chocolate, and passionfruit curd.

It was only when she'd finished and refused the offer of coffee, that she picked up her bag and made her way over to them.

'Good evening, Gordon,' she said, pleased to see the surprise on his face. 'Are you going to introduce me?'

'Jo,' he blustered, 'I didn't know you were here. This is Sally. She's… my daughter.'

Jo turned to face the embarrassed woman who, as Rob said, bore a striking resemblance to Gordon's mother.

'Hello, Sally,' Jo smiled. 'So you're my ex-husband's newly-found daughter. And I understand you met one of my sons last night?'

Sally dropped her eyes. 'Yes. I was curious. I heard this restaurant was owned by two of the Slaters and I wanted to see…' her voice trailed off.

'You were here last night?' Gordon stared at her incredulously.

Sally looked even more embarrassed. 'Sorry, I should have told you. Sorry,' she repeated, raising her eyes to meet Jo's.

Jo drew in a startled breath. Not only did Sally resemble her late mother-in-law, the wide dark eyes which met hers were identical to the eyes she'd fallen in love with all those years ago. This child of Gordon's was more like him than any of his legitimate offspring.

'You look very like your father,' she said drily.

'Yes.' Sally's eyes dropped to the table where she fiddled with her cutlery.

'Doesn't she?' Gordon said, the note of pride evident in his voice. 'Why don't you join us for coffee?'

'No, I have to go.' Jo gave an insincere smile and moved towards the door, where Rob joined her and gave her a heartfelt hug.

'You met her? What do you think?'

'She's definitely your father's daughter,' Jo said, her voice muffled by the hug, her thoughts going to her daughter.

How would Eve ever forgive her dad for this?

Forty-one

'Have you thought this through?' Col peered at his partner across the desk.

Gordon had arrived in the office full of a plan to get his children together – all four of them. He pulled on one ear. 'Probably not,' he said, 'but they need to accept Sally, and if they meet each other… She's already met Rob – and Jo,' he added reflectively. 'We went to The Riverside for dinner last night.'

'Hmm.' Col wished he'd been there. He should have been. If only… But it was done now. He'd made his decision.

'What about you? You're still bent on retiring?' Gordon asked.

'Yes. I'm thinking I'll head north around the end of June. That should give me time to settle things here, and the end of the financial year would make good business sense.'

'You're really leaving town?' Gordon's eyes widened.

'There's nothing to keep me here,' Col lied, seeing his partner mentally process his reply, which was designed to dismiss any doubts Gordon might have had, dispel the rumours he'd heard about Col and Jo.

'Right.' Gordon walked out, leaving Col with the decision he'd forced himself to make, telling himself it was for the best; he was doing it for Jo and her family – even for Gordon.

He puzzled over it all afternoon, finally deciding it was all too hard, before packing up early. As usual, on his way to the car he passed the real estate office of an old school friend, and a sudden impulse took him inside.

'You're a stranger,' Ken greeted him. 'Looking for an investment property, or can I finally persuade you to part with your lovely home?'

Ken had contacted Col when Alice died, thinking he'd want to downsize from the large family home they'd enjoyed all their married life. At that time, it was as much as Col could do to be civil to the guy. But now it was a different matter.

'What's the market like at the moment?' he asked, not really wanting to know, hoping for a negative response.

'Picking up,' Ken replied. 'There's been a bit of a demand for old places like yours and Alice's.' He coughed, perhaps wondering if he'd said the wrong thing.

'So if – only if, mind you. If I was to put my place on the market…'

'You'd be pretty certain of a buyer.' Ken's face visibly brightened at the thought of securing Col's property. 'Are you…?'

'Thinking about it – yes. I'll be in touch.' Col walked out. His phone buzzed, and he checked to see several missed calls from Jo. Tempted to reply, he hesitated, before returning the phone to his pocket. If he was to do this, he needed to be strong, and hearing Jo's voice would weaken his resolve. He continued to where he'd parked his car, got in, and drove home.

But, once there, he was unsettled. He wandered around the house, picking up objects and laying them down again – the large cone shell Alice had found on the beach on their honeymoon at Great Keppel Island, their wedding photo which still sat opposite the bed, the polished wooden box she'd given him on his fiftieth birthday and they'd laughed that it would hold his ashes. It never occurred to them back then that she'd be the first to go.

'Am I doing the right thing, Alice?' he asked. He'd been convinced she approved of his relationship with Jo, welcomed it even, if that were possible. But now… He shook his head, wishing she could answer him.

He poured himself a beer and turned on the computer, finding himself browsing real estate sites for Queensland. When Alice was alive, they'd often talked of retiring there – to Noosa or Yeppoon, places where they'd enjoyed holidays. After she'd gone, he'd chosen to stay in Granite Springs close to old friends. But maybe now things were different? Could he settle in a new place all by himself? Was he too old to pull up his roots and start again?

What if the alternative was to remain here and watch Gordon and Jo together? He knew he couldn't bear it.

Finally, he opened an accommodation site. It wouldn't do any harm to go up north for a few weeks, sound things out, check out a few of the homes for sale. That didn't commit him to anything, and it would get him away from here and out of Gordon's hair.

Half an hour later, he closed the application. He'd booked accommodation in a luxury hotel at Airlie Beach – a place that held good memories – for the beginning of July. That should provide ample time to put everything in motion here, then he could put this whole sorry mess behind him.

Forty-two

Jo gazed at the FOR SALE sign in dismay. What had Col done? What had *she* done? She'd spent the past two days trying to reach him to no avail, before deciding to drop round. Now it looked as if he'd been avoiding her. She was torn. Did she walk up to the door and demand an answer or turn away and go home, tail between her legs?

No. She'd come here to see Col. With a leaden feeling in the pit of her stomach, she walked up the path to the front door and rang the bell. This was a house she knew almost as well as her own, but she'd never approached it with such trepidation. As she waited on the doorstep, seeing the outline of a figure coming towards her through the stained glass, it occurred to her that Gordon might still be here. How would she explain away her presence if it was her ex-husband who answered the door?

Then she exhaled. There was nothing surprising about her dropping in on an old friend.

The door opened.

'Col!'

'Jo!'

They stood looking at each other, then Col moved aside. 'You'd better come in.'

Not exactly the welcome she'd been expecting, though what had she expected?

'Tea or…?' he asked.

'A glass of wine would be good.' Jo followed him into the kitchen. She needed something stronger than tea.

While Col removed a bottle of white wine from the fridge and two glasses from a cupboard, Jo gazed around the room. It was the same kitchen it had always been. Nothing had changed – except the atmosphere. She took a seat on one of the high stools by the kitchen bench, her feet on the bar, and pulled back her shoulders. She could do this.

'I saw the sign,' she said.

'Oh, yes.' Col placed one glass in front of Jo and took a gulp from the other, remaining standing on the other side of the bench.

'When did you decide to sell?' she asked. Then, losing all semblance of the calm she was attempting to display, she added in a broken voice, 'How could you?'

'It's *my* house,' Col replied in a measured tone which infuriated her. 'And I did mention I was thinking of retiring.'

'But…' His retirement was to have been *their* time together. Col sounded like a stranger. Was this the same man she'd known almost all her life? The man who'd made such passionate love to her only days ago? The man with whom she'd imagined having a future? She could feel tears come to her eyes and blinked rapidly. She wouldn't cry. She wouldn't.

'Why?' Jo knew she sounded weak. She couldn't believe Col would make such a decision without talking with her about it. Surely she deserved that, at least?

He put down his glass and leant on the benchtop, both hands flat on the surface.

'It's no good, Jo. You must have realised it, too, when you told me to leave. Your life is complicated enough without *me*. It's best I get out of Granite Springs. Leave you and Gordon to work things out without me around. Your children need you right now – Eve, especially. I'm going away for a bit.'

Jo stared at him, feeling the colour draining from her face. She turned away, a hand going to her mouth. She felt dizzy. She couldn't speak.

'Are you all right?' Col's eyebrows drew together.

'I will be.' Jo took a swallow of her wine which suddenly tasted bitter. 'I should go.' She tried to slip off the stool and almost fell.

Col moved quickly to support her. 'You can't go like this. Let me get you some tea.'

'No.' She shook off his hands, finding a resolve she hadn't thought herself capable of. 'I'm fine,' she said, uttering the words of so many women over the ages. But she was far from fine, and the touch of his hands reawakened the feelings she thought she'd managed to quash.

About to leave, she turned to face him. 'I can't believe you'd do this. I trusted you. I thought…' She choked back the tears as she pushed past and out of the house.

Driving away from Col's, Jo called herself all sorts of a fool – a fool to have fallen under his spell, a fool to have believed his lies, for that's what they must have been, a fool for imagining life had anything more to offer her.

She was heading home when she realised she couldn't bear her own company, that if she went home, she'd spend a sleepless night in tears. Changing direction, Jo made her way instead to Kay's house on the other side of town.

*

'What's the matter?' Kay appeared surprised to see Jo at her door. Jo knew she must look dreadful. The tears she'd managed to stem while at Col's had begun to fall as she drove, almost blinding her. And she knew her hair had begun to fall out of its carefully structured topknot.

She pushed past her friend, ending up in the kitchen where she slumped into a chair. 'I should have listened to you,' she wailed. 'You were right. It was too soon – far too soon. I should have realised…' She burst into tears again, using the back of her hand to wipe them away.

Kay silently handed her a box of tissues and took a bottle of wine from the fridge.

Jo waved it away. The wine she'd drunk at Col's was still sitting uneasily in her stomach.

'Coffee?' Kay mouthed.

Jo nodded. It would keep her awake, but she knew she wasn't going to get much sleep anyway.

'Now,' Kay said, when they were both clasping mugs of black coffee, 'Are you going to tell me what's happened?'

'Col's leaving town,' Jo's voice was almost incoherent, 'He's put his house up for sale and he won't talk to me.'

Kay's eyes widened. 'But… I thought you and he…? What…?'

'Oh, it's everything.' Jo hiccupped and slowly tried to explain the events of the past few weeks – Gordon's ridiculous demands, the daughter appearing out of the blue, Eve's pregnancy, Rob and Steve's forthcoming nuptials, Col's sudden coolness. 'And I told him to leave,' she finished with a sob. I know, I know. It sounds like a soap opera. But it's real life – *my* life.' She sniffed.

'Are you sure? I can't believe that of Col,' Kay said, putting a reassuring hand on Jo's arm.

'I know what I heard.' Jo's voice rose. She clenched her hands into fists. 'You weren't there.'

'No.' Kay seemed to give the matter some thought. 'But it doesn't sound like Col. There must be a reason.'

'He went on and on about Gordon and the kids.' Jo put a hand up to her hair which was threatening to fall around her shoulders. 'He seemed to care more about them than about me.'

'I'm sure that's not the case.'

'What is it with you?' Jo demanded. '*You* were the one who told me it was too soon for Col to start a new relationship. It seems you were right.'

Jo waited for Kay to reiterate her warning. But, to her surprise, her friend said, 'No, I don't think I was. I admit I did think so at the time. I was shocked. But… I've seen you glowing, begin to live again, and… I was wrong. I can see you and Col are good for each other. Men are different. They – at least Col – seem to bounce back quicker – or they have trouble being on their own.'

'Well, *you've* certainly changed your tune.' Jo wasn't sure what she'd expected when she decided to come here. Had she wanted Kay to tell her it was all for the best? Maybe. She certainly hadn't expected her friend to defend Col. She looked at the coffee which was turning cold. The thought of it made her feel sick.

'I should go,' she said, rising. There was nothing for her here either.

But as she left, she heard Kay call after her, 'Why don't you talk with Gordon? I bet you he has the answer.'

The answer to what, Jo wondered as she stumbled out, almost tripping on the step.

Then, as if in response to her question, her phone buzzed, and there was Gordon's face on the screen.

Forty-three

Reluctantly, Jo agreed to Gordon's suggestion they all meet at Yarran, noting Carol's name was conspicuous by its absence. She wished he'd chosen they meet somewhere else and had left her out of it, but could understand how her presence might be able to counteract the inevitable awkwardness of the occasion.

Gordon had lost the plot. Surely he could see how Eve would react? And did he still harbour hopes Jo would let him return? Well, she'd soon disabuse him of that idea.

Poor Scout bore the brunt of her anger as she stormed around the house. First Col's defection, now Gordon's peremptorily demands. She stopped suddenly in the midst of loading the washing machine. Could the two be connected? Then she shook her head fiercely. No way! Col wouldn't be party to Gordon's plotting. But would he?

Jo remembered what Kay had said. She'd been so sure Gordon knew something. But she couldn't be right. Col and Gordon were friends, went way back. And they'd been business partners for years, too. But Gordon knew nothing about Col and her. A chill crept over Jo at the thought of them discussing her. No! Col wouldn't. She could believe it of Gordon, but not Col. He'd always been the more straightforward of the two – honest as the day was long.

But he *was* leaving. There was no getting away from that fact.

Jo sighed, slammed the door closed and pressed the start button. 'Come, Scout,' she said to the dog. 'We need some fresh air.'

Once out in the lane with the fragrance of the lemon scented gum trees in her nostrils, Jo could almost forget her worries. Scout moved sluggishly in front of her, sniffing in every nook and cranny and forcing the galahs, feasting on stray ears of wheat, to rise in fright. Jo laughed, knowing the old dog was no danger to them.

Jo was lost in her thoughts when the sound of her name brought her back to the present. She looked up to see Magda striding towards her accompanied by her two greyhounds. The three dogs sniffed each other then, clearly recognising an old friend, Magda's two ran off while Scout settled down at Jo's feet.

'You look troubled,' Magda said without preamble. 'Is Col not treating you properly? Do you want me to have a word with him?'

'Oh, Magda!' Jo embraced her old friend. 'If it were that easy. It's over.'

'Over? But how can that be? If ever I saw a man in love, it's your Col.'

When? Then Jo remembered. Magda had bumped into them dining one Thursday a few weeks earlier. She'd been very discrete, only saying hello before going to her own table. But Jo had noticed her eyes kept returning to the corner where she and Col were seated.

'Not anymore, Magda. He's planning to leave town.'

Magda's eyebrows rose. 'What has your ex-husband been up to now?'

'He's been up to a lot. But Col seems to have made the decision to leave town all by himself. He won't even talk to me about it.'

'Come back with me for a cuppa and I'll read the leaves.'

Jo was startled. She'd forgotten the other string to Magda's bow. She took advantage of her friend's skills in massage but, in all the years she'd known her, had refused to have her attempt to predict her future. Today was no exception. 'No. Thanks, Magda. It is what it is, and I need to cope with it. But tea sounds good.'

The two women ambled along the lane together, the dogs following, till they reached Magda's cottage. Once inside, Magda made sure all three dogs had water and treated them to a doggy treat, before turning on the electric jug.

'I think camomile,' she said, with a glance at Jo. 'It will calm you.'

About to object, Jo closed her mouth. She did need something to calm her if she was to prepare herself for this fiasco Gordon had in mind. She wondered if Gordon had spoken to their children yet. No doubt she'd soon… She hadn't finished the thought when her phone buzzed – two texts arrived one after the other.

Just spoken to Dad. Is he for real? Call me. Eve

Can't wait to hear Dad's latest plans. Danny

Jo closed her phone with a sigh.

'Trouble?' Magda placed the tea, served in a beautiful vintage-styled cup and saucer, on the table.

Jo sighed again. 'There will be. Bloody Gordon and his ideas.'

'What's he done now?'

Jo realised Magda didn't know. 'This woman has turned up out of the blue. Seems she's his daughter. And he wants everyone to meet her. At Yarran. On Sunday.'

'And Eve and Danny? And the lovely Rob? How are they?'

'That's the problem. Eve's devastated and Danny… I guess he'll take on whatever opinion Kylie has – and that'll depend on what's best for Kylie. Rob's already met her and seems cool with it.'

'And you?'

'I've met her too. She seems a nice girl. It's not her fault. She just wants a family.'

'Her mother?'

'Died recently.'

'So Gordon has welcomed her with open arms? Carol?'

'I'm not sure she knows. It's all a big mess.'

'And he still wants to return?'

Jo nodded.

*

Sunday dawned as a perfect autumn day. The air cool, the sun shining, and a slight breeze ruffled the leaves of the large peppercorn tree in the home paddock. The children all arrived before their father and Sally, and Jo brewed tea while they were waiting. But no one was interested in drinking it, and the plate of brownies she'd risen early to bake remained untouched. *You could cut the atmosphere with a knife*, she thought, as she took a sip of her own drink and gazed around the table.

Brad had taken the children and Scout out into the paddock to keep them occupied. It seemed he didn't feel this was anything to do with him, though he'd have to live with the fallout for Eve if lunch didn't go well. Steve and Rob, who'd taken time off from the restaurant, were trying valiantly to keep some conversation going, while Kylie was uncharacteristically silent. Danny was checking his phone, no doubt hoping for some sign he could escape, and Eve was fidgeting, unable to keep still.

They all heard the car at the same time.

'They're here.' Eve half-rose, then subsided again, her face flushed.

Jo wanted to rush round the table to hug her daughter, to remind her she still loved her, that this new woman wouldn't make her dad love her less. But she managed to restrain herself. It was up to Gordon to decide how to handle this. She was merely providing the venue – and the lunch, she reminded herself, thinking of the quiches, vegetable lasagne and salads waiting in the fridge.

They heard footsteps. Then all eyes turned towards the door as Gordon slid it open and walked in followed by the tall, dark-haired woman. Jo heard the combined intake of breath as they noted the unmistakable resemblance. She risked a glance at Eve who'd turned white, then at Kylie who wore a self-satisfied smile. For a moment Jo wondered, then she realised that Sally, with her unfashionable jeans and shirt, shoulder-length un-styled hair and face free of makeup, posed no threat to her immaculate daughter-in-law.

'Hello everyone. Thanks for coming.' Gordon made no attempt to kiss or hug any of their three children.

Jo tightened her lips. This was not a good start.

'This is Sally,' he continued, seemingly unaware of the atmosphere in the room, 'your new sister.'

You could have heard a pin drop, then Steve said, 'Good to meet you again, Sally. This must all be a bit strange for you. You've already met Rob and me. This fellow beside me is Danny, next to him his wife, Kylie and then Eve.'

Sally smiled awkwardly.

Jo was first of them to regain her composure. 'Sally, Gordon. Would you like some tea?'

'Thanks.' Sally appeared relieved.

'Any beer?' Gordon asked, taking a seat beside Danny and slapping him on the shoulder. 'How's it going, old son?' he asked, as if this was an ordinary Sunday lunch.

'Take a seat, Sally,' Jo said, rising to fetch another cup and a can of beer for Gordon. She was tempted to pour it over his head. How dare he set this up, then be so blind to the tensions he'd created? But that was Gordon all over. She should have known better than to expect anything else from him. He'd always been good at setting up situations, then letting other people diffuse them.

When she returned to the table, it was to find Rob had pulled out a chair for Sally between him and Steve, isolating her from Gordon who was seated opposite and was now engaged in conversation with Danny while Kylie looked bored.

'I'll check on the twins.' Eve pushed back her chair and rushed outside, forcing Gordon to break from his conversation.

'Eve,' he called after her, but she appeared not to hear.

'This is a lovely house you have,' Sally said to Jo, clearly embarrassed by the disturbance her arrival caused. 'Gordon… Dad,' she corrected herself awkwardly, 'told me about it – how you both built it together.' Her eyes flickered towards Gordon as if seeking his help.

'It's my home and I love it,' Jo said, wondering exactly what Gordon had told Sally.

'Where are you from?' Kylie asked, finally deciding to enter the conversation.

Sally turned towards her. 'Mum and I have always lived in Sydney,' she said. 'But now she's gone, there's nothing to keep me there. I've always had a hankering to live in the country. It's lovely here.'

My God, thought Jo, *she's not thinking of moving to Granite Springs*? She looked at Gordon to see how he was reacting, but he didn't seem to have heard. *Maybe they'd already discussed it.*

'What sort of work do you do?' Kylie seemed determined to find out all she could about this cuckoo in the nest.

'I'm a nurse,' Sally replied easily, 'so I can pick up work wherever and… Dad seems to like the idea.'

I bet he does, but what will it do to Eve?

'I'll organise lunch.' Jo rose and signalled to Rob to follow her. 'Check on Eve,' she whispered into his ear. 'I could strangle your dad. He brings Sally here, then practically abandons her. And has no thought for the three of you.' *At least*, she thought, *he's treating this new daughter with no more consideration than his other children.*

'Danny seems to be okay and Kylie is being her usual self,' Rob murmured, before giving Jo's arm a squeeze and heading outside to follow her instructions.

While she was taking the lunch dishes from the fridge, Jo could hear Steve making conversation with Sally, trying to make her feel more comfortable.

When Rob ushered Eve back in, they were accompanied by Brad and the four children, whose rowdy behaviour made everything feel more normal.

Lunch passed without any antagonism, though it irked Jo that Gordon was behaving as if he belonged there. After the meal, and at Rob's suggestion, he and Steve served coffee on the veranda. Everyone was standing around. Danny and Kylie seemed to be arguing; Jo was talking with Rob, Steve and Sally; Brad was playing ball with the boys; Eve was having words with her father. The twins were running around getting under everyone's feet, when Livvy pulled on their mother's arm.

'Can we have a swim?'

'No, darling. It's too cool today and we didn't bring your swimmers,' Eve replied, before turning back to her dad who was trying to placate her.

'Aww, please!' Livvy pleaded. She pulled on her mother's arm but Eve, intent on her conversation with Gordon, brushed her off.

No one saw her and Lottie heading towards the pool gate and the little arm reaching up.

Suddenly there was a scream.

Everyone turned to see Lottie standing by the pool gate which had swung open. Livvy was nowhere to be seen.

For a moment, it seemed everyone was transfixed, then Sally seemed to take in the scene in an instant. Without hesitating, she ran through the gate and dived into the pool, to emerge, seconds later with a sodden Livvy in her arms. Eve rushed in and attempted to take her daughter, but Sally pushed her away, laid the little girl down on the wet concrete and began to administer CPR.

Forty-four

Jo's hand went to her mouth. She knew she should help, but her legs had turned so weak she thought she was going to fall. Only Rob's comforting presence at her side and Steve's arm around her waist were keeping her upright. Livvy! What if she died? They'd all been so engrossed in their own petty conversations; it hadn't occurred to them she was able to unlock the gate.

Brad picked up Lottie who was sobbing uncontrollably, and put an arm around Eve's shoulders, while they watched Sally anxiously. Eve was rocking on the spot and looked as if she wanted to tear Sally's hair out.

Gordon didn't seem to know what to do. He stared blindly at the rescue going on beside the pool. Danny put his hand on his father's shoulder leaving Kylie to comfort the boys who were asking to 'see what's happened to Livvy.'

Jo could barely breathe herself as she watched Sally try to breathe life into Livvy's inert body. Then she let out a gasp as she saw the little figure move, cough and splutter. She was alive!

Eve rushed towards her daughter and Jo thought she was going to grab her from Sally's arms, but instead she stood over the pair, tears streaming down her cheeks. She watched helplessly as a dripping Sally carried Livvy from the pool area, yelling that they needed to get the little girl to hospital, that she'd hit her head and was probably concussed.

Suddenly it seemed as if everyone was talking at once, and there was a hive of activity. Brad handed Lottie over to Jo, then he escorted a sobbing Eve, and Sally, still carrying Livvy, to his car.

Everyone fell silent as they drove off. Tim asked, 'Will Livvy be all right?'

'Shh,' Kylie adjured, shepherding him and Liam into the house, before appearing again with her bag. 'We should get home, Danny,' she said, her voice unusually subdued.

'Yes.' But Danny sounded distracted, 'Will you be all right, Mum?' he asked Jo.

'I'll stay with your mum till there's news,' Gordon said, and Jo noticed a relieved look appear on her son's face. Tragedy affected people in different ways, and Danny had never been good in times of crisis.

'I'll be fine,' Jo said, as a weeping Lottie slipped from her grasp only to cling to her legs.

'We need to go, too, Mum. The restaurant…' Rob hugged her and whispered, 'Don't let Dad get you down.'

Jo nodded. She knew he had to be at The Riverside for the dinner crowd. But it meant she'd be left alone with Gordon – you couldn't count a five-year-old. She heard a soft snuffle and felt Scout's moist nose pushing into her hand. Looking down, Jo saw her pet's sad eyes peering up at her. Of course, she had Scout, too.

Jo felt chilled as she watched the two cars leave. She uttered a silent prayer for Livvy, then turned to find herself in Gordon's arms, Lottie still clutching her leg. For a moment, she allowed herself to sink into his embrace. It felt so warm, so comforting, so familiar. It would be easy to stay there, to accept what he was offering, to…

She pushed him away.

'Gramma, where have they taken Livvy? Can I go too?' Lottie sobbed.

'Later,' Jo said, crouching down to wipe away her tears. 'Livvy's gone to the hospital so the doctors can make her better. We need to stay here till your mummy and daddy call us. She's going to be all right.' Jo hoped this was the case, though she couldn't dismiss the image of Livvy's pale face and limp body.

Jo picked Lottie up again and carried her inside, Scout padding silently behind them. 'If you're going to stay, you might make yourself useful,' she told Gordon as he followed her into the kitchen where the lunch dishes were still lying around the sink. 'If you can load the dishwasher, I'll put on the electric jug. How about some hot chocolate for you, Lottie?' she asked the still weeping child.

Lottie nodded, sniffing. Jo handed her a tissue. 'You can help me. Let's find that chocolate.'

'Can I have some on a spoon?' Lottie asked, brightening slightly, reminding Jo how resilient the young were.

'Of course you can.'

While Jo saw to Lottie, she could hear Gordon bumbling behind her as he performed the unfamiliar task of loading the dishwasher. Despite her worry, she couldn't help but suppress a faint smile that he obviously hadn't been any more help to Carol around the house than he'd been to her. Unlike Col.

No! She pulled herself up short. That part of her life was over, almost before it had begun.

The tea made, Jo and Gordon sat opposite each other at the kitchen table. Lottie settled beside Scout with her mug of hot chocolate and a biscuit which the dog was eyeing longingly.

Jo checked her phone for the umpteenth time, even though she was well aware there could be no news as yet. Granite Springs Base Hospital was located on the far side of town and they'd barely have reached the Emergency Department. She drummed her fingers on the table.

'Reminds me of when Eve was little and they suspected meningococcal,' Gordon said after a long pause.

Jo glared at him. How did this compare? And how could he bring up that at this of all times, when the woman who was the result of his philandering during her time in hospital was the one who'd saved their granddaughter's life? Some would call it poetic justice. She didn't know what she'd call it.

'Not exactly.'

Her phone buzzed, vibrating on the table. She grabbed it with relief, but it was only Rob asking for news. 'Nothing yet,' she replied and quickly rung off, unwilling to tie up the line.

'It's too bad about Livvy, but she's strong. She'll be right.'

Jo scowled at her ex-husband from below furrowed brows. How

could he make light of what might have cost their granddaughter her life?

'She's strong,' he repeated. 'And let's look at the plus side.'

Plus side? What on earth was he talking about?

'It's given us this time to be together.'

This was a plus? Jo could think of another name for it. Why was he still here? She wished he would leave and… Though did she really? While he was there, she had his presence to irritate her – to prevent her from thinking the unthinkable, from wondering how long Livvy had been without oxygen, from wondering if…

'I'm not sure that's a good thing,' she said, a bitter note in her voice.

'Come on, Jo,' he said in the rallying voice she used to love and now found infuriating. 'Don't be like that, honey. You know we belong together.'

'What about Carol?'

'That was…'

'Another indiscretion?' she asked with the glimmer of a smile. *Poor Carol.*

Before he could reply, Jo's phone vibrated again, this time it was Brad's face on the screen. She seized it, her hand trembling.

'Brad?' Jo's voice was unsteady, her stomach doing somersaults.

'Livvy's going to be all right.'

Jo sagged back in her chair, suddenly feeling giddy. She saw Gordon's eyes on her – a worried expression creasing his brow. She mouthed, 'All good', and listened while Brad explained the prognosis. 'How's Eve?' she asked when Brad had finished, relieved to be told she was holding up well, especially now they had good news.

'Give her a big hug from me,' she said, 'and Livvy when you can.' She hung up and exhaled.

'Was that my daddy?' Lottie looked up from where she'd been playing with Scout, having discovered an old ball of his. She'd been rolling it towards him to have him pat it back with one lazy paw.

'Yes, it was, my sweet,' Jo said, going over to pick her up and hug her. 'And he says Livvy will be fine.' Jo crossed her fingers behind Lottie's back as she spoke. That wasn't exactly what Brad had said but had been the gist of it.

'I know,' Lottie said, sliding down again. Jo gave her a dazed look, then remembered the special psychic connection the twins seemed to have. 'Can we go to see her now?' She glanced up with such a pleading expression, Jo couldn't resist.

'We're off to the hospital,' Jo told Gordon, adding to Lottie, 'We may not be able to see Livvy, but we'll try.'

'We will,' the little girl said with an assurance Jo didn't share.

'I'll need to lock up.' She picked up her keys and stood in the centre of the room waiting for Gordon to leave.

'Are you sure I can't…'

'No! How can I get it through to you? I have no intention of renewing any relationship with you. As far as I'm concerned, anything we had together was dead long ago. We share our children and grandchildren but nothing else.'

Finally, Gordon had the grace to look disconcerted. His shoulders dropped, he pulled on one ear. 'Hmm. Well, then…'

They were at the front door, when Jo realised she'd forgotten her phone.

'Won't be a moment,' she said, leaving Gordon and Lottie together in the hallway. When she returned, Gordon was fidgeting and clearing his throat. He was shaking his head.

'Something wrong?' she asked.

He shook his head again. 'No... I didn't… Nothing.'

There clearly was something the matter, but Jo didn't have the time or the energy to pursue it. If Gordon wanted to share with her, he would, otherwise…

*

When they reached the hospital, Jo was surprised to discover Lottie had been right. When they arrived at the nursing station, the nurse in charge appeared relieved. 'So, this is the one our patient has been pining for?' she asked. 'You can go right in but be careful not to overexcite her. She's recovering well, but still has a long way to go.' She gave Jo directions, and, with a strangely subdued Lottie, Jo made her way along the corridor.

Livvy looked so small, lying in the big bed, Eve and Brad seated on either side. The little girl's eyes were open. She was very pale but seemed to brighten when she saw her twin. Lottie let go of Jo's hand and rushed towards the bed, stopping suddenly when she reached Eve's side.

'Livvy?' she whispered. 'Can I kiss her, Mum?'

'Go ahead.' Eve said. Her face was streaked with tears. 'She's better now.'

Jo raised an eyebrow.

'They were afraid of brain damage, but it seems Sally got to her in time. She saved Livvy's life, Mum,' she said, her voice breaking. 'They're just making sure there isn't any damage to her lungs. She should be able to come home tomorrow, all being well.'

'Where *is* Sally?' Jo asked, remembering that all three had come to the hospital with Livvy.

'She left when we got here, said she wasn't needed and she had to dry off and change her clothes. The poor girl was still soaking wet and shivering. But we need to see her – to thank her. What if she hadn't…? It doesn't bear thinking about. Where's Dad?' she asked, looking past Jo as if expecting Gordon to appear.

'He's not here. We… we had words and… He left when we did. I don't know where he went.' It hadn't occurred to Jo to ask Gordon if he intended to go to the hospital too.

'Typical. He's never where he should be. I saw the way he was with you today, Mum. It was as if he was trying to pretend he'd never left. I feel sorry for Carol. And for Sally.'

'For Sally?'

'I was wrong about her. It's not her fault Dad… She seems nice and she saved Livvy. I was wrong about a lot of things.' She paused, her eyes filling. 'This has made me think and… I'm sorry; sorry about all those things I said about Uncle Col. I know he'd never hurt the girls. And, for a while there, you looked happy – happier than I've seen you for years. If you *are* seeing Uncle Col, it may be a good thing. I realise you and Dad… If it's true about the other women…' She shook her head. 'I wouldn't stand for it if Brad did that to me.'

Jo hugged her daughter, sad it had taken her so long to see sense.

And now it was too late!

Forty-five

The sound of rain battering on the roof matched Col's mood when he opened his eyes on Monday morning. He stretched and rose, his eyes blurry from lack of sleep. Staggering into the kitchen to make coffee, he berated himself as a fool. He needed to forget any dreams he'd had of a future with Jo and get on with his life. But he was finding it difficult. It was almost as if he'd been bereaved for a second time.

To make matters worse, his car wouldn't start, and he was forced to walk to the office. It wasn't far, and a trip he often made on foot in finer weather. But this morning he cursed as he strode along the busy thoroughfare, brandishing an umbrella and managing to step in a couple of puddles as he crossed the wide main street and dodged the oncoming cars. By the time he reached his destination, his shoes and the bottom of his trousers were soaked, and he was in a foul mood.

'Good morning,' Dot greeted him chirpily.

Col grunted.

'Someone get out of bed on the wrong side?' she asked.

He ignored the remark and headed straight for his office. A few minutes later, Dot appeared in the doorway. She had a mug of coffee in one hand and one of his favourite pastries in the other.

'You looked as if you might need these,' she said, placing both on his desk,

Col sighed and drew a hand through his hair. 'Thanks, Dot. Sorry,' he called after her as she backed out. It wasn't Dot's fault he'd made such a hash of his life.

It was lunchtime before he remembered yesterday had been Gordon's much-vaunted meet-his-new-daughter lunch at Yarran. He wondered how it had gone, surprised his partner hadn't already come in to share his success and rub his nose in his reconciliation with Jo.

'Gordon not around?' he asked Dot when, around lunchtime, he'd poked his head into Gordon's office to find it empty.

'Didn't you hear? One of the little girls had an accident yesterday. There was some family do out at Jo's place, and she fell into the pool.'

Dot continued to speak, but Col didn't wait to hear any more. All he could think of was Jo and her lovely twin granddaughters. He took out his phone and pressed the speed dial to connect to Jo. It rang and rang, then went to voicemail. He almost threw his phone down in frustration, before realising that, of course, Jo would be at the hospital – or at Eve's.

He dashed out of the building, his head pounding, unclear where he was headed. He bumped into Gordon on the pavement.

'Steady on, mate. Where's the fire?' Gordon asked.

Surprised to see his friend appear so calm, Col stopped in his tracks and grabbed him by the arm.

'Dot said… one of the twins… what…?'

'Livvy. She'll be fine. Gave us a shock at the time, but…'

Col sagged and pressed his palms to his eyes. He felt the tension drain from his body.

'How's Jo? he asked weakly, too anxious to worry about what Gordon might think.

'We need to talk about her.'

Col felt a curl of fear twist his gut. Not now, not when he'd tried to put it all behind him and made plans to get out of town.

'Just need to check something with Dot,' Gordon said, in a better humour than Col had seen him for some time. 'See you at the RSL in…' he checked his watch, '…twenty minutes?'

Col nodded, but it was several seconds before he felt his legs would carry him. Fortunately, the rain had stopped, and the fresh air began to revive him. Once at the club, he ordered a beer and, gradually, his heart, which had been racing, returned to normal. By the time Gordon arrived, his glass was empty.

'Sorry I took so long. Another?' Gordon pointed to the empty glass.

Col nodded and watched Gordon amble across to the bar as if he had nothing to worry him.

Gordon soon returned with two tall glasses of beer and slid into the seat opposite. He took a long draught, licked his lips and smiled. 'It's been quite a weekend.'

Col flinched. He was eager to hear about Livvy's accident but dreaded what Gordon might have to say about him and Jo. He thought he'd managed to come to terms with the possibility of their reuniting, even set things up to facilitate it. But now the moment had come, Col knew he was far from ready to hear it.

'Let me start at the beginning,' Gordon said, leaning back as if he had all the time in the world. Perhaps he had. It wasn't *his* future that was in tatters.

'The lunch was a tad awkward,' Gordon began, then continued, skimming over the conversations at the meal and Eve's antipathy towards Sally. 'Then,' he said, 'poor wee Livvy managed to get herself through the fence and into the pool. If it hadn't been for Sally's quick thinking…' He shook his head.

'Sally?' Col wondered what Sally had to do with it.

'Sally – my daughter. She's a good girl. Her nursing experience came to the fore. She had the kid out of the water and was performing CPR before any of us realised what had happened.'

'And?'

'They've kept her in hospital to check for any complications, but Sally says she'll be out today.'

'Sally?' Col asked again. He was confused. Why was Sally still in the picture?

'She saved Livvy's life. Eve…' he coughed, '…Eve changed her tune when that happened. Wouldn't be surprised if they became bosom buddies.'

Col thought bosom buddies might be going too far, but he could see how Eve would be grateful to the woman she'd repudiated only a day before.

'And Jo?' Col reverted to his original question.

'Jo. Well… that was a surprise, too. After all your protestations.' He pursed his lips and raised one eyebrow. 'She sent me packing after all the others left and…' There was a strange gleam in his eye. '…that old rain jacket of yours – the one you used to wear to golf. I saw it – or its twin – hanging on the hallstand at Yarran.' He paused as if waiting for Col's reaction.

Col felt a chill go right through him. So that's where he'd left it! He'd been meaning to check around and had forgotten wearing it out to Jo's some time back.

'I…'

'It's okay, mate. Threw me for a bit, I have to say. But it made me realise it's not me Jo wants. You're a dark horse,' he chuckled.

Col's eyes bulged. He couldn't believe his ears. 'You mean…' he stuttered. Had his altruistic action been in vain? Had he and Jo broken up needlessly?

'May the better man win. And Jo seems to think you're the better man. No accounting for taste, though…' he gave a wry smile, '…you always did have a better moral compass than I did. That's why I never guessed… Even when Eve mentioned you both in the same breath, it was easy for me to dismiss the idea as a figment of her overactive imagination. Pregnant woman, you know.' He smirked.

So why was he looking so cheerful?

'I thought… you and her…'

'I did too, mate.' Gordon rubbed his chin. 'But it was a pipe dream. We can't put back the clock.'

'So…?' Col exhaled, stunned at this about-face and wondering what Gordon would do now. He didn't have long to wait.

'The past few weeks… living at the Crown… made me realise I'm no good on my own. Need a woman to keep me on the right track. So…' He took a deep breath, looked sheepish, and added, 'Last night, I went back to see Carol, grovelled a bit, and the upshot is… we're going to give it another go.'

'Well!' This was the last thing Col had expected. 'And she…'

'Oh, she's set all sorts of conditions. I've even agreed she can go off the pill. Keeping my fingers crossed on that one,' he grinned – the old wily Gordon surfacing again. 'Eve would never forgive me if I landed her with yet another sister – or brother.' He took a long draught of his beer.

'So, how about it, Col. Won't you reconsider this retirement idea? I'd be willing to bet you were keen to put a distance between you and my ex-wife, but now…' He cocked his head to one side.

'No. My decision stands.'

Col knew retirement was the right thing – right for him, right for Jo. If they could renew what they had, what they'd begun – maybe he could stay in town. There was no guarantee she'd be willing to take him back after he'd behaved like a thwarted teenager.

But he had to try.

Forty-six

Jo was glad to see the sun rise through the hospital window.

She'd spent all night at Livvy's bedside with Eve, while Brad took Lottie home. Her back ached from the hard hospital chair which hadn't been designed for anyone to sit on for any length of time. But her reward had been Livvy's bright face when her eyes opened this morning. The nurse said they'd be doing a few more tests and, all being well, she could go home later in the day.

Standing up and stretching, Jo was glad she'd soon be able to go home to bed. She felt she could sleep for a week. Maybe coffee would help. Eve had already gone downstairs to see if the café was open.

A nurse bustled in. 'We'll be with your girl for the next little while if you want to take a break,' she said.

Relieved to be excused for a moment, Jo took a trip to the ladies' room and splashed cold water on her face to waken herself up. She was returning to the ward when Eve appeared carrying two coffees and looking flustered.

'What…?'

'Everything's okay. The nurse is with Livvy, so I took the opportunity to freshen up. I hope Brad had a good night's sleep.'

'Not a lot,' Eve yawned. 'But he'll be in later and I'll go home for a bit. Lottie's home. He couldn't persuade her to go to school. I need to close the shop – leave a note on the door. Do you think…?' Her forehead creased.

'I think you'll be taking her home before much longer. The nurse said only a few more checks today, then she'll be right.'

Eve let out a huge sigh of relief, pressed a hand to her heart and muttered, 'Thank God. I was afraid... Brad said she'd be fine – Lottie did, too. I sometimes wonder how she and Livvy can read each other so well – even when they're not together.'

'Twins.'

'Mmm.'

By this time, they'd reached the ward.

'Mum!' Livvy's arms reached out to hug Eve, the sight triggering tears to gather in the corners of Jo's eyes.

It was a few minutes before they parted, by which time Jo had collected herself and managed to drink most of her coffee.

'You can go now, Mum,' Eve said, her voice calmer now she could see Livvy looking so much better. 'You probably need some sleep too. Thanks for staying with me and Livvy. I really appreciate it. These chairs aren't too comfortable.'

'You're right.' Jo felt a spasm shoot up her back and winced. 'If you're sure?'

Eve nodded and turned back to Livvy.

Jo hugged them both, then left, giving up her own thanks for Livvy's recovery and her daughter's reprieve as she rode down in the lift to the ground floor.

*

But once back home, Jo didn't immediately head for bed. First there was Scout to attend to. The poor animal had been left alone all night and he didn't leave her side as she fixed herself some breakfast and filled his bowls with food and water. The toast, liberally spread with ginger and lime marmalade, stuck in her throat, but the cup of Earl Grey tea was welcome after the muddy liquid the hospital called coffee. Maybe a walk would help. She called to Scout and they set off along the familiar lanes.

The house had felt cold and unwelcoming when she walked in from the hospital. She shivered at the thought that – but for the quick actions of Sally – Livvy could have died. Maybe the time had come, she mused. Maybe she should move into town, look for something smaller – though not one of Danny's ultra-modern villas. She'd be closer to the girls, to Eve with the new baby. And Danny could give Kylie what she wanted. Everyone would be happy. But would she?

When she found herself at Magda's gate, Jo hesitated. The open door seemed to beckon her and, seeing Magda's small figure through the window, she pushed open the gate, and let Scout in to sniff around the garden before he slowly followed her to the house.

'I wondered when I'd see you. Is everything all right?' Magda's knowing eyes regarded Jo, while drawing her into the kitchen. It was warm from the Aga and filled with the aroma of freshly-baked bread, reminding Jo of times spent in her grandmother's home as a child.

'Yes and no.' Jo collapsed onto a chair while Scout made his way to the two greyhounds who were lying by the stove.

'It's one of the twins, isn't it? But she'll be fine – back to normal in no time.'

'How…?' Jo began. But she knew. Although it felt weird when her friend revealed her uncanny sense of intuition, over the years she'd learnt to trust it. 'That's part of it,' she said. 'I just got back from the hospital. I was there all night.' Jo went on to explain what had happened.

'And now what you need is a rest, but you're too wound up to fall asleep. Why don't I give you a nice massage, and make some camomile tea, then you need to go home and lie down in a darkened room and… What?' she asked as Jo began to chuckle.

'I was just thinking how this kitchen reminded me of my grandmother's and here you are sounding exactly like her, too.'

'She must have been a wise woman.'

'She was.' Jo could picture the old lady as she was the last time she'd seen her – her face wrinkled, her white hair beginning to thin, but her indomitable spirit shining through, and still handing out advice.

Jo followed Magda into the darkened massage room. She felt better already, breathing in the familiar scent of bergamot, lavender and geranium as she slipped off her outer garments and lay on the narrow bed, hoping she wouldn't fall asleep right here.

The hypnotic movement of Magda's hands didn't quite put her to sleep but did succeed in helping her relax. The feeling continued afterwards while she drank the soothing tea.

'But Livvy's not the only thing bothering you,' Magda said when the tea was almost finished. 'It'll all work out – you'll see.'

This time, Jo felt sure Magda was wrong. *How could it all work out?*

'I think I've finally got Gordon to believe me,' she said. 'But Col – that's over. And I'm thinking maybe I should go along with what Danny wants. What do I need that big house for? This morning it felt…' she shivered, '…so empty.'

'You may find you need it,' Magda said with another of her knowing looks.

Damn the woman! But her words gave Jo food for thought as she and Scout made their way back home.

Forty-seven

The dull buzzing of the phone wakened her. It was still light, but Jo had no idea what time it was. She'd fallen asleep as soon as her head hit the pillow. She reached out and answered without checking the screen. 'Hello.'

'Mum. We're home!' Eve couldn't disguise the relief in her voice.

'Oh, I'm so glad.' Jo pushed herself upright and took a firmer grip of her phone. 'Tell me what the doctor said.'

By the time she finished the call, Jo was wide awake and saw it was almost four o'clock. She rose with a sigh. Time to feed Scout and think about her own dinner. The evening seemed to stretch ahead of her. Empty. Lonely. She hadn't felt like this before she and Col started their relationship, so why did she feel that way now – as if life had no meaning?

She knew she had lots to feel happy about – Livvy's recovery, the new baby, Rob and Steve's wedding, even Eve's change of heart. Why then, did she feel as if something was weighing her down?

Trying to dispel the sense of hopelessness, Jo poured a glass of red wine and began to make shepherd's pie – comfort food that always reminded her of happier times, her own childhood, and the years when her children were small.

But once it was cooked, Jo found her appetite had deserted her. She was unsettled but couldn't pinpoint what the matter was. She picked up the phone.

Half an hour later, Jo parked outside Rob and Steve's home.

Fortunately, Monday was their day home when the restaurant was closed. For a few moments she sat in the car, wondering what she was doing there. The impulse that had made her call her younger son and drive here no longer seemed important. She was tempted to turn around and return home. But all that waited for her there was the large empty house and her loyal Scout.

The light shining out through the fanlight window tempted her inside so, with a sigh, Jo levered herself out of the car.

'Mum!' Rob greeted her at the door with a hug. 'Great news about Livvy. Eve just got off the phone. Have you been round to see her?'

'No, I…' Jo allowed herself to be led into the warm living room where a fire glowed in the cast iron wood stove. 'It's not really cold enough, but we thought it would cheer the place up,' Rob explained. 'Steve has been marking assignments all day and it was getting him down.'

'Jo!' Steve rose to greet her, scattering a pile of papers in the process. 'Oops! It'll take me forever to put these back in order again.' He gathered them into an untidy bundle and slid them onto the coffee table.

'I didn't mean to interrupt…'

'You didn't. It was time he took a break,' Rob said, smiling at his partner. 'He works too hard. Now, what can I get you? Wine? Coffee? Tea?'

'Tea would be nice.' Jo was aware she'd have to drive home again and had barely eaten anything all day.

'You don't mind if we finish off the wine we had with dinner?'

'Not at all.'

'So if you haven't been to see Eve's lot, what brings you into town on a Monday night?'

Jo fidgeted in her chair. How could she explain to these two young men how lonely she was; how, all of a sudden, she felt isolated in the house that had been her home for what seemed to be a lifetime; how the company of her loyal dog wasn't enough to dispel the loneliness?

'Leave your mum alone,' Steve said, coming to her rescue. 'Can't you see she needed company? Have you forgotten what it was like to feel like that?'

'Sorry.' Rob's lips turned down, then he smiled. 'I'm glad you chose us.'

'Who else?' As she spoke, it occurred to Jo that, of her three children, Rob was the one she could turn to; the one who was non-judgemental, accepting; the one in whose company she felt most relaxed. 'Thanks for being here for me.'

'Heard the latest about Dad?' Rob asked, when their glasses had been filled, and Jo was sipping a welcome cup of her Earl Grey tea.

'Your dad?' Jo was puzzled. The last she'd seen of Gordon was when they left Yarran the day before. She took Lottie to the hospital and had no idea where he'd gone. She only hoped he'd finally accepted they had no future together.

'I bumped into him this afternoon. He was looking very chipper,' Rob said with a grin.

'He doesn't still think…?'

'He and Carol are back together.'

Jo almost choked. 'That was quick. How…'

'He didn't go into details, but he was loading up his car in the Crown carpark when I saw him. Something about resolving differences, a fresh start.'

Jo's only feeling was relief. She couldn't understand why Carol had agreed to take him back unless… 'Has he agreed to her demands for a child?'

'Don't know. Hope not. That'd be gross. It's enough he's presented us with one new sister – though I rather like Sally. Do you think she'll move here?'

'Who knows? Talking of moving… I've been thinking…' Jo voiced her earlier thoughts. 'I know how I've always said I wasn't going to leave Yarran, but maybe I was wrong. Maybe Kylie and Danny are right, and I've been selfish. It is a big place when there's only me and… if I moved into town… Oh, not into one of those dreadful villas of Danny's,' she said, seeing the shocked expression on Rob's face. 'But something more manageable, less...' She spread her hands out to encompass all the emptiness she'd experienced earlier.

'Of course you're not selfish,' Rob assured her. 'But I can't imagine Yarran without you. And talking of my esteemed older brother and his wife, Steve noticed there are some one-acre parcels of land coming up close to the university. They'd suit Danny and Kylie a lot better than the old homestead.'

Jo chuckled at Rob's term for the house he'd grown up in, but the news intrigued her.

'They could build something modern which I think would suit Kylie better. No offence, Mum, but the old place is looking a bit tired. I've heard how Kylie talks about it. She's told Danny they'd have to do a lot of work to bring it up to scratch. This way, she'd be able to have exactly what she wants. Plus, she'd be closer to town. And old Danny might find one acre easier to manage. Best of both worlds.'

It was an appealing idea. 'Who's going to bring the blocks to Danny's attention?'

'Oh, I bet he already knows about them. It's just a matter of drawing Kylie's attention to them and persuading her it's all her own idea.'

All three were silent as they considered how this could be managed, though Jo wasn't completely convinced it was the right thing to do. It wasn't going to change how empty her house now felt or lessen her loneliness. But it would give the boys room to run around and would be easier for them to be closer to town than on her own acreage.

'I know,' Steve said when Rob had disappeared into the kitchen to refill their glasses. 'The annual Elizabethan Dinner is coming up at the university and, this year, it's being preceded by a parade along the road leading to University Avenue. That means it'll go right by the huge sign the developers have erected. I can get tickets for everyone. Kylie can't miss it. Then, all we have to do is…'

'Hope like hell she takes the bait,' Rob finished, coming back to join them.

'It's a good idea, Steve, but there's no guarantee they'll appeal to Kylie or Danny,' Jo said, feeling a trifle uncomfortable at this plan to manipulate her son and his wife. 'Though,' she added thoughtfully, 'Danny will go along with whatever Kylie wants.'

'Leave it to me,' Steve said. 'I promise she'll never realise, and it can't do any harm.'

The conversation moved on to other matters, and by the time Jo finally left, she was feeling a lot better.

'Thanks for your company, boys,' she said, hugging them both at the door. You've managed to work your magic again. You've cheered me up.'

As she drove through the quiet town, Jo was tempted to make a detour past Col's house. If she did, would the FOR SALE sign still be there, or would it already have a SOLD sticker plastered across it?

She couldn't bear to find out.

Forty-eight

Col was still trying to work out how best to approach Jo. He knew he'd only have one chance at this and was terrified of blowing it. It was almost a week since Gordon had dropped his bombshell, and Col had thought of little else since.

He knew he should have contacted Jo right away. Seeing Gordon whistling to himself as he went about his daily tasks exasperated him when he thought of how he'd thrown away his own chance of happiness for his partner's sake. But Col knew he had no one to blame but himself.

Col packed his golf clubs into the boot of the car and gave one last look at the house before driving off. He'd debated taking it off the market, but Ken had persuaded him to let the one open house planned for this afternoon go ahead. There was little chance it'd sell right away. He sighed. If the house did sell, it would be the end of an era for him. But he knew he'd never have brought Jo back here to live. It was Alice's house. In his mind it always would be. Maybe selling it was the best thing. He'd still have his memories.

'Ready to be thrashed?' Gordon greeted Col at the foot of the clubhouse steps. Being back with Carol seemed to be agreeing with him. The sullen, morose Gordon had disappeared to be replaced with this bluff, affable man.

The game over, even Col's winning score didn't seem to faze his friend, who slapped him jovially on the shoulder as they made their way into the clubhouse for dinner.

'Been in touch with my ex yet?' Gordon asked as they downed their first beer.

'Not yet.' *Why was he so cheerful?* 'Things seem to be going well for you now.'

'They are, they are. Happy wife, happy life.' He chuckled.

'I can't see you with a young baby. I remember your complaining bitterly when your three were little. You seemed to spend more hours in the office to get away from them.'

'I remember,' Gordon looked up reflectively. 'That's why I've taken care of things this time.' He tapped his nose. 'Don't know why I didn't think of it earlier. Would have saved a lot of aggravation.'

For a moment, Col was puzzled, then the penny dropped. 'You mean…?'

Gordon nodded. 'Had the snip. Now there's nothing to worry about.'

'But, Carol?'

'No need for her to know.' Gordon drained his beer. 'Another?'

Col was shocked. He'd always known his friend was devious, but this was taking it too far. He'd deceived Jo with other women, now, it seemed, he was deceiving Carol by having a vasectomy while pretending to be happy about the prospect of becoming a father again. He shrugged and nodded to the offer of another beer.

They took their second beers over to a table and ordered their usual post-golf fare of roast beef with accompanying vegetables. They were halfway through the meal when Col's phone buzzed. It was Ken, his realter.

'Col here.'

'Col, the open house went well. I have a couple who're very interested. They want to have a building report and valuation done next week. That work for you?'

Col agreed, finished the call and clasped his phone, lost in thought.

'Something wrong?'

Col pulled himself back into the present. 'Sorry. No, nothing.' Then, seeing Gordon's puzzled expression, added, 'I might have a buyer for the house.'

'Isn't that what you wanted?'

'Ye…es.' But was it? He'd put it on the market in a moment of pique and now… Col shook his head. He didn't know what he wanted – except to be back with Jo. Why hadn't he been in touch with her? By now she probably knew Gordon and Carol were back together. News travelled fast in Granite Springs – and they were family. What was he waiting for? He made an instant decision.

'I need to go.'

Leaving his half-eaten meal, and with Gordon gazing after him in amazement, Col rushed out of the club.

Forty-nine

Jo poured herself a glass of wine and was about to slide a dish of lasagne into the oven when the sound of a car driving up stopped her in her tracks. Scout roused himself from his spot by the Aga and gave a gentle bark before settling back down again, head on his paws to indicate it was a friend. Surely Gordon hadn't come back to hassle her again? According to Rob, he was back with Carol.

It was beginning to get dark, so Jo switched on the outside light and went to the door. The car wasn't Gordon's, but *was* one she recognised. Her heart gave a now familiar lurch. *What was Col doing here?*

She had barely time to prepare herself before he was standing in front of her, his expression impossible to read.

'Can I come in?'

Jo realised she'd been blocking the doorway and had neither smiled nor greeted him. 'I suppose so.' She moved aside, unsure how to behave. But Scout had no such problem. He immediately left his warm spot to thrust his nose into Col's hand.

'Hello, old fellow,' Col said, clearly finding the dog easier to talk to than Jo.

The pair stood facing each other, neither willing to be the first to speak.

'Why are you here?' Jo asked finally. 'I thought we'd said all there was to say.'

'My rain jacket. I think I may have left it here.'

Jo felt let down – like a suddenly deflated balloon. She swallowed hard. *His rain jacket?* She remembered the old worn waterproof jacket he usually kept in the boot of his car – said he often wore it to golf on wet days. *Why had she imagined he was here to see her?*

'I haven't seen it,' she said shortly, 'but it may be on the hall stand. What makes you think you left it here?'

'Can I sit down? You're making me nervous standing there.'

Nervous? What was he nervous about? It was only an old rain jacket.

Jo pulled out a chair from the table and perched on the edge of it, indicating Col should do the same. She gripped her hands in her lap, the nails biting into the flesh of her palms.

Scout had followed Col to the table, and he scratched the dog's ears before speaking. 'Gordon said he'd seen it here.' His eyes met Jo's.

'Gordon! You mean he…' Her eyes widened.

'He saw it here and worked it out. Not too difficult, I imagine, after you gave him his marching orders.'

'Oh!' Jo remembered leaving Gordon and Lottie in the hallway while she fetched her phone. That must have been when… He hadn't said anything but had been noticeably odd when she returned.

'The thing is… Oh, hell, Jo, I don't know how to say this. I'm no good with words. Alice always said so.'

Jo's heart lurched again. *What was he trying to say?* She wished she hadn't left her glass of wine on the benchtop. She gripped her hands even tighter and pressed her lips together.

'The thing is,' he repeated, 'seems I made a total error of judgement.' He shook his head. 'I should have known better. I should have trusted you, trusted us – what we had together. Instead I…' His head dropped to his chest, and he muttered in such low tones Jo could barely make out the words. 'I let myself believe that it was in your best interests, the best interests of Gordon, your family, everyone, if I let you be to sort things out. I imagined…' He raised his head and met Jo's astonished eyes. 'I imagined if I was out of the picture, you'd take Gordon back, be a family again and everyone would be happy.'

Jo couldn't believe her ears. How could he be so mistaken? She'd credited Col with more sense than this.

'Gordon's my friend,' he continued, 'We've known each other all our lives – all the part that matters, anyway. It seemed the right thing to do.'

Col dragged a hand through his hair, the gesture reminding Jo how it felt to run her own hands through it, the sensation of the thick coarse strands between her fingers.

She gulped, stunned by a flash of desire, which she quickly suppressed.

'When you told me to leave, I thought… I was miserable. I couldn't think straight. That's why I…'

'Put your house on the market and decided to leave town? Wasn't that a bit drastic?' Jo tried to control the tremor in her voice.

'I couldn't bear to stay and see you and Gordon together again playing happy families.'

'As if.'

'What I'm trying to say, Jo, is… can you forgive me?'

A warm glow started in Jo's feet and began to spread up through her body, but she didn't intend to give in so easily. Col might think he meant what he was saying right now, but what if…?

She opened her mouth to speak when the timer went off on the oven.

'Is that something you need to take care of?' Col asked.

'Yes.' Relieved to avoid saying something she might regret, Jo rose and removed the steaming lasagne, placing it on the table, the warm and enticing aroma rising to waft through the entire kitchen.

'Mmm. Smells good.'

'Would you… would you like to join me? There's too much for one.' Not the most welcoming of invitations, she realised as soon as she'd said it.

'I'd love to.' Col rubbed his hands together and gave her a strange look out of the corner of his eye.

Jo squirmed. She knew she hadn't answered his question. She hadn't said whether or not she forgave him.

While Jo fetched plates and cutlery and threw together a quick salad, Col took another glass from the cupboard, topped up Jo's and filled one for himself.

As they sat opposite each other, eating dinner, it was as if he'd never left. The house felt like a home again. Even Scout seemed happier, lying under the table at their feet, snoring gently.

All through the meal, Jo thought about what Col had told her, what he had asked of her. Neither said much.

'Well?' Col cocked his head on one side when their plates were empty, and they'd finished the wine.

Jo knew she couldn't put it off any longer. She looked across the table at his familiar face, his tentative smile, and was engulfed in memories of their days – and nights – together.

'I'll just take these,' she said rising, collecting the plates and taking them to the sink. She was starting to rinse them, when she became aware of a presence behind her and a pair of warm arms wrapped around her. 'Jo, Jo,' Col murmured. 'What happened to us?'

Jo turned into his embrace. As his lips moved on hers, Jo realised it was simple. She'd come home. This is where she wanted to be. 'I'm sorry,' she murmured. 'There's nothing to forgive. It was my fault. When I told you to leave… I was in a bad place. I…'

Col's lips silenced her again, and it was some time before they drew apart.

'We're good?' Col asked, entwining his fingers with hers.

Jo nodded and, gripping his hand tightly, led him to the bedroom.

Fifty

4 months later

'Here we are,' Jo carried the cake covered in pink icing out onto the veranda and placed it on the table.

The family were gathered together to celebrate the new addition to the family. Emily Rose had been born a few weeks earlier – a sister for Lottie and Livvy, who'd completely recovered from her ordeal.

'Another girl!' Liam had groaned when her birth was announced, but he had become just as enamoured with the new baby as the others and vied with his brother for his turn to push the pram or read her a story.

It was like Easter lunch all over again, Jo thought looking around the table. Except, this time, Col was here beside her, having moved into Yarran when his house sold. Gordon and Carol were here too – and Sally.

In the past few months, after her difficult introduction, Sally had become part of the family, her actions in saving Livvy's life having endeared her to everyone. After a quick trip back to Sydney to resign her position and put her mother's house on the market, she'd returned to Granite Springs to get to know Gordon better and check out the employment situation. Now she was renting a unit in town and working in the maternity ward of the Base Hospital.

'Reminds me of Easter,' Eve said, echoing Jo's thoughts.

Except, thought Jo, the family had now grown to encompass three more. It was partly due to Col she'd agreed to bury the hatchet with Gordon and Carol. She still didn't find it easy to spend time in their company but, for the sake of the children and the grandchildren, she made an effort. And today it was paying off.

'I'm glad you and Col are together now, Mum,' Eve said. 'It's nice you have someone to keep you company in your old age. You deserve that.'

Old age? Jo glanced at Col. He nudged her under the table and winked. But Jo was glad Eve had finally come to accept Col was part of her mother's life.

'How's the house going?' Rob asked Danny.

'Coming along. We should be in by Christmas.'

'It was lucky you found those one-acre blocks,' Jo said with a smile.

'Wasn't that clever of Danny?' Kylie asked, unaware of the machinations that had gone on behind their backs. 'It's so much better for the boys than here, Mother Slater,' she said smugly, completely oblivious to her complete about-face. As soon as she saw the blocks and discovered they could build the modern house of her dreams there, all thoughts of moving into Yarran had been forgotten. 'This is a nice house, but it's so dated. We'd have had to redo the kitchen and bathrooms… and the boys… with the dam…' She shuddered.

Jo hid a smile.

After lunch, everyone, except Jo, Carol and, of course, baby Emily Rose, went for a swim. Livvy's near death experience hadn't put her off swimming, though Jo noticed Eve never took her eyes off the twins.

While the others were in the water, Carol cuddled Emily Rose, a tender expression in her eyes.

Jo felt sorry for her ex-husband's young wife. She'd make a good mother and clearly still yearned for a child of her own. It was unfair of Gordon to keep his secret from her. Still, Jo sighed, she'd no doubt find out one of these days. And when she did, Jo wondered how long the marriage would last. Sadly, she didn't think there was too much else to keep it together.

Once the family had left, Jo joined Col on the wide veranda where he'd poured two glasses of champagne.

'That went reasonably well,' he said, raising his glass to hers. 'To us.'

'To us,' she replied. 'To our life together.'

'To the life you deserve,' he said, his eyes so full of love Jo felt like weeping.

It had taken a long time, but she could finally relax, knowing her future with Col was assured.

THE END

If you enjoyed this book, I'd love it if you could write a review. It doesn't need to be long, just a few words, but it is the best way for me to help new readers discover my books.

Now read an excerpt from the next Granite Springs novel, *The Life She Chooses*, which is Kay's story.

Prologue

Something wakened her.

Kay Jackson reached across the bed to touch her husband, only to find her hand encounter a cold, empty space. Her eyes shot open as she surveyed the vacant spot where David should be lying. She started up, then fell back, her mind going around in circles. He was probably in the kitchen. Since the rumours had started – four weeks ago – he'd had trouble sleeping, often getting up to drink whisky and gaze unseeingly out into the darkness.

The first few times she'd found him like that, she'd coaxed him back to bed, but now she knew it was best to let him be, to face whatever demons he had, alone. There was nothing she could do to help him, try as she might.

She knew the rumours were untrue. They had to be. Her David was a gentle creature. They'd been married for over thirty years. She knew him inside out. There was no way he was a child molester. She couldn't even utter the word paedophile. It was a mistake. It had been someone else. Or the girl had some grudge against him. She tried to ignore the fact that, in the past few days, other girls had come forward to tell the same story.

But David was a respected member of the community – the local dentist, a friendly figure to the girls in the netball team he'd coached for what seemed forever. They'd realise their mistake, and life would go back to the way it had been.

Kay closed her eyes again, but sleep eluded her. She got out of bed, pulled on her soft blue robe and slid her feet into her sheepskin slippers. It was cold at this time of the morning, and the kitchen tiles were unforgiving on her bare feet.

In the kitchen, Milly, their old cat, stretched in her basket by the Aga which kept the room warm all night. But she knew it was too early for her breakfast, so immediately curled up again, purring loudly. It was a comforting sound, and Kay needed comfort. She filled the kettle and measured the tealeaves into the teapot she and David had chosen together in better days – days when the dental practice was growing, and the future looked bright.

There was no sign of David. Kay assumed he'd gone for an early morning run. He'd be back soon.

She stood, staring out the window watching the sun come up. She used to love this part of the day, but now it filled her with apprehension as to what the rest of the day might bring.

When the rumours first began, when the first girl made her accusation, David had brushed it off as the wild imaginings of overactive teenage hormones. But as those rumours grew, it had become more and more difficult to dismiss them.

Despite Kay's suggestion they take time off, go away till it all died down, David had been unyielding. He'd gone into the surgery each day, regardless of the cancelled appointments, the sly whispers. And she'd been there beside him, receptionist, wife and supporter, putting on a brave face and offering a tight smile to the critics.

She sighed, slid a slice of bread into the toaster and took a tub of butter and a jar of marmalade from the fridge while she waited, though she had little appetite.

Breakfast over, Kay gazed anxiously out the window, but there was no sign of her husband. He was usually back by now, ready for a second or third cup of coffee. He wasn't eating much either, a sign the gossip was affecting him more that he was willing to admit.

By the time she was ready to leave, David still hadn't appeared. Now Kay was really worried. She opened the garage door and gave a sigh of relief. His car was gone. He must have decided to go in early. Maybe today would be different; there would be no more cancellations; the rumours would die down; they could get on with their lives. But, deep down, Kay knew life could never be the same again.

To Kay's surprise, the office door was locked. David wasn't there. A curl of fear flickered in the pit of her stomach making her fingers clumsy as she fitted the key into the lock. But, once inside, the morning routine took over. She greeted David's partner with a smile, managed to make civil conversation with Denise and Alanna, the two dental hygienists as they arrived, and to welcome the first patients of the morning.

A check of the diary revealed David had no appointments till close to lunchtime, so maybe he'd gone for a drive to *get his head together* as he put it.

The door opened. Kay glanced up, ready with a welcoming smile, only to have it disappear when she saw the sombre face of a police officer.

'Mrs Jackson, is there somewhere we can talk?'

Kay felt her head spin. She could barely breathe. She thought she was going to collapse.

'Are you all right, Kay?' Denise emerged from behind her.

'No, yes. Can you take over for a bit, Denise? The officer wants to…'

She led him into the small staff-room.

'I think you should sit down,' he said.

She did, clasping her hands tightly in her lap and trying not to imagine the worst. Had David had an accident? Was he badly injured? Why was she sitting here when she should be rushing to hospital?

'I'm sorry to tell you, Mrs Jackson, Kay, that early this morning, your husband's car was found on the outskirts of town. It appears he took his own life.'

One

The pall of smoke from the recently extinguished bushfire hung over the town as Kay made her solitary way to the cemetery. It was three years since David died, and each year on the anniversary of his death, she'd made this lonely pilgrimage. It would have been nice if her children chose to accompany her, but Adam, her son, lived in England, having taken a position there over ten years ago, and her daughter…

Zoe lived in Brisbane, had rejected her dad as soon as the rumours started, and refused to return for the funeral or to visit his grave. It was up to Kay to make the trek to Brisbane if she wanted to see her grandchild.

She knelt on the parched grass in front of the simple stone to lay flowers on the grave, her eyes filled with tears. Why couldn't he have stuck it out? But, despite all her denials, in her heart Kay now knew David had been guilty of everything they'd accused him of. That was why, after his death, she'd left the practice, had practically become a recluse. Granite Springs was a small town in New South Wales and, like all small towns, had a thriving gossip mill. She couldn't bear the pity, the words of sympathy, the way people whispered behind her back.

She sighed as she made her way back to the car and drove home, the house enveloping her in its warmth. Milly, the black cat who'd been her sole companion for the past three years, was lying in a puddle of sunlight and opened one eye when she walked in.

The message light on the phone was blinking. Kay debated ignoring it, but suspecting it was her good friend, Jo, she pressed *play*.

She was right.

'Hi Kay. I know this is a difficult day for you. I just wanted you to know I'm thinking of you.' There was a pause, then, 'If you'd like to meet for coffee, I'm available all day, but I understand if you want to be alone.'

The message ended with a silence that filled the room. Kay slumped into a chair. Did she want company? Even the company of the friend who'd supported her through her grief might prove too much to bear. She knew Jo thought that, after three years, she should be making a life for herself. She just didn't understand.

The trouble was, Kay knew, Jo understood all too well. She'd lost her own husband through divorce six years earlier and a good friend to cancer over a year ago. But Kay felt her own grief to be unique.

As if sensing her dilemma, Milly stretched and sauntered over to jump up on her lap, kneading it with her tiny paws. Kay's fingers automatically reached down to scratch the cat's soft fur. Milly strained upwards into her hand.

'Oh, Milly. What would I do without you?' But, of course, there was no reply.

Kay sat like that for a few minutes before deciding what to do. The lonely day stretched out before her. There was still another week of holidays before she was due back at the university. The job she'd taken there a year earlier had been a godsend. Getting back into the workforce had been an impulsive decision, but a good one. She enjoyed the day-to-day buzz of the university office, the demands of the staff and the liveliness of the students. It was only here, at home, that the loneliness set in.

She rose, the sudden movement forcing Milly to tumble from her lap with a loud meow. Coffee with Jo seemed like a good idea.

*

'How are you, really?' The woman sitting opposite fixed Kay with concerned eyes as she held her coffee cup in both hands, her elbows on the table.

'Okay.' Kay brushed a strand of hair out of her eyes wishing she'd taken time to do something more with it. Maybe she should get it cut, but David had liked her shoulder-length dark hair. She gave herself a shake. David was gone. 'I am. Really. It's just this time of year. It all comes back.'

Jo's hand reached across the table to cover hers. 'I know.'

The two sat in silence, then Jo asked, 'When do you go back to work?'

'Next week. I'll be better then. The office is busy; the faculty is busy. I don't have much time to think.'

'It's been three years, Kay.' Jo's voice was gentle, but Kay was aware of the implicit criticism. In her friend's mind she should be moving on.

'I'm not ready.'

Kay wondered if she'd ever be ready in the sense Jo meant. Unlike her friend's new husband who had got together with Jo only a year after his wife's death, there were extenuating circumstances there, she allowed. And men were different – they needed a woman in their lives. *She* couldn't imagine sharing her life with anyone else.

'How's Col?' she asked to change the subject.

'Good. Did I tell you we're talking about taking back the far paddock, and Col has it in mind to plant lavender? He's full of ideas. A lavender farm one day, a pig farm the next. I was worried he'd have time on his hands after retiring, but it's lovely having him around all day. Now I'm worried he's trying to do too much.' She laughed – an indulgent laugh.

'And the grands?'

Jo's face broke into a wide smile. 'They're wonderful. Lottie and Livvy are excited to be going into grade one. They're hoping Allegra will be their teacher. Did I tell you she's been offered a position at Granite Springs Primary?' she asked, referring to the girl who, in her final year at university, had been babysitter for Jo's twin granddaughters the previous year. 'And Emily Rose, she's growing so fast. It's difficult to believe she's only three months old. What about your little Noah? How was Christmas in Brisbane this year?'

Kay sighed. She worried about Noah. A lovely little boy, now almost five, her grandson was alert, curious and turning into the image of his dad, but Kay was concerned his mother regimented his life too much. Surely at his tender age, he should be allowed more independence?

'Zoe hasn't changed,' Kay said. 'I was glad to get home. I don't know how Eric puts up with her. She seems to forget she's not a manager when she gets home from work and wants to organise all our lives. I suppose he's used to it, and he's not home much. His work keeps him busy. Nan's lovely though – his mum. She was there too this year. She's a widow like me. We…' she paused, about to say they had a lot in common. But had they? Nan Bailey's husband had died after a lingering illness, mourned by friends and family, neighbours and former workmates. He was still spoken of highly by Zoe and Eric. How could that experience compare with the rejection and humiliation Kay had suffered?

'It's good to have you back.' Jo's gentle voice was reassuring. Here was someone who understood what she had been through, was still going through.

'And you're still thinking of moving?'

Kay hesitated. She'd mooted that idea with Jo before leaving for Brisbane, but since coming back the idea of packing up the house she and David had shared, the one they'd moved to after Zoe and Adam had grown up and left, all seemed too hard.

'I've been too busy to think about it.'

'Maybe you should.' Kay saw Jo bite her lip. 'I know I fought against leaving Yarran when Danny and Kylie had their eye on it, but it's different for you.'

She didn't need to say any more. Kay still had nightmares about the media frenzy outside the house.

'Maybe,' she said, picking up her cup and finishing the now cold coffee. She grimaced.

But Jo wasn't prepared to leave it at that. 'It's not as if you raised your family there. And surely the memories…' She buttoned her lip as if knowing she'd said enough.

'I should go.' Kay ostentatiously looked at her watch, as if she had she had some pressing engagement. She could see from Jo's sympathetic expression she hadn't fooled her friend for one second.

But Jo made ready to leave too. 'Remember,' she said as they hugged before parting, 'You can always call me if…'

'Thanks.' Kay turned away and hurried off. Jo's sympathy was more than she could bear. Maybe Zoe had been right when she suggested

Kay should see someone, that she was clinically depressed, that by now – three years later – she should be getting over David's death.

Two

'Damn!'

Nick Kerr stood watching helplessly as the bulky bundle of papers slid to the floor and scattered. He thrust a hand through his short thatch of thick greying hair, tugged at his beard, and scowled. He should call it a day. Dean of the School of Education at William Farrer University, he'd been in his office since the crack of dawn, pretending he needed to prepare for the start of semester. It was past six o'clock. He should go home. But there was nothing for him there.

When his wife had left the day after New Year, she'd taken their teenage son and daughter with her, along with half the furniture. The house now had an unlived-in appearance without the dining table, one of the sofas and the widescreen TV. He knew he should get around to replacing them, but it was easier to spend his time here in the office and pretend it hadn't happened.

At least Sam would be back in time for school to start, but that was weeks away. At seventeen, she'd refused to make the move with her mother, demanding to know why she should be disadvantaged and separated from all her friends in her final year of school just because her parents couldn't see eye-to-eye. Never mind that it was Michelle who'd chosen to move north with the man Nick deridingly referred to as her *toy boy*.

He checked his computer again, hoping he'd misread the email that had appeared in his inbox that morning. As if his personal life being in chaos wasn't enough, Fran, his trusted personal assistant, had been summoned to her mother's bedside in the UK and needed to take leave for the entire semester. Where would he find someone to replace her? He supposed one of the office staff could be seconded to fill the position on a temporary basis. He sighed. This was going to be a difficult year.

Unable to contemplate the empty house that awaited him, Nick drove instead towards the river, coming to a halt in the carpark of The Riverside, the restaurant owned by Steve's partner. Steve was one of the few on the faculty who'd shunned the annual rush to the coast by most of the other staff. It would be quiet there at this time midweek, and Nick would be sure of a good meal.

As he pushed through the glass doors, Nick was met with an assortment of delicious aromas, and greeted by the tall broad-shouldered man he was more accustomed to seeing in the university hallways or presenting the union's case in faculty meetings.

'Good evening, Prof Kerr. Table for one this evening?' Steve glanced behind Nick as if expecting to see Michelle, impeccably made-up, chestnut hair sweeping her shoulders.

'Yes.'

So the word hadn't yet got around about Michelle's leaving? It wouldn't take long. Granite Springs might be becoming a larger regional centre, but the gossip mill was still as effective as it ever had been.

Shown to a corner table already set for two, Nick studied the menu before ordering a Cascade Light and a dish of lamb shanks. While he was waiting for his meal, he checked his phone to find two texts from his daughter.

Yeppoon sucks. And Terry's a wanker. Cn I cum home? Samx

Can't stand it here much longer, Nick. Cn u talk to Mum? Samxx

Nick gave a wry grin. In the past year – since turning seventeen – Sam had decided she was grown up enough to drop the *Dad* and call him *Nick*. He missed the little girl who'd called him Daddy and hung onto his every word, and was finding it hard to come to terms with the stranger who'd taken her place. Now he sighed and rubbed the back of his neck.

Poor Sam. Although he dearly wanted to give in to her plea, he'd made a deal with Michelle and the deal was that both Samantha and

Ryan would stay with their mother until the end of January. Then Ryan, who was only fourteen, would start school up there while Sam would return to finish school in Granite Springs. Who knew what would happen then? He'd like to see his daughter follow her parents into teaching, perhaps even enrol in the education program right here at William Farrer. But he knew that wasn't likely to happen. This coming year would most likely be the last he'd have with his daughter before she headed off to another university and greener pastures.

'Evening, Nick.'

He looked up. Standing by the table was a woman he had every reason to dislike. A good friend of Michelle's, Nick was pretty sure Faye had conspired with his ex on more than one occasion to give her an alibi, pretending the pair were out together when the deceitful minx was otherwise engaged with her new partner.

'Hello, Faye.'

'Happy New Year! Heard from Michelle?'

What was happy about it? But Nick put a smile on his face and replied, 'You're more likely to have heard from her than I am.'

'Don't be like that.' She pouted – not an attractive look on someone who'd never see fifty again – and took the seat opposite him. 'I thought you might be a tad lonely. I heard the kids are spending the holiday with their mum. You must be rattling around in that big house without them. Maybe you'd like some company?' She gave him what he assumed she thought was a winsome smile, which only served to alienate him further.

Was the woman really suggesting…?

Fortunately, he was saved from replying by the arrival of the waiter with his meal. 'Would madame like to order?' he asked Faye, who was making herself at home opposite Nick.

'Madame was just leaving,' Nick said, glaring across the table. 'Sorry, Faye, I can't help you,' he said, hoping she'd understand his meaning.

Not now, not ever. He was done with women for good.

From the Author

Dear Reader,

First, I'd like to thank you for choosing to read *The Life She Deserves*. Having spent seven years teaching university and living in an Australian country town, I felt it was time to write a series with a rural setting. This is the first book in the series set in a fictional country town of Granite Springs.

If you'd like to stay up to date with my new releases and special offers you can sign up to my reader's group.

You can sign up here
https://mailchi.mp/f5cbde96a5e6/maggiechristensensreadersgroup

I'll never share your email address, and you can unsubscribe at any time. You can also contact me via Facebook Twitter or by email. I love hearing from my readers and will always reply.

Thanks again.

Acknowledgements

As always, this book could not have been written without the help and advice of a number of people.

Firstly, my husband Jim for listening to my plotlines without complaint, for his patience and insights as I discuss my characters and storyline with him and for being there when I need him.

John Hudspith, editor extraordinaire for his ideas, suggestions, encouragement and attention to detail.

Jane Dixon-Smith for her patience and for working her magic on my beautiful cover and interior.

My thanks also to early readers of this book –Helen, Anne M. Anne S, Maggie and Louise, for their helpful comments and advice. Also to Annie of *Annie's books at Peregian* for her ongoing support.

And all of my readers. Your support and comments make it all worthwhile.

About the Author

After a career in education, Maggie Christensen began writing contemporary women's fiction portraying mature women facing life-changing situations. Her travels inspire her writing, be it her frequent visits to family in Oregon, USA or her home on Queensland's beautiful Sunshine Coast. Maggie writes of mature heroines coming to terms with changes in their lives and the heroes worthy of them. Her writing has been described by one reviewer as *like a nice warm cup of tea. It is warm, nourishing, comforting and embracing.*

From her native Glasgow, Scotland, Maggie was lured by the call 'Come and teach in the sun' to Australia, where she worked as a primary school teacher, university lecturer and in educational management. Now living with her husband of over thirty years on Queensland's Sunshine Coast, she loves walking on the deserted beach in the early mornings and having coffee by the river on weekends. Her days are spent surrounded by books, either reading or writing them – her idea of heaven!

She continues her love of books as a volunteer with her local library where she selects and delivers books to the housebound.

Maggie can be found on Facebook, Twitter, Goodreads, Instagram or on her website.

www.facebook.com/maggiechristensenauthor
www.twitter.com/MaggieChriste33
www.goodreads.com/author/show/8120020.Maggie_Christensen
www.instagram.com/maggiechriste33/
maggiechristensenauthor.com/